# NATALE STENZEL

# PANDORA'S BOX

LOVE SPELL  NEW YORK CITY

*For Jenn, Kathy, Carolyn and Tracy,*
*who encouraged me to walk all the way out on that limb.*

LOVE SPELL®

February 2008

Published by

Dorchester Publishing Co., Inc.
200 Madison Avenue
New York, NY 10016

ISBN 10: 0-505-52752-9
ISBN 13: 978-0-505-52752-3

Printed in the United States of America.

10 9 8 7 6 5 4 3 2 1

Visit us on the web at www.dorchesterpub.com.

# PANDORA'S BOX

According to Greek mythology, Zeus created this woman named Pandora. I'm advocating that she was their version of Eve, by the way, since this is my blog and I'm entitled to express my opinion here. As per archetype, evil Woman is created for Man's pleasure but, due to her weak character, becomes his downfall.

Anyway, so we have Pandora. And all the gods got together and put evil things inside a box, like plague and hatred and whatnot. But also inside this box, they placed hope. Then they gave it to Pandora and—how cruel is this?—didn't tell her what was inside, just told her not to open it. But, as "evidenced" in nearly every culture's folklore, women are weak and easily cave to evil temptation. Thus, Pandora inevitably disobeyed, opening the box and loosing evil into the world. Ironically, in opening this box, she also revealed hope. . . .

# CHAPTER ONE

"I inherited a rock? Some distant relative I've never met willed me a rock? You can't be serious." Was that supposed to be an insult? Mina wondered. *You've been a bad little descendant, Mina, so here, accept this rock as a sign of my eternal contempt. . . .*

"Pandemina Dorothy Avery, right? The thirty-one-year-old unmarried daughter of Elizabeth Avery Dixon and Duncan Forbes?" When she shrugged and nodded, the attorney smiled. "Then, yes. A rock. But more than that. It's actually a cornerstone from a little cottage in Wiltshire, England, last owned by your distant cousin and my firm's client, Gladys Avebury. It's been in the English branch of your mother's family for generations. I assume you've heard of cornerstones?"

She thought about it. "Well, sure. So the cornerstone's a keepsake?" Leave it to her mother's family to pass a sacred rock down through the generations and call it a legacy.

"That, too, but cornerstones are also an old tradition. People sometimes use them as a personal time capsule, to contain mementos and information about the property and its owners. If a building is significant in any way or large, the cornerstone might also contain information about the structure itself. Since in this case we're talking about a simple, if very old, cottage, it's more likely you'll get your hands on some family history. Which, quite frankly, could be fascinating."

Fascinating. No doubt. Mina pondered diplomacy. "Look. I have to be honest. This inheritance might be better off in somebody else's hands. I'm afraid information about distant relatives just doesn't intrigue me like it might some others. The only people I've ever called family are my mother and stepfather—and then, only when they're behaving, which is about fifty percent of the time."

And yes, here now was the guilt. She shouldn't have said that last part. At least her mom and stepfather loved and acknowledged Mina as family. That was more than she could say for the pompous hypocrite who'd fathered Mina and abandoned mother and child before she was even born.

And then there were the loving grandparents, who unanimously denounced Mina's birth as an abomination. Seriously. All because of a little premarital sex and a reproductive oops.

Mina could only assume that her mother's life during pregnancy had been a living hell. On the rare sentimental occasion, Mina even tried to set aside their very real differences in an attempt to build a friendlier mother-daughter relationship. But then her mother would invariably shove some rare crystals or yet another ancient talisman under Mina's nose, thereby driving her daughter to distraction all over again.

"I suppose everyone is entitled to an opinion. You'll have to do as you see fit." Still, the attorney's manner had cooled.

Poor man had been so excited when she walked in the door. He'd wanted to play Santa Claus and deliver his special lump of rock, and her jaded-kid routine wasn't satisfying in the least.

Well, what did he expect? She'd never even met this Gladys Avebury, and Mina just didn't have it in her to weep or gush with sentiment over the death of a stranger. Generalized but sincere regret was about all she could manage.

"Look, I'm sorry if I seem less than enthusiastic about all this. It probably just hasn't sunk in yet." Well, that was certainly possible. Maybe she hadn't completely processed the situation yet. She mentally paused a moment. She'd inherited a rock . . . from a distant cousin across the ocean . . . Hmm. No, a rock's a rock's a rock. She'd inherited a rock, and not of the faceted variety. That was about as "sunk" as it got, she decided, not without regret.

Sort of like her, unfortunately. A monetary inheritance from some mysterious relative she'd have welcomed with embarrassment and sheer gratitude. So, call her materialistic, but now that Jackson, her live-in boyfriend, had dumped her and moved out—leaving her with a mortgage and repairs she couldn't afford—she was desperate.

Thanks to Jackson's vindictive—not to mention married—new girlfriend, Mina had lost her job right along with her boyfriend and potential husband. Then Jackson, in his infinite generosity, had offered to continue the mortgage payments on the house they jointly owned until the house sold. In return, Mina would pay for renovations necessary to make the house sellable.

Right. With what money, exactly? The laughable balance in her checking account? Or maybe she could borrow ahead on a nonexistent salary?

"Ms. Avery?" The attorney had a tight look on his face, as though he'd tried gaining her attention a few times.

"Sorry. Just thinking." Being rude was more like it. Honestly, would it kill her to show just a little interest, out of simple good manners? Sentiment in this case was beyond

her, but curiosity she could do. "So, why me? No disre-
spect, of course, but why didn't Gladys leave her . . . her
*legacy* . . . to somebody she'd at least met?"

"Because you, Pandemina Avery"—he paused, obviously
trying to emphasize the drama of Mina's situation—"are
the 'sole surviving unmarried female descendant of the
Wiltshire branch of the family who still bears some version
of the family name.'" He paused to take a breath.

And no wonder. If she hadn't already verified the attorney's credentials she'd suspect him of trying to con her
with that absurd list of criteria.

"You do realize, of course, that the family name is actually Ave*bury* over in England. It was shortened to Avery
when your great-grandparents moved to America." He
smiled, obviously delighted on her behalf.

No *of course* about it; but Mina wasn't about to enlighten
him and play Scrooge to his Santa all over again. "I . . . Sure.
That's great." She forced a smile. "Look, Mr. Reynolds. No
offense, but don't the requirements for this inheritance seem
oddly stretched to you? The sole surviving whatever of the
whatever and so on and so forth? I'm sure the family history
stuff is fascinating, but why go to all this time and expense
for the sake of a cornerstone?"

"I couldn't say for sure in this case, but I'd suspect sentimentality. When you don't have a spouse or children to inherit your estate, you go searching for descendants just to
feel like you're leaving something of yourself behind when
you die. No one wants to be forgotten." He paused, letting
her absorb his words.

And those words were well chosen. Mina could understand being alone, given her current situation as resident
pariah. She was used to that role, honestly, having played
the neighborhood freak so often as a kid. Isolation was a
bitch. But how much worse would it be to actually outlive
the few people in this world who bothered to acknowledge

the worth of your existence? When you died, would you just . . . cease to exist? Would your absence even register beyond a minor, paperwork-based ripple in the world around you? Mina could identify to some extent.

"So when should I expect this ro—cornerstone to arrive?"

"Possibly as soon as tomorrow. I do have the paperwork here, however." He riffled through his briefcase and, as if he'd had a sudden thought, glanced up. "Speaking of paperwork, you're not to worry about the legalities of transferring property from the UK to here. We've taken care of that. The cottage itself, minus the cornerstone, was donated to the historical society, which may have smoothed the way a little.

"Not that there was any real objection to the cornerstone leaving the country." He looked mildly puzzled. "Given the age of that cottage, I thought the Brits would balk at letting go of any part of it. But that wasn't the case. I suppose it helps that the cottage wasn't located in the historic section of the county. It wouldn't be as valuable."

"Well, that's good, I guess." Mina smiled politely. "So what's the rest of the paperwork?"

"Just the typical forms saying you accepted the property, that I read you the exact terms, etcetera, etcetera." He pulled out a stack of paper. "I'll need your signature here." He pointed to an *X*, flipped to the next page, "and here, as well as initials on these other pages, and then here, here and here."

She skimmed and scribbled where indicated, until she came to the final *X*. "What's this about a guardian? I'm accepting guardianship of the cornerstone and all its contents? What does that mean?"

The attorney frowned, then shrugged. "Just that you're responsible for them. That you own them. I gather they were pretty special to Ms. Avebury. She was probably just concerned that you might accept them too lightly."

Mina grimaced. That was exactly what she'd done, too. Okay, she'd be good now. Money wasn't everything, right? A woman's last wishes deserved respect. "Okay." She signed more carefully and handed the stack of forms back to the attorney.

He accepted it. "Oh, and one last thing. There's a letter from Gladys Avebury herself." He riffled through his files again. "I don't know the contents, just that they were intended to be confidential." Finally locating the proper document, he extended a sealed envelope to her. "Here you go."

She accepted the envelope from him and studied it with fresh curiosity. It was a standard envelope, but the paper had yellowed with age. Still, it was free of creases and unstained. Like the attorney said, it had obviously been important to someone. She ran a finger down the seal, slipped her nail into the corner—

"You should probably open that in private."

She glanced up. "Private even from you? Her attorney?" Eccentricity and sentimentality were all well and good, but this was just odd. "What is it? A confession?" She laughed a little. "Did Cousin Gladys kill somebody with the cornerstone and decide to confess all to her descendants?"

He smiled. "I doubt it. Although, I have to admit I don't understand what the secrecy's all about either. Maybe it's information regarding a scandal or something valuable. Or it could be that Gladys suffered from simple, generalized paranoia. It's hard to say. I never actually met the woman; she dealt with my firm's affiliates overseas.

"As for the letter," he nodded at the missive, "like I said, all I know is that it was Ms. Avebury's wish that the heiress—that would be you—should be the only one to read it. My job is to respect the client's wishes."

"Of course."

Twenty minutes later, Mina emerged from the attorney's office, envelope in hand and mostly unopened. She supposed a properly respectful descendant of the great Avery—no, Avebury—family would be jumping all over a letter from deceased Gladys.

Sure, Mina wondered what kind of letter would merit secrecy even from the woman's attorney. But right now, she was going to be late to meet with her new contractor unless she kicked it into gear. She just hoped he hadn't already given up and left. And—ugh—charged her for a wasted day's worth of labor.

Mina squinted into the sun, finally locating her ancient Ford Escort in the crowded line of cars parked along the busy downtown Richmond street. She climbed into the car and prayed to all the gods of motor vehicles that the engine would start at least one more time. She had half an hour's drive back to Oakville ahead of her and she didn't want to break down this far from home.

But start it did. Smoothly, in fact. "Okay." She merged into traffic, pleased to see that, for once, traffic lights seemed to be working in her favor. Maybe her luck was improving?

When she finally pulled into her own driveway, she was further cheered to see the contractor's truck still sitting in front of her house. Noticing that the cab of the truck was vacant, she decided he'd probably gone around back to survey the job ahead of him. So she trotted around to the backyard, only to discover that the contractor had already started working. Excellent.

"Hello?" She glanced around, looking for a face that would fit the voice she'd heard over the phone. That voice had certainly made an impression. What kind of face would go with tones as richly textured as crushed velvet? she'd wondered.

A man squatting in front of blueprints spread neatly on the grass rose to his full height. He turned to face her.

Oh. Sure, that would do it. Rough-hewn features, silky-looking black hair, and a shadowed jaw square enough to

put a comic book hero to shame. Ooooh, and then there
was the body, also as hot as she'd fantasized. He was big and
rugged and trim, but weathered just enough, so he was
probably in his thirties.

Even better, humor lined the corners of twinkling green
eyes. And he had a very nice mouth, sculpted and bracketed
by attractive dents that deepened when he smiled. "Mina
Avery?"

"Wuh?" As in, *duh*? She cleared her throat. She'd probably been staring too long, damn it. "Yes, I'm Mina. And
you are—"

"Jonathon Teague. You can call me Teague, though." He
held out a hand.

She stepped forward, attempting with effort to stave off
hyperventilation, and clasped it. His hand was easily twice
the size of hers. Warm and calloused. Of course it would be.
No soft and clammy grip would do it for a guy like this. She
reluctantly released him. "Nice to meet you, Mr. Teague."

"No, it's just Teague." He shoved one hand in his back
pocket and shaded his eyes with the other, squinting against
the evening sun to see her.

"Just Teague, huh? Like Cher, just Cher?" She was
shameless—but any heterosexual woman would be, in Mina's
shoes. "So you're a temperamental artist, then?"

He laughed. "No, just practical. My family's got a
Jonathon, a John, a Big John, a Little John, a Johnny, a Jay,
a Jon-Jon, a JT, a Junior, a Third and a Senior."

"Big family."

He shrugged. "Traditional family. They like the name.
So do I, but it can get confusing. And I ran out of options.
So, ever since I turned twelve and declared myself a manly
adolescent, I've gone by Teague."

"I see." And she did. There was rough affection in his
eyes and voice when he talked about his family. "That's kind
of nice. Family pride."

"Nah, we just lack imagination. And girls. My family produces a lot of boys."

She laughed, mildly dazzled. An educated woman shouldn't take this much pleasure in chin stubble, should she? Obviously, there was something insidious at work here, a common denominator among post-pubescent females.

The blue-collar worker fantasy. Dum-dum-dummmmm.

Cheesy and trite, but there it was. Guys stared helplessly at big boobs, both in cartoons and in real life. Similarly, a female saw a tool belt hanging low on slender, denim-clad hips, and defined pecs stretching the material of a soft, white T-shirt and . . . she drooled. Simple cause and effect. Add to that sufficient body heat to comfortably wear short sleeves when it was only fifty-some degrees outside, and factor in the implications thereof. . . . Well, that was a fantasy for you. Nothing politically correct or evolved about it.

Mina squelched her drooling and attempted professional conversation. "So you've made some headway, I see." A responsible homeowner, however temporary, should show at least mild interest when someone prepared to rip holes in her house. Teague had already done some measuring and marking up, she could see, and apparently, had the tools available to start yanking out damaged windows whenever.

"Yeah, we finished this morning's job earlier than we expected and I wanted to get a jump on your project before the rain this weekend. Since we already had the verbal agreement, I didn't think you'd mind if we got started while you were gone."

"Not at all. This is great."

"Good." He smiled and gestured behind him. "I thought we'd take care of this window first, then see how bad the water damage is around the next one. Might have to replace some of your wallboard and maybe even the supports if the wood's bad."

And, given her homeowner's luck, she could almost guarantee the rotted status of the wood. "Of course."

"Anyway, I'm thinking we could have this done right on schedule, rain or no rain." He smiled at her, obviously expecting modest applause.

It was a peculiarly male phenomenon, this expectation of praise for doing the job required of him. Jackson, for example, had always required a little ego stroke every time it occurred to him to pick his smelly socks off the floor or put his dirty dishes in the sink. Mina wondered if Tiffy did the stroking now.

As old vibes dredged up ugly memories, Mina's toolbelt lust cooled just a little. No, she wouldn't immediately convict every guy of Jackson's crimes, but she'd be an idiot to fall for the first attractive man she met after her breakup.

Dumb, Mina. Ever heard of rebound relationships? Those never work out. Try for a little caution.

She forced herself to smile only politely. "Then I'll just get out of your way so you can get back to work. Let me know if you need anything." She turned briskly and strode off, determined not to look back.

Still, she never heard the man move again until after a yell from one of his men. "Hey, Teague! Get the lead out. Thought you wanted to . . ."

Smiling just a little—hey, a girl was allowed some vanity, wasn't she?—Mina jogged up the front steps and kicked her toe into something hard.

"Ouch, damn it. What—" A package lay on her front porch. She frowned and shoved at the box with the heel of her bruised foot. A damned heavy one, too, given that it was only about the size of a shoebox. She bent to read the return address. England, as in Wiltshire? "Already?"

Hefting the box and wrestling it onto her hip, she dug for her keys and let herself in. Silly to lock her door, considering people were preparing to bust the window out of her back wall, but whatever. She dumped the package onto her couch and stared at it. All this fuss over a damn rock. Okay, a rock containing what might be interesting family history, but still.

"So, open it already." Yes, she talked to herself. Maybe she should get a roommate. Or a pet.

Pulling the package closer, she pried up a corner and yanked at the tape. Tough little thing, and reinforced with half a pound of twine. She stood up and went in search of scissors. Instead she found a knife. "This'll work." She plopped herself down on the couch and slipped the blade between packing paper and box and sawed away at it. Dull knives. Not unexpected.

Ten minutes later, she opened the box flaps and stared inside. "A lot of cushioning for a rock. Sheesh." She dug through the wadded up paper. Newspaper? Very old, very thick newspaper. It didn't even appear to be newsprint. The ink was blurred to the point of illegibility. Odd. But then, a woman who bequeathed a rock to a stranger had to be pretty darn odd herself. Gladys was probably one of those pack rats that held on to newspapers for months, even years, before disposing of them. Maybe they'd been stacked all over the cottage.

Then Mina pulled up a last fold of paper and there it was: just an ordinary, grayish stone, obviously chipped and ground into a roughly rectangular block a few inches longer and wider than a standard brick. "Great. My inheritance."

Yes, she was an ungrateful, materialistic jerk, but wouldn't it have been great to inherit enough money to pay Jackson off so she could keep her home? She'd love to be able to thumb her nose at Jackson *and* his agreement by waving a hefty inheritance in his selfish, betraying face. And then there was the obvious advantage of keeping a roof over her head. A cornerstone, valuable as a keepsake though it might be, wouldn't do much in the way of providing shelter for a recently unemployed woman with a fast-dwindling bank account. So she was gaining a cornerstone and losing a house. Gee, there was irony.

Still, the attorney had mentioned old family papers. What if some of these papers were valuable? She lifted the stone out of its box. It was heavy, but not as heavy as it could have been. Hollow, obviously. She upended it and noted a sealed portion. Sealed with mortar? Or was that metal, just corroded to a point where it looked like stone? It was hard to tell. She scratched at the seal until a corner of it, already cracked, chipped away, leaving a tiny opening. But it wouldn't budge any further. She'd need something besides a paring knife to open it. A flat surface would help, too.

Hefting the stone, juggling its weight, she carted it out to the kitchen. She wondered what would be inside. She honestly was curious. Even if the papers inside weren't valuable—she reasoned with silent, recently rediscovered virtue—they would still be kind of neat to read—

*Boom!* And a second crash, as shattered glass and debris flew at her. Mina stumbled backward, half out of the kitchen. Tripping over her own feet, she banged up against the door-jamb on her way to the floor, with debris and shards of glass clattering around her. She heard masculine yells and one odd whooping sound as something hard hit her in the forehead. Then the hazy room went dark.

# CHAPTER TWO

A murmuring began low, then built to a rumbling, almost musical cadence.

*Well, fine, then. You just lie down and take a little nap, why don't you? Like I have all day for this. You know, I have some serious celebrating to do. Places to go, people to see, things to do. Damn, but this feels good. I can look around and—*

*Oh . . . heyyy. This place is wrecked. You live in this? Sheesh. I'd heard you Americans were spoiled, with your riches and your toys. But I thought, given your lineage, that you'd at least have a decent work ethic. Obviously I was wrong. I mean, sure, all hell broke loose when I popped my top, but you can't blame this hellhole on me. Just look at the piles and the dirty pots and now the rest of this mess, and—*

"Oh, my god!" A different voice. "Mac, call 911! We need an ambulance." Footsteps approached, ending in a thump as a man-sized weight dropped to the floor next to her. "Mina." She felt hands brushing her hair back, and gentle, unsteady pats to her cheek. "Come on, lady. Open your eyes."

"Where'd I put the damn phone?" A third voice was

muttering, and Mina distantly registered footsteps and rummaging. "What the hell happened? We barely even touched that window. Why'd it go down like that? And, hell, where'd the wall go?"

"Right now, the client's wearing part of it. You got that phone going yet?" the voice—Teague's?—barked overhead. But everything, even Teague's urgency, sounded muffled as though she were listening from underwater.

"Hang on. It's around . . . Here it is." A click. "Damn. It's dead."

"Find another one, damn it."

Another voice, farther off and faint: "Looks like everything blew from over here. Maybe it was something in this cabinet." She heard shuffling steps and the clank of cabinet doors. "Whatever it was blew off the cabinet door and there's nasty shit sprayed all over. Smells like chemicals . . . turpentine, I think. Doesn't explain why the window blew *in*, though. The window should have cracked, maybe, or even blown *out*, not . . ."

Mina felt hands plucking at her clothing and skin, as though carefully picking away bits of debris. She should try to open her eyes. It just hurt too damn much. And the light seeping through her eyelids was already driving stakes through her forehead.

"Mac, try the land line." The voice rumbled from close to her head, less muffled than before. "Dean, what else you got over there? Anything volatile? Last thing we need's a fire in here."

"Radiator's by the cabinet, next to the window." The response came from across the room. "It's a mess, like everything else. And still hot. Maybe it had something to do with the blast?" More shuffling and rustling, but muffled as though inside a cabinet. "Damn. There's rags and everything under here. She's lucky she didn't burn the place down a long time ago."

Oh, crap. So she was liable for *this* now? But that cabinet of rags had to be Jackson's mess. For all his charm and book smarts, the man was dumb as dirt with his hands—not that he'd willingly accept liability for anything. Great. Just what she needed. Another headache to go with her throbbing temples and the financial problems. She really needed to open her eyes. To argue . . . to explain. But it was so hard. She felt so floaty still.

A distant curse. "Land line's out."

"Check the lady's purse, then. She probably has a cell phone. Dean, take care of the rags and radiator along with anything else flammable or compromised." Shaky sigh, closer again. "Oh, hell." She felt a feather-light probing. "She's bleeding, too. Mina? Doll, you gotta wake up." Fingers brushed her throat, held, and she felt a long whoosh of breath. "She's got a pulse at least. But that's one helluva knot. Whatever it was must have corked her good."

*Damn. I guess I underestimated the physical effects all this would have. You weren't supposed to get hurt. My apologies. Mina, right?* It was an oddly hollow voice. Very close.

"Mmm."

"Hey, she's coming around!" Different voice, from just above her head. Then closer, murmuring in her ear. "Mina. Mina, it's Teague. You know, just Teague, like just Cher?" That voice was rich and soothing, and she clung to it. "Don't move yet, doll. But please, try to open your eyes if you can hear me."

Oh, man. This was really gonna hurt. No sense in putting it off any longer, though. They'd think she was in a coma. With effort, she parted her lashes just enough to see green eyes and a familiar, stubbly chin. It was Teague in all his rough working man's beauty. But very pale. She closed her eyes against the light. Licked her lips. "Hurts."

"I'll bet it does. Sorry about the flashlight. Any chance I could see your eyes again? I need to check out your pupils."

"Mm-hmm." She opened them, briefly, then winced and closed them again.

"Do you know who you are? Can you remember what happened?"

"Yes." She tried to raise her head.

"Whoa. Just relax. The ambulance should be here soon." He shouted over his shoulder. "Mac, did you put that call through yet?" He turned back to her. "There's glass everywhere, and I don't know what injuries you might have—"

"No ambulance." It would cost a fortune. No insurance.

"Don't worry about—"

"*No ambulance.*" She took a breath, then another, then carefully tried to wedge an elbow beneath her. Gritty bits scraped against her skin as she levered herself slightly upward.

"Wait—"

The whole freaking world started whirling. "Oh, god." She closed her eyes against the dizziness and slumped back again. "Could you help me up? Please? The floor's a mess." And she didn't like three big men hulking around while she was flat on her back. Stupid, but she felt at a disadvantage.

"No, you stay right where you are. You could be concussed or worse."

"Fine." She'd get up under her own steam. The guy was probably worried about liability. Opening her eyes, she raised her head and carefully focused on the guy Teague had called Mac. "Do *not* call that ambulance." The guy with the phone—*her* phone—paused, then held up a hand, obviously conceding for the moment. She closed her eyes, hoping efforts to regain her upright position wouldn't land her flat on her back again. She slid her arm behind her, trying to brace it to take weight.

"Christ, but you're stubborn." This from a disgruntled Teague. "Fine, I'll help you over to the couch. But slowly."

Teague sounded so harassed she might've even smiled if

her head didn't hurt so damned bad. Her shoulder was numb, too. "Thank you." She shifted more and winced.

"Hey, I said *slowly*."

She squeaked acquiescence. Good thing he was helping because, despite her threats, she knew she was all talk. It hurt too much to move. Alone, she'd probably just lie on the floor all day and wait for healing.

"Good. All you gotta do is be still. I'll move you." When she nodded just slightly, he carefully slid a hand under her knees, then paused. "You'll tell me if anything hurts? You can feel my arm under your legs, can't you?"

"Oh, yeah. I hurt from the back of my head on down." Except the shoulder. Oh, crap. Take that back. She could feel the shoulder now and it was throbbing like a—"Could we move, please? I think part of that stupid window's poking me in the butt right now."

"Seriously?"

"I sure hope not." Wouldn't it be fun to dive right into bankruptcy just so she could pay a doctor to dig glass out of her butt? "Never mind. Are you going to help me up or not?"

*Cranky wench, aren't you.* The words seemed to echo in her head. As if from far away and yet right there.

In her head? She rubbed one ear in a vague attempt to adjust her hearing. Was there debris inside her ear? A pressure difference? A damaged eardrum? "Hey, you'd be cranky, too, if a couple of windows blew in on you."

"No doubt." Teague, who sounded normal again, slid his other hand under her shoulder. Not the sore one, thank heavens. Then he lifted her, slowly, his attention obviously trained on any wince or out-of-joint portion of her anatomy.

At least he sounded right again. A cautious shifting of her weight, and then he lifted her, cradling her close to his big body. His handling of her was so careful, his attention focused so intently on her every expression, that she felt safe. Almost . . . cherished. Embarrassed by her yearnings, Mina had to object. "And where do you get off calling me a wench, anyway?"

He swung her sideways to fit through the doorway, his hold gentle but the movement a little too swift. "I didn't—"

"Ow! Watch it, would you?" She groaned, squeezing her eyes shut as the world spun and pain thundered between her ears.

"Sorry."

"I swear, it's a wonder you have any clients, what with the smart mouth and exploding windows. Not to mention crappy bedside manner."

"Now, wait just a minute. I didn't explode any damned window. That window was stable until whatever you had in your cabinet blew everything to smithereens." He sighed. "Hell, I don't have a clue what really happened. Even with the cabinet and all, that window shouldn't have fallen like that." He set her carefully on the couch, then glanced briefly through the doorway at the wrecked window. "At least it's not raining yet. We'd have a hell of a mess otherwise. The clouds looked heavy and green for a bit there. Guess it blew over."

"Great. Thanks for the weather report. Any chance you guys could clean up this stuff? You know, *before* the rain comes?"

He scowled at her, but raised his voice slightly. "Guys, could you clear out some of the debris? Lady's been hurt and needs medical attention."

"Hey, sure. No problem."

"Hope she's okay."

Once she heard footsteps retreating, Mina spoke through her teeth. "I said I don't need medical attention."

"What, do you have a phobia or something?"

"Yes. It's called fear of bankruptcy. I don't have health insurance." Dumb. Stupid. Tell her contractor she has money troubles right after he knocks down her wall.

He lowered his voice. "Look, you need to see someone. Most of these scrapes look okay–I could even clean them out for you if you want. But something slugged you damn hard. You were out cold. You might even need stitches there at your temple, and there's no telling what kind of internal damage you've got."

"I'll be fine."

"Look, I get the insurance problem. A visit to the emergency room could be pricey. But I can't just leave you like this. What if . . ." His eyes, which had gone stormy with worried impatience, suddenly cleared. "Hey, I got it. It's perfect. My neighbor's a doctor. Let me just call her and ask what I should do for you. If she says you need to see someone we can—"

"I don't want charity."

"You're not getting charity." He raised his eyebrows, his smile grim. "I'm covering my butt. Get it? This is purely self-interest. Does that work for you?"

She studied him through squinted eyes, not quite buying the self-interest argument. The guy's first instinct had been charitable, which could only raise the hackles of an otherwise responsible, proud-of-her-independence single female. Especially when it was so tempting to play damsel to his rough-edged white knight. Remember caution, Mina?

"Hey, I'm a small business owner. Legal liability is something I have to take seriously for me and my employees. And no money's gonna change hands, if that's what's bugging you. We're just bartering. My neighbor owes me, seeing as I fixed her door last weekend."

Mina didn't respond.

"You could consider her like a subcontractor, already included in that bid I made you. Sound reasonable?" *He* certainly sounded pleased with this interpretation.

Well, it was pretty ingenious of him, she had to admit. "Yeah, fine. Whatever." She closed her eyes again. It wasn't like she really had a choice at this point anyway; Teague fully intended to call his neighbor and was arguing now just to appease Mina's dignity.

*So much for gratitude.* A snide rumble of a voice. Hollow again.

Which irritated her. "Look, I'll be grateful later, okay? My head hurts."

A pause. "Sure, okay." Teague sounded doubtful and very alert. "Let me call the doc now and see if I can put some ice on that head."

She closed her eyes, vaguely registering a muffled click and conversation.

*Whine much lately?*

"What?" She opened her eyes and saw that Teague was attending solely to his cell phone. She blinked, then glanced over his shoulder to see two men on the far side of her kitchen, busily sweeping up debris in front of her cabinets. They seemed to be razzing each other in between instructions. Neither was even glancing in Mina's direction, much less talking to her.

*From what I've heard, you people have been whining for three hundred years and counting. Still, you used to be a hardier bunch. Old Gladbags wasn't such a whiner. She didn't have much, but she worked her tail off and she was an ex-pat. So it must be the soft living, then.*

"Oh, god." Her uncertainty mounting, Mina glanced from corner to shadow to window, from person to person to person. Nothing. What the hell? She worked her elbows under her with a groan and tried to—

"Damn it, I told you not to move. Hold on, Nell." Teague set his phone down and stalked over to her. "You. Lie back down. Or I'm hauling your ass to the emergency room."

"But, I heard—"

"Yeah, she's coming over. The woman's married to her Hippocratic Oath. Whaddya want? You'd think people would appreciate that in this day and age. Janelle just cares about people and she takes her job seriously. So lie still, damn it." He raised his eyebrows.

With a baffled grunt, Mina carefully slid low on her elbows and let her head sink back into the couch pillow. Honestly, it felt a whole lot better when she didn't move, but what *was* that?

*Lousy conk on the head. Big deal. You'll be fine in a bit.*

Heart pounding, Mina raised her head to glare past her chin at nothingness. "Damn it. What the hell's going on?"

Teague, who'd just clicked off the phone, looked over at Mina. "Doctor's on her way. She said ice was okay, so that's what I'm getting you." He paused to study her dubiously. "Are you going to pass out on me again? You look white as hell. Whiter than a few minutes ago, even, and you looked like a ghost then. Maybe we should—"

"No. Ice is fine." She sounded faint even to her own ears. Maybe her hearing was screwed up? She'd heard buzzing in her ears before. Ringing, too. So maybe this— what sounded like a voice but probably wasn't—was all just her imagination. She'd been knocked unconscious, after all.

*Hmph.*

She stilled, gazing around suspiciously as she rubbed at her ear. "I think I'll just rest now. If that's okay."

"It's all I wanted."

*Some people got it good.*

"Yeah, I got it good all right. No money, no insurance, a car older than my students—my former students, rather— and now a hole in my wall. Got it just great." Not that she was in the habit of feeling sorry for herself, but the unplanned ventilation of her house—okay, so it was planned in a manner of speaking, even if the head conk wasn't—was sort of jarring. And now she either had a concussion or she was just going nuts.

*Got it better than I do. Haven't had a good night's sleep since Maegth sicced her—Aaaargh!*

"Ouch." Mina cringed, raising a hand to her temple. "Will you please stop yelling? My head is killing me."

Teague raised his voice just above his men's chatter. "Guys, less talk and more action, okay? Injured client."

"Sure thing, Teague."

*Two thousand years and you'd think I would have learned not to say her name. Guess I've gone too damn long without a good—ahem. Sorry, Mina. I forgot about the lady in the room. Although, for a lady, you have some kind of mouth on you.*

"I know. I cuss like a trucker with hemorrhoids. It's been worse since my breakup, too, but then what do you expect?" She muttered it resignedly, still studying the inside of her eyelids. Everything was a funky reddish black with painful glowing splotches that were probably lights just waiting to nail her when she opened her eyes. "I'd like to see *you* discover your live-in boyfriend in bed with a bimbo named Tiffy. Bet it does wonders for your X-rated vocab, too. What a stupid name. Like you'd need a nickname for *Tiffany* for pete's sake, but I guess three syllables is just one too many for her to handle. Her spastic little brain shorts out after the schwa sound."

"Um. I'm sure you're right?" She heard a click and mumbling. "Yeah, Nell. Kick it in gear, please. She's sounding a little odd. Anything I should watch for?"

Mina kept her eyes closed throughout. Her head just plain hurt, damn it, so she was allowed to sound a little off, in her opinion. A moment later, she felt a cold bag of something touch the side of her head. She flinched. "That stings."

"Easy, honey. It'll help. Doc's orders."

Grimacing, she felt him replace the pack. After a few

moments, she had to agree. Cold felt better. "Got another one of those for my shoulder?"

"Your shoulder? You didn't mention your shoulder before." He sounded alarmed.

"That's because my head hurt too much and my shoulder was still numb."

"Damn it, you didn't say anything about a numb shoulder. Nell—"

"It's not numb anymore, genius. That's the point. It hurts like hell." She enunciated carefully, then heard a sigh and retreating footsteps.

"Any reason why you keep hurling insults at me?" The words came from the other room—her destroyed kitchen, she was pretty sure, which was downright airy now, thanks to her new, unobstructed view of the outdoors.

"You called names first." She sounded like a sulky brat, but it was true. After the last name-calling encounter with her ex-boyfriend, she'd sworn not to put up with that shit from any man. Even if the man in question did look too sexy for his tool belt. And his jeans. She was above all that. Although, she supposed, Mr. Sexy Teague was turning out to be darned helpful for a simple contractor. A lot of guys would have called the ambulance and shipped her off as fast as possible, not put up with her grumbling and nurse her in spite of herself.

Footsteps returned. "Which shoulder?"

"The right one." He gently settled a second pack against her shoulder as closely as possible without jostling. "Yeah, there. Thanks."

"Can you move your fingers?"

She wiggled them obligingly.

"Any nausea? Janelle said to ask."

"No."

"Confusion?"

"Huh?"

"Never mind." He sounded grim and worried again.

Okay, sure, she was confused. He would be too, if—

"Now hold still. You're bleeding and I need to see how bad it is."

"I am?" She felt pressure, then shooting pains across her forehead. "Ow, damn it!"

He pulled back, waited a few moments, then gently reapplied the towel to her temple.

She winced but, braced this time, didn't protest. "Is it bad? Do I need stitches?"

"Mmmm. Probably not. Bled like hell, but it doesn't look as bad as I thought it might. Can you see okay? How many fingers?"

She squinted at his hand and closed her eyes. "Three. Look, I can see as well as I ever could. The light just hurts my head."

"Okay. Well, good." He sounded marginally relieved.

"So . . . did your neighbor mention anything about hearing-changes?"

"You can't hear?" So much for relief, marginal or otherwise.

She shot him a look through lowered eyelashes before closing her eyes again. "Changes in, not loss of."

"Oh. Like ringing in your ears? That blast was pretty loud, so I wouldn't be surprised."

"Um. N-no. Not ringing. Exactly."

"Buzzing? Like a hollow sound maybe?"

"Hollow's getting there. But it sounds more like a . . . voice?" That sounded nuts even to her, and she opened her eyes slightly to gauge his reaction.

As expected, Teague looked appalled. "Oh. Shit." He dug in his pocket for the cell phone. "That does it."

*Hospital.* Stupid. She should have known. "No. Wait. Just . . . I was joking. Really. My hearing's just a little off. It's probably from the noise, like you said. That blast was loud."

He stilled, eyeing her dubiously. "You sure?"

"Sure, I'm sure."

"Maybe we should ask—"

"I think I'd be the one to know exactly what I'm hearing, wouldn't you?" Uh, *no*. She didn't know what the hell she was hearing. She just couldn't chance an emergency room bill.

But that *voice*. Yeah, but what voice? And she'd never heard voices before. Never verged on insanity before either, thank you very much. It had to be her imagination, right? She was just a little shaken by the whole window-smashing business.

*Damn. This guy's looking a little pale. You'd better take it back like you mean it, lady, or you're going to find yourself in the loony bin. Trust me on this. My hostesses and the loony bin experience go waaaaay back. At least they don't burn people at the stake anymore for witchcraft or demonic possession. That's sheer agony, babe. Hell, I remember this one time—*

"Stop!" She slapped her hands over her ears, trying to shove that damn voice back into silent oblivion where it belonged. She was losing it. Would the state pay her bills if she went nuts? Maybe they'd find a way to saddle Jackson with the expense—since he was probably responsible for driving her nuts in the first place. Actually, inconveniencing Jackson would almost be worth her insanity, except she damn sure didn't want to end up locked in an institution doodling with finger paints all day.

*Fine, then. Lord, but you're touchy. Just a little human contact was all I wanted and you deny me even that. Consider me gone.*

Mina swallowed. She hadn't heard that. She hadn't. She'd just rattled her brains a little. Carefully, she lifted one hand off her ears.

Nothing.

Other hand.

Still nothing.

Cautiously, she opened her eyes. Teague looked rattled. And, yes, he was shouting into the phone.

"I swear to God, Janelle, you get here right now. I don't know what the hell to do. She's not making sense, talking about voices and—"

"Teague."

He pointed a finger at her, his eyes hot. "You just lie still a minute. This shit's just wrong—"

"It was a joke, Teague. You know, a *joke*? A bad one, granted." That stupid voice was right about one thing: she'd better make Teague believe her voice comment was a joke or she'd be looking at an emergency room visit, if not more. "I guess I should give the lame humor attempts a rest until my head's better, huh? Sorry about that." Teague was still freaked and angry—and Mina would bet the good doctor Janelle's ears were ringing every bit as much as her own right now.

Ringing. That's what it was. "It's just that my ears kept ringing. And you shouting was making it worse. Teague?" She tried for a sane-but-bravely-enduring smile.

Teague focused a set of seriously harassed-looking green eyes on her. "Well, guess what? I don't believe you. I'll bet you even have a concussion. A bad one. Your brain probably imploded just like the window did."

Mina dropped the smile. "Gee, that's mature. Why don't you let *me* talk to your friend?"

Teague looked undecided, and Mina heard the echo of chatter over the phone. Mina held out a hand.

Reluctantly, Teague passed her the phone. "She says talking to you would be a good idea."

Mina accepted the cell phone. "Hi. Janelle, is it?"

"Officially, it's Dr. Janelle Corrington, but if you're a friend of Teague's, Janelle's great. So, you must be my patient."

"Sounds like. Look, your buddy Teague's just a little panicked over here."

Janelle laughed wryly. "So I gather. How do you feel?"

"Bruised and tired and rattled."

"Sounds about right. Any nausea? How's your vision?"

"No, and fine. Just a rotten headache—and Teague already stopped the bleeding, so that's not a problem. Even he admits the cut doesn't look bad."

"A cut? On your head?"

"Well. Yeah."

"I still want to see you, in that case. Just to be on the safe side. I'll be there in ten minutes. Try to keep him calm in the meantime, if you would."

Mina laughed a little, but stopped when it made her head pound. "Sure." She hung up.

Mina glanced at Teague. "Janelle's on her way. She sounds less than stressed, so take it easy, please. You don't even know me."

"Well, hell, your kitchen blows up, part of your wall falls down, and you wind up unconscious on the floor. Since I and my guys were on the other side of that wall, we feel just a little responsible. I don't like that."

"Relax. I'm not suing." She muttered it tiredly. "I don't have the cash for an attorney anyway."

"You don't? Am I going to get paid?"

"Sure, *now* you worry about my money."

"Well, it looks like you got a little boo-boo head to me." Dr. Janelle Corrington gave Mina a wide-eyed look and Mina snickered over Janelle's shoulder at Teague.

"Smart ass." Teague was looking harassed, but less freaked.

Janelle winked at her. "Just keep it on ice and take it easy. No driving for today, either. I want you to call me if the pain gets worse, or if you experience memory loss or confusion, blurred vision, inability to move your limbs or nausea. Got it?"

"Maybe."

"Here's my number." She held up a business card and set it on the table next to Mina's head. "And I want an update from you tomorrow, regardless. Understood?"

Mina nodded. "Thanks."

"Is that it?" This from Teague. He sounded doubtful. "That's the official doctor's exam of a head injury?"

"Well, I can't exactly open her skull to physically probe her brain—"

"What about CAT scans or an MRI or all that other fancy stuff? Shouldn't she have something like that?"

Janelle spoke patiently. "Her pupils are fine. The bleeding's stopped. The bump is protruding, which will, with any luck, rule out any internal swelling. And the cut, as much as it bled, doesn't even need stitches. She got lucky."

"So today's my lucky day," Mina mused brightly. "Who'da thunk it? First I inherit a rock and then I have a wall blow up in my face and I don't even die. Obviously, it's all just a matter of perspective."

Teague turned a scowl on Janelle. "See what I mean? She's been spewing nonsense since she hit her head."

"Oh, like that's different from any other day." Mina carefully tipped her head so she could meet his eyes. "You hardly know me. Maybe I always spew nonsense."

Janelle started laughing.

"Oh, and Teague?" Mina raised her voice to be heard over Janelle. "Don't even *think* about leaving until that wall is capable of repelling thunderstorms."

"Yeah, fine. Women."

Mina turned back to Janelle. "Amazing, isn't it? I just met Teague in person for the first time today, but we bonded over pain and panic. Sweet, huh?"

"Very." Janelle gave her an odd look.

"No worries. I'm not hitting on him. You're his neighbor, right? I get it. Dibsies. I don't poach."

"Oh, but he's not—"

"Nell." Teague gave the doctor a sharp look. "Leave it alone. Seriously. The woman's just plain scary."

Janelle sighed and looked ready to clobber Teague harder than the wall had clobbered Mina. "You're annoying. Why couldn't the wall fall on you?"

He smiled. "Because then Mina would be liable. And she doesn't have insurance."

Mina frowned. "No, it's money I don't have. And medical insurance. I think I have homeowner's insurance, though. Don't I?"

"Hell. Yeah, you probably do." He looked thoughtful. "I don't know why it didn't occur to me before—guess we were both distracted—but . . ." Teague spread his arms and let them slap against his thighs. "There's your answer. That wall of yours has to be defective or it wouldn't have come down like that. The window busting, fine, but not tossing big chunks of your wall out with it. I'll swear to it. Give the insurance company a call. Have them check it out and pay my bill for you. We'll call it restoration."

Mina stared. "Seriously?"

He shrugged. "It should work out that way. Call 'em."

"Who would have thought a wall blowing up in my face would be nothing less than a stroke of good fortune? So to speak."

Janelle shrugged philosophically. "Well, I'd better get back to my office. Take it easy."

"I'll walk you out." Teague dropped a big hand on Janelle's shoulder and followed her out the front door.

When the door closed behind them, Janelle glanced quickly over her shoulder, then turned back to Teague. She spoke quietly. "Is she the one, then?"

"I don't know. I think so, but I just don't know yet. Hell, she's *got* to be the one. Everything points to it. It looks like her. The house is right, too." He eyed Janelle intently.

"And she keeps talking about voices. I thought at first she was just off her rocker . . ." He sighed shakily. "That head injury was damn close, though. Scared the hell out of me. I seriously thought she was dead at first. What would I have done if . . ." He shook his head.

"Hey, don't think like that. Everything's fine. And you're so close to getting everything now. You've come so far." She touched his arm. "Just hang in there a little longer. You can do this. You have no choice."

"Well, I'm damn sure going to try." He met her eyes. "You're sure she's going to be okay?"

"As sure as I can be."

"I need better than that. What can I do?"

"Not a lot, honestly. Stay with her as long as she'll let you. Call her later tonight. If you see or hear anything out of the ordinary, call me. If she loses consciousness or seems to freak way out, get her to the hospital. No arguments. Okay?"

"Okay." Watch over her. He could do that. "Thanks, Nell. I owe you one."

"No you don't, you idiot. And if you find out she's not the one you're looking for . . . maybe you should ask her out anyway?" She grinned. "Hey, I know you're on a mission, but you're still entitled to something of a life, aren't you?"

"Will you please just give it up?" Like he wasn't already tempted enough. For such a smart mouth, Mina looked like a frothy dessert, with creamy pink skin, chocolaty brown eyes, and wild, strawberry blond curls dancing around her shoulders. All topping off some lush curves that just begged for cuddling.

"I saw you looking at her," Janelle taunted, almost singsong. "Big, dazed green eyes. And you were hovering over her. Like some mutt drooling over a juicy bone."

He scowled down at her. "I was not."

"You were."

Was he? Crap. "Yeah, well, you're annoying." So he was reduced to the lowest common denominator around Janelle. Regularly. She was like the bratty little sister he never had and maybe wanted just a little.

"And you didn't answer my question."

"Which means absolutely nothing other than that you were sticking your nose way into my business."

"Somebody has to. You've been disturbingly monk-like in the past few years."

"Oh, now that's out of line." He gave her a disgusted look. "One of these days, I'm going to overshare just as badly as you want me to. Then you'll be sorry. See if I care."

"You couldn't shock me if you tried. You see, *I*"—she raised her nose with great superiority—"am a doctor." The pose, plus a sprinkling of freckles across her cheeks and nose, made her look about twelve years old. "And I've worked the emergency room on a Saturday night. You know what that's like? I've heard and seen everything. Wanna talk overshare? You wouldn't believe what some people do with rodents. Even vacuum hoses."

He groaned. "Oh, that's just sick."

"Nothing wrong with your imagination, I see." Janelle cackled, blue eyes flashing wickedly. "How I wish you could see the look on your face." Shaking her head, she patted his cheek before trotting down the steps. She glanced over her shoulder. "Oh, and by the way?"

"Yeah?"

"She was watching you right back." Janelle raised her eyebrows above twinkling eyes, then jogged off to her car.

"Women." But Teague was staring into the window now. Mina seemed to be . . . talking to herself?

*At last, we are alone, my Mina with the filthy tongue.*

Mina jumped at the disturbingly familiar voice. Not again. She turned her gaze from the window through which she was trying not to watch Teague and Janelle, and gazed around the room. "Who's there?" She didn't see anything. Was that good or bad?

*Yeah, it's me again. And I know I promised to go away, but good grief, woman. I've been waiting for contact with someone, anyone, for well over a month now. Stupid death law bureaucracy.*

"Oh, god." She squeezed her eyes shut. "If I let them put a straitjacket on me and lock me up, will you go away?"

*Nope. I can't. You're stuck with me.*

"Stuck with you. Who are you? What are you? No—" She stopped herself, hand raised in a halting gesture. "Forget I asked. I don't want to know. But, like, are you another personality, coexisting inside my head? And maybe you just decided to introduce yourself and, now that I'm weakened with a head injury, you're going to take over the rest of my mind?"

*Damn. Now there's an imagination.*

"Well, I do teach creative writing." Or had, up until she was fired for moral objections. Leave it alone, Mina. Rage will not help matters. Concentrate on the disembodied voice. The possibility of insanity. That kind of thing.

*Gladys thought I was a genie.*

"Are you? A genie, I mean? I can't believe I asked that."

*Sure, I'm a genie. You rubbed your head, out I popped, and now you got three wishes. Or not. Do I look like a damn genie?*

"How would I know? I can't see you."

*Try opening your eyes.*

"I don't want to."

*Weenie.*

"For a disembodied voice, you are such a brat."

*So look at me. I haven't had a body in . . . well, a long time. Give it a gander. Tell me what you think.*

Not a good idea. *Not* a good idea. She took a deep breath. Then slitted her eyes open. Shrieked. Squeezed her eyes shut again. "Ohgodohgodohgodnotagoodidea. Badbadbadidea."

# CHAPTER THREE

"Mina?" Teague slammed back into the house and jogged over to the couch. "Are you okay? You didn't try to get up, did you?"

"Nope. Not moving. Never moving again." Irresponsible to move without looking. "Let's go for a ride to the nice funny farm, okay?"

"Huh?"

"You don't happen to see anything over there, do you?" Still not looking—never looking again—she pointed to a spot in front of her television.

She heard a rustling, as he presumably turned to face in the direction she was pointing. "A TV?"

"Other than that. Something you'd remark on, say, *immediately*."

"It's kind of a mess, but—"

"Never mind. Funny farm it is."

Unless she was already there. Hooves belonged on the farm, didn't they? She chanced a peek at where those hooves used to be. But the hooves were gone now, and the voice was silent.

Meanwhile, Teague was staring at her like *that* again—a look no man she'd met just hours ago should be giving her with this kind of frequency. He seemed intrigued, despite himself—right along with rattled and mildly repulsed. And she hadn't even introduced him to her mother yet. A new record for speed repulsion.

"Are you ready to knock off work now?" she asked brightly, and turned her attention to the mess she'd once called a kitchen.

As she'd requested, the guys had covered the damaged part of her wall and window with a sheet of heavy plastic. At least the weather was reasonably mild today. They'd left friendly September well behind and cooler October was finally here and starting to feel like it. Wasn't it odd how weather was such a safe subject, both for polite conversation and for internal distraction from minor hoof and voice problems?

"Is there someone I can call to stay with you tonight?"

"Oh, there's no need for that. I'll be fine." Just her and the TV, blaring at each other all night. She'd drown out the voice if necessary. She was not ready to deal with the implications of hooves and voices. Suddenly, she really, really didn't want to be left alone. At least, not until she felt a little steadier. There was a thought. Maybe this little problem would fade away as her head got better. See? Something to look forward to. That and finding those papers, maybe.

She frowned. "Hey, did you happen to see a big rock on the floor anywhere?"

Teague paused, eyeing her oddly. "A rock?"

"Or a block, really. Made out of grayish stone and about so"—she held up her hands, about twelve inches apart—"big? The proportions of a brick, just a little larger."

"I don't remember seeing anything like that around

here." He frowned thoughtfully. "Why? Is there something special about this rock?"

"I was holding it when everything went boom."

"Huh. Well, I could look around for it, if you want."

"Please. I mean, I'd look for it myself, but I'm pretty sure my head would fall off and make a mess everywhere." Besides, if she did the looking herself, then he would go home—which was increasingly the last thing she wanted, fool that she was. She was scared to be alone *and* scared to reveal her latent freakish side to the hot guy who was being so nice to her. Still, fear of confronting her psychoses trumped fear of exposure, at least for now.

"Well, we wouldn't want that." He smiled distractedly, already scanning the kitchen floor. "The guys did some sweeping in here. I wonder if they chucked it into the can with some of the other stuff they picked up. Let me just check these boxes first and then I'll look outside in the bin."

"My legacy chucked out with the trash. That's logical somehow." She watched him tilt up a corner of a box they'd used to collect some of the larger debris.

"A rock is your legacy?" He spared her a glance as he shook the box slightly to shift its contents.

"That's what I was told. Some distant relative I've never met left it for me in her will. Go figure. Anyway, I was carrying it into the kitchen to get a better look at it when the window blew. It went flying about the same time I did. I'm pretty sure that's what clubbed me in the head."

"Ouch. Rock that size." He shook his head. "You're lucky you weren't hurt worse."

"Probably just a glancing blow. And the rock wasn't as heavy as it looked, either. It was hollow."

"Yeah?" His voice rose with interest. "Was there something inside it?"

She shrugged. "I don't know. I never got the chance to see. The window blew in before I could finish opening it."

"Bummer." He grimaced. "Here's a thought. If the brick was hollow, isn't there a good chance that it shattered like your window did?"

"It wasn't *that* hollow." She frowned, remembering again the blow to her forehead. "In fact, it felt pretty darn sturdy."

"Well, it did hit your head and then the floor. I still think we could be looking for rock dust at this point."

She made a face. "My head's not that hard." She heard mumbling. "What was that?"

He glanced back and grimaced ruefully.

She narrowed her eyes. "Something uncomplimentary, I take it?"

He cleared his throat. "Just one of those reflexive responses a guy should know better than to say out loud." He turned to another, smaller pile of debris the guys had dumped in a box and left in a corner.

"Uh-huh." She raised her eyebrows. "Feeling a little passive aggressive, anyone? You know, if you don't want to look for the rock, then don't. You're the one who offered."

He ignored her passively aggressive suggestion and strove for a change of subject. "Passive aggressive, huh? I thought you said you taught English or writing or something. Not psychology." He pulled a piece of wallboard out of the box, set it aside and reached for more.

Mina watched him, feeling increasingly guilty. For all his muttering about hard heads and stubborn women, the man was still going through the rubble for her. And that was after icing down her bruises and calling his doctor friend to help. Ungrateful bitch that she was, she couldn't seem to stop whining and complaining every time the man turned around. Teague was under no obligation to root through trash for her.

And it certainly wasn't his fault she'd experienced a hoof and voice problem.

She cleared her throat. "You're right. I taught language

arts, with an emphasis on creative writing, at the middle school. But they let me go a couple months ago. I'm still looking for another job."

"Teachers are pretty scarce around here, aren't they? Seems like every public service announcement encourages 'our young people to invest in future generations' by becoming a public schoolteacher."

"It's a campaign the Mason County School District's been promoting. We'll see if it works."

"Still, if they have a shortage, you shouldn't have any problem finding another job, right?"

"Sure." Except for that whole moral grounds issue. Tiffy really needed to die. Preferably with Jackson's favorite body part wedged between her silicone-plumped lips—the exact position they'd assumed shortly before Mina discovered them together a few months ago. In Mina's own bed, no less. Tiffy was quite the hypocritical bitch.

"So that's good, then, right?" Teague gave her a probing look, obviously realizing there was more to the situation than Mina was saying. "You'll find a job pretty easily?"

"Let's just say it wasn't a genial parting of ways between the school and me. I'll probably have to move and start over somewhere else."

"That bad? What did you do, sleep with the school principal?"

Mina blinked in mild surprise. "No, the superintendent."

"Oh. Well." He choked back a laugh. "Guess you didn't do that halfway, did you?"

"No, I left that to Tiffy, who happens to be the stepmother of a student of mine. *She* did him halfway. I was just stupid enough to cohabit with the man while she was half-doing him. Then she got me fired."

"Over . . . ?" He looked amazed and confused and mildly . . . titillated? No doubt he was picturing a hair-pulling, girl-slapping catfight in the school cafeteria. Pervert.

She scowled. "The school board objects to its teachers living indiscreetly with their unmarried lovers. Tiffy simply brought my particular indiscretion to their attention, and that was that."

"Seriously? That's why they fired you?"

"Morality clause. Setting an example for the kids, blah, blah, blah. I could have stayed on, but they obviously wanted to make me miserable enough to leave. So I left."

"What about the superintendent? Was he fired, too?"

"Nope. He's still superintending. Since his position is purely administrative, he's not, technically, mingling with the kids everyday. He's less likely to contaminate them with his questionable morals."

"And the stepmom he was screwing?"

"No proof of that, other than my immoral word. Meanwhile, Jackson and I signed our names to a single mortgage. Proof."

"That. Really. Sucks."

She relaxed and even managed a smile. "Yes. It. Does."

"And so does she, apparently. *Tiffy*? Sure she's not a dog? It sounds like a dog's name."

Mina, who'd dropped the smile at the "so does she" part, snorted in amused surprise. "Wellll . . . sort of depends on your perspective, I suppose. Although I have to admit she did seem to enjoy going down on all fours."

"Ooooh, that's bad." But he was laughing.

"You know, I could really like you, Teague." In a purely platonic manner, of course. After shenanigans between Tiffy and Jackson, no way was Mina going to occupy a corner of yet another lovers' triangle. Nope. An ethical woman observed dibsies, and apparently Janelle—whom Mina had liked, damn it all—had dibsies on her hot neighbor. That meant paws off for Mina. "I wasn't sure about you at first, what with all the wench comments, but this woman or dog question gives me a whole new take on your personality."

"Wench comments?"

She waved a hand, smiling generously. "Don't worry about it. We'll just put it behind us."

He frowned. "You're sure you're okay?"

When she groaned, he held his hands up in surrender. "Just asking. So how big was this rock again?"

"About—"

"Wait a minute." He shoved aside a filthy pile that used to be kitchen curtains and reached behind them. "Is this it?" He held out a chunk of familiar gray stone so she could see it.

"It sure is." The corner was chipped and the seal was gone, but the brick was otherwise intact.

"Well, the thing's empty now. Any idea at all what used to be inside? Papers, objects, anything?" He studied the rock, as though looking for some fragment that might give him a clue. "Just so I know what else I should be looking for."

"Like I said, I never got the chance to check. The attorney said there might be family papers or keepsakes inside. Like a time capsule, you know? But he was only speculating. He didn't really know either."

"I see." Moving closer to her remaining kitchen window, he held the rock out to capture the slanted rays of sunlight and peered into the opening. He carefully poked a finger inside, skimming the interior. "There's no sign that anything was ever in there. No bits of paper or plastic or dust other than rock."

She smiled ruefully. "Not a big surprise, I have to admit. It could be that there never was anything in there. And wouldn't that just figure. My inheritance from a mysterious relative: a hollow rock."

"But you never know." Turning back, he gave her a kind look. "It wouldn't hurt to look around a little more just to see. I mean, the rock's not too damaged. Maybe the contents—if there were any—made it through the blast okay, too." Carefully, he set the rock down within her reach and turned back to the dusty heap he'd abandoned. "So, we're looking for old paper, maybe? Or just anything that didn't used to be a wall." His expression invited a smile.

The man was humoring her and then some. He didn't have to do this. "Have I mentioned yet how much I appreciate you doing this? I know I haven't been very nice to you today, considering all you've done, but I honestly do appreciate it."

"Eh, don't worry about it. You should see Janelle when she's on a bitch. Ug-ly."

Mina laughed and watched as he continued to search. After twenty minutes of that, during which time she felt guiltier and guiltier, she finally called him to a halt. "Hey, Teague? Really, thanks so much for everything you've done, but it's probably not worth your time to search anymore. For all I know this block was empty when they delivered it to me. A shame, but there it is."

Teague straightened and turned to her. "You sure? I don't mind looking some more."

"I know. And you're making me feel like crap now." She grinned at him. "You know, for the bitch part."

"Not a problem." After returning her smile, he glanced around, obviously a bit surprised to realize they were alone in the tiny house. His men had left almost an hour ago. "I guess whatever it is will turn up if it's meant to, right?"

"That's how it usually works." It was late. She'd imposed on the guy enough. "So, you probably need to go, don't you."

He paused, hand stuffed in his hip pocket. "Maybe I could get you dinner or something? To make you more comfortable?"

The guilt compounded. "No, really. You've done too

much already. I'll be fine." Besides, it was time she worked up some courage to face her demons alone.

"How's the head? Any double vision or funky hearing or anything?"

"I'm fine. Just sore. So, I'll see you in the morning, then?"

"I—yeah. Bright and early. Don't get up. I'll lock up after myself." He eyed her window doubtfully. "Not that it does any good."

"I'll be fine."

He still didn't look happy. "Please, just let me call someone to stay with you. A friend or a neighbor, even someone who could just look in on you?" He sounded almost pleading.

Mina glanced away. Honestly? There wasn't a soul she could call on for help—and not just because of her talking demon delusions, although exposure of her insanity could be problematic. No, Mina might as well be living on a deserted island right now. Such a switch from as little as six months ago, when she and Jackson were, as far as she knew, living the perfect little life, with the house, the white picket fence, careers they loved, the future on a platter, even friends and co-workers who wished them well.

Now . . . hell, now she might even prefer living on that deserted little island. It was all gone. Everything she'd ever wanted had almost been hers, and boom, it was gone. Not just the boyfriend who, she now admitted, had probably been a mistake. But everything else that had felt so blessedly normal. People, for pete's sake. Small talk, smiles, friendly gestures. That was gone, too.

Busy with work, a new house, and her now-defunct romance, Mina had lost touch with friends she'd made in college. No doubt they were all pursuing their own, very different lives as well. As for her more recent acquaintances, well, losing her job due to her great acts of immorality tended to stigmatize a woman who lived in the same neighborhood where she worked. Ever since Mina's professional fall from grace, the coworkers and near neighbors she'd once called friends—or at least acquaintances—had given her a wide berth. Friendly greetings had turned to speculative, even suspicious glances. So Mina was the neighborhood freak all over again. She had no one.

Well, except for her mom. And tonight Mina just didn't feel up to enduring a séance or exorcism or whatever horror her mother would deem appropriate to banish the voice and hoof problem. Wouldn't the neighbors just love that?

Silently cringing, she forced a smile for Teague. "No, you don't need to call anyone. I'll be fine. But thanks anyway."

His brow furrowed briefly, then cleared a little. "Look, call me crazy, but would you do me a favor?"

"Um, sure. I guess. What?"

He dug in his back pocket, retrieved his wallet, then slipped out a worn-looking business card. He handed it to her. "This is my number at home. And Janelle left hers on the little table here. You start to feel weird at all—I mean *anything*—call me or call her. Promise?"

"Aw. Just Teague. Are you worried about me?" She was touched, damn it. The man didn't have to go this far.

"Well, do you blame me? You took a brick to the head just a while ago, fell down unconscious. I don't feel right about leaving you here."

"I appreciate it. Really. It's . . . a lot more than a lot of guys would do. Even ones on the payroll." She smiled. "I'll be fine. But, yes, if I start feeling like my head's really busted, I'll call. Okay?"

He didn't look happy, but he nodded. "See you tomorrow, then, if not before. Honestly. Don't hesitate to pick up the phone. It's no trouble at all and I don't live that far from here."

She raised both hands helplessly, palms out. "I believe you." She smiled again. No doubt she looked like a love-

crazed—or at least lust-crazed and soft-brained—idiot.
"Thanks."

Reluctantly, he gave her a little wave and left, locking up
as promised. He really, really was a nice guy. If it weren't
for the wonky head and another woman's dibsies, she might
try following up on that one.

*Shameless hussy. I saw the way you were looking at him.*

She jumped, then sank slowly into the cushions. Right.
That little problem she'd been having. To think she'd actually dreaded the dead silence of an empty home. "You're
still here."

*Well, yeah. It's not like I have anywhere else to go.*

Gee, that didn't sound promising—and this hearing-of-
voices-in-the-head really had to go. The least her twisted
mind could do was provide an acceptable visual to go with
the aural half of this figment of her imagination. Still, any
visual was better than no visual. "Okay. I'm ready for it.
Show yourself again. If I'm having a nervous breakdown,
I'd like proof from at least two of my senses."

*Sure about that? You really freaked last time.*

"Oh, no. I'm braced for it this time. Give me your worst."
She stared, hard, at the place where he'd last appeared.

The air in front of her TV seemed to thicken, the colors
and lines blurring and darkening. Hooves shimmered into
view, followed by long, slender legs, muscular flanks, belly,
chest, and arching neck. The very last to come into view
was perhaps the weirdest, at least for her. Yellow eyes. A
black stallion with eerily glowing yellow eyes. He swished
his tail at her and said, "You know, the stallion's one of my
more attractive embodiments. Women usually find it . . .
exciting."

"Oh, my god. A lecherous horse who talks. This is too
much. You're right. It's been way too long since I got laid if
I'm picturing literal stallions. And you know, some things
should really never leave the metaphorical level." She was

shaking her head, simply rejecting what her eyes were telling her. It just couldn't be. "So you just stay here. I'll go get Teague back and shamelessly jump him and then you can go away. Sound like a plan?" She bared her teeth in a brittle smile.

"Now why would I encourage you to jump some other man? I'm here and obviously as potent as anything you can conjure in that inflexible little brain of yours."

"Ooooooh. Ickickickick. Blech. Propositioning from a horse. What, do I look like Catherine the Great?"

"Actually, I have it on excellent authority that she really did not do horses."

"You do. Great." She frowned, intrigued despite herself. "Whose authority?"

A lecherous grin—on a horse, for pete's sake—slowly curled his lips. "My own. Naturally."

"So what did you—" Mina stared, ideas gelling into visuals she couldn't possibly entertain. "Never mind. I don't want to know."

The horse shifted its weight and turned its head with the equine equivalence of coy modesty. "Although I have to say, once I shifted to human form, she was really quite impressed."

"Lalalalalalala. I'm not lissst-en-innnnng. Hm-hmmm-hmmmmmmmmm-hm-hmmmmmmmmmmm."

"Oh, lighten up. I was just teasing. Like a Russian empress would rendezvous with a condemned puca. You are so gullible. You know, I'd almost forgotten about that puritanical aspect you Americans have. You consider yourselves such rebels, but let anyone admit to a few creative sexual urges and you get all uptight and judgmental. Narrow-minded prudes."

"I was not—and it had nothing to do with—aaaargh. So why am I being lectured by a horse? On the subject of sexuality, no less?" She slumped back on the couch. "You know, this is really not my day. I started out this morning thinking—foolishly, of course—that there was a possibility I could pay up on my mortgage and keep a roof over my head. I end the day with a rock instead of cash, my wall imploded, a possible concussion, and a horse lecturing me about sexual inhibitions."

"I was just saying—"

"Right. Forget sex. I'm not talking to you or acknowledging your existence further until you answer some questions. You did say you've been deprived of human contact for a while? I could make it a whole lot longer." Could she? Was she really getting caught up in this little hallucination she was having?

"Fine. Ask away." A bored horse. This wasn't right.

"What are you? Mr. Ed? And why are you here? Assuming I'm not nuts—and that is a stretch, I have to admit—can anyone else see you or am I the only one blessed with this lovely vision? And last, what the hell do you want from me? Why me?"

"*I*"—the horse raised its chin and tail, appearing almost regal for a moment—"am a puca." It widened its eyes for effect. When Mina didn't react, the horse dropped its tail back to normal position. "I really hate this. You've never even heard of a puca? What's the problem with the last three generations? I just do not get respect anymore."

Mina shrugged. "We call you guys horses around here, but generally, our horses don't talk."

"Oh, pah!" In a shimmering flash, the stallion shifted from horse to eagle to goat to muscular nude man blur and back to horse.

Mina blinked, dazed by the sexy man blur. She couldn't see the human form or face clearly, the flash had been so brief—just a stirring impression of charisma and sensual arrogance potent enough to kick her in the libido. Then he was back to equine form. "Okay. A little more than a horse . . ." Her damn heart was palpitating, in fact. That last image . . .

The horse showed his teeth in a slimy grin. "You liked that one, didn't you?"

"One what?" She frowned, defensive now. He was still a horse, damn it all. Shut up, libido. Nobody asked you.

"The human form." The horse tipped its head with false modesty. "I understand it's easy on a woman's eyes. And other parts."

Mina scowled. "Back to the definition part. You said you were a puca. And . . ." She blinked, remembering blurred shapes. "I mean you . . ." Nervous, she licked her lips and tried again. "So yooouuu . . ."

"So I . . ." Ducking his head slightly, he followed her helpless gaze and her drawn-out word, then ended her question for her: ". . . shape-shift?"

"Yeah. That." She blinked, then frowned. "No, not that. This just can't be. It's all in my head."

He snorted impatiently. "Do you want your answers or not?"

"You call these answers?"

"Yes, I do." The horse was calm.

"Then, fine. Let's go ahead and weave this fantasy a little more. Why not? I can still call the doctor later."

"Oooh." His ears pricked up. "The sexy she-doctor who attended you earlier?"

"Down, boy." She paused. "Oh, good grief."

"Yeah, horses don't rear much. So, on to your next question, which I believe was a rather rude 'why are you here?' I'm here because you inherited me."

"No, I inherited a rock. No one told me anything about a horse."

"I'm not a horse. I'm a—"

"For now I choose to call you a horse and will continue to pretend that this conversation was conjured out of a busted brain. You're just part of a freaky dream I'm intended to interpret and analyze when my head's fixed."

The horse sighed.

A horse— No. She couldn't keep doing this.

"Didn't you read the letter from the old lady?" The horse did a cheerful little shuffle step. "Obviously not or I wouldn't be free, now would I?"

"Huh? You mean, the letter the attorney gave me?" She glanced around for it.

"That's the one. And before you ask, no, I don't know what's in the letter from your cousin Gladys. I'm not allowed to look. Only you are. But I gotta figure it's full of rules and spells and dictates and no-nos, or why else would they keep it from me?"

"Rules—"

"But I'm free! At least a little free. I mean, sure, I can't exactly go anywhere exciting or shift into anything truly effective until I satisfy a vengeful Druid priest. But at least I'm not locked inside that dank little . . ." The horse's gaze—and Mina's—slid to the rock lying next to her.

"No. In there? You were inside the cornerstone? But you wouldn't fit." She was scowling even before the horse tipped its head in a mocking manner. "So, what, did you poof yourself into a little gray mousie and squeeze yourself inside the rock?"

"I wish. No, that was my disembodied form in there. Which, like that envelope you never opened, is just one more thing we should probably discuss."

Mina closed her eyes. "Right. How did I get myself into this, anyway? Obviously, through sheer idiocy. When it comes to legal paperwork, one should always, always be suspicious. 'Guardian' of a rock, my ass." She sighed and refocused. "So, let's try this one: Why me?"

"Why were you picked to inherit me?"

She nodded.

"Well, there's your lineage, of course. You know, the whole Avebury thing. Oh, and by the way, the pronunciation's more like *Ay*-bry, not Ave-berry. I think maybe your ancestor had a cold when he stepped foot on American soil and offered his name."

"Gee. Fascinating. I know an attorney who would just love to chat with you. Can we skip semantics, though, and get back to the fun inherit-a-puca fantasy?"

Long ears tipped back just a little as yellow eyes narrowed. "I was just explaining. So, like I said, first there's the Avebury lineage. But that wouldn't do it by itself. No, what it all boils down to, baby, is *spinsterhood*."

"Oh, please. Like anybody even uses that word anymore. Lots of people voluntarily stay single well into their thirties, forties, even longer."

"Hey, I'm just answering your question. You should have married your little boyfriend when you had the chance instead of just shacking up with him." He snorted in what Mina could only presume was mocking equine laughter. "Ironically enough, my ex-girlfriend's outraged daddy didn't think my female jailer needed to be virginal. Virginity is not the standard; the unmarried state is."

She scowled. "Why should either be an issue?"

"Practicality. This way you can devote all your time to watching over me, instead of taking care of a husband and family. Sure, a virgin guardian sounds so otherworldly on paper, but virginity's no longer the prize it once was. Consequently, a virginity requirement would disqualify too many potential guardians. Such a shame for you that the Druid priest Akker saw far enough into the future to realize how mores would change over time." He shrugged. "So that means your marital status counts. Your sex life, however, is completely inconsequential."

"Oh, nice. You sound like my mother now."

"Hates sex, huh?"

Mina gave a short laugh. "Oh, no. Just the opposite. She thinks I'm one mass of inhibitions and hang-ups just because I prefer serial monogamy to perpetual slutdom." Okay, so that was a mild exaggeration. Lizzy Dixon never wanted her daughter to engage in mindless, meaningless sex, but she also thought Mina took the act a little too seriously.

"A little repressed are we?" The stallion made sympathetic noises. "Well." And now there was a sly lilt to the horse's voice. "Maybe I could do you a favor before I trot off into the sunset. You know, once we've broken the curse, saved the day, all that good stuff."

"A favor? What kind of favor?" Mina eyed him suspiciously.

"Well, it sounds like Mommy dearest is recommending a little sexual adventure for you. I'm thinking if I promise to go adventuring with you, you'll help me figure out how to lift this stupid curse."

"Oh, I see. I get to be some horse's pity fuck, and in return for this honor, I have to help said horse break some kind of curse. What about this doesn't seem fair? And what the hell am I saying? I need help."

"Have I mentioned your language? No, I take it back. It's unattractive in an *uneducated* woman, but you keep lacing it with these witty zingers. I'm finding myself a little, well, stimulated."

"Retract that thing before I cut it off."

"Huh? What?" Horseface whinnied and ducked his head before glancing away in near embarrassment. "Uh, sorry. In this form, I really have no self-control."

"So why don't you pick another form, hornball, so we can talk." She thought a moment, then warmed to her subject. Sizzled, really. "Human would be great, might make me more comfortable—"

A shimmering—

"No, wait," she yelped. On second thought, she did not

need to be turned on by a shape-shifting puca, thank you very much.

—flash and—

"Eeep. Um." Mina stared at gleaming muscles, shoulders to make a woman drool, short gleaming curls of black silky hair. All spoiled by—

"Sorry about the face. I can't show it to you. It's in the fine print of this Druid curse. If you—as my unmarried and nubile female guardian—can't see my face, it's harder for me to distract you from guardian duty. I understand I'm generally hard to resist in unblemished human form." And there was definitely a leer somewhere in that blur he once called a face.

"Yeah. Okay." Still, she continued to stare. This was so over the top. Honestly, the blurred face was almost welcome, given her original reaction to this form, but the rest . . .

A broad, tanned forehead creased attractively above a blur that replaced his face from brow level to chin. There was just a sensation of those same golden eyes he'd had as a horse and an impression of features just beyond her conscious eyesight. He tipped his head forward to survey himself, from plum-colored sleeveless tunic, cinched lightly at the waist with a silver braided belt, to black breeches and leather boots.

Apparently satisfied with his appearance, he shrugged and turned his attention back to Mina. "Why are you still staring? I'm clothed. I explained the face. And I'm not offending you with stallion woody anymore. Hey, and speaking of stallions, I gotta tell you, we're both just lucky I didn't mess up when you distracted me mid-shift. Try to be more careful in the future. So. What now?" A pointed, silky ear twitched.

Mina ran a hand over her hair, touched her ear. Decided not to comment. This really was for the best. Blurred face might not have been sufficient to repel her depraved libido. Blurred horse-eared freak, however, might actually do it. "Never mind. So, um, back to answering my questions."

"Your questions. Yes. Can anyone but you see me? In my human form, not at all. In other forms, not unless I will it. So far . . ." He shrugged and she had the impression of wicked humor in his stance. "I haven't willed it."

Mina eyed him warily. "So, for now, I'm the only one who sees and hears you. I only have my own eyes and ears to believe. You know, I'm not sure if that's a good thing or not. A second set of eyes would at least give me proof of the state of my sanity, but then where would that get me? Either I'm stuck with a puca or I'm nuts. All lose-lose, as far as I'm concerned."

He lifted a sculpted shoulder carelessly. "And what do I want with you? I believe that was your final question?"

"Not the last by any means, but maybe the last one I mentioned on that list you seem to have memorized. So, yes. Give me your best shot. What exactly do you want with me?"

"This has nothing to do with want. It just is. I'm stuck with you. And you're stuck with me. You're my guar-di-an." He drew the last word out, mocking both of them.

Stuck with her puca buddy and his little rock home. Gee, that was so cheering. "For how long?"

"Until death do us part. Or until the curse is broken." He chuckled a little. "So I guess you could say what's between us is sort of like a warped marriage, eh?"

Oh, God. For life? Mina stared, her mind blanking. "No. There has to be some way out of this—"

"Like I said, you help me break the curse."

"What makes you think I can do that?"

"It was foretold long ago that my first guardian instated after the turn of the second millennium—that's you— would be the key to my freedom." He cleared his throat and raised his chin slightly to quote: " 'Much like Pandora, the curious woman who opened a dangerous box, this guardian will free the puca to face another trial. The subsequent November Day will be his judgment day.' " He lowered his head and tilted it thoughtfully. "Given that my little cage there busted wide open as soon as you started chipping away at it . . . I gotta believe there's something to the prophecy."

Mina was frowning. "What's November Day?"

"November the first. Traditionally, this is considered the puca's day, the one day each year when a puca must be civil, even in the face of condemnation. And, occasionally, the puca will hand out prophecies to lucky observers. In my particular situation, however, November Day will mean a full trial in front of the Druid Council."

Mina goggled. "*What* kind of council?"

"Druid Council."

"You've got to be kidding me. Aren't those guys long dead now? Are we talking about a jury of ghosts?"

"No. Modern-day descendents of hereditary Druids. There's a grove meeting regularly in a state park right here in central Virginia."

She gave him a deadpan look. "Right. And the pixies all meet in a Philadelphia bingo hall."

"It's true. Well, about the Druids, not the pixies." He blinked in wide-eyed innocence. "I think the pixies patronize a sports bar in Detroit. Don't look at me like that. I'm kidding. Who believes in pixies anyway? You know, it's probably no coincidence that the Druids have been meeting right in your backyard, so to speak. I think they've been waiting for this. For you."

She shook her head. "We'll leave that alone for now. Back to judgment day."

"Right. November first. By that day I must either make amends or break the curse. Otherwise, I poof back into my cornerstone. Since it's hard to make amends to dead people, I'm thinking that breaking the curse would be our best option."

"Uh-huh." Leaving that one alone as well. "So, we have the who and the when. What's the how?"

"How do we break the curse? I'm not exactly sure, but I've heard rumors suggesting that a human sacrifice might—"

"No. *Oh*, no. Voices in my head and talking horse types urging me to kill. I can't think of a better definition of insanity."

"But I'm sure there's some way around—"

"Nope. All done. Go night-night. I'm going to bed now. With any luck, I'll be normal in the morning. Good night, figment."

"This isn't going to go away just because you want it to."

But Mina had already turned, hands raised and waving distractedly as she wove unsteadily toward her room. After changing into sweatpants and a T-shirt—comfort clothes to ease her broken brain—she fell into bed and shut down. The last thing she heard was what sounded like a lullaby in a tongue she didn't recognize.

"Good mooooooorrr-ninnnggg."

Mina jumped, cringed, wished herself inside her pillow. "Oh. God. Who? Ow." Between the phone ringing what seemed like half a dozen times last night, and this rotten headache that wouldn't quit, she needed to start the night's sleep over. She'd heard from Teague she didn't know how many times. Granted, the contractor was worried about her, which was probably why Janelle called, too. But right at this moment, Mina's head could be falling off or exploding, it hurt so much. And she was so damned tired.

"Oh, the head. I forgot. Sorry about that."

That voice. "No. It didn't happen."

"Hey, I tried to let you sleep as long as I could. Wasn't that patient of me? It wasn't easy either, you know. With Gladys kicking off almost a month ago, I've been living in that rock with no one to talk to, so I have a lot of words stored up, all waiting to be said to someone. Are you ready? To hear them all?"

"No. You're not here." She burrowed deeper into her pillow.

"Sucks, huh? Sorry about that. Okay, I'm not sorry about that. To be sorry about that, I'd have to wish myself back into that damn cornerstone. I'm talking hell on earth. No way."

She turned her head on the pillow and opened her eyes, slowly, reluctantly, to focus on . . . the faceless man. She rolled to her side and eyed him doubtfully. It was so wrong to have her nemesis encased in such a good-looking body. One long black ear twitched. Oh, the ears. That helped. A tail, too, she remembered.

"I'm happy to be here, Mina. I just wish it didn't bother you so much."

"Oh, don't go starting with a guilt trip. I have a talking, shape-shifting, faceless man living in my house. Do you have any clue how this complicates an already messed-up life?"

"Well, at least I'm not complicating your *perfect* life. I'm just wrecking a mess instead of perfection this way. Isn't that much better?"

She scowled.

His tone lowered provocatively. "And there just might be something I can do to rectify your mess, if given the chance."

She eyed him doubtfully but crawled out of bed, heading toward wonderful coffee that had yet to be made.

He followed. "Seriously. We just have to get to know each other, decide how we can best scratch each other's back."

She glanced over her shoulder, saw his cocky stance that somehow managed to express amusement.

"And I don't mean that in a sexual way, since that freaks you out so much."

"Oh, good lord." She remembered her kitchen, now open to the outdoors. She wondered if the electricity still worked. She hadn't bothered to check last night. She flipped a light switch. Nothing happened. "Great." So, no coffee. She headed toward the cabinet. A whole refrigerator and freezer of food going bad. Just what her already distressed budget needed.

"So, let's start with the explanations. Suppose I introduce myself?"

She didn't respond, just pulled out bread and peanut butter.

"I've been called lots of names over the years, but the name you'd recognize most easily would be Robert Goodfellow."

She froze. Robert—Oh. No. She opened her mouth. Nothing came out at first. She cleared her throat. It just got better and better. "I thought it was *Robin* Goodfellow. The, um, devil?" So that was it. She was entertaining the devil and therefore damned straight to hell. She'd always wondered if that would be her fate, but never suspected that a horse-eared, faceless man would confirm it for her.

"Nope. Not Robin—and not really the devil either, so don't faint on me. Robin's my older brother and, according to gossiping mortals, born to a human woman and son of Oberon, king of the fairies. Well, Robin and I share a father, but apparently, Dad begat me while drunk on ambrosia and horny with the village idiot. Hmm." He frowned, then shrugged carelessly as he watched her shakily smear peanut butter on a slice of bread. "That's what Robin always said anyway.

"So, all in all, I guess you could say I'm the black sheep of the family. I had a bit of a . . . tempestuous adolescence, and then there was the Druid curse, which was an embarrassment to the name. They try not to talk about me much."

"A *Goodfellow* cursed. I see what you mean." In a surreal sort of way. She took her makeshift breakfast over to the dust-covered table. Paused. She'd stand and eat.

"No kidding. Eventually the word *goodfellow* came to have a double meaning, thanks entirely to me. Either boon companion or . . . thief. All that was before your time, of course. Still, worse than any offense I might have committed was the humiliation of being cursed by a *mortal*. Granted, Akker was a really, really pissed-off mortal with his own share of power. Druids were such a strange bunch," he mused distantly, his voice almost affectionate. "Bloodthirsty little devils, but they were so clever. A lot more entertaining than the nature worshippers who call themselves Druids these days. Dilettantes."

Then he shrugged. "So, there you have it. You can call me Robert or Bob if you want." The voice deepened devilishly. "Or the BobGoblin. Or there's also Rioghbardon— Riordan for short—which is what my father called me when he was still feeling the love. I actually liked that one. But I anticipate that ours could be a long marriage so I suppose I should leave the choice up to you. Please be kind. Or at least creative."

"Marriage, my ass. So to speak." She eyed his tail. Given his semitransformed state, the guy looked like a sexy, cross-dressing satyr. Appealing in a repulsive way. "Look, Robert. Puca. Bob. Riordan. Whatever the hell. You need to leave. Really. It's time to go. Hocus pocus, abracadabra, whatever. Surely there's some way I can make you disappear from my semiconsciousness so I can get back to recovering."

His cocky stance subtly wilting, he seemed a little hurt.

"Well. Thanks to the curse, I can't exactly leave you, but if you ask nicely, I could give you a little privacy. For a while."

Now she'd insulted a hobgoblin named Bob. This was really getting spoofish. She was starting to sound just like her mother, bless her weirdo but goodhearted soul.

Weirdo—"Oh. Of course." She'd call her mom. If she could tell anyone about a puca in her house, it would be her mom. Inspired, she focused on the puca. "Bob."

He sighed, almost wistfully.

She relented. "Riordan, then?" At least she wouldn't dissolve into hysterical giggles. A puca named Bob just sounded funny. And she would not, could not call him the BobGoblin. That sounded way too much like role-playing for the serious fetishist. Blech.

He dipped his head, seeming pleased by her choice of moniker. Then he turned his attention toward the light switch she'd tried earlier. It flipped. The lights went on.

Mina started and gazed around at her illuminated kitchen. It wouldn't short out or catch fire, would it? "Oh. Um, thanks?"

He responded with a casual bow that was somehow courtly despite tail and ears.

She nodded, a little awkwardly. "So. Riordan it is." She cleared her throat. "Riordan . . . would you please honor me with your absence? Until I call you back—"

A shimmer and he was gone. Except for a hollow voice echoing in her head. *No, your kitchen won't catch fire. Just give me a yell when you want to talk. And, speaking of fire, you might want to avoid the phrase "speak of the," you know. Guy from the hot place.*

"Why? What happens then?" She shouldn't ask. She knew she shouldn't ask. But maybe forewarned was better?

*Out I pop, in full view of everyone, in whatever form happens to be on your mind at the time. Things could get dicey.*

"I'll bet. But I thought you said you weren't the devil."

A sigh. *Oh, come on. Has no one ever called you a cute little devil? It doesn't mean that you are literally the devil, but things can get blurred in my part of the world. Metaphorical and literal blend a little more here. So, basically, if the king of the fairies makes a practice of calling his troublemaking halfling son something like that . . . well, scary shit happens.*

Really, really, really scary. "Bye, Riordan."

No response.

"O-kay." Mina took a deep breath. Then another. Then finished her cold breakfast. She looked around her now-silent kitchen. It was still her house, at least for now. Same as it always was. Well, except for the new ventilation, courtesy of her contractor Just Teague and, possibly, a puca.

A puca. Courtesy of a puca. She really needed help. "Yes," she said, talking to herself out loud. "Call Mom. Even if I am nuts, she'll never know it. I'll just be one of her kind. Finally. A true-blue member of the abnormal Avery-Dixon family."

After wending her way back to her room and throwing on some jeans and a T-shirt, she gingerly picked her way through the living room and glanced around for her purse. The house really was wrecked. She'd left it messy to begin with, and then the contractor and his guys had moved a lot of stuff from the kitchen to the living room. Locating her purse on the floor by the couch, she pulled out her cell phone and hit speed dial.

"Good evening, darling."

"Mom. Thank God you're home." Mina inhaled deeply to calm herself. Her mother was bonkers all by her endearing little self, so she was in no position or frame of mind to judge. Having a bonkers daughter would only make her proud—not inclined to notify the nearest mental hospital. "I have something to tell you. No, ask you. And it's going to sound weird, so—"

"Then let me make it easier for you. I heard Cousin Gladys died. Her attorney contacted me, looking for you. So, am I to understand that you've inherited the family puca?" Her mother sounded wickedly amused—even smug.

She knew? "No. Nonononono." In a truly mature move, Mina hung up on her laughing, protesting mother. "It can't be real." Her mother's wasn't exactly the most reliable opinion on occasions like this. She needed someone objective, someone scientific. Yes. So, maybe . . . Janelle the doctor? Yes, she'd call Janelle. Where was the damned business card again?

She stumbled over to the end table, ignoring a wave of dizziness. See? More proof that she just had a really bad head injury. That was all. A physical problem, easily cured. She carefully keyed in the phone number and listened to the rings.

"Hello—"

"Janelle! Look, you've got to help me. I've . . ."

"—can't come to the phone right now, but if you leave your name and number—"

Not home. Mina hung up. She closed her eyes. What now? What else was there? "Riordan." She smiled grimly, her inner vision a wickedly appropriate one. "Speak of the devil."

*Flash-shimmer* and the puca landed on his ass. An ass landing on his ass. Now that was a sight for sore eyes. The ass glared at her. "Hey, I turned your electricity back on. Well, flipped the switch in the fuse box, anyway. Still, it was a favor. Aren't you supposed to be nice to me?"

"Yeah, but you're supposed to not be real."

"But this?" He glanced down at himself. "I suppose you think this is funny?"

"I think it's fitting. If I'm going to have a psychotic episode, then I'm damn well going to be in charge of it."

"Ever piss off a puca before?"

"No. But what are you going to do? Take my house away? Blow a hole in the back of it? Bust my head? Bankrupt me? Drive my family to insanity? Saddle me with a curse and a smart-mouthed, perverted puca? Gosh, I'm scared."

He frowned and scrambled to his feet. Hooves. "Look—"

The doorbell rang. Mina froze.

Riordan the talking ass stilled. Then narrowed his eyes over what had to be a calculating little smile.

Mina stared at that smile. "No. Oh, no."

"Mina, open up." It was Teague.

# CHAPTER FOUR

"Well, damn." Mina heard Teague muttering, presumably to himself, just outside her front door. "She's probably sleeping it off. I'll just go around—"

"No!" Mina shouted in a near panic. "I'm. Um. Not dressed. Give me. A minute." She glanced around wildly. It could be the ultimate test, or—

"So what's it going to be, lovely Mina?" No ass should be able to croon in such a mocking manner.

Nerves clanging, Mina lowered her voice and tried for an ingratiating, borderline butt-kissing tone. "Um. Riordan? I'm really, reeeeeaaaally sorry about calling you up like that. Any chance you could just poof yourself back into—"

He was already shaking his head. Didn't seem the least bit disturbed about it either, the ass. "You commanded the form and when you command it, it's solid. No invisible asses for you, sweetie. Say goodbye to disembodiment. Didn't I mention that part? It's all in the adjusted rules of my semi-confinement, so I must have forgotten. Or it could be that I'm still learning them myself. Hmm. After this little lesson, we should probably proceed with caution, don't you think?"

"What are you talking about?"

"I'm saying you can ask and we can all be polite about it, come and go as we please, but commanding is different. Once you command me to a solid form, I can't voluntarily return to disembodiment anymore. I'm here. Hey, you know, I did try to warn you about that phrase and what would happen, but noooooo. You got mad at your puca and called upon the hot guy. So here we are. You and your ass. And now you're in a bind." He sounded absolutely delighted about it, too.

She glared at him. "Hey, you did that on purpose."

"Well, maybe I did. But nobody forced you to be rude to me, now did they?"

She groaned, wringing her hands and nearly dancing in place now. A malicious puca—or even a talking ass—was not what she needed right now.

"Although . . ." The ass shuffled coyly.

"What? *What*?" Mina tossed a panicked look at the door then back to the puca. "Anything."

"Anything?"

Mina groaned at the lilt in his voice. "I'm not going to like this, am I?"

"Well, if you ask nicely, I could always shift—"

Another knock on the door. "Mina, just let me in. I'm a thirty-four-year-old man who's been around the block a few times. It's not like I haven't seen everything before."

Gaze still on the puca, Mina raised her voice. "Well, you haven't seen mine, buddy."

"Yet." The puca muttered it speculatively.

"What? Never mind. I never like the answers." She whispered it furiously. "Now change—or shift. Whatever. Something he won't be able to—"

A shimmer-flash, and the puca ass shifted to a dog.

"A dog?" She blinked. Okay, a dog was at least a little more explainable—

Glowing yellow eyes peered up at her.

She stumbled back a step. But . . . at least a dog wasn't immediately objectionable. Right?

She eyed the puca cautiously. "If you're real, he'll see a dog. Right?"

The dog wagged his tail. "Yeah. You like?"

She pondered, desperately, then groaned. "A talking dog with demon eyes. I'm telling you, this is not going to work."

"Um. Ahem. Bark?" More tail wagging. Canine brows rose in question over slitted eyes that only mildly spooked.

She winced. "Maybe you could be a mute dog?"

"Picky, picky."

Maybe Teague wouldn't even see the dog. Maybe it really was just some kind of ghost or even a figment of her busted imagination. Gee, there was a cheery thought. Which was better? A busted imagination or a puca for a ward?

Heart pounding, Mina walked toward the door.

"Mina?" Teague's concern and probable intent spoke loud and clear.

"Right. I'm coming. Sorry." She disengaged the deadbolt and opened the door.

Teague. In all his hotness. A rugged hotness equal to challenging the sexy faceless man Riordan had shifted to earlier. Better yet, Teague had a sexy, gorgeous face and no confusing horse ears and tail. She almost whimpered in gratitude. "I am so happy to see you, Just Teague." Dibsies. He belongs to Janelle. Remember dibsies, Mina.

He looked surprised. Pleasantly so. "Yeah?" Then he frowned. "Is something wrong?"

"I . . . No. Why don't you come in?" She stepped back. *You know, subtlety's not exactly your strong suit.*

She jumped. Riordan could talk in her mind even when

he was sort of, well, physically there? Not that she'd completely accepted that he might be here. She could still be
nuts. But if she wasn't, there was no way that dog could actually pass for a dog. Not on close inspection.

*Say no more, my guardian.*

"Bark." A black blur passed her and skittered off toward
the back of the house.

Startled, Teague glanced after it. "Hey, you have a dog."

"Yeah." Not nuts. Was that good or bad?

"So, what kind of dog is he?"

"He's a puc—Uh. *Peekapoo.*" Almost busted herself. A
flustered Mina was not good at subterfuge.

"Pookapeekapoo?" He grinned a little. "Wait, I know.
Like a cockapoo and peekapoo crossed?"

"Something like that." No, more like a smart-mouthed
hellhound. Which he very well might be.

*I noticed you forgot the cock part of that concoction of yours.
Never forget the cock.*

She choked.

"I dunno. I didn't see him all that well, but he looked bigger than that. Like a chow-shepherd mix maybe."

"That, too. He's a mutt. Um, the other was a joke. The
peekapoo part. Cockapeekapoo. Pookapeekapoo. Whatever."

*Smoooooooth. Maybe you should leave the talking to me?*

"So." Mina raised her voice, struggling for distraction
from the demon pet. "What brings you here?" Stupid question. Dumb, dumb, dumb. He's your contractor. Why do
you think he's here? To work, idiot. "I mean, in my house
here. Y-yesterday you just went right to work. Outside. No
need to even see me." She shifted her weight and tried to
arrange her features into an intelligent expression. "So are
you guys working inside the house today?" Still very, very
lame, no matter how hard she tried to save it.

She heard a puca snort in her mind.

"I just wanted to check on you before I get started mucking through what's left of your kitchen wall. How's your head?"

"My head?" You have no idea, buddy. "It's okay. A little achy, naturally, but not broken." Debatable, Mina. Seriously debatable. "Thanks for asking."

"Hey, what's this?" Eyes narrowing, Teague bent past her. Bracing herself, Mina followed his gaze and saw a white corner visible from beneath her armchair. Teague snagged it and turned back to her.

The envelope the attorney had given her.

"Is this what you were looking for yesterday?" He held it out.

"Sort of." She accepted it from him and flipped it over, regarding it more seriously than she had before. Hey, when a girl inherits a puca, she realizes it would be good to have an owner's manual to go with him.

*If I were you, I wouldn't open it in front of this guy. Unless you think he'd love to meet a puca in person? Or, rather, canine?*

Mina started, glancing around discreetly for the whereabouts of her non-dog.

*Oh, come on. I'm out of sight. Being good. And now I'm just trying to help, based on past, extensive experience with guardians who thought for sure they could convince other humans to believe in me.*

"Are you going to open it?" Teague looked curious. "What is it, anyway?" He shook his head. "Never mind. I'm just curious, but maybe you don't want to read it in front of me."

Mina pondered—to open or not to open—then spoke slowly. "No, that's okay. I don't mind."

*Suit yourself, lady. Don't say I didn't warn you.*

"This is the letter the attorney gave me when he told me about my inheritance."

Teague raised his brows. "Really. Sounds interesting."

"That wasn't my thought at the time, but now . . ." She carefully broke the seal and slipped out a folded sheet of paper. Just plain old notebook paper. She didn't know whether to be relieved or let down by the lack of a flattened, centuries-old scroll of parchment.

*Last chance, baby. Keep in mind Cousin Gladys was pretty batty and outspoken as all hell. You didn't know her, but I did. You could maybe stand a chance—romantically speaking—with this guy if he doesn't think you come from nutty stock, right?*

The damn dog might as well have read her mind. Her history. She couldn't count the number of boyfriends who'd ditched her once they met her mom and stepdad and realized what they were getting themselves into. A talking puca would have fit right into her teenage household. Just one more meddling nutcase with a fixation on the otherworldly.

"Well, maybe I will wait to read it until later. My head still hurts and besides, how urgent could a letter accompanying a rock be?" She slid the paper back into the envelope.

No, she didn't do it because she thought she really had a shot at Teague, romantically speaking. She mentally glared at the puca. The man was taken, she reminded herself. But maybe she didn't want to witness the expression she knew she'd see on Teague's face once she revealed herself for the freak she was raised to be.

"You're right, the letter's probably not too urgent. Still, aren't you curious? Maybe it gives you some idea what used to be in that rock of yours. Or where you could find copies of whatever was in there. Didn't you say it was probably family history stuff? Mementos?"

"The attorney was just speculating. He also implied that Cousin Gladys was pretty eccentric. Maybe even downright nutty. For all I know, she collected empty Dorito bags, and just decided one day to stuff her 'treasures' in that rock."

*Dorito bags? That's going a little far, don't you think? I mean I'm all in favor of discretion and reading that letter in private, but you could show the lady some respect. She didn't eliminate me when she had the chance.*

He could be eliminated? He could? How?

*I know what you're thinking, and don't even go there or I'm going talking dog all over your little date here. And yes he is, too, your date. Or will be.*

"Listen, I have to be honest," Teague was saying. "I wanted to see you this morning. You know, to find out how you're feeling after yesterday, but maybe it wasn't the only reason." He laughed a little. "Well, this is going to sound stupid, but . . . are you seeing anyone?"

"Wha—?" Mina glanced around nervously. The puca had been talking only in her head, right? *Right?* "Um, who exactly should I be seeing?"

"I mean . . ." Teague frowned. "Look, my timing sucks as usual, but I was wondering if you wanted to go out with me. Tomorrow, maybe? Unless you're otherwise occupied . . . or committed?"

"Oh, you mean *seeing* someone, seeing someone. I thought— Never mind." She frowned. "But what about Janelle?"

"What about her?"

"Well, I thought you two were . . ." She raised her eyebrows.

"Nah. I mean, sure, I did ask her out once, but she turned me down. She said I looked too much like her ex, which was a big turn-off to her." He grinned ruefully. "But we got to be friends in spite of my ugly mug."

She smiled. Damn, but he was a cutie. And he was available. And he was asking her out.

Oh. The dog was right. Teague was asking her out. So was it simple observation, or could the puca read minds or . . . oh, shit, she hoped he couldn't read minds.

*Told you so.*

"Stop that."

"Huh?"

"Not you. The dog." Oh, good grief.

"Huh?" Now Teague looked uneasy again.

She laughed nervously and shrugged. "Just one of the perils of living alone. You start talking to your dog and figure they're talking back to you. Sometimes he gets this look and I'd swear he was thinking about something besides dog biscuits and trashcans."

*Oh, thanks. I'm so flattered.*

"Don't mention it."

"I . . . won't?" Teague tipped his head, obviously amused. "Why, does someone think you're nuts for talking to your dog?"

"My mom would." No, she wouldn't. Woman was nuttier than a fruitcake. Nuttier than Mina, until now. And why had she brought up her mother? Self-sabotage, no doubt.

"Hey, moms are like that." He moved closer. "Don't worry about it. Dogs are pretty smart, anyway. I wouldn't be surprised if he could hone in on what you're feeling sometimes. Hell, I could almost envy a dog of yours. I wouldn't mind being able to read what you're thinking right now." Still smiling, Teague peered into her eyes. His own narrowed, emphasizing a ridiculously attractive spray of laugh lines around the outside corners. He could almost be laughing with those sparkling green beauties. He was so hot. And he was obviously flirting with her. She'd wondered before, but now—

"Woof." Riordan spoke his spooky bark from the other room, and she jumped.

Stupid puca. She'd really be enjoying this one on one with Teague if the damn puca weren't eavesdropping.

*Think no more, sweetie. Consider me gone.* A galloping click of nails and Mina felt a discreet tug as the envelope was plucked from her slackened grip. She glanced down in time to see a black blur hurtle into her bedroom.

"Hey!"

And slide under her bed? Sure enough, she saw a shadow darkening the bedskirt. Was he eating the letter now?

*Now don't start whining about the letter. No, I don't eat paper, and loverboy didn't see me take it from you. I'll keep it safe so he doesn't open it when you're not looking.*

She stared after the dog. "Oh, shit." Well, that was one question answered. He could hear her thoughts? He could hear her thoughts. Not just talk to her in her head, but actually pick out and listen to any darn thought she had.

*Oh, cripes. I can hear them when you shout them. If you don't want me to hear every little hormonal sigh and moan, keep it down and I'll try to be polite. Unless I'm bored.*

"You don't want the dog in your room? I can get him out for you if you want . . ." Teague took a step in the direction of her room.

"No, that's okay." She laid a hand on his arm, trying to conceal her panic at his words. Best to keep man and dog at something of a distance. The dog really couldn't bear close inspection. Those eyes were too . . . otherworldly to be canine. "Really. I just realized—forgot—" She laughed. "Never mind. So you were saying?" She raised her eyebrows.

"Right. About dogs understanding their masters."

Masters . . . was she the puca's master, then? She mentally cleared her throat. Hey, Bob. Am I your master?

*So now you want to talk to me. No, you're not my master. No Druid, however powerful, could subordinate me to a mortal and have that relationship passed from generation to generation. No, you're more the keeper of the key to my cell.*

Key? What key?

*Damn. If you don't know, then we're both in for the long haul, aren't we? Now pay attention to the guy. He's horny, too. You could get lucky and spare me the trouble of boning you later. Get it? Boning you. Hahahaha.*

Sick, sick puca.

"Mina?"

"What?" She turned impatiently to Teague.

"Maybe I should go."

"No. Yes. I mean, no."

*Mina, you're blowing it, babe.*

Stop that, you demon dog, and stay out of this. We'll have us a little talk later. You, me and an envelope, you thief. That was my letter, not yours.

Forcing a bright smile, she turned back to Teague. "I think maybe you make me a little nervous. In a good way, I mean."

His eyes crinkled at the corners, attracting her full attention. What was it about that little spray of wrinkles around the eyes that was so blasted sexy? On a woman, they were called crow's feet. On a guy, they just looked rugged.

*That's it. I think I'm gonna hurl.*

"Shut up." She snapped it at the bedroom.

Teague jumped, smile and crinkles completely gone as he backed his way toward the front door. "Yeah, I really think I should go. Get to work, I mean."

"Really?" She followed him anxiously toward the door.

"It's what you pay me for, right?" He smiled, but it was strained, and reached for the doorknob. "So—"

"Wait. Teague?"

With obvious ambivalence, he paused. "Yeah?"

"Please. Do you think maybe we could start over?" She glanced toward her bedroom in time to see a fuzzy black tail disappear under her bed. She wavered. "Tomorrow, maybe? I still have a splitting headache, so I don't feel quite like me yet."

He relaxed his grip on the knob. "A headache. Of course you have a headache. Why wouldn't you have a headache? Damn brick clobbers you and . . . Yeah. Are you okay?" Releasing the knob, he turned to face her fully, that wonderful face with its wonderful creases expressing such delicious concern. "Can I get you something before I go to work?"

She smiled, forcing a brave look onto her face. Maybe all was not lost.

A hollow snort echoed in her head, but this time she had the intelligence to ignore it.

"I took some pain relievers a little while ago. They just haven't kicked in yet. I probably just need time and rest."

"No doubt. Well, I won't keep you, then."

"Um . . . tomorrow . . . ?"

He leaned against the doorjamb, those green eyes surveying her from head to foot. "Yeah. What time?"

"Seven okay?"

He smiled. "Seven's great."

"Oh. Great." She smiled brightly.

The desperation in Mina's eyes was still fresh in Teague's mind as he closed the door behind him. He dropped the smile, his thoughts grim and seriously conflicted. "Well, I guess that answers a whole lot of my questions."

And, as a result, he felt both wonderful and completely duplicitous. Not that anything would change his course now. He was what he was, and his choices, frankly, were a rock and a hard place. When he saw the curtain flicker, Teague forced his feet to move, striding off toward his truck to gather equipment.

Mina dropped the curtain, then turned back to her unfinished business. "Bo-ob!" She watched golden eyes and floppy ears peek around the corner.

"You howled?"

"Oh, shut up."

"Okay."

Remembering her dismantled kitchen, which did nothing to muffle sound, she lowered her voice. "Explain yourself."

Golden eyes blinked. *Hey, I tried. I was ready to leave you two in peace, but it was too painful to listen. Your moves need work, babe.*

"Out loud." Mind-speech or telepathy—whatever a damned puca would call it—was just way too intimate.

"You want me to start over and . . ." Canine sigh. He spoke in a bored singsong. "Hey, I tried. I was ready to leave you two in peace, but it—"

She groaned. "Will you stop that?"

"Women. One contradiction after another."

She took a deep breath, lowered her voice to a squeaky whisper, and attempted reason. "Look. I thought you wanted me and Teague to get together."

"It's not what I want or don't want. It's what I know."

"You know? How could you know?"

"How can I change into a horse or a dog or talk inside your head? I just can and do."

She slumped. "I asked for that."

The dog tipped its head to the side in an alarming, human-like shrug. "Well, yeah. Pretty big of you to admit it, though. So maybe I could be convinced to forgive you for the ass transformation."

"Ooooh," she whispered furiously. Forgive? He, forgive her? When he—"Sure, just picture me on my knees and groveling for your gracious consideration."

"Such sarcasm. Aren't you a little young to be so jaded?"

"Spare me. Look, Riordan." She glanced past him, saw the guys heading into the backyard, then closed the double doors connecting kitchen and living room. She turned back to Riordan. "You need to promise me something."

"Ooooooh. Guardian in my debt. Whatcha got?"

Mina groaned. "Nothing that's going to inconvenience your puca self too much. Just . . . while the men are here, you have to be a dog. No puca sightings, no talking animals, nothing to make them suspicious enough to call the white coats for me or the X-file people on you. Reasonable?"

He sighed, as if put upon. "Yeah, fine."

"Good."

And he was actually true to his word, napping all morning in a sunny corner like a cat.

*Hey, I object. You know, there's a very good reason why I never shift into cat form. Felines are glorified roadkill.*

"You are such a heathen."

Mina spent the day skimming want ads and doing job searches online. She even updated her resumé, which had seemed such a daunting challenge only last week but today wasn't all that difficult. Now that she had a puca to put it all back in perspective, and a sexy contractor to make her eye the future a little more kindly . . .

*Blech.*

"So stop eavesdropping." Feeling creakier now than she had that morning, Mina paused in her work and glanced at the puca. He just mindlessly lay there while she worked. Squatter.

*Hey, I'm only doing what you told me to do. Being a dog. You know, a dog's life isn't such a bad thing.*

Mina snorted.

*And I might be an unwelcome tenant, but you gotta admit I don't take up much space.*

Tenant . . . room and board. Horrified, she spun around to face him. "What am I supposed to feed you? Do you eat?" She hadn't even thought—

*Aw. I'm touched.* And there really was an odd look in his eye. Yearning almost; not that his timing was in any way appropriate. *You'd really feed me? Even though you don't want me here?*

"It's either that or get picked up for animal abuse. So, what, you're in the mood for a doggy biscuit now? Great timing, pooch. Maybe I should call you a poocha instead of puca."

Canine ribs expanded on a sigh. *Just when I think you're getting used to me, you have to go and say something like that. You know, that was just mean.*

"Yeah, well this is even better. I will *never* get used to you. How the hell does a normally sane woman get used to sharing her home with a—"

"Mina?" Teague's voice, and a knock on her door.

Mina jumped and winced when her body protested the sudden movement. Creaky, creaky, creaky.

*That'll teach you to say mean things to me. Now stop growling at me and go answer the door.*

"Coming." Mina creaked her way to the front door and, as she opened it, heard a skitter of toenails on hardwood floor. The dog was making an exit, she realized. Thank heavens.

Now, seeing Teague standing so politely on her front doorstep when the back of her house was half missing, she had to grin. "You know, since I know you're here already, you could have just walked through the kitchen wall instead of knocking on the front door."

"We-ell, I didn't want to startle you." He gave her a teasing look. "You seemed to be having a conversation with your dog again."

Mina laughed a little nervously. "Yeah, you caught me. Just talking to my dog again."

*Oh, good grief. Have you never lied convincingly?*

Shut. Up.

Teague, who was eyeing the doorway to Mina's bedroom, looked puzzled. "That dog of yours runs away from me every time you open the door. Not much of a watchdog, is he?"

Mina laughed, scrambling for explanation. "He's just shy. I'm sure if someone tried to hurt me he'd go feral in my defense." She grinned at the thought. Actually, spooky yellow eyes would be all it took.

*Feral, huh? And all in defense of a helpless damsel. That's so naïve, but very sweet actually. In a teddy bear, baby chickie and smiley face kind of way. Blech.*

Teague ducked his head a little closer and lowered his voice. "I just wanted to tell you I was finished for the day. Are we still on for tomorrow night?"

"Sure. Of course." She eyed him, dazzled by his nearness. The guy was a solid shot of testosterone. Even a mostly modern-thinking girl could talk herself into swooning with that much masculinity—*available* masculinity—staring into her eyes.

*Again, blech.*

"Good." He reached out and touched her cheek. "How's the head doing?"

She grimaced. "Let's just say I'm creaking a little."

"I'm sorry. Can I get you some ice for it? Do anything for you?"

She shook her head. It was time Teague stopped seeing her as a headcase with an injury and saw her as a woman. "I'm okay. And I'm looking forward to tomorrow night."

"Good. I'll see you tomorrow morning first, though."

She smiled and tipped her head to the side. "Yes, you will. Isn't that nice?"

He laughed. "Very."

"Hey, Teague!" a man's voice called from several yards behind Teague. "Where should I put this? Your truck or mine?"

Teague gave her a wry look. "Bye."

"Bye."

He turned and strode off. "You're starting the Jenson project tomorrow, so you hold on to it." He continued issuing instructions while Mina shamelessly watched. His butt.

*Oh, come on. Ever see a dog puke before?*

Mina jumped. Seethed. She closed the door and turned to see her canine puca strolling lazily into the living room. Just like he owned the place, the cocky little scamp.

*Your puca? And cocky, too? Hey, you remembered the cock. I'm so proud.* Obviously recognizing violence in her gaze, the dog attempted a winsome pant.

"Give it up, Riordan." She heard a truck engine roar to life. And another. "Now. We're alone. You and I need to have ourselves a little talk—out loud—and then you're going to zap yourself into whatever never-never land you came from and let me lead my life."

"Sure, we can talk, and if I could zap myself somewhere, I'd do it. Just for you." The dog sat and gazed up at her eerily. "Like I said, though, I'm as stuck as you are. Unless you help me."

"Help you? What about helping *me*?"

"I'll be happy to help you. Hey, ever have a puca in your corner? Seriously excellent luck if you play your cards right."

"What do you mean?" She remembered the light switch earlier. And gazed at him, wide-eyed.

"Sounds like you want a demonstration. I can do that. Just give me a minute." The puca raised a hind leg to scratch behind his ear, narrowing his yellow eyes in thought. He lowered the leg. "I know. The bitch your boyfriend was sleeping with. She really did that to you, right? Got between you and the boyfriend, then got you fired? No exaggeration or fabrication?"

Mina gave him a disgruntled look. "Yes. She really did all that. No exaggeration or fabrication necessary."

"Perfect. Call her."

"Why would I do that? Just to ruin my day?"

"No, to get her over here. You need to bring her here and let her inside the house. You won't be sorry."

"What are you going to do?" Mina eyed him warily, half intrigued and half appalled. "Give her a tail?"

"Better. I promise. And I say this with all due restraint, you understand. I personally would prefer the tail, but I think you'd prefer what I have in mind." Riordan let his tongue loll out in a doggy grin.

What did she have to lose? Her job? Her boyfriend? Her home? Her sanity? "What the hell." She was curious.

She went into the extra bedroom and pulled the phone book out of the closet. Then she dragged it back to the living room and paged through it. "Tiffy. Gotcha." She dug through her purse for her cell phone and glanced back at the puca. "Now, whatever you're thinking, don't cross me. We already talked about angry pucas, but have you ever seen an angry desperate woman? Your fur would be history, buddy."

The puca sat up straighter. "Don't threaten me. You wouldn't like it. That tail? I could still entertain myself." He dropped his gaze to Mina's as yet tailless butt.

Riordan was obviously a loose cannon. No wonder he needed a guardian. Carefully, she lowered the phone and lifted the phone book to close it.

"Wait! I was bluffing about the tail. I can't do that, I swear—it would go contrary to your karma. Just give me a chance here to show you what I can do for you. I promise you'll like what I have in mind for your pal Tiffy. All good stuff."

Silently debating, Mina regarded him. The puca still wanted something from her, so it wouldn't make sense for him to cross her. Maybe he was trying to win her favor after all. Could be he was telling the truth. "All right. I'm probably going to regret this, but let's see what you can do."

She picked up the receiver and dialed the number. When someone picked up, Mina studied Riordan while she spoke in a careless tone. "Hey, Tiffy. It's Mina. . . . Yes, *that* Mina. How's it going? . . . Right. Hey, I found Jackson's video camera, and *wow* but that boy took some wild footage. Have you seen it yet? . . . *Oh*, yeah. And as I understand it, there's a huge market for amateur porn, especially on the Internet. What an interesting opportunity for me, don't you think?" Mina batted her eyelashes just a little.

"So I thought I'd just go ahead and upload some of these fun party pics of you. They'd be perfect. Yeah, there's this website I found and— Oh, you don't think so? But they'd pay me an *awful* lot of money and you know I'm unemployed now and—Tiffy? Tiffy, are you still there?" She hung up the phone. Turned back to the puca. "I think she's on her way over now."

He was already snorting, probably a dog laugh. "I like you, Mina. We could have some fun."

Pondering Tiffy's outraged shriek, Mina couldn't suppress a grin of her own. "Think so?"

"Oh, I do. So come on, you've got to tell me." He pranced around, his dog butt bobbing with excitement. "*Was* there a camera running? For real? Can I see?"

Mina groaned. "Just when I think we have a chance at getting along, you go all perverted on me. Pleeease—"

"All right, all right. But do you know how long it's been since I enjoyed some skin slapping? Or even some fur plumping—"

"Oooh, yuck." Mina pressed the sides of her head, trying to distract her mind's eye from . . . yuck. "Why do you say these things? Now all I can see is—ugh."

"Hey, it's not a perfect life, but a puca's gotta do what a puca's gotta do."

"Right. Fine. Too much, *way* too much information."

"I'm just teasing. Man, you're easy. No, I don't do animal sex. That's way beneath me. No, baby, I'm a sexual connoisseur." The puca's eyes glowed. "Seriously. Anytime you want a sampling of puca pleasure, you just come talk to your buddy Riordan. I'll set you up."

"You sound like a sleazy pimp. Or a drug dealer."

"Only because I'm in my—what did you call it?—cockapucapeekapoo form. It's real hard to seduce like this, I'm telling you. But if you want, I can shift—"

"Change the subject. What are you going to do to Tiffy?"

"Just teach her a lesson."

"Yeah?" A lesson from a puca. Somehow Mina thought it might be a poetic one. "Can I watch?"

"Now there's a girl after my own libido."

"Sick puca. Bad puca. This better not be some twisted and torturous thing you're going to do. Or at least, I better not get blamed for it."

The puca sighed, shook his head, ears flopping just a little. "I can do subtlety. Like I said, you won't be sorry."

Ten minutes later, there was a frantic knocking on the door and feminine threats. "Pandemina Avery, you better not have played those movies for anybody or I swear I'm going to—"

Mina swung the door open. "Hi, Tiffy. So you like to play porn star. That's so enlightened of you. Not that I personally would participate in anything like that. I do have a reputation to think about. Although . . . I guess I could do just about any sleazy thing I want to now. Morally speaking, I'm a free agent since the Mason County School District banned me from its hallowed classrooms. Isn't that right?"

"So that's what this is about? You're out for revenge?" Every bleached blond hair on the woman's head stood on end. Could be it was from the hairspray holding it in place. Or maybe the severely taut skin of her face-lifted forehead and scalp pinned it upright.

"Tiffy. Honestly. That claw thing you do with your bangs? That went out of style decades ago. Time for a new 'do."

"You're just jealous because I—"

"I'm sure you're absolutely right. So—"

*Okay, that's all I needed. You can throw her out but leave the door open for me. I shouldn't be long.* The voice dopplered eerily as he became a blurred, not quite substantial form that kept to the shadows leading toward the door.

Mina watched still-yapping Tiffy with mild concern.

*You're on, babe. Toss her butt. Unless, of course, you haven't finished talking to the woman.*

No, I'm done. But you're not going to do anything illegal are you? Or universally taboo, or just really, really bad . . . right? Riordan?

*A little trust, please?*

She groaned. But she knew she was going to let him do it. The puca didn't strike her as evil, and she was, technically, his guardian and could pull him back just by spouting a little speak-of-the-*blank*, right? She hoped.

Okay, Riordan, you're on. I had to actually invite the woman into my home and I feel really dirty now. Make it better.

*Yes, ma'am.* There was a smile in his words.

"Bye, Tiffy."

"Where is that camera?" She shrieked the question.

Mina grinned. "I don't have Jackson's camera. I was just bluffing. Thanks for sharing, though. It's been educational." Mina herded her toward the door.

Tiffy's big eyes seemed to cross just a little, and her carefully plucked eyebrows knit in confusion. "But . . . You mean you . . . Well, of course you didn't. It's not like I actually—"

"Right. You can go now." Mina sought distraction. "Where's your stepson? You didn't leave Nathan home by himself, did you?"

Tiffy looked affronted now, but she was through the door finally and standing on the porch. The shadows seemed to envelop her as she stepped back. "Nathan's a responsible boy. Almost a teenager. I can leave him alone for a few little minutes, you know, and—Oh! He-ey!"

Mina jumped but couldn't really see.

*Just turn around and go back inside. You don't need to watch this.*

Aw, come on, Riordan. Are you goosing her?

"Oh, my god! What are—whaaaaa!" Not pain. Fear. Tiffy had moved off the step into the shadows.

Uh, Riordan. Don't, like, really hurt her, okay? I don't like the woman, but I'm not loosing a puca hit man on her either.

*Have a little faith, please. No lasting damage—I swear. This is all good stuff. Go inside and relax. Read or pluck your nose hairs or do whatever women do when no one's around to watch. I'll be back.*

Well, she'd gone this far, so why not? Mina turned around and strode evenly toward her bedroom. She heard the faint *clop-clop* of . . . horse hooves?

Startled, she pivoted to look through the open doorway. There was nothing there. No sign of the puca or Tiffy. Just Tiffy's car, with its door wide open. Mina wavered. Maybe she'd been irresponsible. She hated to actually claim guardianship of the puca, but if he really was her responsibility, maybe . . .

*Have faith, Mina. Like I said, I'll be back in a flash. So to speak.* A wicked chuckle echoed faintly in her head.

# CHAPTER FIVE

"Okay. You can close the door now."

Mina jumped awake, the eerie voice still echoing in her head. It was the stuff of nightmares and fantasies—and wow, but she'd had a few. She slumped weakly back in her armchair. She'd only fallen asleep for a moment, although during that brief moment she'd managed to entertain all manner of wild dreams. Cornerstones and shape-shifters and demonic dogs and talking horses and . . .

"Hello? I'm here. Not a dream."

Heart sinking, she reluctantly opened her eyes. Blinked. "Oh, god."

"No, *Riordan*." The puca chuckled. "Hey, I'm in dog form. You seemed to prefer that one, so here I am, fuzzy and courteous. Hey, I even invited you to close the door so I wouldn't be tempted to cause more trouble. Pretty mature of me, I thought. Noble even."

Mina glanced at the mantel clock. It was two in the morning; she'd been waiting for hours now. She'd occupied herself briefly by setting up space heaters she'd rescued from the attic—relics of her rental past and, likely, her rental future. Then she'd gone and stuffed towels under the door to her kitchen as crude insulation and attempted some decluttering of her ransacked house. Exhausted even by that, she'd collapsed in the living room chair where she now sat.

Reluctantly, she turned to face the puca, blinking a little distractedly at the glowing eyes.

"I can't help the eyes. They are what they are. Get used to 'em."

"I'd rather not." She studied Riordan a moment. He seemed unscathed. He also seemed to be lacking a certain boyfriend-snatching fiend. "So, should I ask?"

"Which question? The door one or the bitch one?"

"Since I'm terrified of your answer to the Tiffy one, we'll start with the door. Can you just leave this house whenever you want? And what kind of trouble can you cause me, anyway?"

"Well, you are my guardian after all. A ward can wreak all kinds of havoc with a guardian's life. But I didn't do that. See how well-behaved I was?"

"We'll get to the well-behaved part in a moment. Can you just leave whenever you want?"

"Hey, you can always call me back. Remember the 'speak of the' thing I told you about? It still works."

Puca was stalling. Not good. She narrowed her eyes. "Answer the question. Can you leave at will?"

"No. Well, not ordinarily, anyway. But significant exceptions do apply under certain circumstances."

That sounded bad—like small print about guardianship in a seemingly harmless last will and testament. "Like?"

"Hey, what happened to two questions?"

"You're still answering the first one. Explain these exceptions and circumstances."

"Bossy. Fine. If you invite someone in and leave the

door open behind them, I can, well, escort them to some extent."

"Define escort."

"Do you really want me to?" That was a definite doggy grin.

"Oh, god."

"No, it's Riordan. You're having a little trouble with that tonight, aren't you?"

"You're going to hell for that."

"I know."

"So. Escort?"

Riordan sat on his haunches. "Okay, this is where I educate you on the puca and legend. First, the overview: A legend only has as much power as belief lends it. Get that much?"

She nodded.

"According to the most popular legend surrounding my brother and myself—as in, the one most commonly believed and therefore the strongest of the puca's powers—a puca in stallion form can take humans on what's considered the ride of their lives."

"A ride on the puca? That's not a euphemism for some kinky sex act, is it?"

"No, although given my obvious prowess, I could see where you might think so." If a dog could grin lasciviously, then that was exactly what Riordan was doing.

"Riordan—"

"All right, all right. It's just a wild, possibly frightening but mostly traditional, gallop to wherever my little heart might desire. After this ride, the human returns to civilization . . . er . . . *changed*. I regained this power when I left the cornerstone, just as I suspected I might, but I can only use it if certain circumstances are in place and if karma supports my intentions."

Mina shot to her feet. "Changed? What do you mean

changed? Oh, no. You really did give her a tail. No, you made her a horse. Or a swine. Or—"

"Not changed like me, you dope. Changed . . . internally. Mentally."

"What, a few more screws loose upstairs? She's a blithering idiot now?"

Another doggy grin. "Now that would be fun, wouldn't it?"

"I'll admit to a fleeting temptation. And I feel really bad about that, by the way. You didn't, did you?"

"No, the change is more like a life lesson. The experience of a lifetime to make you question who and what you are, and what you might do with your life if the wild ride doesn't end in horrible death. You know, that kind of thing."

"No. Way."

The puca shrugged, unconcerned.

"So you mean like a change of heart? Attack of conscience?"

The puca shrugged again.

"Dogs don't shrug."

"Sorry about that. No one's around but us anyway, except . . ." He cocked an ear.

The doorbell rang.

More doggy grin. "Showtime."

"Mina? Mina, please open up. We need to talk. I—"

Mina heard sobbing through the door and glanced, appalled, at the puca before running to open it. "Tiffany?"

The woman was a mess. Her blond spikes were flattened on one side and sticking out every which way on the other. Smudges of dirt had mixed with the tears and makeup on her cheeks, and her tiny cardigan was stained with . . . paint? A smeared red cross, maybe? No, a *T*—make that a huge, if blurred, letter *T*. With a backward *e* in front of it. Both in red, with smears of yellow and black . . . What the hell had happened to the woman?

*Isn't it obvious? She got puca'd.* He sounded obscenely satisfied.

Shut. Up. "Tiffany? Are you okay?"

Tiffy seemed flustered. And she was attempting further speech. "I have to . . . I've got to . . ."

"Use the bathroom?" Mina guessed.

"No." Tiffany took a breath, grabbed Mina's upper arms and stared fiercely into her eyes.

The woman was actually focused—feverishly so—and Mina had always doubted Tiffy was capable of anything beyond momentary concentration. Normally, her eyes seemed to work independently of each other, much like her mouth and brain.

"I've been wrong. Spiteful. I never should have . . ." Tiffany swallowed hard, her eyes glazing slightly as she ran down a mental list. "I'm going to call the school board and tell them I was mistaken. You're a wonderful teacher and I need therapy." She refocused. "You're entitled to a private life and I had no right to publicize the details or judge you. And I never should have cheated on my husband. I messed up both of our lives. Four lives. No, five, if you count Nathan. He was hurt by all this, too. That's wrong." She looked like a religious zealot riding a caffeine buzz.

"Well. Yeah." Mina blinked, a little dazed. "So you're going to—"

"Call the school board. First thing in the morning. I'll rally the PTA behind your cause if I have to. Anything. We'll get your job back."

"Seriously? You're not sleepwalking or anything, are you? Do you have a head injury? Because I understand head injuries. They can do some freaky stuff to your mind and—"

"No. I've just finally seen clearly. And I am *sorry.*" Tiffany's eyes were feverishly intent and her voice shook with the intensity of her emotions. Maybe she was sick? No, she was just really, really, emphatically sincere.

Mina studied her a moment. "Apology accepted. Thank you."

"I'll call tomorrow. I will." Tiffany backed out the door.

"Watch out!"

Tiffany tripped on the step and Mina reflexively lunged forward, but Tiffany stuck an arm straight up, already scrambling to regain her footing. "I'm fine. Just a stumble. I'll call. I will."

"Thanks." Mina stared, almost speechless, as the woman sprinted to her car, launched into the front seat and sped off.

Mina watched the taillights disappear around the corner, until something nearby caught her attention. A presence. Eyes in the dark? She squinted. Freaky night, head injury, Tiffy with a brain infarction . . . and now someone watching all of it? Just what she needed. Tiffy—

"You might want to close that soon. It's getting a little breezy in here."

"Huh?"

"The door." The puca padded toward her and nudged the door closed with his nose.

Mina absently pushed it the rest of the way home and set the bolt. Then she stared down at her puca. Her puca.

"Feeling possessive now that I've strutted my stuff?" The puca gloated.

"You."

"Yes?"

"You're like . . . like . . ."

"For a writing teacher, you really have a way with words."

"A loaded weapon. A time bomb. A body snatcher. What did you do to her? She's not herself. Is she?"

"Sure, she is. She won't be quite so religious in her quest tomorrow, but she'll still be determined. That's how it's always worked. She's finally seen the light." He panted, tongue hanging over his left jowl. "I'm good at showing it to them."

"But that hardly seems ethical. Or fair. You're messing with her head and twisting nature around and—What am I saying? You're a wonderful, wonderful puca. She seemed like a human being. And I'll get my job back, too?"

"That's the plan."

Then her heart sank. "No, I won't. There's still the mortgage, which is in my name and Jackson's. They can't ignore it now that she's shoved it in their faces."

"Funny thing about that mortgage of yours." If she didn't know better, she'd think the dog was checking out his front toenails, in a manicure inspection sort of way.

"What about the mortgage?" Mina stared at the dog. What had he done? Oh, no. Could she lose the house now? Maybe it was some kind of payback thing? She could keep the job but at the expense of the house? Hell, she didn't know how this whole puca karma thing worked.

"Soon it'll be in your name only."

"My—"

"The house is yours. Only yours. Thanks to Tiffy's intervention, Jackson will accept your generous offer to buy back his half and the paperwork will go smoothly. I guarantee it." The dog, seriously, batted its eyelashes at her. Its eyes looked like two flashlights performing a duet in Morse code.

"But I never made an offer to buy him out. I don't have that kind of money." She gave him a panicked look. "He didn't accept an offer from someone else, did he? Am I going to be out on the pavement next week?"

"No. The offer was made in your name. And don't worry about the money. It's being taken care of."

She eyed him with suspicion. "Don't worry about the money? What are you talking about? Where did the money come from? Is this even legal?"

The dog cocked its head. "Do you really care? I swear the closing date will be two weeks from now."

She stared. "And then the house will be mine? But how?"

"All yours. And do you honestly care how it happens as long as it does?"

"I . . . *should* care."

"Suit yourself." The dog paused, as though gathering its thoughts and wondering how best to express them. "The offer was legal. It was just . . . expedited. I paid it. I have assets and I chose to invest in you. I trust you won't take advantage."

Mina stared at the dog, who stared right back, yellow eyes unblinking and utterly serious. No threats. Just a promise and a lot more going on in that head than she'd guessed. Mina closed her eyes, then determinedly opened them again. "I'm going to hate myself for asking this. What kind of assets does a puca have?"

A doggy grin. "Wouldn't you like to know."

"You won't tell me?"

"I'm not that trusting, sweetie. So, do we have a deal?"

"You . . ." Deal? Did she make a deal? Her mind scrambled, sought some kind of foothold. Did she actually think, even for a moment, that she had any sort of power in their relationship, such as it was? Guardian. Ha. She knew who held the cards. And it certainly wasn't the penniless, unemployed, soon-to-be-homeless, rejected and obviously undesirable schoolteacher.

"Correction. You're not broke. Just very close to it, which doesn't matter so much since you will be employed after tomorrow. You can keep your home if you want it badly enough. And the rejected part? I think the ex did you a favor. He was a jerk unworthy of your time, especially if he preferred somebody like Tiffy to you. You're better off without him.

"And as for undesirable, hey, what about the attentions of a certain horny contractor—whatshisface, Teague? You know, the one you've been entertaining fantasies about?

Looks like a reciprocal situation to me. The man's hot for you even if you've been acting like a nutcase since you met him. Nothing like a little ego stroking to help you get over a breakup, eh?"

"Fantasies—!" He was spying on her while she slept? Or daydreamed? "Hey, you can't do that!" So what if she'd passed the time enjoyably while the puca had been out doing God knows what. She'd needed to keep her mind busy so she wouldn't imagine the worst, and frankly, it was downright pleasant to picture Teague in any number of positions, whispering naughty and wonderful things to her. Riordan had no right to spy on them.

"And you call me sick. I was so embarrassed. Nearly lost my footing once or twice. Sorry about the mess in the school football field, by the way."

"What mess?"

"Hooves on turf . . . never a good combo. Anyway. So we were discussing a deal, but I didn't mean to get ahead of myself. My assistance with Tiffy and the job and the house was simply a demonstration. A good faith gesture, if you will. Your life no longer sucks. Any chance you could help me make mine suck less? I could be one helluva grateful puca. And, as you can see, grateful pucas make excellent friends."

"Spell it out, Riordan."

"Help me break the curse. Please. You won't regret it."

Mina raised her eyebrow. "You don't think so?"

"Well, maybe briefly, but in the long run, I swear we'll both be better off. Aren't you in a much better frame of mind now than you were an hour ago?"

"Sure, I guess so. But you paying off Jackson is only postponing me losing the house. I can't afford these payments on my own."

"Oh, please. I took you for a resourceful woman. Use your head. Refinance the mortgage. Haven't you built up any equity in the place? Work with it. Get your payments lowered. If you want it enough, you can do it."

Mina's mind raced. Damn dog was right. She could do this. If she wanted it badly enough—and she did—she could keep the house. Especially if Teague was right about insurance covering the renovation work.

"See? Now stop calling me a damn dog."

"Okay, let's get something straight. I'm grateful—no, *overwhelmed*—if you've somehow managed to turn things around for me so completely. But you've got to stop reading my every thought."

The puca sighed. "I know. But it's so much more efficient than waiting for you to transfer thought to speech. I'm also just a little anxious to hear what you think about this deal. This could be win-win for both of us, you know."

That was reasonable. "Okay, we can talk. Exactly what would I need to do to make your life suck less? And would making your life suck less make mine suck more in any way, shape or form?"

"Depends on your definition and performance."

"Explain."

"Well, for my part, I'm going to want my freedom—which I think is reasonable—and I'm going to want free use of the powers that are rightfully mine."

Mina studied him. "I guess that's understandable. So how do we get this for you?"

"Like I said, we break the curse."

"Yeah, I get that part. Over and over, in fact. But you're going to have to be more specific. Have I mentioned my complete inexperience with curses and the breaking of such? I'm a total novice. Completely ignorant. I don't even believe in curses."

"Don't believe—! Hello? Remember my cornerstone? There's a clear imprint of it on your forehead. That would be evidence of a curse. Plenty of basis for belief."

"It's just a rock." Still, Mina eyed him uneasily.

"Distinction: that 'rock' was part of a Sarsen stone that once stood among hundreds of others like it in the sacred stone circle of Avebury in Wiltshire County, England."

Tiny hairs rose on the back of Mina's neck. "Oh, lord. I shouldn't ask. I know I shouldn't ask. But . . . by stone circle, do you mean Stonehenge?"

"Oh, please. Of course not Stonehenge. You people are so predictable."

Mina relaxed.

"Stonehenge might be a pretty little circle, but it's all theatrics. No, Avebury's older, bigger, more effective and, frankly, less well-kept. It's a shame really. If people only knew. Well . . ." He eyed Mina's no doubt appalled expression. "Maybe it's better they don't."

Mina worked her jaw for a moment. "And I'm supposed to believe all this?"

"A smart woman will generally take on faith a few things once she's seen a few related ones, yes? Have I said anything that hasn't come true yet?"

No. He hadn't. So that meant the cornerstone really used to be part of some mysterious stone circle. She licked suddenly dry lips. "So. Is this the part where you tell me how my life is going to suck?"

"You know, I thought you had a little more courage than this. Not everyone would have the guts to start renovations on a house while facing down unemployment, bankruptcy and homelessness. To a sensible person, that's terrifying."

"True."

"So what's a stone circle or two when you're teamed up with a puca who can do good things for you? I made the unemployment go away. I made the specter of homelessness go away. So listen to your puca. Take a risk. Live a little."

"Sure, talk to me about risk. Here you are, a shapeshifter. What do you have to worry about?"

The puca's eyes glowed. "I've been living under this curse for a millennium or two. There's more to worry about than you know."

"Gosh, that's convincing."

The puca dropped moodily to the floor, muzzle buried in his paws.

"Oh, don't even do bloodhound on me. I'm impervious to puppy dog eyes, especially spooky yellow ones."

The eyes looked up at her, all signs of humor leeched from them. Staring into them, Mina saw utter weariness and desperation. It gave her pause. A millennium or two. Just the way he'd said the words, enunciating each syllable as if he felt the weight of every year of his term of imprisonment . . . and no human could possibly comprehend that length of time. He'd spent every year, every day, every moment of it in captivity. Disembodied.

She tried to imagine not feeling her limbs, not really seeing or sensing anything or anyone.

"To be technically correct, I have been able to communicate with most of my guardians. None of them as well as you, though."

"And everything else?"

"I wasn't aware of anything or anyone else. I had some limited perception before they busted up the Sarsen stone, since it was grounded in the earth, but once they did that . . . nothing." His yellow eyes were flat now. "Just conversations with my guardian of the moment, whatever she might care to share with me. Gladys was actually really generous on that score, sharing her day-to-day thoughts and worries with me. Sometimes, when she was in the mood, she'd even read from the newspapers to me. I liked that. She was originally an American, like you."

"So that's why you don't have much of an accent. Years of living with Gladys."

"That and American TV programs. She loved her imported cooking shows and sitcoms. And the woman was a complete movie addict—loved American films. The raunchier the better. Whatever she watched, I could watch. Otherwise . . . it was just limbo for me." He shrugged. "So I watched."

Mina nodded, thinking. Limbo. Disembodiment. What was that like? It must have been so disorienting. Like forever wandering in the dark without being able to feel or see, to smell, touch or taste. It would drive anyone literally insane. Who would do that to another being? What would merit a punishment like that?

"I seduced Archdruid Akker's daughter when she was engaged to another man."

"Oh." Mina winced.

"Yeah, I know how you feel about cheaters, but I swear I wouldn't have done her if I'd known she was engaged to someone else. I don't remember that night, but I do know an engagement would generally hold me up." When Mina's expression and mindset didn't alter, the dog slumped further. "Hey, I like sex as much as the next guy, but I have one or two standards. Besides, I was a handsome guy. Pussy wasn't that hard to come by. I wouldn't purposely go after somebody else's girl when an unattached one is so much less complicated."

Mina stared, hard, then shook her head. "I don't get it. I was waiting for world-altering offenses. Stomach-churning horrors. Instead I get locker-room logic and a soap opera drama? You guys—puca, Druid, whoever else you're not telling me about—for all your powers and your 'millennia' are as petty as humans. What's the deal?"

"Hey, nobody said we had different problems. Just that our temper tantrums were a little more extreme."

"No kidding." She dropped into a chair. "I can kind of see where the guy's coming from, though. I mean, Tiffy and Jackson pissed me off royally." She shrugged. "I might have done a few petty things to get back at them." She paused, remembering the porn-related suggestion she'd made just tonight over the phone, and grinned ruefully. "And maybe I'm not done being petty either. I'm not sure what I would have done with powers like yours or this Druid's if I'd had the chance." She pondered a moment. "But weren't Druids human? I mean, how would this Druid guy stand a chance against you?"

"A righteously pissed-off Druid, you mean, which is important . . . and me with my hands tied."

"What do you mean?"

"We have our rules, too. For example, puca magic generally has to follow the path of karma, so as a result, only the deserving benefit from our intervention and the undeserving lose as a result of it. In addition to a few other complications, I violated that flow. As a result, I lost the ability to protect myself from, or retaliate against, revenge by a victim of my magic."

"So the Druid girl did this to you? But I thought—"

Riordan was shaking his head. "This is where it gets sticky for the puca. A victim is defined as anyone who is hurt by puca magic, including pissed-off fathers of compromised daughters. The pissed-off daddy in this case also happened to be a powerful Archdruid with an amazingly detail-oriented gift for spell casting and an eternal thirst for vengeance."

"I see." She eyed him. "So, are you sorry? That you made love to the girl?"

He stared at her, his eyes glowing almost neon with frustration. "I guess I should be. I don't know. I can't remember her. I don't remember the night I did her, even."

"But you're sure that you did."

"I'm sure. But part of the curse was not remembering her or the act itself. And I can't say her name without experiencing this pleasant, implosionlike sensation in my head.

Akker decided I didn't deserve the knowledge or the memory of his daughter. He said I had no right to them and he was just reclaiming them for her. So I have the physical and mental conviction that I really did have sex with a girl who was intended for someone else, but I have no memory of the act itself. I don't know how we touched, what she said, if she liked it, if I liked it, how it started, how it ended . . . *anything*."

"Oh, goody. Amnesia, too? Why does this sound like a soap opera? Look, are you damn sure you did this?"

"I had sex with her. I'm sure of that. And I must have wronged her or her father to some extent or I wouldn't have been vulnerable to the curse. I'm also sure, though, that the sex was consensual." He frowned. "Mostly."

"Mostly? *Mostly* consensual? Well, screw that." She stood up, with every intent of dismissing him and his problems. "I don't cut deals with rapists." Let him rot in his damn cornerstone.

He lunged to his feet. "I don't mean that. I wouldn't rape a woman."

She waited.

"But I might have turned on the charm a little. And maybe I wasn't head over heels in love with the woman, just wanting to get laid. Maybe I exaggerated things a little. I don't know."

She gave him a contemptuous look.

"Hey, I'm trying to be honest with you. I swear I don't force any woman. I don't have to. If I want a woman, well, I generally get her. It was always that way. Or it was back then, anyway. I have no recent experiences to offer as proof. Disem-*body*-ment means a whole lot of sacrifice, you know?" He looked brooding. "Anyway, I'm into kinky but I've never been into violent kinky. If that makes sense."

She sighed and slumped back in her chair. "Yeah. I know

what you mean. So you probably tried some stupid line on her, did the wild nasty, and . . . and what?"

"I don't know. I don't know. That's the problem. I can't remember anything about that night. Except for a wild and wicked ceremony in Avebury after the fact, and a whole lot of nights stuck with that damned stone. But at least I could see and hear the world at first. I was under the stars. Later, after the stone was busted up and Akker's followers made some adjustments, the confinement got worse." He gave her a woeful look, obviously inviting sympathetic questions about his punishment.

It was enough to jade even the most optimistic woman, and Mina was certainly less than. "Sounds like something a decent fraction of the frat boy population has done at some point or another. Both the mysterious sex and the freaky ceremonial. Hell, even the curse and blackballing. Aren't you guys supposed to be above at least some of this crap?"

"We've already discussed this part."

"I know." She stared at the clock. "And I'm too damned tired for this right now. No way am I cutting wee-hour deals with a cursed shape-shifter when I have a knot on my head and too little sleep. We'll talk more tomorrow. Fair enough?"

"Sure."

She stood up and stretched, then padded her way into the bedroom. Hearing footsteps following her, she halted in her doorway. "Oh, no. No pucas in my bedroom. I don't swing that way, remember?"

"Oh, come on. Have a heart. It's been literally centuries for me. And if you'd prefer the human form—"

"No how, no way, no matter what form you take. Do we have that straight?"

"Sheesh. If you have a headache tonight, just say so."

That glint in his eyes . . . he was teasing, right? She was

almost certain he was teasing. But she wasn't taking chances. "Hey, as far as you're concerned, I have a headache *every* night. Got it?"

"Humans. You guys take this stuff way too seriously."

She glared at him until the glint faded. "And you don't take it seriously enough. Maybe the Druid knew what he was doing when he cursed you."

"Oh, that was low." The puca slunk back into the living room, tail down, and collapsed on the rug.

Mina leaned against the doorjamb for a moment. Given what he was, what he could do, and what he'd just shared with her, she should really be afraid of him. But she wasn't.

"Well, you shouldn't be. Pucas are playful. Haven't you heard? We don't like pain and we don't inflict it. Much."

Mina groaned. "I think it's that 'much' part that concerns me. Good night, Riordan."

Canine sigh. " 'Night, Mina."

Too tired to do much but carefully wash her face and dab at the ugly bump on her temple, Mina changed into the most modest pj's she could find and crawled into bed. Just as she was drifting off, she reminded herself to find that missing letter in the morning. It would be interesting to get Cousin Gladys's take on pucas and their curses. Maybe she had some secrets to impart, too. Something about eliminating a puca?

*Hey, I heard that.*

Mina smiled a little at his peevish tone, already drifting off. Maybe it would also tell her how to break the curse. . . .

# CHAPTER SIX

"Hey, beautiful." Cinnamon-flavored breath warmed Mina's cheek. "Are you in there?"

She groaned without opening her eyes. "Oh, Riordan. Not again. Really. A girl needs her beauty sleep." If he woke her up one more time to ask if she'd made a decision, she was damn well deciding against him. She had half a mind to do that anyway. A sane woman would. What chance did a schoolteacher have against a two-thousand-year-old curse?

"Riordan?" The voice, deep and masculine, came from farther away. And from about three feet above her head.

Not Riordan's voice. Sounded familiar, though—

"Teague?" She opened her eyes.

"Sounds like you're used to company early in the morning." His voice was bland—as bland as crushed velvet could get, anyway—and his gaze was steady.

Damn, but he looked good. Even early in the morning when her eyes were swollen and her body ached as though she'd been the one on the back of a stallion last night.

Oh, no. Where was the puca? He wouldn't—?

"Bark." The hellhound.

Teague closed his eyes at the sound. She couldn't blame him, really. That unholy bark was downright unnerving.

Mina listened to the moist huff of canine panting under her bed. "That's Riordan."

Teague's expression relaxed. "Oh. Interesting name."

Thank God the puca had brains enough to assume doggy form.

*Give me a little credit, please.*

Don't screw this up for me. Or I swear you can damn well live with that curse.

*Does that mean you'll help me?*

She snarled. "Will you just stop pushing me?"

Teague removed his knee from the side of her bed. "Sorry."

"I—"

*I'm shutting up. I swear. Just let me know if you need a matchmaker. I think I'd be really good at that shit.*

She growled under her breath.

*Keep talking to me like that and you're going to mess things up with this guy. Is that what you want?*

"Hi, Teague. Sorry I'm so testy. I just feel like a wall fell on my head this morning." She tried to sound pathetic.

"No wonder. Doesn't help to wake up to a strange man's face hovering over you, either, I bet. I tried knocking, but you didn't answer. I was worried about that head of yours, so I went around back and came through the section of your wall that's still open. Hey—" He whipped around, his focus arcing low to follow the path of a dark blur. "What the hell?"

Riordan, obviously. He'd bounded out of the room and soon thereafter Mina heard scratch-shuffling as the dog squirmed his way under . . . the couch, she had to presume. Didn't sound comfortable.

*It's not. But thanks so much for your concern.*

Just an observation.

*So have you—*

And don't ask that question.

"Does your dog run away from everyone or just me?" Teague turned back to eye her quizzically. "A guy could get a complex."

She grinned. "From a dog?"

"We-ell, I guess you could say I'm a little at a disadvantage to start with. Vulnerable, you might even say."

"Right." Mina snorted.

"Hey, isn't it just possible that *you* make *me* a little nervous, too?" He raised his eyebrows at her. "You know. 'In a good way.'"

Mina remembered her excuse from the other night. It had been an excuse at the time, but . . . honestly, he really did make her nerve endings go all bouncy. So, his went all bouncy, too? How very interesting.

"Great. Now you look smug."

And he looked less than nervous, but that was okay. She smiled. "So do we have a date tonight still?"

"Yes, ma'am. Feel free to come as you are." His gaze dipped lower and she followed the direction—

Snagged the blankets back up, but it was too late.

He was laughing.

She groaned, mortified and amused at the same time. "I didn't buy it. Blame my mother." The woman had much to answer for, including the tawdry pj's. Hey, she normally slept in a flimsy tank top and panties, but no way was she waltzing around Riordan and his stallion woody while wearing next to nothing.

So she'd settled for pajama pants and a T-shirt describing the various suggestive positions of the "comma" sutra.

"If you hate it, why wear it? Maybe you should give it to the dog to sleep with." He raised his voice. "Yo. Riordan. Come here, boy."

A warning growl rumbled from beneath the couch.

*Your new boyfriend's a laugh a minute. Maybe I should give him something to—*

"Riordan. Hush."

*Hey, watch it, babe. I'm not your lapdog to order around.*

"So, Teague. Know of any good vets? I should probably do the responsible thing and get my dog fixed."

*Oh, now that's just plain mean. Like I'd ever sit still for something like that.*

Teague was frowning. "Oh, now that's just plain mean. Poor dog. He's just nervous having me around. Give him a break."

"Men." She glanced from Teague to Riordan. "You guys all stick together when it comes to the jewels, don't you?"

Teague shrugged, looking innocent. "Fellow feeling?"

"Uh, so to speak?" she asked in the same tone.

He grinned. "So, about tonight."

"Our date tonight?"

"Yeah, that one. I was thinking dinner at that new steak place across town. Unless you're a vegetarian? Not that that's a problem. We could do something else—"

"No, steak sounds wonderful."

*Yeah, I just love steak. I can't wait. The last time I ate a steak was . . . damn, I can't even remember. This is just great, Mina. And he's paying, right?*

Mina froze. You mean—

*Just like a marriage. Whither thou goest also goest I. Or something like that. My grasp of Old Testament lingo is kind of rusty. Not a good era for me.*

Spell it out, dog.

*You know, I could start taking offense at all these dog references and demands you make—*

Riordan!

Canine sigh—and she could hear the whisper from under the couch in the living room. *Look, it's not like I have a choice in the matter. The Druids took this whole guardianship deal seriously. Now that I'm locked into physical form, I can't be apart from you.*

Well, what about that puca ride? The one you took Tiffany on? I wasn't there then.

*An exception to the rules.*

So make another exception.

"Mina? So we're on for tonight? The steak house?"

"I—" Riordan, you'd damn well better give me an out for this one. Somehow. This isn't fair.

*Live in a cornerstone for two millennia as punishment for one night's disgrace and then tell me about fair. Look, I didn't make the rules and I can't change or break them. I'm bound to you, remember?*

"I . . ." Mina stared at Teague, mind racing for an explanation, alternative, solution, recipe for puca poison—

*I heard that.*

"Is there a problem?" Teague eyed her cautiously. "We could go somewhere else if you'd rather."

"I . . . What if we ate here?" Oh, thank God. Oh, dear God. She had to cook? "Or maybe do take-out." Brilliant, Mina.

"Sure. I guess." He glanced around doubtfully. "I just thought . . . you don't seem to get out much. And then I come here to work all day. A change of scenery might be good."

"Well . . ." She scrambled. Okay. What were her options? Tell a guy before their first date that she's tied to a shape-shifting puca who lives in a rock? Right, that would work. More likely, it would kill the possibility of any romantic relationship. It might even lose her a contractor who refused to work for the criminally insane. What about partial truth? "Okay, I'm going to level with you. I can't leave my dog."

*Aw, that's so sweet. I'm touched.*

If you can't help, the least you can do is butt out.

*Okay. Butting out for now.*

She smiled, just a little evilly. "Actually, I just recently adopted him and he's still nervous about me leaving. He gets . . . incontinent when he's nervous and I get a mess. I'm sure he'll settle in eventually, but for now—"

Teague was nodding. "Okay, I get it. Maybe you both could come over to my place? Unless he'd make a mess there, too." Teague was frowning a little, obviously not eager for dog feces in his home. Not that she could blame him for that.

Can I do that? Riordan?

*Thought you wanted me to butt out, sweetie.*

Oh, cut it out and tell me. Can we leave here together?

*Yeah, sure. I think so. I'm still feeling out the rules for this new existence of mine, but so far it sounds possible.* He paused. *Actually, it might be kind of nice to go somewhere. I get to ride in a car, right? I've never been in a car. Does it hurt? Will you hold my hand if I get scared? Paw. I meant paw. You'd rather I stay doggy-style, right?*

Riordan, you are one sick puca. Yes, probably a car.

And maybe a little part of her softened at the idea of giving the puca a new experience. He'd missed so much, living inside that rock since well before the industrial revolution.

Meanwhile, Teague was eyeing her, still with question, but a question that would expire soon unless she responded. "Yes, Teague. Riordan and I would love to have dinner with you at your place. He'll be good." He'd better be.

*Er, bark?*

"Excellent. I'll pick you both up at seven, then."

"Or I could just drive over—"

Teague was already shaking his head. "Now that would just be sabotage. If you can't tell, I'm trying to impress my date with old-fashioned chivalry."

"Oh, really." Mina smiled. "In that case, I'll just be sitting here all damsel-like and waiting."

*Make that "barf." I'll bet he sobs his way through sonnets, too.*

"Excellent. See you at seven."

With a salute of a wave, Teague eyed her pj's one last time, his grin deliberately teasing, then left.

Mina, meanwhile, decided to tackle the obvious. "Riordan. Get in here." She hissed it, waiting until the dog trotted into her bedroom before closing the door.

"You do like to order me around, lady."

"Yeah, I know. And if you weren't playing hell with my life right now, I might find it in my heart to be nicer to you."

He gave her big, sad puppy dog eyes, spoiled by the sulfurous glow emanating from their eerie depths. "You were nicer to me last night. Has something changed?"

"Yeah. See, last night I thought you were tied to me metaphorically, as in, can't leave my house or always in my head. Now you tell me I'm tied to you physically? You can't leave me? And you can't poof yourself into disembodiment?"

"Well, disembodiment is out—I already explained that— and as for the other . . . Unless I'm performing the puca ride ritual—which is tied up in more red tape than you want to think about—I have to stay within certain physical bounds."

She frowned. "How narrow are these bounds?"

"Let's see, shall we?" He raced for the door, abruptly rebounding off of it while Mina winced right along with him. "Whoops? Still getting used to embodiment. Must obey most universal laws. Got it. So, would you mind?" He glanced at the door, then back at her.

Mina opened it for him, then followed him out into the living room. She could hear voices coming from behind the kitchen door, which she'd at least thought to close last night. Quietly, she opened the front door for him. "So, I wait here?"

"Yep."

"Oh, and, Riordan? No talking dogs, okay? The guys are right around back."

*Check.* He strutted out onto the porch, with tail and chin

high, excitement tautening his entire body. *Oh. Outside. Air. Grass. Sky. Sunshine. This is awesome. You gotta help me—*

And boom, he ran into an invisible wall cutting him off just short of the front porch steps. He sat down hard, thought for a minute, then glanced back at Mina. *Probably this building and no farther.*

Frowning, she stepped out onto the porch with him and approached the steps.

Riordan stood up again, alert as before. When she descended the stairs, he trotted easily after her, then leapt into the grass to roll and bark and squirm.

Soon, Mina was laughing and plopping her butt down on the bottom step. For the first time, Riordan looked sincere, oblivious to her presence and completely guileless. He looked just like a happy canine, his eyes closed, mouth hanging open and all four paws kicking out at the air and grass. His long tail wagged madly as the furry body squirmed and attacked every itch, reveled in every texture. Finally, he lay still. He turned a sleepy gaze toward her. *Thank you.*

Resting an elbow on her knee, she braced her chin on it. "My pleasure." And it was. She could feel his joy at finally being able to physically experience the outdoors again. "So this is how it works? Your boundaries move with me?"

He cocked his head, seeming to ponder something. *Yeah. That makes a lot of sense now. Akker liked to speak in riddles and he mentioned something about a moving sphere of freedom? Mobile cage? I'm not sure of the translation.*

"He set out rules for your embodiment and disembodiment when he cursed you?"

*The man was a contract attorney before his time. Small print stuff was his specialty and the bane of my existence in every form. It would be great if he'd given me a written copy of the rules himself before he did this, but Druids didn't believe in writing stuff down. Not that he would have gone to the trouble for a victim of his curse anyway.*

She nodded. "It must be hard to live by rules you don't completely understand."

*You said it.*

"So if I go inside the house and get dressed, you could still sit out here on the porch without me, right?"

He stilled a moment. *You wouldn't mind?*

"Jeez, I'm not an ogre, Riordan. No, I don't mind. I'd stay out here longer, if it weren't for the skanky pj's." She glanced down at herself.

He gave her a slack-jawed doggy grin. *I think I like your mom.*

"Gee, there's a shocker." She rolled her eyes at him, then stood. "Don't do anything I wouldn't do." As Riordan trotted up the steps beside her, she frowned and rephrased. "Don't do anything a real dog wouldn't do."

*Got it. I'll be a perfect dog.* He dropped to his haunches in front of her on the porch, a picture of doggy obedience. Except for the mischievous glow in his eyes.

She smiled ruefully. "I'll believe that when I see it."

Twenty minutes later, showered and dressed, she stepped out onto the porch to find Riordan barking his fool head off at the mailman. "Riordan!"

*Would you rather I bite him?*

"Oh, good grief." She restrained him, one hand on his collar, and smiled an apology at the mailman. Poor man all but tossed Mina's mail in her face before retreating to the relative safety of his vehicle.

*Hey, I had no choice. You wanted me to be a dog, so I channeled dog, and no dog endures the mailman, right? I thought I was doing well.*

"Right. Fine. I'm going in for breakfast." She eyed him. "Do you eat?"

He paused. "Not like you. Not in a long time."

"Well, come on, then."

Uncharacteristically quiet, he followed her inside.

She led him to the kitchen. "So let's give this a shot, then, shall we? Just remember . . . dogs don't talk. The contractors are right outside."

*All right.*

She swung open the refrigerator. "So what do you like?"

*Anything you like.*

"Gee, that's awfully agreeable. Still, I'm in the mood to take you at your word." She opened the fruit drawer. "Just tell me you're not a strict carnivore. I have fruit here and that's what I was getting for myself."

*I like fruit.*

"Great." She pulled out a bag of red grapes and carried them over to the counter. She broke off two big bunches, rinsed them in the sink, then set them in two bowls. She glanced out her one unbroken window, smiled a little when Teague caught her eye and waved to her. She waved back, then hesitantly turned back to Riordan. "Maybe we'll take these into the living room. Just in case."

Again Riordan followed her, oddly obedient and even more oddly quiet.

Mina sat on the couch then paused, unsure of procedure. "So, are you eating these doggy-style?"

*Hey, I like how you say that.* Still, it was a half-hearted jab, as though the puca were deep in thought.

"Let me guess. You haven't eaten a bowl of grapes in as long as you haven't rolled in the grass. Am I right?"

He plopped down on his butt in front of the low coffee table and watched as she set them in front of him. Hesitantly, ears cocked up and eyes only on the glistening fruit before him, Riordan carefully plucked a grape with his teeth. It fell. With an audible groan, he tried again. Same result.

"Problem?" Mina delicately inquired.

"Well . . . I haven't eaten solid food in a couple of millennia now. And even way back when, I generally dined in human form. Doggie jaws . . . I dunno."

"I see." Mina stood up, drew the blinds, locked the front door and carefully closed the kitchen door. "Okay, go ahead. Do the morph thing so you can eat."

His gaze on Mina, Riordan flash-shimmered and suddenly a man sat on her couch. The same faceless guy—minus ears and tail—who'd disarmed her just the other day.

*I caught on to the ears and tail. It just took a while. Your little joke on me, huh?*

Somehow, she had the impression that he was nervous. "What's up, Riordan? They're just grapes. Nothing poisonous in there for me—and nothing that would hurt you, right? Is that the problem? You don't know?"

*They won't hurt me.* He slowly reached into the bowl and plucked one of the grapes. Then, hesitantly, brought it to where his mouth would be if she could see it.

Mina blinked. The grape was there . . . and then it wasn't there. Just disappeared into the blurred maw of his face. Then she saw his jaw move, pause, then move quickly, efficiently. His throat worked as he swallowed. He didn't say anything, then leaned back in the couch.

"What's wrong? Are they sour?"

*I wouldn't know.*

"What do you mean?"

"I can't taste it."

"You mean because it's a grape or . . . You can't taste *anything*?" Mina was horrified. "Oh, because of your face. Okay, well, hey, you just morph back into the dog thing and . . . and I'll cut them for you. That might make it easier."

He was already shaking his head. *It will be the same. I managed to bite into one of those grapes before I dropped it. No taste. I'd hoped I was mistaken, but . . . it's something else Akker took from me when he . . .* Riordan broke off and looked away. She had the impression there was more he could say, but he'd chosen silence.

Probably devastated, poor guy. She sat next to him. "I am sorry. That must really suck."

He gave a low, humorless laugh.

"There's nothing I can do for you? How do you eat, then? Don't you eat?"

"I don't have to. A body needs food. I've come to the conclusion that I'm sort of suspended between body and not body right now."

"You didn't tell me that before."

He shrugged. "I'm as new to this as you are, and Akker spoke his curse and conditions long eons ago. I'm still putting things together."

"I'm sorry. And this is just a tease, isn't it?" She looked at the grapes. Big and red and pretty—and probably sweet. "Maybe I should take these into the kitchen and just eat there."

"That's not necessary. In fact, if you don't mind, I'd like it if you would eat here. Maybe I can smell them or something."

"Maybe," she murmured doubtfully. Still, she picked up a grape and, instead of popping it into her mouth, deliberately bit it in half, carefully holding the remaining half between two fingers. She offered it to him.

Hesitantly, he bent toward her hand, sniffed. Bent closer, sniffed again. Then he pulled back and sighed.

"Nothing?"

He shook his head, then halted a moment, his attention obviously caught by something on her face.

"What? Oh, juice, right?" She fumbled for a napkin, but Riordan was already dabbing his fingers along a juice trail down her chin. Startled, she contracted her fingers reflexively, squeezing more juice from the half-grape to run down her hand. "Oh—" She popped the remainder of the grape into her mouth and licked at her palm.

His hand still on her jaw and throat, Riordan froze. "Mina!"

"What?" She finished chewing. "I know. Great table manners. Sorry."

"Never mind that." He seemed so intense. "Do me a favor. Eat another grape." He still held a hand to her neck, his fingers splayed over her chin and throat.

She frowned, wondering. "Like this? But—"

"Please. I'm begging you. Just like this. Another grape."

Moving hesitantly and feeling awkward, she reached into the bowl for another grape and brought it to her mouth.

Riordan seemed to stiffen, and she could almost swear she saw a familiar glow of yellow in the depths of his blurred face. "Go ahead," he whispered. "Put it in your mouth."

She did so, closing her lips around the fruit. She bit into it, feeling the grape's skin burst and the juices and soft flesh bathe her tongue. Riordan groaned, his fingers caressing her face as she manipulated the fruit with tongue and teeth. Slowly, she chewed, watching him all the while. After an uncertain moment, she swallowed the grape and licked juice from her lips.

"Another?" He sounded like a little kid begging for candy.

"Um, question first. This isn't a sexual thing, is it? Because I have a few inhibitions and, well, performing food kink with a guy who was a dog two minutes ago really rubs up against some of them."

"No. Not sex." He rubbed her jaw, his fingers trembling a little. "I can taste the grape. Through you. Somehow, some way, when you eat that grape and I'm touching your mouth or your jaw or your throat . . . I can experience some of it with you."

"You're eating vicariously?" She eyed him in bafflement. "Seriously?"

"In a way. It's like an echo of the experience. I can feel it, like a ghostly grape in my own mouth, the flavor faint but there. I don't know if it's the mind link we have or if it's just my imagination . . . no, I swear it's not my imagination. Could we do it again? Please? I have to know."

Intrigued, Mina picked up another grape and popped it into her mouth.

"Slowly. Please." He groaned. "Oh, yeah. That's good."

Her eyes widened, glancing at the door, she spoke with her mouth full. "You're making sex noises. Keep it down."

"Sorry," he whispered, still sounding enraptured. His chest heaved just a little with his breathing, and he kept caressing her face, her neck, her jaw.

Mina edged back, just a little. She would not, would *not* think what she was thinking. Grapes grapes grapes grapes . . .

"Think whatever you have to think. Just eat the grape. Please." Riordan hummed a little when she popped two grapes into her mouth, cheeks bulging as she tried to chew without spraying all and sundry.

He chuckled just a little, the sound lazy and pleased.

Mina clapped a hand to her mouth, but found his hand already there. His fingers traced her lips, which strained not to part under the pressure of an overfilled mouth. She chewed until the contents had reduced somewhat, then spoke against his hand. "I'm a pig."

"And all for me. I'm flattered, Mina." His voice lowered. "And so grateful. Thank you."

She continued to eat quietly, trying not to feel self-conscious as the big male hand hovered so gently over her jaw and throat. Obviously too pleased to worry about inhibitions himself, Riordan thoroughly enjoyed every bite she took, humming and murmuring. He relaxed bonelessly into the cushions, but for that one, insistent arm and the fingers handling her so gently.

His unconscious sensuality was unexpected. Lasciviousness she'd anticipated. He'd been nothing but a letch in stallion and dog form. Like this, as a man with needs and expressing such honest appreciation for something so basic as the taste of a grape, he was . . . disturbing . . . to her peace of mind. After she'd plucked the last grape and eaten it, she abruptly stood.

As his hand fell away, she averted her eyes, feeling like she'd kicked a puppy. "I'm sorry. I'm—I'm full now."

He nodded. "I don't suppose . . ."

"No, really. I'm full. I'd already gorged myself on a cereal bar before I remembered I had a puca on my porch."

"Oh. Right." He slumped a little in obvious disappointment.

Her heart turned over. "But I'll have to eat later, right? Maybe we could try something else then?"

"Really?"

He sounded so unabashedly hopeful, she nodded enthusiastically. "Sure. I'll even let you pick."

"I'll do you one better. You let me taste, and I'll even cook for you."

She gave him a doubtful look. "You cook?"

"I hung out in Gladys's head for a good decade or two before she passed on. The woman cooked. And she liked to talk while she cooked." He mused, almost affectionately, "I think she was just trying to share her life with me, as simple as it was."

"That was kind."

He nodded. "So, I have some experience based on observation. Plus all those cooking shows . . . so I'm sure I can remember some of it. And, if not, I'm sure you can clue me in."

She nodded, then frowned. "Although maybe I'll let you cook dinners for me instead. Unless the workmen go offsite for their lunch." She raised her eyebrows meaningfully.

"Oh. Right. Your boyfriend. You don't want him to catch your dog or your faceless tenant making meals on your stove."

"He's not exactly my boyfriend."

Riordan shrugged. "What else would he be?"

"Well, I only met the guy a few days ago. We could just say he's Teague. Doesn't have to be anything in relation to me."

"You don't want him to mean anything to you?"

"I didn't say that. I said I just met the guy, and only a fool starts thinking in terms of relationships this early on. He's Teague. He and I are going out tonight. It's no more than that. However, I don't want to explain how my dog can talk and turn into a faceless man, either. Makes for odd employer-contractor relations and really uncomfortable dinner conversation." She frowned. "Speaking of which, we've got to do something to keep you from blowing your dog cover."

"Like what? Four legs, floppy ears, wagging tail—what else do you need?"

The yellow eyes. "Can you squint? And play mute?"

"You know, some people might be satisfied with my ability to shift shape, to bend time, space and matter and assume the form of a different species. But you? Oh, no. The puca must playact as well. You're so picky."

"Yeah? Well, for a supposed dog, you have demon eyes and you can't bark. That's a problem."

"Fine. I'll be careful. Squinting and muting. Got it. So we're going out—Oh, *steak*. You were going to have steak until you guys decided against a restaurant. Oh, pull-lleeeeeeeease." He sounded like an adolescent boy who'd eaten nothing but broccoli for a week.

"Oh, give me a break. There's no way I could—"

"Doggy bag. You could just cut your meat in half and bring home your leftovers to eat when we're alone together."

"That sounded really, really bad, Riordan. That whole sex noise thing? Now you're making sex scenarios. Stop that."

"Okay, okay. But let's work on the steak scenario. Deal?"

She rolled her eyes, grinning reluctantly. "We can work on it. Another night we'll broil steak or something."

He whimpered.

"If you're going to whimper, maybe you'd just as well zap yourself into Riordan the dog again."

"Oh. Already?"

"We-ell . . ."

A reluctant flash-shimmer and she had a dog sitting on her couch. One with annoyed golden eyes staring at her. And she completely ignored her own relief at seeing his familiar canine self. That other . . . That had been strange, disturbing, exciting, weird, just plain odd. A question mark she didn't want to answer. Dog was so much simpler. "I'm sorry. It has to be this way when the contractors are here."

"Just remember that I. Am. Not. A. Dog."

"Fine. You're not a dog." Not that it made sense to be saying such to a four-legged creature with floppy ears and tail. Factor in the freaky eyes and command of the English language, however . . .

"So, what do you think your buddy Teague will make for dinner?" Riordan let his tongue loll out of his mouth while Mina groaned.

# CHAPTER SEVEN

"I don't know. I was just in the mood for steak tonight."
Teague smiled a little sheepishly as he showed Mina and
her dog into his townhouse that evening. "I hope that's
okay. They've been marinating and I thought I'd just toss
them on the grill for a while along with some potatoes. I
have salad makings, too, if that suits you."

"Sounds great." Mina snuck a glance at Riordan, who
was prancing with excitement.

Teague was also watching the restless canine. "Does he
need to go out or something?"

"Hmm?" Mina glanced up. "Oh, he's just excited. I think
maybe he likes you."

*The man's cooking steak. What's not to like? Tell him you
want yours rare. The bloodier the better. And I want butter and
sour cream on the potato, but you can do whatever you want with
the salad. I was never much for vegetables, so that's all yours.*

Gee, thanks. She gave him a sarcastic look before turning back to Teague, who was bending down to Riordan. As
he met Riordan's eyes, a startled Teague rocked back from

his haunches to land flat on his butt. "This dog . . . Hell, that's no dog. He's Satan with ears. Holy shit!"

*Ooops.*

Mina growled silently at Riordan. *I told you to keep the eyes slitted, demon boy.* She turned to Teague, who looked as though he wanted to search out a crucifix and holy water. "Teague, I'm sorry. I should have warned you. He has . . . an eye condition. Sees mostly shadows and light." *Run into something, would you?*

"But they're yellow. Yellow eyes? That's not natural."

"No, actually, they're a pale—really pale—hazel. The light just catches them funny. Now, please, be nice to him. He's had a hard life. The eyes seem to scare people." When Teague still regarded the dog with suspicion, she gave Teague a wide-eyed, appealing look. "In fact, I think his eyes are the reason his previous owner used to beat him."

That did the trick. The suspicion fading to surprise, Teague met her eyes for a moment, then, hesitantly, turned back to Riordan. "Beat him? Who the hell would beat a dog? Well, maybe *this* dog. I swear it looks possessed, Mina. You're sure?"

"That's what the animal shelter told me before I adopted him. He's been abused." *And if he doesn't remember to hide his damn eyes from now on, he's going to be even more abused.*

*Right. Squint so as not to scare the wimpy humans. You guys are so superstitious.*

*So says the puca cursed by ancient Druids to live inside a rock. Why in the world would people be superstitious?*

"Well, okay." Frowning, Teague rolled onto his knees and, after thinking a moment, held out a hand for Riordan to sniff.

*Oh, come on. Do I gotta?*

*If you want steak, you damn well better.*

Silent doggy groan before Riordan reluctantly approached Teague's hand, arrogantly sniffed it then—

Don't even think about peeing on his floor.

Riordan lowered the leg enough to turn the gesture into a brief scratch. *There's absolutely no dignity in this. What is with you people? Your ancestors used to revere me. Or at least fear me. Now I'm reduced to doggy status to keep you guys from peeing all over yourselves in terror.*

That doesn't give you an excuse to pee on an innocent man's floor out of spite. Now think steak and try to behave.

Still grumble-growling under his breath, Riordan slunk off to a corner and curled up for a nap.

Thank God. Mina turned back to Teague. "Thanks for being patient with him."

"No problem. Like I said, the dog's eyes do throw you when you first look at them . . . but I never could stand the idea of somebody abusing the small or helpless."

More grumble-growling in the corner, which Mina ignored.

Instead, she concentrated on the man in front of her. "That's because *you'd* never do something like that." He really was a nice man. The dog unnerved him that much and he could still feel sympathy for it and show patience for a grumpy temperament. And she couldn't forget his kindness to her on the day they first met. Kindness to a grumpy stranger and freaky dog. "You'd never intentionally hurt or use somebody just to achieve your own ends."

Teague stared a moment, obviously disarmed. "No. Well, I hope I wouldn't." He frowned. "So. What can I get you to drink? I have water, soda, OJ, wine, beer . . ."

"Wine sounds good. Thanks." She followed him into the kitchenette, which was separated from the dining and living areas by a small bar with stools. An impressive array of pots and pans hung from hooks on the wall. "You cook."

Teague followed her gaze to his wall and grinned a little sheepishly. "That would be my mom's doing. Both the stuff hanging from the wall and knowing how to use all of it."

"Useful skills." She raised her eyebrows at him. "So the man can build a house and he can cook a meal in its kitchen. You're some kind of catch, Mr. Just Teague."

He flashed a cocky grin. "Don't I know it."

She rolled her eyes, laughing. "What can I do to help?"

He pulled open the fridge, grabbed bags of greens and veggies and set them on the counter. "Do you chop?"

"I chop." She rolled up her sleeves and accepted the knife and cutting board he handed her.

"Great. You'll find a bowl over there if you want to finish up the salad while I see to the steaks and potatoes."

With a smile, he strode past her and headed out to the balcony. He closed the sliding doors behind him, shutting out the smoke from the grill and leaving Mina alone with Riordan.

"So, are we liking this guy?" Riordan piped up broodingly.

"Yes. We are. Is that a problem? Even better, do I really care? This is *my* life I'm trying to lead. In spite of you."

"Believe it or not, I don't like screwing up your life."

She eyed him a moment before pulling a head of lettuce out of a bag. "Believe it or not . . . I do believe that. I also think we have a problem on our hands. A long-term problem."

"That's what I've been trying to tell you—"

The sliding door snicked open and Teague strode in. "Just a little while now and everything will be ready."

"Great." She smiled. "It smells wonderful."

Later, they sat down at the little table, smiling at each other across candles Teague had been sweet enough to light. A man who remembered his candles definitely had a romantic streak, she decided. That was a plus.

As she bit into a piece of steak, she was well aware of Riordan's eyes fixed covetously on her mouth. Darn it, she couldn't even enjoy a meal without him butting in.

*Sorry. Just . . . doggy bag? Please?*

She cleared her throat, trying not to lose her smile. "This is wonderful. Much better than any restaurant."

"You know, I think so, too. Not because I think I'm some incredible chef, but because now we have privacy—and no annoyingly helpful waitstaff dropping in every five minutes." He nodded at her plate. "You sure your steak is okay? I can cook it a little longer if it's too pink for you."

"Oh, no. It's perfect." *A little too pink, but not the* bloody *that Riordan had requested. So sorry, mutt, but I refuse to introduce myself to my food before I eat it. Yuck.*

*Beggars can't be choosers.*

*It would be nice once in a while if you remembered that.*

*Hmph.*

"So tell me, Teague. How did you get into the home renovation business? Something you always wanted to do or a side road that led you from an original ambition?"

He shrugged. "A little of both, actually. I studied originally to be an architect, but I really, honestly like to have my hands all over the job, too."

"Control freak," she teased him.

He laughed. "Yeah, some of that. But I like to see a job through from beginning to end, from the planning to the doing. This lets me do that."

"Sounds satisfying."

"Yeah, it is. When it's not a complete headache." He smiled, then, studying her, let the smile fade. "What about you? Is teaching what you love? What are you going to do now?"

"Yes, teaching's what I've always wanted to do, and"—she laughed, a little uncomfortably—"believe it or not, it's just possible that I'll have my job back next semester."

"Seriously?"

She shrugged. "I guess my nemesis had a change of heart and convinced other people to have one, too."

"That's wild. I mean, in a good way, but really wild. I

would have thought the paperwork and red tape would be too ugly to allow for a change that quick."

"Go figure. I guess my"—she glanced in the corner at the seemingly snoozing Riordan—"*guardian angel* was working overtime." And then some. No one had been more amazed than she was this afternoon when Tiffy, still flying high on her religious experience with the puca, had called, all hyped up about her efforts on Mina's behalf. Mina really and truly would have her job back after semester break. They hadn't hired a replacement, other than a substitute to fill in for half a year, so the red tape had actually been minimal.

Naturally, Riordan had assumed the worst about Tiffy's methods of persuasion. Not that he was necessarily wrong. It was quite possible that Tiffy *had* screwed more than one school administrator, thereby giving her all kinds of leverage. Which she'd used on Mina's behalf. Poetic justice? Possibly. Mina was just happy to see satisfying employment in her near future.

"Well, that's great. What do you do in the meantime?"

"Play fast and loose with my credit cards, I guess. I do have some savings. I'll do okay."

He frowned. "Well, if things get tight—"

"Don't even say it. Really. We're not going there."

He shrugged. "I was just going to offer to let you make payments at a slower rate. Not charity. Just consideration."

"Let's see if insurance takes care of it like you said, though."

"I'll call tomorrow."

"Thanks."

"And that's it for the business talk. Agreed?"

She laughed. "You got it. So tell me about the neighborhood. I read recently that . . ."

Conversation flowed, and Mina found herself relaxing with Teague more than she ever remembered relaxing with Jackson. Her ex had always expected her to be on her toes.

Politically correct, academically accomplished, everything. With Teague, she was just herself. Occasionally goofy, occasionally bawdy, and always natural. He seemed the same with her.

So it was with regret that she called it an early evening. She knew he had to be up early the next day and, frankly, she knew she was pushing her luck with Riordan, whose glowing yellow glares were increasingly belligerent. Hey, she couldn't help it if Teague ate the rest of her steak. It was rude to ask for a doggy bag in somebody else's home.

She did feel bad for Riordan, though. Maybe a great breakfast in the morning would cheer him up.

*You wish.* He scrabbled around on the back seat of Teague's car, obviously looking for a comfortable spot. *I can't believe you made me miss out on steak. That was cold.*

It just wasn't appropriate. I'm sorry. You can share breakfast with me tomorrow.

*Didn't I see ice cream in the freezer? I think I'd like to try ice cream.*

You've never had ice cream? She was appalled.

Sullen silence.

She felt even guiltier.

Soon, they were pulling up in front of the house and Riordan slunk out of the car like a wolf, waiting—and obviously resenting it—for Mina to catch up so he didn't run into one of those invisible walls again and land on his butt. She hurried ahead and unlocked the door, letting Riordan plod past her before turning to Teague. "Want a drink or something? Coffee?" A kiss . . .

Riordan grumble-growled and slunk off to the bedroom in obvious disgust.

"Sounds great." He stepped past her, looking around. "You're not having too much draft coming in through the kitchen, are you? I'm sealing that wall off as fast as I can."

"I know you are. I'm doing okay. Good thing it's been so warm this past week."

"Good." He smiled. "Now I have a confession to make."

"What?"

"I don't want a drink and, honestly, I wasn't all that worried about a draft. I really just wanted to get the girl on the couch to steal a kiss."

She laughed and lowered her voice to a whisper. "Maybe I have a similar confession to make."

"Oh, yeah?" Grinning, he snagged her hand and tugged her along with him. He rounded the coffee table and dropped onto the couch, pulling her down with him. "Now, let's see. How about . . ." He tipped his head from side to side as though weighing his options. "Yeah, I really do think . . ." He teasingly tipped her across his lap and lowered his smile to her lips.

Laughing, Mina slid her arms around his neck and met his mouth with eager curiosity. A gentle, teasing hello of a kiss lengthened and deepened into something warmer, then hotter. Soon hands were growing restless, exploring shoulders and tender ribs and venturing further. Just as Teague started tugging at her shirt, Mina heard a scuffle in the bedroom.

Dog toenails against hardwood floor.

Riordan. Mina broke off the kiss to stare dazedly into Teague's eyes. He looked as blurrily aroused as she felt, then bent to her mouth for more.

Another scuffle.

Mina pulled back. This was unreal. Mr. Fairytale, right here, big as life and in the mood to prove every inch of himself . . . and she had a puca in her bedroom, privy to her thoughts and their every move. Not a damn thing she could do about it.

"Mina? What's wrong? I thought—"

"Yeah." Her breath caught. "I did, too. I just—"

*You're gonna make him stop? But it was just getting good.*

Shut up, you voyeuristic perv.

*Now I'm hurt.*

Riordan. Just hush. Please. So I can think.

Silence.

Mina focused on Teague. "We're moving too fast." Yeah, there was a good generic. A complete lie. Or maybe not? "I just don't want to mess things up by missing a step. Or something."

"You think we're skipping a step now?" He combed his fingers through her hair, sliding them gently against her scalp.

"Not yet, but if we . . ." She raised her eyebrows.

"Oh. That step." He looked just a little wistful. "I really like that step."

"Yeah. I'm looking forward to it myself."

When he bent close again, she pulled away. "But it's not the next step. Not yet."

"Oh. Well, damn. You're sure?"

She sighed, torn between amusement and frustration. "I'm afraid so."

"And that whole leapfrogging over steps is a bad idea?"

She nodded.

He gave a huge, exaggerated sigh. "Whatever the lady says. Any chance you could tell me what the next step might be?"

*I think I'm gonna hurl.*

Oh, shut up. This is all your fault.

*My fault? How do you figure? I didn't stop you.*

Sick puca. I'm not an exhibitionist.

*It's only exhibitionism if you do it in front of other humans.*

I've seen you take human shape. For my purposes, you qualify.

*Man, I just can't win. I'm a dog if I make moves on you and a man if some other guy does. You are cruel beyond words.*

Obviously not, since you still won't be quiet so I can converse without your voice blathering in my head. Can you and I talk later while you just be still now?

*I do and I do and I do for you. Fine, okay. Shutting up.*

Thank you.

Silence.

She focused on Teague, who was frowning now. "Where did you go just now?"

Mina tried to look innocent. "Nowhere? I haven't moved."

"No, but you ran off somewhere in your head. What were you thinking about so hard? Is the next step that complicated?"

Next step . . . ? Oh. "No. I'm just thinking about it. And you. You are nearly irresistible, just so you know."

His frown eased until his eyes were twinkling just a little. "That is good to know. Although I wish like hell we could eliminate that 'nearly' part."

"I'll bet you do." She smiled at him. "I just think we ought to take things slower. Play them by ear. Now doesn't feel right. Not yet. But I had a great time tonight."

"And that would be my cue?"

"The man's a genius. I swear it. A genius with the hammer, the spatula and even the subtleties. You do impress me. And I hate booting you. I just think it's the right thing to do."

"Fair enough." He helped her to her feet, then rose from the couch. Still holding her hand, he trailed her to the door, then turned to face her. "I'd like to see you again."

"Good." She smiled. Then, lifting up to her toes, she kissed him softly, lips clinging and reluctant to leave his, before she settled back on her heels with a sigh. His eyes stayed closed for mere moments after hers opened. Just long enough for her heart to do a wistful little sigh. "Good night."

"Good night, Mina."

She watched him take the stairs at a leisurely jog, then, once he climbed into his car, she gripped the doorknob.

"I think he likes you."

At the familiar voice behind her, Mina narrowed her eyes, finished closing—or, slamming, rather—the door, and turned to face her faceless nemesis. Dog had shifted to man. "*You.*"

"Me?"

"Can't you let me have a life? I meet a nice guy, go on a date, and I can't even have a few moments of privacy."

*Flash-shimmer* and he was a dog again. "Want me to go live in the doghouse?"

"Gee, there's a thought. Maybe I could build a damn doghouse and keep it on my porch."

"Aw, Mina. You wouldn't. I swear, this isn't my fault. Well, maybe I talk in your head when you guys start embarrassing me a little, but I can't help that. And I'd give you peace and solitude if I could, but good old Akker saw to it that that was impossible. I'm here. Maybe you could just explore your inner exhibitionist?" Now he sounded eager.

Mina glared down at him. "You're so lucky you're in dog form right now."

"Because you don't kick dogs?"

"Not unless seriously provoked. So be careful. I have my limits." She stalked into the kitchen.

"So, what are you going to do about this guy?" Riordan followed. "Hey, are you hungry? Do you want something to eat?"

"No, I'm not hungry."

"Figures." He slumped onto the floor, muzzle propped on his paws. "So, about the guy? What are you going to do? Maybe he likes celibacy. You could explore that instead."

She growled.

He raised his chin briefly. "Or maybe he'd like it if you

and me and he all . . . you know." No dog should be able to waggle his eyebrows that lasciviously, but that's what he did.

"You are one sick puppy." And so were the images playing in her mind's eye. She would not let those be communicated to—

"Whoa, baby. I had no idea you were that kinky."

"I'm not. And I'd never. Just because you planted some sick pictures in my head doesn't mean I'd ever think of acting on them. I'm looking for a relationship, not a depraved sex act."

"Oooh. Well, that knocks out several possibilities. I guess it's going to be celibacy then. Damn shame. You're a good-looking woman, Mina. I'd hate to see you shrivel up and uglify before experiencing a satisfying sexual wingding with a guy."

"Yeah? Well, me, too. What am I going to do about you?"

Carefully, Riordan pushed himself up and flashed to human form. "You could always help me break the curse. It would solve both your problems and mine." He spoke in all sincerity now.

She pondered. Did she really have any choice? Either she condemned herself to life with a puca looking over her shoulder, or she helped free him.

"Or . . ." She raised her eyebrows in sudden thought." I could just wait until the first of November, when you'll disappear inside your rock again. Correct?"

Silence. "I suppose that is an option for you. If you're only worried about my physical presence here in your home with you, then yeah, that would take care of the problem."

"So this shape-shifting stuff is all short-term for me." Thank God. A life back. Soon. She just needed to keep Teague from losing interest for a few more weeks and they could work on leapfrogging some steps.

"But even after November Day I would still be in your head. I could talk to you. My voice will always be here." He raised his chin, continuing to speak quietly. "Hard as he tried, not even Akker could completely silence me."

"You'll be in my head? Always and indefinitely?"

He nodded. "Until you die or marry."

"Until I . . . But you'd be gone once I married?"

"Sure, if you could tune me out long enough to concentrate on another man and marry him."

Could she do that? Ignore his presence in her thoughts, his voice in her head, enough to fall in love with another man and marry him?

Worse . . . a little voice—*her* voice—whispered in her head. Could she live with herself if she ignored Riordan's voice? Ignored his plight? Knowing there was something she could do to help him? The man was being tortured, had been tortured for two thousand years. Until now, the Druids were responsible for his misery. After now, if she did nothing, she would share the blame for his suffering. Could she live with that?

"That wasn't me talking in your head. That was all you."

"I know, damn it." She scowled at him. "You really think there's something I can do to help you? Realistically?"

"I know you're my only hope."

"And what we have to do is break this curse. That's the only solution."

"It's the only one I'm aware of."

She sighed, dropped down into the couch. Again. Did she really have a choice? It sucked to be her, but it could suck a whole lot more for her . . . and dear God, but it sucked to be Riordan. She watched him, still standing there and looking damn near noble in his quiet dignity. If she could help him . . . how could she not? "All right. I'm in."

\* \* \*

"Yo! Teague! Open up! Come on, it's raining out here."

Concerned, Teague ran to answer his door. Janelle hurried inside, shedding raindrops all over his floor, while he peered outside into the darkness. "It's raining? Oh, shit. I hope it's not getting into Mina's house. We covered that wall with tarp, but—is it windy outside? Windy enough to lift a tarp?"

She scowled at him, peeling off her jacket to reveal badly wrinkled scrubs. "Gee, thanks so much for your concern, Teague. You are such a pal. No, I'm fine. Just a little damp. No need to fret over me."

He gave her a lopsided grin. "Sorry. But really—"

"No, it's not windy." She let out an explosive sigh. "It's just a steady, gentle rain. Your Mina's going to be just fine."

"Good." He surveyed his friend. "You, however, look like a drowned rat."

"Finally. Sympathy."

"Hot chocolate do the trick?"

"I love you. I do. Really. If I didn't know about your Mina, I'd jump your bones right here and now."

Chuckling, he backtracked toward the kitchen, pulling out chocolate and milk, then reaching high for a small saucepan. Once he had the milk warming, he turned back to her. "Long day?"

"You know it. Thank God I'm off tomorrow. Now shut up about my day and tell me about your date. Did you tell her? What did she say? Did she believe you?" Janelle leaned against a counter.

"Of course I didn't tell her. How the hell do I tell her something like this? She'd never believe me."

"Well, why not? If she's so wonderful, she would. I believed you."

"Yeah, well, I've had a good five years to break it all to you gradually, too. And pouring a few beers down your throat when you're insane with sleep deprivation helped suspend that lousy disbelief considerably. This isn't the kind of thing you spring on someone all at once."

"Oh, come on. You're not trying to tell her you can fly like a bird."

"No." He lowered his voice gloomily. "I'm just trying to tell her I've always had visions about a man who could."

"Visions aren't that creepy."

He raised his eyebrows.

"They're not. They're just . . . evidence of some kind of über-sensitivity. Or something."

"Or something is right. Either an active imagination or sheer insanity. I wonder which she'd believe."

"Oh, you big weenie. You're just scared."

"Well, hell, wouldn't you be?" At a hiss from behind him, Teague spun around and lifted the bubbling milk off the burner to let the frothy stuff settle. Then he turned off the heat, accepted the mug she handed him and poured.

"Well . . . yeah, I guess I would be nervous about her reaction. It's just that you've waited your whole life to gain some closure to this."

He slumped. "Yeah, but now that I finally meet her, recognize her . . . it's just not that easy. I mean, how do you tell the woman of your dreams that she's, literally, the woman *in* your dreams?"

# CHAPTER EIGHT

"Okay, it says here that not only does your species not exist in real life, but that you personally don't exist even in mythology or folk tales." Mina frowned at the computer screen. "As far as I can tell, there's only supposed to be one puca, not a puca and his black sheep brother."

"Yep, that's me." Riordan nodded carelessly. "Just a figment of your imagination. I thought you weren't supposed to believe everything you read."

"True enough. And I'm still checking out all the accounts of your existence." She backtracked a page and clicked on another link.

Riordan folded his arms over his chest, his attention on the screen of Mina's laptop computer. "I'm telling you, this Internet of yours isn't going to have our answers."

"And how am I supposed to help you if you're so negative about all my ideas? Whatever happened to me and my ideas being your ticket out of that cornerstone?"

"I never said anything about your ideas or actions breaking the curse, just that you were key to my freedom."

She slanted him a miffed look. "So if all you need is my unintelligent, unmoving presence to somehow gain your freedom, why did you bother begging for my help in the first place? I have all kinds of things I'd rather do than sit here and be insulted by a mangy, two-faced—"

"Hey, hey. There's no call to get nasty." Riordan attempted conciliatory speech. "I just don't think Druids would willingly reveal their remedy for a curse, much less publicize it."

"Just consider the odds, all right? I know you think you're special and all, but do you honestly believe you're the only guy who's ever been cursed by a Druid?"

"No, but I think the remedy to that curse is something a Druid would keep secret. If the remedy's well-known, the curse has no power."

"I guess you have a point. But you'd be amazed what you can find online. All these references to puca—"

Riordan scoffed. "References, ha. This is ridiculous. I mean look at this. A *rabbit*? Why would I take the form of a rabbit? Talk about spoiling my badass image. Who does this Jimmy Stewart guy think he is?"

She turned to him, spine straight and shoulders thrown back in challenge. "Other than deceased, to my everlasting grief? The most perfect man in the world. Do not diss Jimmy."

"Fine, I won't diss Jimmy if we can set this contraption aside and try something a little more logical."

"What's more logical than research?"

"Well, for starters, I personally have existed on this planet a hell of a lot longer than your machine here has."

She eyed him skeptically. "Yeah, but if you had all the answers, you wouldn't have spent the majority of your existence inside a stupid rock."

"Oh, that's nice. I never said I had all the answers. I just think, at the very least, I should be able to tell if you're on the right track or not. Unlike some of these quacks you're reading who profess to be experts."

"So—"

"So my thought is, the solution would be a combination of your experience and mine. So I want you to think curse in general. Breaking a curse. What do you do?"

"Break a curse. Break a curse. How does one break a curse?" Mina pondered quietly, feeling Riordan's gaze on her. She frowned. "Seek out an expert? A respected one, in person? Hey, at least it's more accountable than the Internet."

"Good luck with that. The only experts you'll find these days are classified as nuts and dismissed by society."

Nuts? "Of course! My mother!" Mina grinned at him. "I'll invite Mom over and we'll brainstorm. See? It's perfect. My mother is, after all, part of my personal experience, right? And she qualifies as both an expert"—Mina frowned doubtfully a moment before shaking it off—"in her own way, and as research. What do you think?"

"Can't hurt, I guess."

"Will she be able to see or hear you?"

"Does it matter to you?" Riordan regarded her quietly.

Mina thought about it a moment. "Yes, it matters. Please don't communicate with her or show yourself. Actually, shouldn't you be in dog form anyway? Just in case Teague—"

With a sigh, Riordan flash-shimmered into his canine alter-ego. "So, fine. About your mother. Why shouldn't she see me?"

"If she knows she can see and speak to a real live puca, I'll have her visiting every other day."

"That's a bad thing?"

"Are you kidding?" She inhaled, feeling guilt ride her. Again. Guilt sucked royally. "I love my mother. I do. She just drives me crazy. No offense, Riordan, but the woman's obsessed with your type of thing. Paranormal, supernatural, crystals, spells, Wiccan, Druidry. You name it, she's tried it on for size. I think she desperately wants to answer her 'true calling' in the universe, and believes magic is it. She just needs to find the variety that actually works for her." Mina puzzled a moment, shook her head, then picked up the phone. "Seriously, Riordan. Let's just pretend that there's no way you can show yourself to her or make yourself heard. Or I won't hear the end of it."

"Hey, if you're willing to help me, I'm more than willing to make a few concessions."


"So what shapes do you prefer?" Leaning forward, Lizzy Dixon smiled, utterly enraptured with canine Riordan. Mina scowled from across the room.

"Stallion's my favorite, but this dog persona's a lot more convenient." Riordan tipped his muzzle almost apologetically. "I'm afraid, due to an unfortunate curse, that I can't do human with anyone but my guardian—your daughter."

"Oh, but that is a shame." Lizzy's tone was certain and meaningful. "I've heard such stories . . ."

"Mo-om!" Mina felt her cheeks go red, even as Riordan snorted a doggy laugh. Lizzy Avery's carnal nature, a constant embarrassment to her daughter, now was obviously a source of unholy amusement to the BobGoblin. Pervert.

"I was just mentioning that your black sheep puca has a bit of a . . . reputation." Lizzy winked at Riordan, then slanted a glance at her daughter. "And you have him all to yourself. Aren't you the lucky girl?"

Mina slapped her hands over her ears and glared. "Oh, ick! Will you just stop it? He plays horse and dog. Like I could even consider him in the light of a man, let alone as my—Ugh. This is completely outside of my comfort zone and totally unproductive." She eyed them both. "Now, if you don't mind, I'd like to get back to the subject. Riordan's on a deadline, remember? You don't want him condemned for another millennium just so we can chitchat and trade twisted innuendo, do you?"

Noting the sheepish look on her mother's face, Mina let her hands slide back to her lap. "Now. Curse-breaking. And Druids."

Lizzy brightened. "Oh, good. I can't tell you how much I've looked forward to discussing this with you. Finally."

"So glad you're pleased. Any chance you could share instead of gloat?"

"I'm not gloating." At her daughter's raised eyebrow, Lizzy shrugged. "Well, okay, maybe a little. But you've always made fun of this kind of thing."

"With good reason. My childhood was hell, thanks to all your dabbling."

"It was for a good cause."

Mild doggy cough. "Um, could we get back to the Druids and curses subject? Not that this isn't fascinating, but I thought you had an appointment to keep, Mrs. Dixon?"

"Lizzy, please." Mina's mother smiled. "And yes, I do." She turned back to her daughter, then hesitated. "I've waited so long for this moment that I've forgotten the phrasing I was originally going to use. He forbade me to ever bring up the subject myself. In fact, he threatened some really ugly consequences if I did. But he never said *you* couldn't introduce it, or that I couldn't answer questions. Two entirely different scenarios, right?"

Mina frowned. "He, who?"

Lizzy fiddled with her skirt, then gestured vaguely with one hand before answering. "Your father."

Mina groaned. "Oh, good God. We're not going into that subject, now are we?"

"Ask me some questions, Mina." Lizzy spoke low and pointedly. "Some questions you asked me just a moment ago."

At the look in her mother's eyes, Mina paused. "About Druids?"

Lizzy just waited expectantly.

Mina spoke slowly. "Is my father an expert on Druids?"

"Oh, yes. Definitely."

"I thought he was an accountant."

"That, too."

"Did he study it or—"

Riordan buried his muzzle under his paws, obviously in some distress.

Lizzy regarded him sympathetically. "Your puca can't discuss it either. This is all on you, Mina. Right, Riordan?"

Doggy nod.

Mina eyed them both. This had to be good. "So Duncan Forbes studied Druidry. Right?"

Her mother nodded.

"He's a scholar?"

Her mother shook her head. Riordan shuddered and buried his muzzle deeper into his paws.

"So he studies it, but not on an academic level . . ." Mina raised her brows in wonder. "He's a practicing Druid? No way."

"No." Even Lizzy looked impatient now, trading looks with Riordan. "Well, yes and no."

"Yes and no. He's torn?" She raised her brows in question.

They both nodded.

"This is worse than charades."

More emphatic nods.

"He's torn between practicing and not practicing . . . so maybe he's drawn to it against his will?"

More nods.

"Like an addiction?"

Groans.

Racking her brain for appropriate questions, Mina studied the crystals draped as necklaces around Lizzy's neck, and the titles of books she'd brought with her, books exploring various pagan beliefs and ancient lore. Mina knew what it was to feel torn. She'd so wanted a traditional mother instead of a hippy with her own brand of bossiness. Mina had only ever wanted a normal life. "His family is the reason he's torn."

Emphatic nods and keep-it-going gestures.

Lovely. So Mina and Dunky shared common ground. Why was that not reassuring? "His family is trying to force him into the Druid scene?"

Less emphatic nods, implying close but slightly off course.

Mina stood and began to pace. Maybe if she came at it from a different but related angle. "Okay. I'm Riordan's keeper. The Druids cursed the Avebury family and Riordan so that, come today, I would be a puca's guardian. And I didn't exactly have a choice in the matter either." She glanced at them. "It was a condition forced on me by my ancestors' actions. By heredity?"

"Bingo!" Lizzy clapped her hands. "You always were such a bright girl. I'm sure you get that from me and not from that shortsighted nitwit who fathered you."

"Great. So, since we're on that subject anyway, suppose you guys tell me exactly what some Avebury ancestor did to put me in this position. What's the crime?"

"Conspiracy." Mina's mother spoke with a decisive nod.

"More specifically?"

She shrugged. "A matchmaker role, one might say."

Mina raised a cynical eyebrow. "What else might one say?"

"All right. So it amounted to arranging the whole tryst on their behalf and keeping it secret from . . . others."

Riordan cringed while Mina sighed. "Good lord."

Lizzy waved impatiently. "But back to your father. And heredity. You have to say what you're thinking exactly so I know for sure we're on the same path."

"He's a—Like witches, maybe he's a *hereditary Druid*?" She felt foolish even voicing as much.

Lizzy nodded and Riordan relaxed finally.

"So that's what we're dealing with. A man who resents his Druid heritage, but at the same time, seems drawn to it. By family, by guilt, by various forces he wishes he could control."

"And the lady wins the prize." Riordan sat up, looking downright proud of her. "We're going places."

"Lucky me," Mina murmured. "So what else can you tell me?"

"That's it, I'm afraid. You'll have to go to your father and ask him directly for anything else you want to know." Lizzy shrugged apologetically. "This is as far as I can take you. It's what was preordained for me."

"Preordained for you? I don't understand." Mina eyed her mother and then Riordan, who seemed to understand.

Riordan tipped his head. "Ever heard of divination?"

"Predicting the future?"

"Yep. Didn't I mention before that I'm a prophet?" Riordan let his tongue loll out the side of his mouth.

Mina narrowed her eyes. That tongue-lolling thing was so deliberate. Purely for effect? He did that on purpose. Why?

"Just part of my charm. So. Shall we visit your father? Honestly, your mom can't tell us anything else without putting a serious whammy on her karma. I can't be responsible for that."

Lizzy fanned herself flirtatiously. "Oh, how gallant."

"Yeah, my dog's gallant. He couldn't even keep himself hidden from you. Even though I begged him to."

"Hey, how was I supposed to know she'd turn on the charm like that? I couldn't be rude." He looked upon Lizzy with fond respect. "Hospitality rules, so here I am."

"Oh, Mina. I just wanted to see him. Was that so terrible?"

"You're not going to be on my doorstep every day just so you can flirt with a dog, are you?"

*Stop calling me a dog. I'm a puca. And, yes, I'm doing this for effect.*

But why?

Riordan looked uncomfortable. *It just makes people more comfortable with me if I act as they think I should act. Your mom expects a canine scamp. So that's what I do.*

But there was more to it. Mina just knew it.

"No, I promise I'll call first. Deal?" Lizzy smiled brightly, then glanced at her watch before standing.

"I guess." Mina eyed her mother with doubt and Riordan with growing suspicion.

After her mother left, Mina turned to Riordan and watched him flash-shimmer into his manly form. Thank God. Attributing human aspects to a dog was really starting to wear thin.

"I like your mother, Mina." There was amusement in Riordan's deep voice. "She's very charming. Spirited, too."

"Oh, don't start." Mina held up a hand, waiting for the word *sensual*, or worse, *carnal* to enter into the conversation.

"It's true. You might stop and think for a moment, too. You call your mom a weirdo for her beliefs and interests, but here you are with a millennia-old shape-shifting puca under your guardianship. Who's the weirdo now?"

"Smart-ass. So, are you ready to go?"

"To your dad's?"

She winced. "Please don't call him that. It conjures up all these visuals of chubby babies, piggyback rides and father-daughter dances. Honestly, not Dunky's style."

"So you don't acknowledge him as your father?"

She smiled tightly. "*He* doesn't acknowledge *me*. As a pissed-off teenager, however, I decided to make it a reciprocal insult and not acknowledge *him*. For the sake of my own dignity."

"A real fun guy, huh?"

"You don't know? I thought a 'canine prophet' would know everything."

"Nope. Just parts of the puzzle. Not the whole."

"Any parts you'd be willing to share with me?"

"I'm bound by rules, Mina. You know that. I share and it's all a waste anyway. Break the rules, renew the condemnation. I'd be back in my cornerstone."

"They'd know?"

"They'd know."

"Just sucks to be you, doesn't it?" Mina felt dirty and mean, but darn it, this wasn't any cakewalk for her either. And *she* wasn't the one who seduced some Druid's precious daughter. What had it been like to have a father who loved her so dearly he cast life-altering spells over pucas and generations of a human family just to avenge her?

When Riordan seemed to be watching her too long—and too knowingly—Mina whirled and snagged up her purse on the way out the door. "Let's go."

"After you, babe."

"Low profile, please. And, um, the face thing?"

"Right." He sighed and flashed into his dog form.

Inwardly protesting the idea of seeing her father again—hey, if he didn't want to see Mina, then Mina damn well didn't want to impose her soiled presence on his exalted self either—she wrestled the steering wheel and ancient gears until she'd gained the interstate. Halfway there, she was gazing absently out the window, when she noticed a brand-new sign advertising the county's campaign to recruit teachers. She frowned, staring more intently, until realization had her reflexively stomping on the brakes.

"What—whoa!" Riordan landed on his butt on the floor mat.

Mina parked on the shoulder to stare at the billboard. The *T* and *e* of *Teacher* were smudged—and familiar. She remembered the huge lettering on Tiffany's stained cardigan. The puca ride. She unwillingly pictured the puca in stallion form . . . galloping along the framework of a billboard? No. That billboard had to be thirty feet high. How would he get up there? Fly? She stared at it, then at Riordan, who regarded the sign almost fondly. "You didn't. You couldn't have."

"Would you like a demonstration?" This from a very smug-sounding puca.

"No. I don't want to know. I'll just—no." Conscious of— and completely ignoring—Riordan's disturbing amusement, Mina carefully put the car in gear and merged back onto the interstate. Twenty minutes later, they stood outside a dignified brick building with its tasteful sign proclaiming the offices of Forbes & Forbes, Accounting and Financial Services.

Mina studied the sign. It was new. And smudge-free— but no, she wasn't going there. Her head would explode. The second Forbes on the sign, Mina knew, referred to her half-sister, who appeared to be infinitely more acceptable as a daughter. Mina had never met the girl and, frankly, knew nothing about her other than that she had somehow managed to earn favor in Duncan Forbes's warped eyes.

"So this is the domain of *the* Duncan Forbes? Somehow I never pictured your mother getting it on with an accountant."

"Dogs don't talk," she muttered and, dismissing the sign and her thoughts, stalked up the steps and opened the door.

Absently, she held it open for Riordan to trot inside after her. Then she turned to the gaping receptionist, who'd jumped to her feet and was now pointing at Mina's canine companion.

"No dogs in the office!"

"He's a working dog." Mina raised her eyebrows for emphasis and attempted to look dependent.

*Man, are you going to burn for that one.*

Why, did you have a better argument to offer?

*Not at all. Fabricate away, my beautiful Mina.*

I'm not your anything.

*That's not what the Druids say . . .*

Riordan's singsong response echoed in Mina's head as she turned abruptly and strode down the hallway to her father's office. If she had the receptionist announce her, no doubt Duncan Forbes would keep Mina waiting for twenty minutes while he slunk out the back door. That's what he'd done the last time she tried to talk to him. The time before that . . . she'd rather not recall, if at all possible. Pain and humiliation were bad enough to live through the first time without enduring a mental replay. Ugly scene.

"Ma'am? Ma'am! You can't go in there!" The receptionist hurried after Mina, but Mina just strode on.

*Lady, you have balls. I'm so impressed.*

No, I'm just desperate and well aware of the cowardice of good old Dunky.

Mina popped a hand out in front of her and simply smacked her father's office door open. As the receptionist squawked protests to Mina and apologies to the tall man seated at the desk inside the office, Mina ignored her. She simply held the door open for Riordan to enter and followed him in.

When Riordan fixed his eerie gaze on Mina's father, the man shot to his feet, eyes wide and staring at the puca. "You."

"Sir, I tried to tell her we didn't allow dogs—" the receptionist hurried to explain.

Duncan Forbes merely waved her away, then sank slowly into his seat. "It's all right, Wendy. I'll handle it."

Looking relieved, the receptionist hurried out, closing the door behind her.

After a silent few moments, Forbes raised his gaze to Mina. "So, it's happened. Just like she intended."

"Like who intended?" Realizing Forbes wasn't going to do the polite thing and offer her a seat, Mina presumptuously dropped into a chair without invitation. Riordan seated himself as well, his chin raised to fully meet the man's gaze.

"Why, that lying bitch who gave birth to you, of course. Who else?"

Mina saw red, but kept her voice icy. "Say what you will about that 'lying bitch,' but at least she was 'man' enough to stand by her own child. Where were you? Coward."

Forbes glared. "I don't have to listen to this."

"Yes, you do. Unless you'd like to pay up on the eighteen years' worth of child support you owe my mother. Funny thing, how paternity tests have become so much more sophisticated since I was first born. And how would your wife and acknowledged daughter take the news that you had another family you never mentioned to them? Kind of a big secret for a staid old accountant." She paused. "Much like your heritage is."

"Heritage?" He cast a nervous glance at Riordan, who seemed to be smiling, Mina decided. Riordan was incorrigible. Undoubtedly one of his more attractive qualities.

*You humble me.*

That'll be the day.

Doggy snort.

"So what do you want from me, then? Money? The name of a vet for neutering this thing?"

"Just some answers. That's cheap enough, don't you think?"

Her father leaned back in his chair, eyes speculative as he folded his arms across his chest. "What kind of answers?"

Damn good question. What kind of answers do I want, Riordan?

*Ask him if he knows me.*

"Do you know my friend here?"

"The dog?"

Mina shrugged. "Sometimes."

Duncan Forbes looked even more forbidding. "I've never seen him before."

Mina raised her chin. "Duncan Forbes, meet Riordan. Also known as Robert Goodfellow, puca."

"Nice to meet you, dog."

*The man needs a lesson in manners.*

Tell me about it. "So you've never met him. Do you know *of* him?"

A long pause. "Yes." A single, grudging word.

"Ah, we're getting somewhere. What do you know of him? And how?"

"Just silly stories. Myth. Legend." He paused, then continued with ironic candor. "Frankly, I never thought to actually lay eyes on him."

"But as soon as you did, you knew who and what he was and implied my mother was involved?"

"No implication needed. The woman tricked me."

"How?"

"*You.*"

Mina swallowed. This shouldn't hurt. It shouldn't. Obviously, she never learned. "She tricked you into having me. That's what you said when I first talked to you."

That first time Mina had walked into his office—which then bore only one Forbes on the sign outside—she had been so hopeful. He was normal. An accountant, for pete's sake. Maybe he'd welcome her with open arms. She'd even looked for and found some resemblance, in their coloring— the light skin and strawberry-blond hair—and something about the set of her eyes. But there the connection ended. Her Daddy fantasies were nothing but that. Fantasies. She'd decided she didn't want to claim a man as cowardly as Dunky anyway. So there. Take that.

Dunky was scowling. "That's because your mother *did* trick me. If it was up to me, she never would have gotten pregnant."

"So you were helpless. Used and abused. My mother *forced* you to have sex with her. She *raped* your sorry self. Right?"

"No, I'm saying she lied about being on the pill, hid her identity from me, and seduced me just to have my baby."

"She wanted me." God, that wasn't supposed to come out sounding so weak and needy. But at least it was true. Her mother wanted her, even if the man who'd fathered her didn't.

"Yes and no. What she wanted was a child from our two bloodlines." He raised his eyebrows.

*Make him spell it out for you. I think he wants to, but mostly to hurt you and divide your sympathies.*

Mina glanced at Riordan, but the warning was unnecessary. The malice in twisted old Dunky's eyes was pretty damn obvious. As was, now that she looked more closely, the rage and anxiety. She chose her words carefully. Tried to remain objective. "Why would she want a child from your bloodline and hers . . . and what do you mean by bloodlines? Why is this important?"

"Obviously, you already know about your mother's bloodline." He glanced at the puca and back to her. "You're descended from the Avebury family and, apparently, a viable guardian for this freak."

"Some people might condemn a man who abandoned his child as pretty damn freakish. And cruel. Riordan's never been cruel."

"Not to you."

Riordan shifted, but no comment sounded in Mina's mind.

"Not to me. That's right. And, what's more, nobody in this room is a saint. We can all acknowledge that and move on. So, tell me about your bloodline."

Forbes grimaced. "It's very simple really. Your mother was descended from the peasant family found guilty of aiding and abetting this jerk. I—my family—are descended from the woman he wronged. And descended from the Druid who condemned the puca." His eyes narrowed. "And you, my daughter that should never have been born—"

Riordan growled. *Somebody's in desperate need of a puca ride.* But Mina buried a cautioning hand in his fur.

"—you are descended from both Avebury and Druid. You have blood ties to both the condemned and the condemner. The perpetrator's conspirator and his victim." He smiled, and it wasn't a nice smile. "Feeling a little torn, daughter?"

"Not really. You don't act terribly victimized. And Riordan has paid over and over for what he did. Aren't two millennia of torture and isolation sufficient punishment for his crimes?"

"That's a matter of opinion, and frankly, not your decision to make."

"Yet." Riordan spoke aloud, drawing Forbes's attention.

"So the spook speaks. How quaint. I'll bet you could tell some tales after living all these centuries."

"Not as many as you might think. I spent most of those lifetimes locked inside of a rock."

Forbes sneered. "What, am I supposed to feel sorry for you? From what I've heard, you only got what you deserved. You thought you were so powerful as to be above human ethics and morality. Apparently not. Look what a human did to you."

Riordan nodded, seeming more thoughtful than affected. "I've heard it said that with great power comes great responsibility. It only follows that wrongs committed by those in great power should garner great punishment. And so mine did," Riordan acknowledged evenly. "I might also add that lifetimes spent in contemplation tend to change a person. I'm not the mere child I was when I was condemned. I've changed and learned."

"So you say."

"So I say." Riordan deliberately lowered his voice. "But what I wonder is . . . have *you* learned anything in the years since you abandoned Mina?"

Forbes sputtered in outrage. "I didn't abandon her. She wasn't supposed to even exist. She's Elizabeth Avery's creation, not mine. It would have been different if she'd been accidentally conceived. But she wasn't. She was the product of an act of manipulation committed by her mother. I refuse to bow to anyone's manipulation."

"Gentlemen, could we please get back to the point? Look, Dunky, Daddy, Mr. Forbes, or whatever the hell you think I should call you"—it had been a contentious point during their last conversation—"I frankly don't give a shit whether you wanted me or not. All I want from you now is information. You owe me answers." Mina stared at the man who'd fathered her, refusing to feel anything but frustration. She just wanted those answers and a ticket out of this hellhole.

Forbes studied his daughter, then averted his gaze. "You'll leave when you have your information?"

"Happily, freely and immediately."

"Fine. What else do you want to know?"

Her heart pounding with emotions she refused to entertain, Mina paused to arrange her words. "You say my mother wanted to give birth to the product of two bloodlines. The condemned and the condemner. The perpetrator as well as the victim. What is the significance of this? Tell me why this is important."

Her father scowled, obviously wishing her question was anything but this one. So she wasn't supposed to take this leap? He'd obviously intended only to drive a wedge between her and Riordan with his revelation, not lead her to another conclusion and disturbing question.

"Answer her." Riordan spoke compellingly, and his eyes glowed.

You can compel him to answer me?

*Not by using magic. I'm using the man's guilt against him. He and I both know what we're about. He can't stand to have you here, forcing him to acknowledge to himself what he did to you.*

Mina couldn't breathe. Just waited.

"It means," Forbes spoke reluctantly, "that you and only you can free him from the curse. You're the key to the freak's freedom. It was foreseen."

Once the words were out, Riordan bowed his head, as though a burden had been lifted from him.

Mina stared at her father and then at Riordan. "So, it really is true."

Forbes shrugged. "Is that the last of your questions?"

"No." Mina swallowed and glanced away. Then she returned her gaze to her father, almost angrily. "My sister, the accountant. What's her name? What's she like?"

"That's none of your business."

"Yes, it is."

Again, Forbes couldn't hold her stare. "She's . . . smart. Hardworking. Loyal. Beautiful."

In short, perfect. "What's her name?"

Forbes seemed to be biting back fury and anguish. "Why do you want to know? She's nothing to you. Leave her out of this."

"She's my sister. I've never had a sister." Mina spoke softly.

"Her name is Daphne. And she would want nothing to do with you. I guarantee it. Now, will you please leave? This is a place of business, not a soap opera set."

"Daphne Forbes," Mina mused. "Daphne means laurel in Greek. Did you know that? So is Daphne your laurel, Duncan?"

"No, damn it. She's my daughter. The only daughter I have. Now go."

"One more question."

"This better be the last one."

"How old is Daphne?" Probably fresh out of college. Mina wondered if there could be any common ground between them at all. The bastard thirty-one-year-old daughter on the fast-track to freakdom, and the bright and ambitious, legitimate younger daughter, the very apple of her respectable father's eye.

Duncan looked furious. "That's none of your damn business."

"Tell her." This from Riordan, his eyes glowing with knowledge and threat.

"Daphne's thirty-one. Just turned."

Mina stared. "But I'm . . ."

"Thirty-one?" Duncan asked her angrily. "Yes, damn it, I know. I was already married and, during a weak moment . . . Your mother was a mistake. You were a mistake. You understand now?"

"Obviously, Mina was the best mistake you ever made." Riordan spoke with soft threat. "And thank God for mistakes. Thanks so much for your trouble, asshole." *Stand up, Mina. Turn and walk out the door. Do not look back. Come on, babe. I've got your back.*

Numb and speechless, Mina responded to the voice in her head and felt a muzzle nudging her hand, urging her onward. She walked. Opened the door. Walked through it, past the staring receptionist and out the door.

Then she kept walking.

*Mina? Hello, babe. You're scaring me. Are you in there? We just passed your car.*

Mina slowed, turned and walked back to the parked car. Then she unlocked the door, let Riordan leap past her into the passenger's seat, before climbing in herself. There she sat in silence.

"Mina, I'm sorry," Riordan said aloud. "I am. I had no idea he was that bad or what it would cost you to do this.

What an asshole. May I just say you won the gene pool? I like you. You're an amazing woman and a credit to the human species. Unlike jerkface in there."

Mina inhaled. Exhaled. She could breathe again. "You know. I was prepared for him. At least, I thought I was. I knew he didn't want me. Granted, I didn't know he also considered me an offense against the natural order of things—you know, on a universal level. I also . . . I didn't know . . ."

"That he was married when he met your mother, and then got both women pregnant at the same time?" Riordan sounded thoughtful, too. "If it helps any, I think the man's been terrified for thirty-one years. He's a coward, too scared to do anything but lash out."

"He believed what he said."

Riordan couldn't deny that. "This was his way of justifying it in his mind. Unless he continues to believe that you shouldn't exist, then he has to believe himself guilty of abandoning you and ignoring you all these years. He's a weak man, Mina. He doesn't deserve you. Hell, I can't imagine having a man like that raise you, either. Can you? Your mom loves you."

"Yes, she does. I think. Still, that whole manipulation thing in the beginning . . ."

"That was before you became a person. Her love for you is obvious to anyone who cares enough to look. Hold on to that."

Mina nodded, then tried a laugh. It came out creaky. "You know, I really thought I was past all that abandonment crap. I'm a thirty-one-year-old woman. I've been on my own for years, answerable for my own actions and dependent on no one. This shouldn't matter. Nothing he thinks should matter. I no longer need a daddy to wipe the tears and rock me to sleep at night."

"Mina."

Lost in reverie, she didn't respond.

A flash-shimmer caught her attention. Riordan had shifted to human form. Faceless, but a man nonetheless.

"What are you doing?"

Riordan took her hand in his and spoke low. "I want to make you a promise, Mina. There are men who say my word means nothing, but I'll swear it to you anyway. It's all I have."

Mina eyed him warily. "Okay."

"I promise you, whatever comes of this quest of ours, whether I'm back in that damn rock or a free man finally, I will only be a call away from you. Speak my name and I will hear you. *I swear I will never abandon you of my own free will.*"

# CHAPTER NINE

Mina stared at Riordan, aghast. "But, I don't get it. All you've ever wanted is your freedom. Why would you tie yourself to me now with a new obligation?"

"If I do gain my freedom, it will be thanks to you. I'll never forget your efforts and sacrifices on my behalf. And I will never willingly abandon you. You can count on me."

Mina gazed at him, shaken and so touched. . . . This wasn't the BobGoblin. "Riordan, you are a complete sham."

He sat back in his seat. "This is what I get for offering my lifelong allegiance?"

Mina was shaking her head, a wondering smile growing, easing away the day's strain and disappointments. "You've outed yourself, buddy. I was starting to catch on earlier, but this little speech betrays you completely. What's with the BobGoblin act? You're so much more than the goofy dog you portray."

He shrugged. "I'm not usually in dog persona. Horse was my favorite at first. Then it was all disembodiment. The dog was for your benefit."

"As was the act," she mused. "I wonder why that is?"

Suddenly, Riordan flash-shimmered back to dog, just as a knock sounded on the driver's side window. Mina jumped and saw a hand motioning for her to roll down her window—and a policeman's uniform right behind it. Her heart still pounding, Mina rolled down the window. "Yes, Officer?"

"Everything okay, ma'am?" The man bent and peered into her car to glance around. Riordan, thank heavens, kept his eyes lazily slitted and his tongue hanging out in friendly greeting. "I saw you get in your car a while back but you didn't pull out, so I thought I'd check on you. We've had some cars vandalized near here."

"Oh. I didn't know. But everything's okay as far as I can see."

"All right, then. Have a good day." The policeman straightened and Mina rolled up the window.

"Good lord, but that was close."

"Bark," was Riordan's dry response.

Still unsteady, Mina was content to drive home in silence, which normally talkative Riordan never broke. After parking and letting Riordan hop out, still on the familiar all-fours of a canine, she unlocked her house and let them inside.

After she shut the front door, she turned on a light and froze at sight of a man sitting on her couch. "Teague?" Okay, that was a little unnerving. She couldn't quite bring herself to be spooked by him, but finding him in her house while she was gone, even if he *was* doing renovation work for her . . .

He cleared his throat. "Yeah. Kind of awkward, huh? Sorry if I scared you. Some lady let me in. She said she was your mom? And that you might be upset about something?" He seemed uncomfortable but concerned. "Look, I know this looks bad, and if she hadn't said the part about you being upset, I wouldn't have waited here without an invitation from you. I swear I'm not some stalker type."

Mina relaxed. Of *course* her mother would let a good-looking man into Mina's home. Apparently, there was at least one member of the Avery/Avebury family who'd never learned to stay out of the matchmaking business. Mina glanced covertly at her "dog," grateful to see Riordan hadn't shifted to man form yet.

*Hey, I can be discreet. And I can even be sensitive to budding romance, if you want.* He trotted into her bedroom and crawled under her bed, leaving Mina and Teague virtually alone.

Teague shoved his hands in his pockets. "Is this okay?"

"I . . . sure. So, my mom was here?"

"She said she skipped an appointment to wait for you, then when I showed up . . ." He shrugged. "We got to talking and I mentioned that you and I were dating. She seemed to think you'd rather see me than her, whatever that means."

Mina felt her throat tighten all over again. How could her mother have done it? Mina had expected the worst from her father. But her mom? Why? "I know what she means. It's nothing you need to worry about, just a misunderstanding." A thirty-one-year-old misunderstanding—or a few of them—but all of it could keep until Mina finished mentally unraveling the mess. She regarded good-looking, seriously normal and honest-faced Teague with no little appreciation. "I'm glad you're here."

"Then I am, too." He smiled, relieved and genuine now, then rounded the coffee table to hold his arms out to her. Mina found it completely natural to just step into those arms and let them envelop her as she rested a cheek against his chest. Just melted right into his body. Oh, nice. Big and strong and safe, but not so safe as to be boring. Damn near perfect, in fact, she decided, enjoying the fizz of growing awareness.

He tightened his arms around her and dipped his face close to hers. "You want to talk about it?" he murmured.

Talk about it? What could she talk about? What was safe? Any of it? Well, some . . . "I went to see my father." Her voice sounded thick even to her own ears. Dear God, but she wasn't going to weep all over the man now, was she? How clichéd could she get?

"Not a good meeting, I take it?" He started walking backward, tugging her along with him until his calves butted against the couch. He sat, giving her hands a little tug to follow him down.

She didn't protest when he arranged her on his lap, just snuggled close to slide her arms around his neck and rest her head on his shoulder. She sighed, letting some of the tension ease out of her. "No. Not a good meeting."

"I see."

She laughed brokenly. "No, actually, you don't. I'm talking a *really bad* meeting. He's never acknowledged me as his flesh and blood, so he's been absentee and living in denial for my entire life. My mom twisted my arm into seeing him today about another matter, so I did. I think part of me wishes he regretted leaving me. That maybe he'd like to get to know me."

"It didn't turn out that way?" he questioned against her hair. She felt his warm breath stir tendrils as she shook her head. "I'm sorry. He doesn't know what he's missing."

Mina frowned a little. "That's what my mom always said. I think that's the standard answer moms give their kids when their fathers don't want them, though." She tried to shrug, but it was halfhearted. "No biggie. Honestly, I was braced for his attitude. I've encountered it before. What I didn't know . . . I found out his other daughter is exactly my age."

"Oh. So you mean . . ."

"Yeah, no wonder dear old Dad doesn't claim me. It

turns out he cheated on his wife with my mother and got them both pregnant at the same time. Nice man."

"Sounds like." He rubbed her back.

She buried her face in his chest to inhale his scent and his warmth. Clean, slightly soapy, lots of outdoors. She let it ease away the polluted feeling she'd endured since talking to her father. Teague was so wonderfully, purely normal. The man probably never met a scandal in his life, or at least not one connected to his family or himself in such an ugly way. "What's your family like, Teague? Tell me about them." She felt like a child demanding a fairytale, which, she supposed, was exactly what she was doing.

"Rowdy, big, close. I've got three brothers, two younger and one older. No sisters." She heard a smile in his voice.

"Right." She smiled against his shoulder, remembering their joke. "Teague, Just Teague. Are your brothers all like you?"

"Big and ugly? Sure. I'm smarter, though." When she laughed, he squeezed her. "We're just brothers. You know. Fighting, arguing, competing. But we can all count on each other. Any time one of us was in trouble, as kids, the rest would drop whatever stupid fight we had with each other and stand together. No matter what. That's just how it worked."

"Fight among yourselves but heaven help the outsider?"

He shrugged. "Pretty much."

"That sounds nice."

He laughed. "You're nuts."

"No, I'm not. And you know what I mean. You have your differences but you're there for each other."

"Yeah, I guess so."

"What about your parents?"

"Mom's a terror. A complete tyrant." But there was a smile in his voice. "Think five-foot-nothing steamroller with pretty eyes and you have her nailed. Dad's big and dumb like the four of us. He thinks Mom walks on water when she's not spewing the fires of hell all over the idiot men in her house."

Mina laughed. "They sound wonderful." A fairytale. Just what she'd always wanted. "Do they live close?"

"North Carolina, so not all that close. But I visit when I can and my damn phone rings nonstop it seems."

She nodded.

"So. Your sister."

"Half-sister." Mina wasn't ready to acknowledge the favored child. Why should she? That kid had somehow managed to score a father and a mother and a normal life. And now she was beloved enough to be her father's right-hand woman. What was that like?

"Half-sister, then. Did you meet her?"

"No. That's the last thing good old Duncan Forbes wants. Living, breathing proof of his infidelity comparing notes with his acknowledged daughter. They're in business together, too. Did I mention that? She's an accountant like Dunky."

He chuckled a little. "Dunky?"

"Cheap nickname. So sue me."

"So she doesn't know about you, either," he mused. "Will you try to meet her?"

Mina thought a moment. Should she? What if the precious Daphne was a horrible person and hated Mina? What if Daphne was every bit as wonderful as her father swore she was? Which would be worse? What the hell would Mina even say to her? "I don't know. Not now. I don't know about later, though."

He nodded. "It's entirely your call. But I say don't let good old Dunky deny you a relationship with your sister if you decide it's something you want."

"I doubt she'd want to know about me. After all, her beloved father would topple off his pedestal if she knew he'd produced me, wouldn't he?"

"Maybe. But," he paused meaningfully, "it sounds to me like you're assuming an awful lot about this woman. How do you know she has Daddy on a pedestal? Maybe she and this father you share aren't as close as you think they are."

"They're partners in business together. How estranged could they be?"

"True enough. But I still think you should try not to lump them together in your head." He gently pushed her away enough that he could look into her eyes. "If you do meet her someday, try to keep an open mind. A sister's not something you should give up without serious soul searching first. And, that said, I'll stop pushing. I just know I'd be missing a lot if I didn't have my brothers. You might find that you have a lot in common with this sister of yours."

"Maybe." It was a lot to think about. She'd admit—as an occasionally discerning adult—that she might be a little biased against this unknown sister. Maybe Daphne was a decent person. And, maybe not. But it would be a mistake to judge her, sight unseen. She nodded, feeling the tug of his fingers, still threaded through her hair. "I'll give it some thought."

"Good." He smiled.

Meeting his eyes, she smiled back. "And as much as I hate to admit it, my mother was right, too. Thanks for being here."

"Well, you know. It was a burden and all. Got a hot woman on my lap, snuggled up in my arms. But I'm willing to sacrifice for the cause." He squeezed her, his eyes glinting with humor. And something more. "So, let's move on to the next subject."

"And that would be?" She contemplated the devilish light in his eyes.

"Well, see, like I said, I've got this sexy woman in my lap. I like that subject."

"You would." She laughed, enjoying it every bit as much as he did, especially when he tugged her hips yet closer to his body. Feeling that fizz of awareness bounce right up to a steamy simmer, she sank into sensation, enjoying the feel of his big body supporting hers.

"I don't hear you complaining. I think you like it, too."

"Oh, I don't know." She tried to look undecided—not an easy accomplishment, given the fact that her nerve endings were all popping away with sensory input. "Maybe I see you as a brother now that we've gone all mushy with the family talk and soul-searching."

"Damn." He frowned in mock concern and she nodded in mock agreement. "Guess I'll have to do something about that." In a deft, breath-stealing maneuver, he dipped Mina backward enough that he could swing one of her legs across his lap. When he tugged her upright, breathless and laughing, she was straddling his thighs. "Now that's much better." He grinned outrageously.

Eyes wide, and intelligent thought only a remote possibility now, Mina gazed down into his glittering green irises. "Ooh. You're smooth."

"Think so? I mean, I'd hate for you to think of me as a brother right about now." Winding her hair around his fingers and cupping her head, he angled his smiling mouth to hers.

Mina met his smile with one of her own, pressing her lips to his. With an appreciative groan, Teague used his hold on her hair to slant her head while he let lips and tongue play over hers. A kiss to the corner of her mouth graduated to a teasing swipe across the seam of her lips, coaxing them to part. When they did so, he slipped his tongue in to probe and savor.

The man could kiss. Sliding closer, her body aching for

more intimate contact, Mina tightened her arms and arched her pelvis against him. He groaned approval. Playing her tongue over his and pressing her body flush against him, she let her hands glide free to explore broad shoulders and biceps, lean ribs—

*Ahem.*

She started, and felt Teague wince, no doubt anticipating intimate injury. "Sorry," she muttered against his mouth.

*Hey, you're the one who doesn't want to play exhibitionist. I'm just doing my duty here. Very kind of me, I thought, considering I have no problem at all with the role of voyeur.*

Mina could have wept as she pulled back from Teague.

"Something wrong?" His breathing was rough, the kiss having taken a toll on him as well.

She met his eyes with silent entreaty. Oh, man, this was just rotten. Here he was and . . . Oh, crap. Riordan, you better appreciate this.

*I'm telling you, I'd be happy to appreciate it if you'd just go on ahead and—*

Shut up.

"So, is it the leapfrogging of steps again?" Teague tried to smile.

"I'm afraid so. That and, as much as I enjoy spending time with you and as much as my mother was right about you being good for me right now . . ." She shrugged fatalistically. "I really should talk to my mom while everything's fresh in my head. We have some things to straighten out."

"I see. I guess that's probably smart. Even if it sucks for me." He smiled crookedly. "I hope things go well."

She relaxed. "Hey, thanks to you, I may refrain from murdering her."

"Wow. I averted murder with a mere kiss," he marveled facetiously.

"Uh-huh. Don't kid yourself. There's nothing 'mere'

about your kisses. Potent, lethal, all that good stuff." Grinning, she stood up and turned to offer him a hand.

He accepted it. "Well, hey. If that's the way you feel about it . . ." He tugged her down for a brief but firm kiss.

Groaning, she gripped his shoulders a moment, enjoying the hot contact, before tugging back. "You don't make this easy."

"Not my job." His lashes drooped low, revealing only wicked slivers of green. "Are you sure I need to go? Now?"

She eyed him wistfully. "Yeah."

With a great but not-bad-natured sigh, he released her and stood up. "So I'm getting booted. You kiss me like a crazy woman and then heartlessly throw me out." He followed her to the door.

*Blech*.

Mina ignored Riordan and unlatched the door. "I know. It's killing me, believe me. Seriously, though, Teague. Thanks for putting things into perspective. That helped a lot."

"My pleasure. So. I'll see you tomorrow?"

"I'm paying you. I damn well better see you tomorrow." She grinned up at him.

"I feel like a gigolo."

She raked a gaze over his fabulous body. "Look like one, too. And with the tool belt on?" She gave a slow, wondering head shake. "Oh, man."

*Really blech*.

Shut up.

Chuckling, Teague bent and kissed her again. Helplessly, she fell into the caress, wishing for more. When he responded with growing enthusiasm, she laughed and protested against his lips. Holding him off finally, she gave him a good-natured little push out the door and watched as he trotted down the steps and walked to his truck.

She frowned at the sight of his vehicle, parked in the

street like that but definitely in front of her house. "I never saw his truck there when we pulled up. Or did I?"

"You were a little distracted." This from behind her. "And probably used to seeing it, so you didn't really notice before."

She turned to glare at Riordan, projecting every iota of the frustration that jittered along her nerves. "Look at me. This is all your fault. I'm shaking, I'm so worked up, and I had to send him out the door. For you. Is that right?"

"Hey, like I said—"

"Oh, don't. I'm real close to violence here." She marched past him.

"Look." He sighed. "I'm sorry. I could—if you want— try to cover eyes and ears and all that, but I can't help the mind link."

"Yeah, yeah." She took a deep breath and let it out slowly. Another. Then turned to him. "I know. You can't help it. But I never did anything to deserve any of this."

"And I did. I know." He shifted uncomfortably. "I thought you were going to call your mom."

"That was just an excuse. I needed to get Teague out of here before I forgot about you—and any shame I might have acquired in spite of my mother's influence—and jumped the guy." She eyed him measuringly. "Meanwhile, I wholeheartedly suggest that we do something about this curse of yours."

"Sounds like a plan."

"And we'll do this my way." She strode decisively toward her laptop.

"Your oh-so-marvelous Internet."

"It's what I know."

After twenty minutes of surfing weirdo websites—which would undoubtedly garner some really scary adware—she had a pile of printouts in front of her. "Okay. Here's what I found. First, the *geas*. Is that what was done to you? It's

Irish or Celtic or something, but we are talking about Druids."

"Yes, that's a big part of it. Akker was descended from the Irish Celts, so he knew exactly what he was doing."

"So explain this *geas* to me."

"What, your research didn't make things clear enough?"

"Riordan—"

"Okay, okay. A *geas* is something a Druid places on someone, usually a warrior, at the time of the man's birth. It's a request that can be anything from don't eat beef, to never cross paths with your father's cousin, to . . . never deceive or take advantage of a human female. If the man breaks the *geas*, usually the result is death or some social catastrophe."

Mina digested that. "So Akker was around for your birth? You must have been a baby when you did the nasty with his daughter. Relatively speaking."

"No. I was born two centuries before Akker's own birth. He did, however, attend my coming of age party, when I first came into my full powers."

"Maturity," Mina mused. "Or more importantly, the birth of your powers."

"Exactly. Rules can be applied differently with immortals, or so I understand."

"And that's when he burdened you with this *geas*?"

"That's my best guess, although you'd think he might have been sporting enough to tell me that."

"Why would he do that to you, though?"

"Well." Riordan cleared his throat uncomfortably. "Like I said, it was my coming of age party. Things got a little wild."

"Isn't that sweet?" she crooned mockingly. "An orgy in King Oberon's fairyland. So, do they call that swapping fairy tails?"

He gave her a bland look. "What can I say? It's a different culture. Anyway, it could be that Akker worried what I might do or become. Or maybe he actually foresaw what would happen." Riordan lowered his voice. "As it turns out, he was right."

"Hmm. Well, at least we know the root of it. So how do we undo a *geas*?"

"I don't know of a way to undo a *geas*. Once the request is made, it's for life, and it's unforgiving, too. One literally does not break the *geas*, no matter the consequences of abiding by it. Ignorance of the *geas* is no excuse and, as far as I know, there is no out clause."

"So. We are seriously screwed."

"But there must be a way around this, out clause or no. It was foreseen. Hell, I'm the one who foresaw it—and you."

She scowled at him. "So why didn't you foresee some of the details, then? They'd sure come in handy right about now."

"No doubt. But it's not something I can control."

She sighed. "I know. You told me. Sorry. I'm a little nervous. Some of these ideas I printed out are pretty weird."

"And having a cursed puca, recently freed from his cornerstone and living in your house, is normal?"

"Good point. Let's try these, then. How about this one?"

Riordan skimmed the page.

"Wait. You can read modern English, right?"

"Yes, yes. Give me the damn paper."

"Well, I just thought, since you couldn't read the letter that Gladys sent me—And where did that thing go, anyway?"

"I can't read it because it was prohibited. More rules, more spells, all that good stuff. And it's around here someplace. I'll get it for you later."

"But—"

"Sssh. I'm trying to read this. It looks . . ."

She hushed and watched until he looked up. "Well?"

"Fire?" His voice rose with disbelief. "We're going to play with fire? Seriously? How and where?"

Mina rolled her eyes. "Oh, ye of little faith." She went to one of the windows and was grateful to see the colors of sunset fading over the horizon. She went to gather some necessities.

Half an hour later, under cover of darkness, Mina placed two metal trashcans six feet apart in her yard. She'd wadded up a week's worth of newspaper she'd saved for recycling pick-up and placed an equal amount in each can.

Riordan studied them skeptically. "These are bonfires?"

"A little imagination, please? I have to believe it's the fire that does the cleansing, not the pile of wood, you know? So we make two fires and you do your thing to effect the necessary cleansing and purification."

"Hmm. Well, for the record, I think you're nuts."

Mina glared at him. "Oh, yeah? Well, for the record, I think you're an ungrateful jerk. I'm trying to help you here. Isn't this what you wanted?"

Riordan dropped his arms to his sides. "Yes, of course it's what I wanted. I just . . . I'm having a hard time believing in the possibility of all of it."

"I guess I can understand that. But consider this. I had a hard time believing in possibility myself. You know, minor things like the possibility of fairyfolk and pucas living among us. Ring a bell? And yet, since you introduced the impossible to me, you've made it possible for me to keep my house and continue my teaching career. The power of possibility."

Riordan pondered for a silent moment. "You make a very good case, Pandemina Dorothy Avery. A very good case. All right. Open mind. I'm visualizing two bonfires. Ready to light them?"

Mina nodded, silently praying for her yard and home not to burn down. Oh, and for the neighbors not to call the fire department on her. That would be good, too. She had to be breaking all kinds of laws to do this. Hoping for the best, she clicked the butane lighter until a flame ignited. Holding her breath, she dipped the flame into one trashcan, waited for it to take, then dipped it into the other trashcan. Soon, both were blazing along merrily.

She stepped back and regarded Riordan, or rather, what little she could see of him in the dark. "Okay. You're on. You know what to do."

"I feel like an idiot."

"So change to dog form. It probably doesn't matter what form you assume."

"No. I committed the crime in human form, so that's the form we'll purify. When and if it works."

"Riordan. *Possibility*? None of this when and if stuff."

"If and when allow for possibility. By definition—"

"Oh, good grief. Just jump, would you? Before the fire goes out or the neighbors bust me." She glanced from one house to the other. The houses weren't built exactly on top of each other, but they were certainly close enough to see flames this bright.

"Wait—" Riordan, eyeing the flames, turned back to Mina. "You have to jump with me."

"What? Now wait a minute—"

"You were condemned every bit as much as I was. In your role of guardian, you pay for your ancestors' guilt in helping me. My crime can't be forgiven completely unless yours is, too. Trust me on this."

Swallowing and unable to argue with his logic, Mina eyed the flames. "O-kay. I think. So . . . how?"

Riordan held out a hand and Mina stepped forward to take it. They stood side by side and about fifteen feet away from the blazing cans, which themselves stood six measly feet apart. The object was to jump between them, not into them. But six feet apart didn't look all that big when two people were trying to squeeze past.

Mina glanced warily at Riordan. "If I catch on fire, I'm never forgiving you. So you can just forget any kind of purification ceremony. Nothing will save you from my wrath."

"Understood." There was a smile in his voice and, she would swear, admiration in his regard of her. "Ready?"

"As ready as I'm going to get."

"On my count and . . . go!" Tightening his grip on her hand, Riordan charged the flames and, at the last moment, leapt, tugging her with him. They landed just beyond the trashcans, with Mina stumbling until Riordan steadied her. She was relieved to find no part of herself consumed by fire.

Then she turned to Riordan. "Well? Did it work? Do you feel cleansed and/or purified?" The jump behind them now, Mina felt almost giddy.

"I don't know. How would I know?"

"Well, do something. Something you couldn't ordinarily do."

"A better idea. My face. Can you see—"

"I can't see anything. Come here."

He did so and Mina angled him toward the firelight. She saw the same blur obscuring his human face. "I . . . no. But wait. Flash to dog, then flash back. Maybe it's like rebooting a computer."

"Rebooting—"

"Oh, come on. Just try it. What can it hurt?"

He shrugged, then flash-shimmered into his canine self. Paused. Then flash-shimmered back to human form.

Faceless human form.

Mina sighed. "No. It didn't work. Damn. I thought—"

Riordan shrugged. "It's okay. Hey, it's our first try."

"Well, yeah, but that was actually a Celtic solution. I thought it was our best shot out of that whole stack."

"Solutions aren't always obvious."

"I guess not." She sighed. "Let's put the fires out."

"Sure." He turned with intent toward the baskets—

"No!" She glanced around nervously. "Don't poof it or whatever you do. What if the neighbors see? Use the water hose. It's already attached to the faucet." She pointed to the faucet and a skein of rubber hose piled by her house's foundation.

"It's too dark for them to see anything. But if you insist." He walked toward the house and, twenty feet later—a mere five feet from his goal—rebounded off an invisible wall.

Mina winced for him. Talk about adding insult to injury. "How about I help you with that?"

He didn't respond, just waited for her to catch up with him, then followed her to the outdoor faucet.

"It'll be okay, Riordan. We will figure this out. We just can't give up hope."

He nodded.

The man was downright depressed. She couldn't stand it. Where was her puca? The man who so cheerfully played BobGoblin? Narrowing her eyes in thought, she casually picked up the hose nozzle and handed it to him. "You hold this. I'll turn it on."

"Okay." He held it gingerly, obviously unfamiliar with hoses and their like.

Which gave Mina an idea. "Oh, not like that. You have to hold it like *this*. Watch for the water to come out and tell me when you see it so I can adjust."

He let her position his hand, then waited while she turned the knob. Water shot out, directly into his face. "Hey—!"

Hooting with laughter, Mina took off. "Oh, yeah. That's the stuff. Put out that fire, baby. You're just too hot for words."

Growling, Riordan charged after her.

"Now don't go crazed puca on me. I was just having fun—" She screeched when she felt a big arm slide around her waist, lifting her off the ground. Retaliation, puca-style. "Hey, no abusing the guardian. I'm going to go tell a Druid on you."

"I'm just staying within my boundaries, baby." He dragged both her and the hose over to the trashcans. Once he'd doused those flames, he looked down at a heaving, still giggling Mina.

"You're drenched, Riordan." She gave an exaggerated sniff. "Sheew. Kinda smells like wet dog around here."

"You think so? And what does wet Mina smell like?"

"Hey—" She broke off on a laughing shriek and scrambled away as he turned the hose on her.

Riordan chased after her, still aiming the hose, until Mina dragged her foot over a small bush and dropped to the ground. "Ow! Oh. My ankle."

"Mina! Are you okay?" Riordan dropped to the ground beside her, released the hose and gently took her foot into his hand.

While he tried to unlace her shoe, Mina made a wild grab for the hose and turned it on him again. Shrieking with laughter over his muttered curses, Mina waved the hose one way then the other, trying to keep it out of his hands. Finally, he lunged high, grabbed the hose, and landed on top of her giggling self.

"Ooomph. Man. For a supernatural being, you weigh a ton." Out of breath from laughing and running, she lay her head back and grinned up at him, still shaken by the occasional giggle. "You were hilarious. Imagine, aiming the damn hose at your face so you could 'watch for the water' while I turn it on full blast. What a genius. That was priceless."

"Oh yeah? Kind of like this is, huh?" She heard wicked humor in his voice as he subtly twisted hips and flat belly against her, making her well aware of her position beneath him. "I can't remember the last time I had a laughing woman squirming under me, so young and strong and wet from play." He paused. "Quite literally, I can't remember. So. Laugh if that's what it takes, but I'll stay right here while you do it."

She'd been had.

# CHAPTER TEN

"Ooooh, you're sly," Mina marveled with pensive admiration. "How did I not remember your weirdo ability to walk around in my head? You knew what I was doing all the time, didn't you? You are so bad."

"Uh-huh. And what about you? Drag your foot across a bush and suddenly you've sprained your ankle and completely lost your balance? Sure, that's believable. I'll bet you killed the damn bush stepping on it like that. Meanwhile, look what *I* get."

He sounded like a boastful little boy.

"Little boy?" he scoffed, still poking around in her head. "Give me a break. I'm no little boy." He paused. "And I'm no dog. I'm a man. And this is something I've needed for a very long time. You feel damn good."

He sounded so smug. And he felt pretty damn good himself. It was such a shame they had this species problem between them.

"You're going to hold that against me now? I can't help it

if I'm puca and you're human. Hey, I can assume human form, so there's a bridge, right?"

"Riordan, please stop reading my thoughts. It's rude."

"It is?" He sounded confused. "Yeah, I guess it is. But it's not like I can help it. Your thoughts are all out there. I can pretend not to know them, if you want."

"Is there any way you can literally *not* know them? Just for my peace of mind?"

He studied her, having never moved from atop her body.

"And could you maybe get off me while we discuss this?"

Reluctantly, Riordan rolled to the side and sat up, helping her push to a seated position. Feeling her butt sink into saturated ground, Mina groaned. "Just let me turn off the hose." Remembering the invisible wall problem they endured, she noted the distance and deemed it acceptable before rising. "I'll be right back." She turned the water off, then returned to where Riordan still lounged in the grass. She dropped down beside him.

"This is nice," he mused. "Playing in the water, rolling in the grass. Enjoying the warming glow of fire in autumn. Even the cold, clammy feel of wet clothes sticking to my skin. All good stuff, Mina." He sounded wondering.

She thought about what it would be like to be him, enjoying the simplest of physical sensations. To have been without for so long that even the feel of wet clothes clinging to one's skin was a welcome sensation. "It must have been hell, existing without a—a physical reality for so long."

"Yeah." He thought a moment. "But back to your request. I can teach you to shield your thoughts from me."

"You can?" She eyed him curiously.

"I just said I could. Why?"

She shrugged. "I'm just surprised you would offer that up. You could have said there was nothing you could do. I would have believed you. Why would you give up an advantage like that?"

He folded his hands and stared at them for a brooding moment. "I'm already taking advantage of you. Just by being here, I'm putting your life on hold. And you've done so much for me." He went on, a smile in his voice now. "You were trying to cheer me up, weren't you? It was twisted, but you honestly did drench me because you wanted to distract me and make me laugh."

She shrugged. "You seemed so sad."

He nodded but didn't elaborate. "So, it's like this. If you want to keep your thoughts private, you have to picture them in your head, except inside a room, or a mental partition. It takes practice, but you do get the hang of it. I had a maze of partitions when I was still living with my brother, so I know it's possible to build and maintain them. It's pretty effortless after a while, like not falling to the ground when you're standing." He paused. "Although it's true that the walls occasionally tumble down when you sleep."

She nodded slowly. "Well, it's not like I have any life-or-death secrets to keep from you. But the occasional stray thought . . . well, it'd be nice to be able to keep it private until I screen it and decide whether it's appropriate for sharing. Like you can do when you think before you speak your thoughts."

"Why don't you give it a try, then? Until you've had more practice, I'd suggest building the walls first and then placing a concept inside them. I'll tell you if I can read it or not."

Mina closed her eyes and pictured a wall. It turned into a cubicle, which made her smile. Actually, a cubicle wasn't a bad idea. It was a familiar visual she could hold indefinitely, and she could always connect other cubicles onto it as needed.

"What's a cubicle?"

Unwillingly, she let a mental picture of a cubicle form in her mind, then turned a frown on Riordan. "Hey, I didn't think you could read my thoughts like this."

He shrugged. "You're thinking about cubicles. Out loud in your head. If you didn't want me to know, you should have put the thought *inside* the cubicle."

"Oh." Turning that strategy over in her head, she closed her eyes again and, holding the cubicle solidly in place, she set a thought inside of it. Tried not to smile. "Okay."

"Pink panties."

Her eyes flew open. "Hey!"

"You put a damn window in the cubicle. I could see them."

She made a face. "Who wants to work in a cubicle with no window?"

He groaned and spoke with exaggerated patience. "Maybe somebody who doesn't want anyone seeing inside the cubicle?"

"All right, all right." Huffing, she closed her eyes again and reformed the cubicle.

"You might want to raise those walls all the way to the ceiling."

She opened an eye.

"Hey, I'm trying to be honest here. I thought that was pretty damn noble on my part."

"It is, it is." She closed the eye, raised the walls, and checked along the bottom, sides and tops. Four sealed walls, a ceiling, a floor, no windows. Carefully, picturing herself inside the cubicle, she framed a thought. Made it an embarrassing thought, so as to offer self-incentive. Then she concentrated on maintaining the image inside the cubicle image. "Okay."

Riordan went silent a moment. "Hmm. Assuming there's something really in there, I think you did it."

"I did? Woo-hoo!" she tossed her arms in the air.

"Um . . ." He choked on laughter. "You have to actually keep the walls in place if you want this to work."

Mina covered her face. "Oh, dear god."

"No kidding." He was shaking his head and laughing. "This is what I look like naked? Seriously? I'm flattered, sure, but isn't it a little overblown? The proportions alone . . ."

She groaned. "That'll teach me."

"I sure hope not. Hey, look at it this way. If your goal was to cheer me up, I have to say you did a damn fine job of it. First the free feel, and now extravagant compliments. Darn good evening, in my book."

"Aaarrrgh. You know, normal people don't have to worry about this stuff."

"Normal's overrated."

"Depends on who's doing the rating." She stood up. "Come on. Put those oversized muscles to work and help me clean up."

"Actually, I thought my muscles were a lot bigger than you pictured, but the *other*, well, now that was exceptionally well done." He rose to his feet next to her. "God only knows how I wear pants over something that big, but I do. Just one more manly accomplishment—"

She elbowed him on the way past and reached for a trashcan while he took the other. "When we get inside, we'll sort through the stuff I printed out and pick out our next experiment."

"Sounds good to me. Does any of it involve you naked and covered in mud? I thought I saw something like that on the television the other night."

"Dream on, puca."

Later that night, after a shower to wash off the grass clippings and dirt she'd picked up rolling around under Riordan—whoa, that was a bad way to phrase matters—Mina sat down on the floor next to him. She tugged the stack of printouts to the edge of the coffee table and started shuffling through them. "Any thoughts? Preferences? And we're talking about ideas that I'm willing to explore, by the way. This human sacrifice crap you mentioned a few days ago just is not happening."

"Okay, okay."

She paused over a page to skim it.

"What's that?" He read over her shoulder. "Oh, Wiccan. Witchcraft."

She shrugged. "They claim you guys, so I thought it might be a reciprocal thing."

"What do you mean?"

"They believe in the power of the Druids. Some liked to think they were descended from Druids. They also believe in fairyfolk—which includes you, too. Through your father."

"Oh, you've met Dad?"

"Can't say that I've had that pleasure, thanks. Or that I want it. Oberon, King of the Fairies. As in, more powerful than puca? I'm not sure I want to go up against that one."

"That's smart. He's a ruthless son of a bitch. I'll give him that. Apologies, my king." He murmured the last out of habit. "He doesn't claim me anymore, by the way."

"He doesn't?"

Riordan shook his head. "Robin's his pride and joy. I was an oops."

"Ah. I can relate."

Riordan nodded. "I guess so. It got worse, naturally, after Akker did his thing. Oberon was mortified and I was banished." He glanced up. "I know, and yes, it sucks to be me."

"No, actually. I was going to say I thought parents should be more forgiving than your average Druid."

"My father didn't kill me, at least. Akker would have killed me if he could. God knows he did his worst. Which is this. But Oberon could have terminated me with a snap of his fingers if that's what he wanted to do. He didn't."

"That's something, I guess," she replied doubtfully. "What about your mom?"

"She's long dead. Since about ten years after I was born. She was human, remember. I hardly knew her."

"Oh." Mina didn't know what to say now.

"Nothing *to* say."

She glanced up in surprise.

"You didn't put it in the cubicle."

"Cubicle. Right. So. About this curse-breaking spell."

He frowned. "Just so you know, I'm not bashing a rotten egg or anything else against my forehead."

"Nobody's suggesting you bash a rotten egg against your head. Next time, read a little more carefully." So saying, she reread the spell herself. "Hmm. I dunno."

"What?"

"Well, I have some of this stuff. Candles, sage, sea salt, a bell, water, black cotton thread and cloth. But dragon's blood resin? And these exotic oils? And heaven forbid I have any fresh rosemary in the house. A rotten egg, however, I can do."

"Why don't we try one of the other spells, then? We can collect supplies tomorrow."

"Yeah. Hold on, though. Let me go take an egg out of the fridge." She rolled to her feet and went into the kitchen to set an egg out to rot.

What about that just seemed wrong? Other than everything.

She padded back to the living room and dropped down beside Riordan, who was sifting through the stack. "Find something?"

He shrugged. "Just picking at random. How about this one?"

Mina skimmed it. "More dragon's blood. I don't suppose you're acquainted with any dragons, are you? No, I did not ask that question."

"Whatever happened to *possibility*? And *accepting the impossible*?" he taunted her.

"I'm slow to accept. So sue me."

"To answer the question you didn't ask, I used to know a dragon, but I doubt he's still alive. Most of them died out as civilization took hold and their hiding places diminished."

"You mean they really . . ." She shook her head. "Never mind. The point is, you can't get your hands on any real dragon's blood right now."

"No."

"I wonder, though, if it's really a euphemism or nickname for something more commonplace. We can look it up later. Meanwhile, I think there are some easier possibilities here." She read through one. "Here's a thought. Ever try a simple prayer to God? Asking for forgiveness and help?"

He snorted. "If you only knew how many times I've tried that. Cursing and begging and bargaining. Nothing works."

She nodded thoughtfully. "I'm not giving up on that one yet. I think there's potential there. But here's one I'll bet you haven't tried, given your recent disembodiment."

"What?"

She smiled. "How do you feel about bubble baths?"

He studied her with new interest. "Are we talking nudity now? I think I could like this one." He continued with casual certainty. "And naturally, since you were cursed every bit as much as I was, I think you should also—"

"Oh, no, buddy. We are not going there."

"Okay, okay. It was just a thought."

She gave him a severe look, attempting without much success to stop the blood from rushing to her cheeks and other places. The first time she ever saw his human form, in a flashing instant, he'd been nude. Impressive. And now, picturing him gleaming with water and bubbles in the candlelight . . .

Riordan cleared his throat, obviously trying not to laugh. "The cubicle, Mina."

"Oh, good lord." Annoyed, she turned back to the page and started reading, pausing to note down necessary supplies. "On the night after the full moon . . ." She glanced up in dismay. "I didn't even notice—"

Riordan looked alert now. "I did notice. Last night was the full moon. Maybe fate's finally in my corner."

"Maybe." Mina studied the spell with new interest. "Just before bed—" She glanced out the windows into darkness.

"Check. Go on."

"Umm . . . light thirteen candles, white preferably. Votives count, don't you think?"

Riordan nodded.

"Fill the tub with water, as hot as you can stand. Add . . ." She jumped up and padded into the kitchen to open her spice cabinet. "Sea salt, sage, lavender and chamomile. I have tea bags for those last two. Those should work, don't you think?"

"I don't see why not. So, we're making puca tea?"

"Sounds like it." She read through the rest. "Turn off the water and let the bath steep in the herbs. Kneel or sit in front of the tub, in the nude." She chanced a glance at Riordan, refusing to acknowledge her thoughts. "And then there's an incantation you repeat. Then you—"

"I'm not going to remember all this. Let's just gather what we need and proceed to the bath." Riordan sounded downright cheerful.

"I could just give you the stuff and let you do it alone."

Riordan was already shaking his head. "I really believe that you should at least be present for all this. Seriously. Yeah, yeah, I'm a letch and probably enjoying all this way too much, but honestly, it was foreseen that you would be key to my freedom. If you're not there, I don't see anything working."

"You really believe in this prophecy stuff?"

"As much as I believe in all the other stuff. And I'm here to tell you that all the other stuff exists. Including the curse. And, this brand of prophecy can be cryptic and occasionally misleading, but usually proves to be correct."

Reluctantly, Mina nodded. "Then let's get what we need." She pulled spices and tea bags from the cabinets, pointed him toward a box of candles and her lighter, then headed toward the bathroom.

Riordan entered and glanced around curiously. "I've always wondered about these."

"You've never seen a bathroom before?"

He shrugged. "No body, no need for one."

"I see." Frowning at the idea of how different they really were, she set the ingredients next to the basin. Then she arranged the thirteen candles around the room and lit them. Satisfied by the glow they cast, she flipped off the overhead light and bent over the tub to turn the hot water on full blast. Referring again to the instructions, she measured out sea salt and sage, then carefully broke open the tea bags to measure their contents. She dumped them into the tub. She hoped all the leaves and twiggy stuff wouldn't wreck her plumbing. Maybe she'd sift it all out later.

Still pondering, she turned around and saw Riordan.

Naked.

And jumped back, nearly toppling into the tub herself.

Riordan caught her hand and steadied her. "Hey, I'm just following the instructions. It said nude, so I'm nude."

"Yeah, but . . . I mean, you could have waited until the tub was full."

"How full does it have to be?"

"Full enough to camouflage some of you would be good."

He chuckled low. "Are you feeling shy, Mina?"

"Well, I don't know if you've noticed, but in modern times, people don't waltz all over creation in the nude."

"So you're not used to it."

"No, I'm not used to it."

"Jackson didn't walk around the house naked?"

Mina pressed her lips together, but the thought escaped before she could check it or hide it.

Riordan snorted. "Seriously? He wouldn't undress with the lights on? What was he hiding?"

"Stop that."

"Then work a little harder on those cubicles."

Still grumbling, she glanced at the water. "There are a few inches in there now."

Riordan followed her gaze. "Turn it off, then."

"But—"

"Hey, we're going for potency, right? Why water down the ingredients?"

He had a point, as uncomfortable as it might make her.

"You think *you're* uncomfortable? I'm the one playing voodoo queen and chanting in front of an audience."

Another good point.

"Thank you."

She considered asking him to stay out of her head, but gave up the effort. He had, after all, given her the means to hide her thoughts. If she chose not to employ it and he merely saw what she didn't bother to hide, it wasn't his fault.

"That was downright sporting of you, Mina."

She gave him a wry grin. "Gee, thanks. So let's get on with this. Your water's going to get cold."

He lifted a leg to step in, and she grabbed his thigh before she realized what she'd done. "You can't just—"

"Mina. *Darling.*" He leaned close, his voice shaking with amusement. "I feel it, too. Just surrender to the lust."

Pulling back, she growled at his teasing. "Shut up. Look, you can't just climb in. You're supposed to sit or kneel in front of the tub and do the chant thing first."

"I am?"

"Weren't you listening earlier?"

"I kind of got hung up on the nudity part. Like you did."

"Not like I did. Never mind. So kneel already."

With a shrug, Riordan sank to one knee, then the other, bracing himself on the edge of the tub. "So, what's the chant?"

"It's several lines long."

"Okay, you say it and I'll repeat it. That way you're participating. Remember the prophecy?"

"That's reasonable. Okay." She found her place on the page and began: "'What was done was done, Be it now undone . . .'"

He repeated it.

"'By the light of the full moon's wane, Cleanse my soul of taint and stain . . .'"

She continued to read, phrase by phrase, each of which Riordan carefully, surprisingly reverently, repeated. Until the last: "'Return my spirit to its grace.'"

After dutifully repeating it, he looked up. "I'm not sure there ever was much grace to my spirit, even in the beginning."

"Given your orgy of a coming-of-age ceremony, I have my doubts, too, but let's give this a shot anyway."

"So what do I do next?"

"Get in."

He stood and climbed into the tub. "Do I sit?" When she nodded, he sank into the water.

Awed by the display of sinew and skin cast in flickering candlelight, Mina determinedly averted her gaze from his lap. It was not easy. It was becoming less easy. And he was—"Hey, you're reading my mind."

"How do you know?"

"Puca junior's growing. Tell him to quit that."

"So stop looking. And thinking." Amusement threaded his voice.

"Can we just get on with this?"

"Hey, I'm doing what I'm supposed to do. You're the one with the dirty mind."

She closed her eyes, hoping for patience. Self-control. A leash for her wayward, undoubtedly perverted thoughts.

"Oh, they're not *too* perverted."

"Riordan!"

"Okay, okay. So do I just sit here now or what?"

She turned her attention back to the instructions, locating her place. "It says you're supposed to cup water in your hands and pour it over your head three times. Wait! Not yet!" She watched him lower his hands. "Each time you do it, you say these words: 'Accept my apologies for what was done. Disperse my spell with the morning's sun.'"

Thoughtful now, Riordan cupped his hands in the water, ducked his head and poured a double handful over his scalp. He said the words. Then he did it again. And then once more. Whipping his hair back finally, sending sprays of droplets around him, Riordan turned his attention to Mina. "What next?"

She shrugged. "You stay in the tub until the water cools. Then you get out and go to bed. The curse should lift at dawn."

"And that's all there is to it? I sit here until my nuts freeze off, then go to bed. And poof. All better. I'm me again."

"Yes. If this works."

He nodded. "I have a good feeling about this."

She smiled. "So do I."

"And it's not just the herbs collecting in interesting places, either. Remind me to try some water fun with you when I'm all better, by the way."

"You're impossible."

"But seriously. This spell could possibly work. Right?"

"Right. So, um. How's the water?"

"Scalding my ass."

So they'd sit there like that for a while still. Him naked, her shamelessly spectating. Maybe she didn't need to be here.

"Please stay." And he was completely sincere. "I want you here. I won't try anything. I just . . . I'd like you to stay."

"The prophecy thing."

"Not just the prophecy thing." He paused. "Did you know, in all these centuries, you're the first guardian who's tried to free me? All the others believed me guilty and deserving of punishment. Even Gladys, although she seemed to pity me at least. But none of them tried to break the curse."

"Maybe you didn't try hard enough to convince them to help you. You worked your tail off—so to speak—trying to convince me."

By thwarting the wants of her libido, naturally. And it worked, too. Very smart puca.

He laughed.

"I really need to work on that cubicle, don't I?"

"Oh, don't do it on my account. Your thoughts generally prove entertaining and even enlightening on occasion. I had no idea I was physical perfection in the eyes of all womankind."

"Don't look now, but your ego's outgrowing the bathroom."

"Your fault, not mine."

She grumbled. He certainly had her there.

"So. Mina." He seemed to be trying for the same playful tone, but there was an uncertain edge to his voice now.

"Yes?" What could make a puca uncertain?

"If this works—if we break the curse—what are the chances of you and me . . . you know."

"You know . . . ?" She frowned, mildly confused.

"Getting together."

"Sex? You're worried about having sex with me? Now? My interest in Teague aside . . . Buddy, you're soaking in chamomile tea and waiting for the inevitable shrinkage as the water cools—that does happen to pucas, too, I assume?—and you're still capable of suggesting we have sex?"

"We-ell . . ." And now he sounded even more hesitant. "Even if there's no sex, I would like to see you again. If you don't mind. Just check in once in a while to see if you're okay. I mean, I did promise not to abandon you. You know, to always show up if you called. But I think I'd really like it if we . . . Well, I mean, I like hanging out with you sometimes, and I'm getting used to those entertaining thoughts of yours and—"

She eyed him wonderingly. "Riordan, are you asking me if I'd like to be friends with you?"

He paused. "Yes. That's what I'm asking. I don't have any friends like that. I've witnessed the feelings of my human guardians when they were with their friends. Equal footing. Laughing, teasing, even arguing and making up. I don't have that. I have people who fear me, people who hate me and people who are stuck with me. If you were given the option to freely hang out with me . . . Sometimes. Like when you're not on a date or busy or naked or sleeping . . . would you want to?"

She was touched. Trying to gather her words together, Mina glanced around a little awkwardly before seating herself on the bath rug where Riordan had knelt just a few minutes ago. From this angle, his distracting naked parts weren't so readily available to her view and imagination. She held out her hand to him and smiled when he took it. "Yes. Surprisingly, probably to both of us, I might like that. I'd like to see you happy one day, Riordan. Happy and enjoying your freedom and maybe sharing more stories of the impossible with me."

He squeezed her hand, not saying anything, but the silence said more than words could. A man without friends had made a tentative gesture toward friendship. And found it accepted freely. He'd been so profoundly isolated. The reality of his existence had to be so much worse than she could possibly fathom. She couldn't wrap her mind around the concept of one millennium, much less two of them—and then filling those millennia with isolation, disorienting disembodiment and sheer loneliness and desperation. "I'm surprised you didn't resort to threats to get me or someone else to help you before this."

He shrugged without answering.

"You know what? I think a lot of people have underestimated you. Akker and his daughter most of all. Their loss. We'll figure this out, Riordan. One way or the other."

Half an hour later, the water had cooled and Riordan climbed out, drying off and draping the towel around his waist. When Mina moved to scoop out as much of the herbs as she could gather, Riordan brushed her aside and took care of the chore himself. They drained the tub, snuffed out the candles, then turned to face each other. Mina was at a loss for words and even shameless Riordan didn't seem quite sure how to act.

"So I just sleep now?" Riordan mused quietly. Then he continued in a tone, half-mocking and half-not, obviously intended to put them both at ease. "But gee, Mom, what if I have blasphemous dreams? What if I wake up before dawn or just can't sleep? Imagine insomnia spoiling my one shot at freedom."

Responding to the undercurrent of concern in his voice, Mina frowned. "Well, it didn't say, but I can't think that it would matter much how you slept. The idea is that the curse would break at dawn. Don't you think?"

He shrugged. "I guess."

"So. Sleep." She glanced around at her bedroom with its bed inside, and then around her home. No other beds. She frowned. "It never occurred to me to wonder—"

"Where I sleep?" He sounded amused. "I know. You assumed I poof myself somewhere. I've been using your couch or, occasionally, the corner rug. Depending on the form I take."

"You can sleep as a dog?"

"Not my preference, but sure."

She nodded. "Well, I can get you some blankets and a pillow for the couch."

"Thanks." He followed her to the hall closet, where she got down the bedding and handed them over. Then she wrapped her arms around her middle and regarded him with some uncertainty. "If this spell works and I'm still asleep when you find out . . . I know you'll have a ton of things you'll want to do, but you won't leave without saying good-bye, will you?"

"Never. I promised, remember? You can count on me."

She smiled for real now. "I guess we really are friends."

"Guess so."

"Good night, Riordan."

" 'Night, Mina."

Mina hesitated, then impulsively grabbed the cornerstone from the table. At his wondering gaze, she shrugged awkwardly. "Thought I'd take it with me. For safekeeping. And luck." Something to stare at when she couldn't sleep either. When he nodded wordlessly, she turned and padded off to her bedroom. She lay awake for long hours, hoping. She considered going out to the couch and just watching to see if his face would appear.

*Go to sleep, Mina.*

You're awake, too.

*Well, it is sort of my face on the line here. Not to mention the rest of my existence, eternity, freedom, all those large concepts.*

Yeah. Is it hard to believe? Are you afraid?

*I don't know. I think I stopped being afraid and stopped really believing a long time ago. I feel more now. Now that I've found you and I've left the cornerstone, there's hope. I do feel that. Hope. Thanks to you.*

Come on, Riordan. Don't go all sappy on me now that we've decided to be friends. She smiled. I'm kind of partial to smart-aleck pucas. I don't know what I'd do with sincere and brooding or hopeful types. Very disconcerting.

She felt, more than heard, him chuckling. *No chance of that. Purification spells just seem to put me in a weird mood.*

That's understandable. Mina let her eyes close and felt her thoughts blurring just a little.

*Let go, Mina. I'll wake you in the morning.*

As though his directive was all that was needed for her to do exactly that, Mina drifted off. The night's events, from fire jumping, to hose wrestling, to nudity in a tub, caught up with her. The experiences tangled with her thoughts and her limbs, and soon her limbs were tangled with the dream of Riordan's long, gleaming arms and legs.

Flesh, slippery from herb-scented water, slid against hers with heated purpose. She wrapped her arms around him, felt his broad chest. Its swirls of hair matted by water rasped against the tender skin of her breasts. Bare now. She was as naked as he. And wet, their skin glistening in the candlelight as they moved together. Tandem, counterpoint, searching, discovering, scenting, tasting. He teased her mouth open and his tongue tangled with hers for a long, skillful kiss.

Mina groaned and tugged him yet closer, rolling over him and on top of him, to ride his big, naked body. She felt the hot length of his erection between her thighs. Wanting him closer. Wanting him inside—

# CHAPTER ELEVEN

"Mina?"

"Mmmmph. Riordan?"

A male chuckle. "Does your dog talk?"

At the words, Mina's eyes flew open and she dazedly scanned the bedroom before focusing on a man standing next to her bed. "Teague?" The man kept popping in at the most startling moments.

"You sleep like the dead, woman. I knocked and knocked, then tried the doorbell. No answer. So I went around and let myself in through the back again. Hope that's okay."

The back? Oh. They'd had to replace her back door and it wasn't quite secured yet, she remembered. Teague had worried about that. "Yeah." She licked her lips and gazed casually around the room. "Sorry. I must have been tired."

He frowned. "You seem kind of warm. Are you sick?"

"No, I'm fine." She frowned in remembered worry. "Have you seen Riordan? Is he in the living room?"

"Your dog? Oh, you're worried he might have escaped."

"Yeah. He can be determined. With the back door loose—"

"And him being so high-strung. I get it." Teague strode toward her bedroom door and reached around the door-jamb to flip the light switch, bringing the living room into dim view. "Yeah, he's out here. Sleeping under the coffee table. Did you have overnight guests or something?"

"Hmm? No. Why?" Why was Riordan under the coffee table? He was in dog form. How could she tell if the spell worked if he was in dog form?

"There's a pillow and blankets out here."

Think, Mina. "I used them. I was watching TV last night and got cold. I guess I left them out there."

"It did get chilly last night." Teague turned back to Mina. She sat up in bed, pushing her tangled curls back off her face to eye him blearily. She was exhausted.

And aroused. All those dreams—

"Wow. I really like the tank top. A whole lot."

Mina glanced down at her nearly transparent white cami. "Oh. I—" She pulled the covers higher.

"No need for that." Teague's voice was husky as he approached her. "The view was excellent. I had a dream about you last night, looking just like that. Until I stripped the tank top off of you."

Mina swallowed. Hard. This was *not* going to happen. She was not going to use Teague just because she had a dream about—

Cubicle walls going up.

And speaking of which. Oh, Lord. She still had a puca in her house, able to read her thoughts. She knew she'd never keep the barrier up if she and Teague . . . Stop!

And that just wasn't right. Doing anything like that with Teague when Riordan was in the house and—Hush!

The mattress dipped as Teague sat on it, facing her. Green eyes glowed darkly beneath that gorgeous sweep of eyelashes. The brackets of near-dimples dented his cheeks, one deeper than the other, as he half-smiled with those sculpted lips. So sensual.

Mina closed her eyes against the sight, felt the mattress sink lower as Teague's mouth touched hers. Oh. Oh, nice.

Oh, *bad* Mina. Wake up. She pulled back, blinking. "I—"

"You what?" Teague murmured. "You look good enough to eat like that. Wearing almost nothing, and all warm and soft with sleep. Curls wild and everywhere. I really, really could eat you up. I wonder. Would you let me? If I'd kissed you while you were asleep, would you have kissed me back?"

Oh, god. Probably.

But it would have been Riordan she was kissing in her sleep. Wrong. It was so wrong. Mina clutched the covers. "Teague." What could she say? What should she say?

He bent close again, and Mina, acting without thought, rolled off the opposite side of the bed before he could plant those yummy lips on hers again. She was really turning into a slut. Two men making her hot. And one of those wasn't even human. What the hell was she going to do?

Break the curse. No other hope for it. Break the curse.

Meanwhile, Teague looked puzzled. Ugh. She was such a tease. "I have to brush my teeth. Morning breath, you know. And cramps. I have lots of cramps." Yeah, that'll keep him coming back for more. Idiot. She groaned inwardly and heard the echo of a chuckle in her head. Riordan?

*Sorry.*

Riordan! How are you? Are you okay? Your face. Do you have a face? Are you free? Are you waiting . . . to say good-bye?

Silence. Then: *No. It didn't work.*

"Oh, Riordan, I'm so sorry." The words burst out without forethought.

"Huh?" Teague sounded confused.

"Dog. I have to feed the dog on a specific schedule. He has a medical condition."

Teague looked baffled. "That is one high-maintenance mutt you have."

"I'm just trying to be a responsible pet owner."

"Hmm. Okay. But before you—"

Sudden pounding thudded against the back wall and a voice rose, muffled but still audible. "Teague? Everything okay in there? Any more walls come down?" Muffled laughter.

Teague glanced over his shoulder, as though he could see through her bedroom and kitchen walls outside to his men, obviously ready to start their day. He raised his voice. "I'll be right out."

"Okay. We're ready whenever you are."

Teague dipped his head forward before meeting her eyes again. "Sounds like I'm being paged."

"Yeah, it does." Nothing like a mixture of relief and disappointment to confuse the morning.

"Can I call you later? Or at least check in with you before I leave?"

"I'd like that." Just keep the lines of communication open. And break the curse.

*I like that plan.*

Mina closed her eyes. Make that, break the curse quickly.

*I like that one better.*

After Teague left, Riordan cautiously entered her bedroom. *Everybody clothed in here?*

"Of course. And of course you know Teague is gone. What's up?" Seating herself on the mattress again, she gave him a sympathetic look. "Other than that spell not working?"

"Well . . ." He seemed hesitant.

"What?"

Restless, he shuffled his feet, if one could accuse a dog of doing such. "Do you remember that letter from Gladys?"

Mina leapt off the bed. "The letter. Of course. Where do you suppose it is now?"

"It's under the bed." Riordan, who hadn't moved, looked even more hesitant. "Because I hid it from you that first day. It's been under there this whole time."

Mina dropped to her knees and lifted the bedskirt. "But why?" She spoke under the bed. When she found she could see nothing, she pulled back to glance at Riordan as she raked the bedskirt higher and out of the way.

"Remember that bit about . . . eliminating the puca?"

Mina paused. "You were afraid I'd really do that to you?"

"Let's just say I could understand the appeal if you were desperate to get rid of me."

"Yeah, but I'm not heartless. I wouldn't just eliminate you unless you turned out to be dangerous to the human race or something."

"I've come to realize that. So . . . maybe you could find it, read it, check for clues. Since I couldn't." He frowned. "I actually haven't seen it in a while. Not since that first day—"

"Well, you know I haven't exactly cleaned the place from top to bottom since then. It must be around here somewhere. Let me get a flashlight. Hold on."

Ten minutes later, Mina triumphantly displayed the envelope for Riordan. "Found it!" She plopped onto the bed, stared at the envelope front, then flipped it over to lift the flap and . . .

Inhaled sharply. "It's empty." She opened it wider, even slid her fingers inside, sweeping from corner to corner. Nothing.

Riordan jumped up next to her and peered into the envelope. "You're sure?"

"Yes." Lowering the envelope, she eyed him quietly. "So,

is this more of the same? Are you pretending to come clean with me so I'll stop pestering you about the letter?"

"No, I swear. It must have fallen out. Come on, I'll help you look for it. It must be around here somewhere."

Twenty minutes later, Mina had counted all the dust bunnies under her bed and resigned herself to the knowledge that the bunnies lived alone. No letter to be found. "You're sure you hid it under here and nowhere else?"

"Yeah." Riordan sounded grim. "Maybe it got kicked out?" They searched the rest of the bedroom but to no avail.

Mina groaned. "Look. Searching for it's not going to work. We'll only find it when we give up hope of finding it. Right? Right. Okay. So . . . let's try to crack this thing without it and hope for the best. Maybe it will turn up."

"Unless it got tossed out with the renovation debris."

"Oh, crap. I forgot about that part. Lots of stuff did get swept up and tossed." An eventuality Mina just didn't want to accept right now.


Over the course of the next few days, Mina and Riordan searched every bin and dumpster that Teague and crew had used. They also visited several shops on the wrong side of town—shops with bars across the windows and scary loiterers circling the vicinity. They interviewed fortune tellers and white witches and iffy witches, collecting—and paying for—various spells and sachets and even a little gris-gris from a voodoo practitioner. Then they talked to a priest, who basically trotted them out of his office before Mina could say five words. Exorcism, apparently, was a sore subject with the Church, while excommunication was not.

Back at home, they tried each and every concoction and combination they could find. Caught up in the experiments and conscious of their deadline approaching, Mina even postponed returning phone calls from Teague until they became less and less frequent. It was disappointing but not exactly unexpected. She didn't have the time to devote to a relationship right now and didn't have the energy to keep putting off a desirable man without driving him away. A clean break was better than messy, she decided, not without regret. After all, he'd finished the renovation project and all that was left was paying the bill, which her insurance company had agreed to do.

Riordan, who didn't tease her about Teague anymore, complained of pruny skin from all the cleansing baths he was forced to take, along with a skin reaction to some of the herbs. Until now, Mina hadn't known a puca could fall victim to hives. Neither had Riordan, at that.

Still, one last spell involved a little bit of everything they'd learned and tried, as though bits and pieces of fire, water, prayer and sincerity of symbolism were combined into one perfect concoction. Riordan, who'd grown jaded with the process before this, even held out hope of this experiment working.

The appropriate words spoken with quiet ceremony over incense and candlelight, Riordan dunked his head as instructed in a baptism-like attempt at cleansing and rebirth. Then he rose from his knees, droplets of water, herbs and ash clinging to his skin, but kept his naked back to Mina.

Mina stared at him, heart in her throat and afraid to breathe. Did it work? Was he free? "How do you feel?"

"Well, let's give it a whirl." Riordan seemed to brace himself. Mina, familiar with his nudity by now but no less affected by it than she was the first time she saw him, waited quietly. She was almost sick with hope. It had to work.

After a moment, Riordan glanced down into the water, peered more closely at his reflection, but then sighed and turned to her. He voiced what she already knew. "It didn't work."

Mina slumped. "Damn it." She watched, helplessly, as Riordan stepped out of the tub and pulled a towel off the rack. He used it to swipe water off himself, then pulled the plug to let the water out. Mina snuffed out candles and incense burner.

Without another word, he grabbed his tunic and pants and left the room. A few minutes later, she heard the back door opening and closing, then silence. Emerging from the bathroom, curious and worried about him, Mina craned her neck to watch and saw his profile through the window, well within his usual boundaries of the back porch. Obviously he needed time alone and Mina couldn't blame him for it. She was failing him. His hopes had to rise with every experiment they performed only to fall when she failed— and he had way more at stake than she did.

Hell, she had nothing to lose. No boyfriend now that Jackson had cheated on her and left her. No prospects now that Teague's interest had so obviously cooled. Sure, it was at least partially her own fault for being so careless with his feelings and attention—after all, the phone lines did allow calls in both directions—but she'd hoped for at least a little more persistence from the man. She'd really liked Teague.

Sure, she had a house and a job back. But that was all thanks to Riordan, whom she was failing. This just really, really sucked. Feeling sorry for herself, she swung open the fridge door and shoved leftovers and milk aside. She pulled out the nearly full bottle of wine she'd ignored for . . . Did wine go bad after a month? Who knew? Who cared?

Seriously wallowing now, Mina plucked a wineglass out of the cabinet and set it down. Then she popped the cork on the bottle and shamelessly filled the goblet to the brim. Hey, maybe there was inspiration at the bottom of a wine bottle.

Setting the bottle down, she raised the glass in an ironic toast and gulped a third of it. Too fast. She choked a little, wiped her mouth, and drank some more.

Bottle in one hand and wineglass in the other, she moved

her pity party to the living room and slumped down on the floor behind the coffee table, her spine braced against the couch. She dragged the latest stack of books closer. Flipping through the pages, she smoothed dog-eared corners of experiments they'd already tried, and turned down corners of pages with new ideas. Was she wasting her time? She didn't know. She just knew she couldn't give up on Riordan. When the back door reopened half an hour later, Mina glanced up. "Hi."

"Hi." He sounded so serious.

Mina's newfound hope crumbled. "I'm so sorry, Riordan. I really thought *this* time—"

"So did I." Carefully skirting the table, he dropped to the floor next to her.

"We're running out of time. And I'm running out of ideas."

"You're just tired." He sounded less upset than she did about it. Hell, the man was comforting her, when her failures could result in him being locked inside that damn stone for another millennium.

He winced. "Could you maybe avoid thinking of it in quite those terms?"

"Well, it's true, damn it." She was near tears. "You could be stuck in there just because I'm not smart enough to figure this out." Her voice thickened. "What if I fail you, Riordan?"

"You won't." He sounded confident.

And different. This was Riordan the man, she knew. Not the farce he so often enjoyed playing. Trickster puca. The BobGoblin. She couldn't believe she'd ever fallen for that act.

He touched her empty glass and turned his face toward her. "Would you mind?"

Her breath caught. He wanted to taste. At least this was something she knew she could do for him. They'd shared evening meals this way for some time now, and she was just glad he felt close enough to her to comfortably ask for a favor like this. "No. I don't mind at all."

Nodding, he poured more wine into her glass, emptying the bottle. Her eyes widened a little. If she finished off this glass, she'd be snoring under the table. But she wouldn't refuse him. It was little enough to offer him and well within her control. Unlike the curse, damn it all. So they would have wine.

She reached for the glass then, gently taking his hand in hers, pressed his fingertips to her jaw and throat. She raised the glass, parted her lips and let the sweet wine flow into her mouth. She held it there for a moment, letting it breathe and wrap around her tongue until her taste buds tingled.

Riordan sighed and relaxed against the cushions.

She swallowed and watched him. "More?"

"Please." He sounded rapt, his fingers still lingering at her throat and lips, while the sweet taste lingered on her tongue. It was much like their other evenings together, and yet different, too. Normally, they shared their meal at the table, where it didn't seem quite so intimate. Eating together at the kitchen table had felt stimulating but mostly harmless, like holding hands with a good-looking but platonic friend. But this was different.

She raised the glass again, sipped more of the wine, taking her time and letting them both take pleasure from it. She'd make this indulgence well worth a morning's hangover.

He chuckled, sounding tipsy.

After swallowing, she smiled at him. "Can you actually feel the effects of the alcohol, too?"

He shook his head lazily. "No. Not literally. I could get drunk from taste alone, though. It's been so long, you see. Sensory deprivation for so long. And now, I feel so much. See? This is what you give me. Friendship. Help. Compassion. Dedication. Kindness and affection. You're amazing to me. I don't deserve you. I know that. But thank you."

"Oh, Riordan." Her breath hitched.

"More?"

He sounded like such a kid for a moment, she laughed again. "I get it. I'm being buttered up so you can get drunk on my hangover."

"Saw right through me, did you?"

Still smiling over the rim of her glass, she watched him, so at ease. She let the wine linger in her mouth, let the tastes and scent waft upward until they tickled her nose.

"I still remember . . ." Riordan sounded drowsy. "The celebration we had for my coming of age, a decade or so before I was condemned. Everyone was dancing, playing, laughing. Eating and drinking the most wonderful things. Anything I wanted to experience, my slightest whim . . . all were granted. My magic, at last mature and mine to wield, swirled around us. It was almost too heady." He paused, obviously lost in the memory, as she took another drink of wine. He turned his head and she felt his gaze caress her, almost a physical presence. "But being here like this, with you, I feel almost overstimulated. More so even than then, and I thought nothing could top that experience."

Feeling drunk now and touched beyond words, Mina covered her mouth, letting the tears well up. "Oh, Riordan. God, it's just going to kill me when you finally hate me."

He stilled, his hand still cupping her throat, fingertips resting gently against hers. "But why would I hate you?"

"You don't now. But when I can't break this curse, you will." Her voice broke. "And you're all I have left." If she were sober, she'd really hate sounding so pathetic.

"Sssssh." He took the half-empty glass out of her hand and set it on the table. Then he tugged her closer, pulled her onto his lap. "You have it all backwards. Don't you see?

You are my everything. And you have been since the moment we met. But you . . . you could have anyone you wanted."

"Oh, right. That's why Jackson wanted brainless Tiffy with the inflatable boobs more than he wanted me."

That surprised a laugh out of him. "Inflatable boobs? They make those?"

"And why Teague's so enthralled with me he hasn't called or visited me in weeks. Obviously, it's because I'm so fascinating he suffers from performance anxiety. He feels unworthy."

Riordan shook with laughter now.

"And that's why even a horny shape-shifter who hasn't had sex in two thousand years finds me so irresistible he hasn't laid a hand on me." She spoke softly now. "Except platonically."

Riordan stilled. His hands, which had been rubbing gently up and down her back and shoulders in an effort to soothe, stilled as well. Then they began to move again. Just as gently, but with leashed intent. She could feel power trembling in his fingertips. Leashed power. Not Riordan's leash. The Druid's leash. But then, the man Riordan was today would know how to leash his own power.

"Mina mine. The truth is, Jackson's a fool for wanting any woman but you. And Teague, if he's too damn blind to see you for the wonder that you are, is completely unworthy. As for your platonic puca . . . if you only knew."

"Only knew what?" She was breathless. Pulling back, she stared hard into the blur that was his face. At times, she could almost see the glow of his eyes, feel his regard. This was one of those times. How she wished—

"How *I* wish."

She could feel the smile in his voice.

"Yeah, sometimes the mind-reading bit is helpful. Sometimes it's dangerous. I've wanted, so many times . . ." He paused, obviously wrestling with himself. He turned his gaze toward the coffee table, where her nearly empty glass and the empty wine bottle sat. Then, seeming to come to a decision, he turned back to her. "I've wanted you more than my next breath. More than my magic. More than my freedom. Of all the punishment I've endured, knowing that I can't have you . . . seeing you and knowing I can never have you . . . that you'll be someone else's—*that's* the hardest. *That* could break a man."

"Oh." Mina stared, moved beyond words. "You . . ." She exhaled shakily. Gaze steady on the glow she saw beyond the blur, she raised her hands. Paused.

He didn't move. He didn't object.

Carefully, she touched his chest. It was hard. Warm. Tingly. She slid her hands toward his throat, where his tunic ended in a V. Settling her fingertips inside the V, she felt the heat rising, felt his breath on her face and moving beneath her touch. Carefully, again giving him a chance to stop her, she slid her fingers to his neck, his throat, where she felt him swallow, then his jaw, skimming the edges of the mystery beyond her sight.

"Mina . . ." But he still didn't stop her.

She slid her fingers higher, felt the crackle of magic beneath them and the formation of . . . lips. His mouth. She stilled, feeling both shocked and exhilarated. His face. *She could feel his face.* Carefully, as if someone might stop her, she slid her fingers higher, to trace lean cheeks, imposing cheekbones, the sharp blade of a nose. "So arrogant." Enthralled, she tried to smile. "You blueblood, you."

Amazingly, she felt his lips curve under her palm. Just an impression, not substantial. But more than she'd had before. Gently, she trailed her touch across what seemed to be eyelashes. They moved. A blink? "Oh, I wish I could see."

"But you do see me. You saw me even when I tried to hide." His voice lowered. "You are my world right now. I have nothing without you. And you give me so much."

"Sssssh." She moved closer, as if, fingertips still lingering, she could finally see his face.

When she was so close she could feel his breath—his breath!—she tipped her face so their foreheads and chins were aligned. Their mouths aligned.

Then, groaning, he seemed to break free and his mouth was on hers. It was and yet it wasn't. She could feel a crackle of hot energy, the will that strove relentlessly to break through the magic and physically form. The crackling remained. But his heart was so close this way. And suddenly her hands had a will of their own, wandering his cheeks, his silky hair, those wide shoulders, a chest that made her heart skip a beat even now.

His wandered just shy of her breasts and she could feel his chest heaving once, twice, before his fingers curled in on themselves. Gently, so carefully, he pulled back. "I can't do this. Mina mine, I swear to God I would have you if I could and savor every moment. How I want to be the man to show you at least a fraction of the love you deserve." He paused. "But I am not. And I wouldn't hurt you for anything."

"But—"

"Can I just hold you for a while?"

She laughed, shakily, her heart breaking a little. "Like you'd have to ask. Yes. Please hold me."

Settling her more comfortably in his lap, he wrapped his arms around her and leaned back against the couch cushions.

Sighing, at peace and yet aching, she dropped her head to his shoulder. She could sleep like this. Her eyes drooping, her head muzzy from the wine, and his arms so warm and encompassing. She felt safe. Loved even. Even if she couldn't keep him. How could it feel so good and hurt so much at the same time?

\* \* \*

Long minutes later, after her breathing had deepened, Riordan dropped his head forward to rest on hers. He held her like that for a long, long time. Until he knew she might wake soon and then it would be too late. He had to erase this. He couldn't let her wake with these memories. It wasn't fair.

Puca to the rescue, he mocked himself. And, as they say, the drunkard's sleep is the puca's kingdom. He'd been completely mindful of this fact when he told her his feelings. The woman had polished off almost a full bottle of wine, all by herself—and had been sweet enough to share the experience with him.

He wouldn't reward that generosity with a broken heart. She deserved the normal life she craved so badly, not life with a damned horse or faceless man, or later, nothing but a nagging voice in her head and a cornerstone hanging from her neck. Mina was wrong. She was the one who would grow to hate him. He didn't think he could bear that.

Resolute and aching, he brushed a hand over her face, laid his cheek to hers and whispered a few words in her ear. He paused, remembering and wishing, but it was done.

She would remember none of this when she woke. Come morning, he would just be her puca again. Her quest and her burden. But at least he'd had tonight with her. He'd have to commit the experience to memory so he could savor it for a long time. Because even if he did manage to break free of this curse, be it days, decades or lifetimes from now . . . He smiled. He knew he'd never find another woman like his Pandemina.

A woman so unafraid to open the box and find him inside.

He'd left her.

The awareness was there even before Mina opened her

eyes. She found herself, not snugly cuddled in the lap of her favorite puca, but tucked in her own bed. Alone.

"Riordan?"

No answer. She frowned. What time was it anyway? She sat up, groaning as the action sent her head pounding. Right. The wine. She should have known better.

Well, actually, she *had* known better. She just hadn't cared. Given the same choices and a promise of the same outcome, she would choose the hangover every time.

Grinning ruefully, she swept the blankets aside to discover she was still wearing last night's clothes. Riordan, apparently, had played the gentleman, which was quite the shame. Or not. She'd rather be completely aware if the guy was going to take advantage. Aware and participating.

Sure, he said a relationship between them was impossible, but there must be a way. Had to be. With that thought, she headed toward the bathroom for toothpaste and ibuprofen. Not necessarily in that order. And when she emerged twenty minutes later, she was freshly showered and anticipating a puca waiting for her.

But he wasn't there. Probably just giving her privacy. After pulling on jeans and a sweater, she went to seek him out. Maybe he was making her breakfast. She remembered the wine and smiled. Something else they could enjoy together.

As she neared the kitchen, she heard faint noises indicating that she'd guessed correctly. Riordan was in the kitchen and he was cooking. Smiling, she snuck up on the chef and wrapped her arms around his waist from behind. "'Morning, my handsome stallion."

He stilled, then laughed shortly. "You'll never let me live down that Catherine the Great comment, will you? Now back off before you get burned." He sounded oddly strained.

She let her hands slide free and backed up a step. Moving to the side, she tried to peer into a face that she knew was there. Had to be there. She'd felt it herself last night. "Is something wrong?"

"Hmm? No, of course not. I'm just making you breakfast. Even swap, remember? I cook, you help break the curse."

"No, the deal is you cook and I let you taste it with me."

He shrugged. "That's okay. I'm good for now." He slid the eggs onto a plate and set it on the table for her. "Chow, baby. We have some curse-breaking to do." He turned back to the counter, set the skillet in the sink and ran water into it like she'd showed him. "I've been reading up—"

"Why are you acting this way?"

"What way? I'm not channeling the BobGoblin." There was amusement in his voice. "This is really just me this time. Why, do I sound goofy?"

"No, worse. You sound distant. I thought . . . what about last night?"

He tensed, the humor, even a pretense of it, leaving him. "What about last night?"

"Well, didn't it mean anything to you?"

"Didn't what mean anything to me?" He sounded alarmed now.

"Oh, good god. So even pucas get cold feet the morning after. This is too much. I didn't ask you for anything. But you gave me the impression that we were on the same page. You know. Feelings-wise."

She raised her eyebrows, feeling increasingly stupid when he didn't reassure her. "Look, maybe you said more than you wanted to say to me. Maybe you didn't even mean half of what you said. You felt bad for me. I get that. But you can't tell me now that you feel nothing for me beyond friendship and gratitude. I remember everything you said and how you said it. I was there."

"Yes. You were, weren't you?" His voice sounded hollow.

Almost as though he were speaking in her head again, but he wasn't. "You remember."

"Hey, I wasn't *that* drunk. Of course I remember. It meant a lot to me. I thought it meant something to you, too."

He didn't move for another few moments, and she felt the intensity of his gaze on her. Finally, he sighed and shook his head. "I'm an idiot. I should have known better. I thought I could glam it up, make you forget—"

"*What?*"

He tensed even further, but more on an oh-shit level than anything else.

"Explain. What do you mean by glam it up?"

"It's a fairy trait I inherited from my father." Riordan spoke with slow reluctance. "Or a skill, rather. To glamour means to . . . achieve an illusion in the human mind. We can cloud perceptions or memories. Influence them. Even painlessly remove them. It's how we protect our culture and yours and maintain the human barrier of disbelief."

"And this is what you tried to do to me?"

Riordan nodded.

Mina stared, taking it all in. "You. Yooooouuuuu. Oh. I can't believe this. The most romantic evening in my life and you were just playing with me. And you intended, all along, to take the memory from me."

"But I didn't mean—"

"Didn't mean what you said last night? Bull. You meant every word of it. Your hands were trembling, you meant those words so much. Why would you want to glamour it off, try to make me forget? Did you think I didn't care the same way? Well I *do*. Hell, you're in my head half the time. Can't you tell what you mean to me?"

"Yes." He spoke softly. "But you'll get over it if I help you."

"That's what this is? You want me to get over you?"

"It can't work between us, Mina. You know it can't. I was just trying to—"

"You wanted to get out of it the easy way—get rid of the memory so you won't have any sloppy tragedy to deal with when it's time to say good-bye. Well, too damn bad. I'm here and I remember. So there."

He sighed. "Obviously. And even more obviously, I should have realized I couldn't pull off a glamour on you, of all people. You're my guardian. No doubt Akker was trying to protect you from my influence."

"No doubt." She bit off the words. "Men. I swear. In every form you can all act like gutless imbeciles, can't you."

So saying, she dumped the eggs he'd cooked for her into the sink and left the room.

Once she slammed the door behind her, Mina paced the bedroom, angry and hurting. Even Jackson hadn't hurt her this much. Jackson was weak; she knew that. In fact, part of her was convinced that he'd wanted her to catch him in the act and thereby save him from the commitment she'd pressed him to make.

That was her own fault. Only a fool presses a reluctant man for a commitment.

And, she supposed, an even greater fool presses a reluctant puca for words of love. Or worse, a future together. And, oh, she could not believe that he would try to tamper with her memories like that. It was no less than a violation. Nobody should play with somebody's mind, especially on such a literal level. Major trespassing. She wouldn't tolerate it.

Just as she headed out the bedroom door to harangue him for this as well, the doorbell rang. She stopped short, then changed directions. Opening the front door, she encountered a face she hadn't seen in a while. Teague.

"Hi, Mina." He offered her an awkward but genuine smile. "I've missed you. Look, I feel like an ass and I need to explain— Can I come in?"

Wordlessly, she stepped back and motioned him inside.

"I'm sorry. I know I haven't called in a while. Weeks even." He turned to face her as she closed the door. "It's not that I haven't been thinking about you."

She cleared her throat and gestured awkwardly. "Yeah. Me too. I took a while returning your phone calls, I know. I guess I just thought . . ."

"That we'd run our course?"

She nodded.

"I could let you continue to think that, but it would be wrong." He eyed her intently. "The truth is, I've been confused and running from things."

"The law?" She tried a halfhearted joke.

That tugged a reluctant grin from him. "No. Not the law. Smart-ass."

She didn't respond.

He cleared his throat. "Look, I have something to say to you. It's something I was running from, but then I realized I couldn't run from it. Didn't really even want to." He met her eyes. "I've fallen in love with you."

She stared. "I think I need a drink."

He closed the distance between them and took her hand. "Yeah, I know. Smooth, suave, and I'm just sweeping you off your feet, right?" He gave her a rueful smile. "I screwed things up. And will likely continue to screw things up, given past experience. You see, I've never been in love before. Isn't that hilarious?" He grinned down at her, inviting her to share the joke.

"I see." She exhaled in a shaky whoosh. "Um. I need a few minutes. To digest a little. Can I get you anything? Something to drink?"

"No thanks." He studied her. "I've made you uncomfortable."

"Well, *I* need a soda." She forced a smile, her gaze sliding over his shoulder instead of meeting his eyes. "I'll be right back."

She escaped to the kitchen, closed the door and leaned against it. "This is seriously screwed up." She closed her eyes. It was really, really good to see Teague again. His handsome face, the sincere look in his eyes, the sense of humor. He was so hot—her dream man—and unlike Riordan, he was saying everything a dream man should say. All the right words.

He was perfect. Perfect for *her*. But how could any man be perfect? How could she believe in the perfect man? And yet, during the past weeks, she'd unbent enough to believe in something as unrealistic as a shape-shifting puca cursed by Druids. Why was it so much harder to believe in the existence of a man who was perfect for one Pandemina Dorothy Avery? Was she that jaded?

Carefully, still pondering, she peeled her spine off the door and aimed herself at the refrigerator. A soda. She opened the fridge, pulled out the milk and reached for a mug. As she was pouring, she focused and realized what she was doing.

"Losing it. Of course that's what I'm doing." She put the carton away, glanced around indecisively for a solution to her mug of milk, then simply poured it in the sink. Sometimes a girl just needed her chemical-laden carbonation. Grabbing a soda from the fridge, she returned to the living room and Teague.

Leaving the kitchen door open behind her, she focused on Teague, who was standing right where she'd left him. Obviously unsure of his welcome. "Have a seat." She wasn't petty. Hey, an I-love-you made up for a certain amount of absence, and she'd accept part of the blame for pushing him away, too. Besides, after this morning's romantic disappointment, a surprise love declaration was balm to a bruised ego and heart.

Teague dropped onto the couch, and she watched how his knees seemed to poke up too high. The man was tall. Easing back a little, he crossed an ankle over his knee and slid his supporting foot out a little. "Have you finished digesting?"

She smiled ruefully. "No, I can't say that I have. You. Here. Saying that out of the blue. Yeah, that was pretty much the last thing I expected today." Riordan. She'd expected Riordan. Curious, she glanced around, wondering where he'd gone.

*I'm trying to give you the privacy I should have given you before. Consider yourself, for all intents and purposes, alone with Teague.*

She closed her eyes. Oh, Riordan.

No response.

She opened them and focused on Teague, who was eyeing her intently. She took a long drink from her soda and set it aside.

"I guess this is overwhelming."

She nodded. He could say that again.

"I'll be honest and say I was hoping to overwhelm you. At least enough to talk you into giving me another chance."

"Another chance?"

"Let me make it up to you. I know you have feelings for me. Or at least you did?" He eyed her in question.

She couldn't deny that. There was a whole mix of feelings she hadn't completely identified. Chief among those had been her yearning for the happily-ever-after that she'd always been denied and always desired. Add to that a body to stop traffic, enough charm to melt her knees, and a sense of humor to soften her heart . . . there was a lot there. She'd been just this side of falling in love with him before. Could she fall now? Maybe she already had and was in denial.

She stood up. Was she infatuated with Riordan and in love with Teague? Riordan, after all, represented fantasy and adventure. Excitement. Lust. The forbidden. Maybe, on a boring day-to-day basis, without the shared challenge of breaking a curse, he'd lose a lot of his charm. Maybe.

Yeah, she doubted it. Not that she could ever have a day-to-day with him anyway.

And so there was Teague. But how could she get any more involved with a man when she was keeping a secret from him—a secret as big as guardianship of a puca?

She should tell him and see how he reacted. Maybe?

She glanced back at him.

"Mina?"

"I just need a minute or two to think. Okay?" More than a minute or two.

He nodded. "Take all the time you need. Just make your answer a yes." He grinned at her.

How about a qualified yes? Or not. If she really cared about him, she should tell him about Riordan. If Teague was the guy for her, she should be able to share with him even her weirdo secrets, lifelong bogeyman or no.

Determined, she turned back to him. "I would like that, too. But first I have to . . ."

He leaned forward attentively.

She couldn't continue.

"But first you have to . . . ?"

"Have to . . ." She swallowed, opened her mouth again. "To . . ."

"End another relationship? Renew your library card? Ask your mother?"

She smiled reluctantly, as he'd obviously intended. Come on. She could do this. Just a short, freaky explanation and she could move forward with this amazing guy. Have everything she ever wanted. Just get the words out. It couldn't be that bad, right? Hey, sexy, fairytale-perfect man, did I mention that I've been living with a shape-shifting puca? Yeah, he's my ward forever unless I break this ancient Druid curse. Teague would be shocked, sure, but she could at least try to convince him she wasn't nuts and that this was a workable situation. Right?

Um. Maybe?

She licked her lips, glanced at him. Steeled herself. Risky or not, she had no choice. Tell him or it had to be over. "First I have to . . ." She inhaled. "Tell you . . ." This was good. She was closer. Just a few more words to start the conversation. "About . . ." Yes. Getting. There.

He waited.

She could tell him. If she loved him, she'd have to trust him in this. If she trusted and loved him, she had to tell him. If she loved and trusted him, she'd feel *capable* of telling him. If she loved him . . . she'd trust him. But . . . She slumped. Apparently she didn't trust him enough. Or love him.

Shit. She dropped back into her chair and buried her face in her hands. Why? Why did this stupid thing always happen to her? She had, absolutely, the worst taste in men. What was her problem, anyway? This perfectly wonderful man comes to her door, tells her he loves her and she can't even bring herself to trust him because—

Shit.

# CHAPTER TWELVE

Mina raised her head and met Teague's eyes. "I'm sorry. Honestly, you have no idea how sorry I am about this. But I just can't. Not because of anything you've done or haven't done, but because . . . I'd be leading you on." She inhaled. Seriously. The absolute worst taste in men. This sucked. "I'm in love with someone else."

Teague stared, obviously nonplussed. Not heartbroken, really, just at a loss. And troubled. "You're sure?"

She smiled a little. "About my decision, or about being in love with someone else?"

He leaned forward, bracing elbows on knees, and met her eyes. "Both. I can give you time. And I'd be so attentive, I swear. You could forget this other guy. Even if you're not in love with me now, maybe we could just spend time together. Help you get over this other guy first and see where things go from there. I mean, it sounds like you know he's wrong for you. Am I right?"

She shrugged. "That doesn't seem to matter. And as for getting over him . . . I don't see that happening anytime soon. I'm obviously a complete idiot. You're a wonderful man and I'm going to hate myself for breaking things off with you, but it's the right thing to do. Goodbye, Teague." She stood up, and Teague reluctantly rose to his feet.

"Sure you don't want to think about it? You might change your mind."

She grimaced a little. "I won't." Because she was an imbecile with stars in her eyes and rocks in her head. Her perfect man, with the bod of the sexiest toolbelt fantasy she'd ever imagined, kind and quick-witted, self-supporting, dreams that jived with her own ambitions . . . "A complete idiot," she murmured, then smiled ruefully at him.

He smiled back, green eyes thoughtful as he studied her face. "All right. This other guy . . . he's one helluva lucky man. I hope he realizes that. Goodbye, Mina." He kissed her cheek, then turned and walked out the door.

Mina stared after his truck as it pulled away, then swung the door violently closed. "Oh. Dammit dammit *dammit*." She kicked the couch. Kicked the chair. Went ahead and kicked the door. "Ouch! *Damn* it!" She staggered a few steps, swinging a moderately wild gaze around the room. "Riordan! Get your horsey butt in here. Now!"

"I'm here." The words came softly from behind her.

Mina jumped and whirled, knocking her shoulder into the doorjamb where he lingered. "Ouch and damn it again!"

Riordan tipped his head forward, obviously training his gaze on her. She couldn't see it, but damned if she wasn't absolutely certain he was smiling.

"Don't you laugh at me. This is all your fault. *Yours*." She poked an index finger into his chest.

"My fault? That you beat the hell out of your own furniture?"

"That's not funny."

"Wellll—"

"Shut up. Just shut up. How dare you come into my life, mess with it, make me fall in love with you. A freaking shape-shifter. I'm in love with a damned puca. A faceless man tied to a rock and doomed to disembodiment unless a schoolteacher—that would be me—breaks a Druid curse for him. Do you know what a loser that makes me?"

"You're not a loser."

"Oh, no? First I can't hold on to the guy I've been sharing a home and a mortgage with, then I reject the guy who actually surpasses my longtime vision of the perfect man, and now I'm hopelessly in love with a man I can never have. A man who's not even human. Sounds loser-ish to me."

"It sounds brave as hell to me. I don't deserve your love." He gently tucked a lock of hair behind her ear.

Mina pulled back until his hand dropped away from her face. "No, you don't—not after you tried to trick me with that whole glamour bit. But apparently, my brain doesn't get a say in this. So what are you going to do about it?" She stared up at him, desperately wishing the blur would magically clear so she could try to read his thoughts. So not fair. This mind-reading bit should be reciprocal, damn it.

Especially when he didn't reply to her question. Mind-reading or no, she had her answer when he dipped his head, obviously breaking eye contact.

"See? Major loser." She turned and stalked into the kitchen.

"Mina."

"Oh, don't bother with excuses. Or explanations. I've heard them all and I don't need the BobGoblin putting his quirky little spin on them. This is humiliating enough."

"I don't mean it to be." He paused, then continued in a lower voice. "I just wanted to tell you that your ex left a message on your answering machine. He's dropping by tonight."

Appalled, Mina stomped back into the living room. "But *whhyyyyy*?" she wailed. "Because I need yet one more social challenge to round out a sucky day?"

"He mentioned a delicate issue involving a former student?"

She stared, her turn to be nonplussed. "Ye-es?"

He sighed. "Tiffany whatserface's son. That's all I know."

"Oh, good god. Just what I needed today."

And, sure enough, later that evening, there came a knock on the door. Mina glared over her shoulder at Riordan. "Go do your doggie poof thing or leave or something. So I can get this." She turned back to the door, waited a few seconds to compose herself. Then opened it.

"Jackson." She spoke with all the enthusiasm of a belligerent child facing the principal. Or of a woman facing her cheating school superintendent of an ex-boyfriend.

"Hi, Mina. Did you get my message?"

"Sure. Whatever. What do you want?"

"Can I come in? I need to talk to you. It's a work matter."

Surrendering to the inevitable, she swung the door wide and stepped back into her living room. Jackson followed, closing the door behind him. "It's about Nathan. Er, Tiffy's son."

"Great."

"Well, first, let's acknowledge that he was an innocent in all this. We all only want the best for him and . . ."

As Jackson rambled on through his politically correct speech, Mina stared up at him, wondering how she could have missed all the signs. Weak chin. Eyes that darted to meet hers and then shied almost immediately away. Sure, they were a deep blue and beautiful as could be. That didn't mean there was substance behind them. And sure, they were kind eyes. When he looked at kids or spoke of them, there was a wealth of kindness in them.

That's what attracted her to him when they first met. A

man who could make children both love him and respect his authority . . . she knew what a narrow line that was, but he walked it well. She could still admire that about him, if nothing else. He was a true children's advocate, regardless of what the morality police might have said about their mortgage papers.

Mortgage—oh, shit. She'd never wondered how Jackson had reacted. He knew she didn't have the money—

*Relax. I took care of it. Tiffy, remember? In her "religious fervor" I'm sure she was every bit as convincing as that buyout offer was legitimate. Jackson now believes an inheritance from your distant Cousin Gladys paid off his half of your house. Which is true, after all. You inherited me and I paid it off.*

Mina chewed on her lip. It sucked to be both indebted to and angry with a man. Puca. Whatever.

*You owe me nothing. I owe you everything.*

Riordan.

"It's like this, Mina." Jackson shifted his weight, frowning in concentration. "The boy wants to rewind his life to the way it was earlier this fall. And that means putting you back in it as his teacher. You know Nathan loves to write, and apparently you brought that out in him more than his current teacher does. He wants you back." He paused significantly. "And Tiffany fully supports this."

"Well, thank God for that."

"Don't be snide. This isn't easy for her either."

"At least she has a decent support system in you, though, huh? Superintendent and all, you can get her anything she wants. Why are you bothering to ask me?"

"Tiffany and I aren't seeing each other anymore. She went back to her husband and refuses to speak to me except about school issues." He paused. "My . . . connection with Tiffany was a mistake on both our parts."

"Bully for you."

He eyed her. "So what's your decision?"

"Of course Nathan can come back to my class. That was never an issue. But why did you bother consulting me? You could have just plunked him down in my classroom one day and never discussed a word further with me."

"I don't know." His gaze slid away from hers. Again.

She sighed. He may not know, but she did. He felt guilty, probably had some regrets about dumping her and their life together. Maybe he was even hoping she'd make the first move. Make things easy for him and offer to take him back.

Tough. "I'll be happy to have Nathan in my classroom. He's an excellent student and a nice young man. Go ahead and pass on the news. So, if that's all . . . ?"

"Mina—"

"Look, I've had a long, rotten day already and I really just want to go to bed and pretend it never happened. Could we maybe discuss this in the morning? Over the phone, even? Where it's more appropriate?"

Nodding, he reluctantly turned back toward the door. Mina followed, refusing to feel guilty or soften toward him. Memories did not a relationship make. Just as he reached for the doorknob, the telephone rang.

"I have to get that. Could you lock the door behind you?"

"No problem."

Dismissing him, she turned back toward the kitchen, hurrying as the phone started its third ring. At sight of caller ID, she slowed and let the phone ring until her machine picked up. Her mother again. Mina knew she should answer, but it was just one more thing she didn't need today.

It was only later that Mina puzzled over the black blur that had swept past her as she listened to her mother's message.

"Hello, Jackson. Interesting to meet you finally." Riordan watched from the shadows as the blond man jumped and turned warily to face in his direction. Walking along the side of a darkened road, lost in thought, Jackson was just begging to be roadkill. So Jackson lived close enough to Mina to walk home? Probably not a coincidence, whether Jackson acknowledged it or not. The man was still drawn to his ex.

"Who are you?" Jackson took a step back, hand unconsciously patting his back pocket where a man often kept his wallet.

"I'm not going to rob you, if that's what you're wondering." Riordan smiled, knowing the man couldn't see him clearly in the dark. He'd taken care to meld his shadow with the bushes and a tree branch hovering overhead.

Hesitantly, Jackson dropped his hand back to his side and shifted his weight. He squinted into the trees, obviously trying to distinguish the speaker from shadows. "So what do you want, then? And how do you know my name? Do I know you?"

"No, you don't know me. But I know of you. I'm here to help you, Jackson. I'm giving you a gift that few men are lucky enough to receive." God knew Riordan himself wasn't lucky enough. No, instead, his was the hell of bestowing this gift upon a man as unworthy as Jackson.

So perhaps it was Riordan's job to ensure the man gained sufficient worth. Determined, if resentful of it, Riordan lunged forward and, before Jackson could do more than goggle at him, swept the man up onto his back.

"What the hell?" Jackson scrambled for purchase as Riordan galloped off the road and into the night.

"You want Mina back." Riordan whispered it into the man's mind.

Jackson started. "Who—"

"Don't turn around." Clouding the man's mind just a little, Riordan purposely implied he was a second rider behind Jackson. "Answer the question. You want Mina."

"Well. Yeah. Sort of. I miss her. Why? Are you her new boyfriend? Hell, I didn't mean to poach, if that's what this is about. She's all yours. Yeah. I mean, women are women, right? I can find another. Mina's all yours."

"Wrong answer." Riordan increased his pace, gazed grimly ahead. It was going to be a long night.

He whipped sharply left, nearly dumping his protesting rider before turning sharply right so the man could regain his balance. "Lesson one: Women are not interchangeable. Each is different and deserving of respect. Lesson two: You don't deserve Mina. At all. Ever. You're going to have to work to get her back and work harder to keep her happy with you. Got it?"

"But I thought—" Jackson broke off on a sharp scream as Riordan lunged into the trees, nearly clotheslining his clumsy rider.

"Wrong again."

"Right. Wrong again. What's right?"

Riordan ground his teeth. "Did you ever love Mina? At all?"

"I—" Another shriek.

"Too slow. Speak up, asshole."

"Yes. Yes, I loved her." Jackson lowered his voice from shriek level to merely harried breathlessness as Riordan eased his pace. "But Mina's different."

Riordan kicked up his back legs, eliciting another yell from his rider. "A qualifier, Jackson. You forgot the necessary qualifier."

"Necess—?" Jackson yelled again. "Damn it, I can't talk or think when you do that. Do you want answers?"

"I want the right answers."

"My right answers or your right answers?"

Riordan slowed fractionally. The man had a point. If they weren't one and the same, this whole endeavor was for nothing. "Answer this straight. Do you want Mina back and are you willing to do what it takes to get her back?"

"Y-yes. Yes. I do. I . . . I've never known anyone like

Mina. She is different—different in a *good* way, so don't try to kill me over the qualifier again." Jackson paused. "So are you, like, her guardian angel?" He laughed nervously.

Riordan tossed his head. "You can think that if it helps. I'm looking out for her is all you need to know."

"Got it. Respectful of Mina or the vengeful guardian angel kills me."

"Now you get it."

"I never meant to hurt her." Jackson spoke low but emphatically. Riordan ducked and Jackson held tight. "I swear I didn't want her to see what she saw. And I left because I couldn't look her in the eye. You're right. I don't deserve her. I never did. I knew that. But do you think . . . I could *work* to deserve her?"

So Jackson was willing to see the light. That should please him. Riordan didn't pause, didn't waver in his stride, but his thoughts grew increasingly erratic despite himself. Could he really do this? This was so far beyond what he'd ever had to do. Even the stone. This was worse. "Can you take care of her like she deserves? Will you stay with her and be faithful to her?"

"You mean forever—like *marry*—" The man yelped, cutting off his own question. "I—yes! Yes. I was getting to that point. Eventually. I just think—" He shrieked again.

It would be a long, *long* damned night. Riordan grimly plowed ahead. "So tell me, Jackson. Ever see the city of Richmond from the rooftops?"

Should she do it? Mina continued pacing, wearing down a path she'd walked for nearly two hours now: around the kitchen, figure-eight into the living room and around the coffee table, back into the kitchen and . . .

Should she? She hadn't pulled that trick on Riordan in a very long time. It seemed so disrespectful now. Sure, in his BobGoblin mode, she'd had no trouble invoking the devil by speaking of him, but now . . .

Granted, part of her didn't want to see him right now. She was too angry. He wasn't even willing to give them a chance. All they had to do was break the curse, right? Then Riordan would be free to be with whomever he wanted.

Mina paused. Surely it wasn't because he didn't want her. He'd sounded so heartfelt . . . but he was a shape-shifter, so maybe . . .

Where the hell was he? Riordan? *Riordan?* He still wouldn't answer. He was purposely tuning her out. "Ugh. It's not enough that real men tune me out, but now even the horsey ones do. This could really give a girl a complex—"

*Knock, knock, knock.*

The door. Why would Riordan . . . ? What if he was hurt? Dear God, if he'd—Mina hurried to throw it open. "Jackson." She breathed again. Annoyed. She focused on the darkness behind him, but though she felt eyes watching her, she could see nothing. Then she focused again on the—sweating?—man in front of her. "Why are you here? I distinctly said goodnight to you earlier."

"Mina, please. Hear me out. Can I come in?"

"Look, this really isn't a good time."

"Please. We were together for years. Surely you can spare me a few minutes. Let me speak my piece and I won't bother you again unless you want me to."

Distracted from her worries by his urgency, Mina focused more intently on Jackson. "Something's wrong."

"No. Surprisingly enough, I think something's finally right. Please, can I come in?"

"Oh, fine. It's like Grand Central Station around here." Remembering her earlier encounters with men today, Mina frowned and grouched back at him. "Just don't bother to declare your undying lo—"

"Mina, I love you."

"Oh, good god. You, too? What, is Cupid taking pot-

shots at men in my living room? Suddenly Mina's wonderful and loveable and everybody wants her except—"

"Please." Jackson snagged her hand and turned her to
face him. "You know me."

"Correction: I *thought* I knew you."

"I know. And . . . look, when I saw that offer from you to
buy my half of this house . . . well, it was something of a
shock for me. Essentially, it was a formal dissolution of
everything you and I had built together. It made me realize
exactly what I'd destroyed. I really screwed up."

"No, actually, I was the one who screwed up. You know,
when I decided I was in love with you. Major, *major* screw-
up." She smiled tightly. "I'm done with that."

"I know. But I can be different now." He ducked his head
to stare intently into her eyes. "I swear it. I'm ready to be
the man you thought I was. I am that man. I can be that
man. Just give me a chance."

"What the . . . ?" This was just plain eerie. Freaky.

He dropped to one knee, his gaze relentlessly holding
hers. "I know this is sudden, but I also know you need
proof. I'm a different man, and I want so much more now.
More of us."

"Oh. My. God." She stared down into his eyes. They
were clear, intent, utterly determined and open. "You're
not going to—"

"Yes. I am." He held her hand tightly in his, his expression almost fervent now. "Mina. Pandemina Dorothy Avery. Will you—"

"Stop. Now." She yanked at his hand but couldn't seem
to budge him.

"I don't want to. Unless you need time. I can give you as
much time as you need to be ready. I have to work to earn
your trust. I know that. I have to deserve you—"

His phrasing was so much like—and the dogged, single-minded persistence—Mina closed her eyes, feeling her cheeks heat with fury and utter humiliation. Without opening them, she muttered low, "By any chance . . . have you been horseback riding this evening?"

He frowned, his grip slackening. "Why, do I smell?"

She groaned, trying to rein in the fury. Rein in. Get it? The whole damned joke was on her. "You need to leave. Now." She jerked her hand away, marched toward the door and yanked it open. Stepping outside, she peered angrily into the darkness. She saw slight movement. Someone was out there, damn it. "Riordan! You just come back here so I can kick your shape-shifting ass. This is outrageous."

"Mina?" A concerned voice from behind. "You said it was a long day, but . . . are you okay?"

She cast her ex a dismissive glance. "You're still here? You need to go. Don't worry. I think the effects will wear off. Mostly. Just avoid dark horses from now on."

Stepping out onto the porch, Jackson moved closer and spoke low. "You know about him? He told me no one would believe me if I said anything."

Mina stumbled, mentally. What was she doing? Declaring to all and sundry that she had a shape-shifter living with her? Ease back, idiot. "It was just a metaphor. Writing teacher, remember? I was trying to sound mysterious. Why don't you go home and ponder it?"

Whirling, she stepped past him and went inside, letting the door slam shut behind her. Long moments later, she heard slow footsteps descending her porch steps. Jackson had left.

Coast clear.

Mina scanned her living room grimly. "Riordan?" No response. She strode through the kitchen, then rounded into her bedroom. He wasn't there either. "Fine, don't answer me. You asked for it. Speak of the devil."

"Hey!" Riordan, in manly form, stared up at her from

the floor in front of her dresser. "I thought you weren't going to do that anymore."

"That's when I thought you respected me. That I could trust you." She bent toward him, hands fisted at her sides.

"But I do."

"So explain Jackson, then. Unless you're going to tell me you didn't pull the puca ride stunt on him?"

Silence.

"God." He might as well have slapped her across the face. "Isn't it enough that you're breaking my heart yourself? Do you have to try to set me up for another fall? Do you *hate* me?"

"I could never hate you. And I didn't brainwash Jackson. He really does love you. He just had some maturity and commitment issues that needed working out."

"So, what, you beat them out of him?"

"No, I just showed him the light. He went toward it willingly, too, by the way. He just needed clarity to envision what kind of future he wants and sufficient motivation to make his life changes now." Riordan paused, his voice lowering. "The future he wants is with you. He really does want you back. I can't make him feel that. That's all him. I swear it."

Mina opened her mouth, wanting to respond but not sure how. Gesturing helplessly for a moment and blinking back tears, she finally dropped her hands with a slap against her thighs.

Riordan rolled to his feet and stood tall before her. "Jackson's yours if you want him. Things can be like you always wanted them. Before I came into the picture, even before Tiffany came into the picture. Better yet, the guy knows what he wants now, so he's not going to repeat his mistakes. He wants you. All you have to do is call him and you can have your life back."

Mina stared up at him, wanting so badly to see his face.

Why had he done this? What was he hoping to achieve? Did he just want to be rid of her?

"No, I don't want to be rid of you."

Mina growled.

"I'm sorry. Your thoughts are at my disposal and I can't help it right now. What I want is simple. It's to *not* destroy your life or make more trouble for you than I already have."

"You—Oh, shut up. I mean it. Just shut up right now. You honestly think I want Jackson back? That I can just pick up my emotions and plop them all over him instead of you? Just because you said I could and told him he wants this?"

"You used to love him, and like I told you, he does want—"

"Yeah? Well it just so happens I don't care what he wants. I care what *I* want." She paused, staring up at him. "Aren't you going to say anything? I know you can read my mind. *You're* what I want. *You*. Somehow. All we have to do is break the curse."

"Mina." He sighed. "Look. I'm so grateful for your help. I am. But the reality is we may never break this curse. You could be saddled with me indefinitely."

"And you think that's a bad thing?" she asked him softly. "Before you, my life was a wreck. Get it? *Before* you, not after you. And I don't just mean the way you arranged it so I could keep my house and get my job back." She paused and shrugged. "Although I have to admit those were some pretty neat tricks."

She couldn't see it, but she knew that was a smile on his face. She reached out and took his hand. "You've opened my world. Cracked it wide open."

He winced. "What a guy. I busted your world for you."

"You know what I mean. I used to see only limitations. Now I see a whole world of possibilities and variation. I used to be so worried about what people thought of me. As if the world were so small that such a thing could be important."

"It did cost you your job."

"And possibly gave me back my job. And more."

"So you're in love with me because I showed you the world was bigger than you knew it was. Is that all you've got?"

She moved closer, letting her fingers trail up his forearms. "You know it's not. And what's more, you love me, too. I know you do. You confessed you had feelings for me—and meant it—when you thought I'd never remember it. You gained nothing from that, other than the chance to share what was in your heart. And that love—and it is love, so don't even try to play semantics with me by saying you never said the word—that *love* was so big you were willing to let me go to another man because you thought he was better for me. Shoot, I could have run to Jackson and forgotten all about you. And you would have let me. November first could have come and gone and you'd be back in your cornerstone. How would you get free then?"

He shrugged. "Another day, another guardian."

"But you can't . . . How could . . . ?" She spluttered. "You are absolutely impossible. I can't say anything right now that you won't deny. Can I?"

No response.

"Ah. I stand corrected. But maybe there's something else you can't deny." Eyeing him with challenge and every wicked promise she could project, Mina slid her hands up his arms to his shoulders and then snaked them around his neck.

"Mina—"

She closed in on him, locking her hand around her other wrist, just in case he tried to pull away. "What? Is this not a good idea? Unwise maybe? I can't believe the puca's preaching caution. Just where did you hide my horny little BobGoblin anyway?" She paused, mildly taken aback. "I didn't really say that, did I?"

"Yeah, actually—"

But she had her lips on his and her tongue in his mouth before he could finish. He held back at first, and Mina could feel his will in conflict, torn between two necessities, until he caved and wrapped his arms around her. When he tightened them convulsively, as though surrendering to a primal need denied too long, she raised a knee and climbed up, up, up that body as she'd longed to do since she first met him.

Shame? Screw shame. She was riding her puca tonight even if she had to force the issue.

Given the hard length she currently cuddled so brazenly as to be considered unfair, she was pretty damn sure force would be unnecessary. Just some truly manipulative coaxing. Who would have guessed a puca would have a freaking honor code, anyway?

"I can still read your thoughts." He breathed the words against her mouth.

"Good. I wanted you to." Smiling against his lips, she let her mouth trail to his chin and neck while grinding her pelvis slowly against his. She could feel him twitching through the material of his breeches. Growing harder, hotter, longer, if that were possible. "Don't you have someplace we need to be? Like on that bed, maybe?"

"Mina mine." He groaned when she tightened her legs around him for a particularly intimate grind. "You don't play fair."

"Park it on the bed, puca, or I won't be responsible for resulting injuries. You're not getting away from me."

So, one reluctant step after another, he finally toppled them onto Mina's bed, with Mina on top and in the mood to be utterly ruthless. "So. Let me go to another man, will you?" She yanked at his tunic and found a cord in her way, securing the garment at his waist. She unwound the cord until she could slide the material free.

"I didn't want to. I still don't want to." He groaned. "But what could I do? I want you to be happy with the house and husband and children you want." Riordan obligingly pulled his arms out of the tunic and wrapped them around Mina again, while she went to work on his pants.

Tugging them free of his waist, she looked into his face, sensing the golden glow of eyes, full of magic, full of love. Only for her. She knew this. "Do you think I want some cookie-cutter, generic husband and family? I don't. I'm in love with *you*, you jerk, and I don't see that changing any time soon. Now lift your butt so I can get you naked." When he shifted, giving her access, she glared at him. "You know, it would be nice if I didn't have to wrestle a man into bed. This is a little hard on the feminine ego—" She broke off on a squeak as he lunged to the side, reversing their positions.

"Is this better?" He rested on his elbows, obviously staring down into her face. She sensed a smile in the blurred depths.

"That all depends." She tightened an arm around his big, naked shoulders, raking the nails of her free hand lightly over his skin. "Are you going to make love to me now . . . or leave me again?"

He buried his face in her neck, his breath leaving him in a long, heartfelt *whoosh*. "Ah, Mina. It was never a matter of me leaving you." He kissed her neck and she felt her pulse skittering under his lips. "I intended for you to fall in love with someone else and leave *me*. Go and be happy and normal. Everything you want. You deserve to be happy. But letting you go to someone else is so damned hard to do." He nibbled lower, teeth raking lightly over her throat. "So hard. And when you're like this I damn well *don't want* to let you go."

"Then don't. Because I'm not going anywhere. And you . . ." She spoke softly, knowing she was fighting dirty. "You made me a promise. You said you'd never leave me. I intend to hold you to that promise." A girl had to do what a girl had to do.

"That *is* dirty." He pulled back slightly to frame her face with his hands. "Ah, Mina. To be a whole man again. To have you and keep you and never let you go. I want those things more than anything else in the world. But I should be strong enough to break my promise to you."

"Gee, that makes sense," she teased him softly. "Be man enough to break your promise to me? That's just wrong, Riordan. Be man enough to fight for us. Can you do that for me?"

"I want to. I want you." He lowered his voice. "I'd do anything within my power to have you if I could. Anything."

"But?"

"Know this, Mina. I love you. I would do anything to ensure your happiness." He seemed to wrestle with himself. "But, dear god, I have to have you. I'm that weak." He groaned. "So be it."

And suddenly his touch was everywhere, inciting a riot of sensation all over her body, from sensitive fingers inching under her top, dragging it up toward her breasts, to wildly talented mouth devouring her lips, her chin, her neck. He dragged her shirt off and, chest shuddering with his breath, slowly lowered his face to her breasts, letting his breath warm them. Rasping breath. Hungry and panting and she met him, breath for breath, heartbeat to heartbeat.

"Make love to me, Riordan. I need you."

"I will. I don't think I could stop now if I tried. God forgive me. Mina forgive me."

"Ha." She gasped when his mouth closed over a nipple through the lace of her bra. "Just you try stopping and see if I forgive you then."

But soon she was beyond speech, almost beyond thought. Riordan seemed to have more hands, more mouths than any mere man. Still seducing one nipple with his mouth, he managed to rake the rest of her clothes off. Soon, she was as nude as he was, arms and legs wrapped shamelessly around him, as though she could stop him from leaving her.

*I won't leave you.*

"I know. I believe you. Ooh." She inhaled sharply when his hands dragged their way, slowly, up the inside of her thighs, to part them wide.

"Pretty, pretty Mina."

She choked off a laugh, both embarrassed and aroused to near insanity. "You just haven't seen one in a few centuries."

"Not true."

"Do I want to know any more?"

He laughed, still so obviously eyeing her body, his hands gentle and affectionate. "Probably not. Let's just say I haven't touched one in centuries. But this . . . why, this was worth waiting for." Brushing her thighs with one hand, he explored her with the other, his fingers carefully trailing through the curls, subtly teasing with gentle tugs, tiny caresses. Wondering fingers rediscovered, marveled, experimented and played. Light strokes flirted with curls before burrowing closer, feinting left . . . drawing closer still . . . then, deliberately, slowly . . . traced a devastating line down the tight, aching nub of her center.

She gasped. Oh, yeah. Here was a man who hadn't played with a woman's body in centuries and centuries. And she would be his feast after the famine. Mina felt her orgasm approaching, just at the thought of it. Hers was the first one he'd had in eons.

Riordan chuckled. "That turns you on?"

She shuddered. "Yeah. So maybe I'm shallow."

"Mmmmm. Think so? Maybe I should check."

Mina arched her hips, coaxing that finger to return for a like caress, but this time it was bolder, inserting itself slightly into her wet opening. She panted, trying desperately not to shriek at him just to—

He buried the finger deep, pulled it out wet, and then

sank it even deeper. As she thrashed on the bed, feeling her body warring with itself, on the verge of an orgasm she'd wanted to slow down and savor . . . wait for him . . .

His lips touched her then and she screamed silently, shuddering as a tongue slipped in to join lips and fingers. The confusion of sensation won an immediate, almost violent orgasm from her shuddering body. As he wrung the last spasms from her, she closed her thighs over hands that still gently caressed. She opened her eyes to see him, but his head was still bowed and she saw only his dark hair and a silhouette in the shadowed bedroom.

"Now? Please, Riordan. Come into me now."

"My pleasure. Honestly. All my pleasure. That was beautiful." He slid higher on top of her, raining kisses as he went. He brought her hands high over her head to twine their fingers together as he slowly thrust himself into her body.

As he stretched her, she felt a zing of pleasure shoot from his body to hers. An aftershock and more. She arched her hips into his, and he surrendered to the pleasure, letting her take his weight as his hips thrust repeatedly against hers. He filled her again and again, savoring every stroke until, with a hoarse shout, he buried himself deep inside her body, shuddering.

"I love you, Riordan." She whispered it into his ear, so close to hers.

"And I love you. More than life itself."

Riordan kept his face turned into her neck, wishing, wishing for so much. A lifetime of moments like this. With Mina. He didn't care about the power and freedom that the Druids would almost certainly forbid him now. He'd wondered, suspected . . . and now he knew. He'd felt the telltale *zing* and tug when they'd made love, felt the shifting of magic that suggested he'd somehow broken the geas. Again. Thanks to his actions tonight, he could practically guarantee that he would never again see the light of day after November 1.

But she'd been worth it. Every minute of their time together had been a lifetime of joy. An eternity of it. It would have to last him. But would she ever forgive him?

"Hey." Mina slid her fingers through his hair, gently coaxing him to turn his face to hers. He didn't want to. As much as he wanted to see her lovely face, he knew what she would see when he did.

"Mina mine." He whispered the words into her moist skin. Moist with their love. "I do love you."

"Aw, Riordan, you say the sweetest things." She was teasing, but he could hear the thickness in her voice. The woman just hated to go soft on him. He loved that about her too.

"If I could, I'd give you sweet words, loving kisses, all the riches and joys the universe contains. You know that, don't you?" Even he could hear the fierceness in his voice. He couldn't help it. Somehow the time for smart-ass comments and bawdy humor just seemed past. At least for tonight.

"Riordan? You sound strange tonight. Is something wrong?"

Oh, yes. And oh, no. Heaven and hell in one beautiful conjunction. And, as sure as he breathed, he knew which realm he represented for her. After tonight, it could be that she'd grow to agree with him. That hurt the most of all.

Still, she deserved to know the truth. He raised his head and turned his face to hers.

She froze, eyes wide, mouth opening and closing in shock. Snatching the sheet convulsively, she pulled away from him.

"*Teague?*"

# CHAPTER THIRTEEN

"I believe I once told you I was known by several names."

Mina choked. Then, holding the sheet close, she tossed the covers and the man—whoever the hell he was—aside. He scrambled after her.

Still, Mina backed away from him, the sheet clutched high, and stopped only when her back hit the rough wall. She heard the lamp rocking on her dresser, tipping until Teague . . . Riordan . . . stilled it with a big hand. He turned that familiar gaze on her. The green eyes. But flecked now with gold. The dark curls. A combination of Teague's face and eyes . . . and Riordan's dark curls. "How? . . . Why?"

"Okay, take it easy a minute." It was Teague's voice, complicated by the more formal timbre of Riordan's. And yet, he sounded normal and soothing. Even rational.

"No. I will not take it easy. Just what the hell is going on here? Who—oh, god, but I swore I'd never be the kind of woman who had to ask this—but exactly who did I sleep with tonight? Who the hell are you?"

"Well, not Bob. Not really. Robert Goodfellow was

more of a joke of a nickname long ago bestowed on me by the locals after my disgrace.

"As for the other names . . . My mother, a human long dead, called me Teague. I was always called Riordan or Rioghbardon by my father and acquaintances. They all mean poet—or royal poet. It was the gift bestowed upon me at birth." He shrugged. "Not that I ever lived up to that gift or anything else I planned for my life."

"So I'm not feeling real sensitive right now, but I don't give a shit about your poetry or your dreams. I want to know who the hell I got naked with tonight. It's a reasonable question."

"Yeah, it is. And I'm stalling because it's complicated and I screwed up. Obviously. The truth is, I am both. I am Teague and I am Riordan."

"And you were going to tell me all this *when*?" She glanced meaningfully at the bed.

"I don't know. Originally . . . never."

"Oh. Gee. I feel so much better now." She tugged the sheet closer. At least a tramp could count on her lover being mortal and of the same species. What sort of obscene depravity had she committed, anyway? "Just what exactly are you? A freaking horse, a man, a figment of my imagination, what?"

"I am a puca. A shape-shifter. Cursed by a Druid to live a fragmented existence. Part of me mortal and part not."

"Huh?"

"The part of me you know as Teague is mortal. Thirty-four years ago, a man named Teague was born to the family he told you about—*I* told you about—and he'll live for another forty or fifty years before his body dies. His half of our soul will be reborn into another baby, who will also be named Teague." He spoke calmly as though reciting a weather report.

"The part you know as Riordan . . . that's my immortal part. As close to the real me as I can be without actually being whole. My powers, my heritage, my personality, even my memories all exist inside this form." He paused. "Before I screwed up two thousand years ago, these two were joined. I never died, but I could live and walk and talk in the free world as a man, and invoke my powers whenever I wished."

"How is that different from now?"

"This half of me, the puca half, was insubstantial and powerless until you released me from the cornerstone. Once you released me, I regained many of my powers but was still fragmented in soul, limited as a corporeal being, and bound indefinitely to you. Other restrictions, intended to protect you, also applied. Like, for example, the blurred face. The only reason you can see my face right now is because we made love."

"So we let that sacred cow out of the barn ourselves, huh? Well, I sure wish I could undo that now."

"I know."

"So you lied to me, all the time, in every form."

"That's not true."

"Gee. So maybe it was lie by omission. What I don't get now is *why*? Why bother? After all the weirdness you made me believe, this was just one more detail. I mean, how hard could it be? A mild little 'hey, honey, you know how most people are just themselves? Well, there are two of me. Sort of.' Okay, so it might have been complicated, but damn it, I thought we were in this together. I deserved to know the full truth." Before I fell in love with you.

He lowered his gaze. "I can still read your thoughts."

She lobbed the lamp at him. Naturally he caught it.

"I'm sorry." He set the lamp down. "I thought you should know."

"I should have known a lot of things." Carefully, deliberately, she imagined a steel-plated wall, joined by three others just like it, and lowered it in her mind to encase her thoughts. Then she slapped an airtight floor and ceiling on it, creating every banker's dream of an impregnable vault. Worked much better than flimsy cubicles, she decided.

He watched her, obviously well aware that she'd shut him out. She hadn't closed him off this completely since he'd shown her how to do it. Little by little, she'd given up even wanting him out of her thoughts.

She regretted that intimacy now.

"I know you have regrets."

She jumped.

"I can't read your thoughts. You shut me out. But your face is another matter. I see regret all over it. I'm sorry for that. More than you know. But I can't even promise that I would have acted any differently had I known how this would turn out. I wouldn't have missed what we've shared for the world. Even for my powers and my freedom back." He quirked the corner of his mouth in a smile so forced it obviously hurt.

He looked so sad. And lost.

Resigned.

But Riordan never, ever resigned himself to anything. Never. Something, other than the obvious disagreement, was horribly, terribly wrong. "What else is going on? What aren't you telling me?"

"Nothing important, Mina. I just want you to know that this wasn't casual for me. I love you. More than I thought I was capable of loving anyone. After all this time, I was pretty damn sure I'd become no better than the beasts I can resemble. Somehow, you made all that fade away and I once more became Riordan the man." Again, that smile that hurt her now. "Instead of the BobGoblin."

Mina tried to harden herself against him, but it was impossible. Even the vault she'd built in her mind weakened and diminished. He'd known so much misery already. No, he wasn't the beast, or even the caricature of himself he'd invented as a defense against the world, the disbelief, the years and the loneliness. So much loneliness. How had he stood it?

"You chased away the loneliness for me. That was worth everything."

There was a finality in his tone that chilled her to the core. Then the import of his words registered. "Everything? What do you mean everything? What have you done? What did we do?" She stared. Into his face. "Oh, Riordan. Why is it that I can see your face now? I thought it was because sex broke the curse, that you slept with me to get your life back, but—Oh, god. It's not, is it? What did we do?"

"It's over. That's all. Come November first, you'll have every bit of normalcy you ever wanted." He shrugged and looked away. "If you want Jackson back, I'm sure he'd come running. You could marry him, end your guardianship duties, and live the life you want. The man has seen the light for real, you know."

"I don't want Jackson."

He turned back to her. "What do you want, then?"

"I don't know anymore. I used to know."

"I've killed it all? What about your beliefs? Your dreams?"

"I don't know. I—*Riordan*?" She stared, horrified, as his body seemed to fade at the edges. "What's going on? Are you leaving now? Well, that's cheap. We're still in the middle of an argument and I still have questions—"

He was shaking his head. He was almost translucent now and as serious as she'd ever seen him. "I have no choice." He glanced at the cornerstone she still kept on her dresser.

Mina followed his gaze, comprehension thudding heavily in her stomach. "*No*. Disembodiment? That's what you meant by over. You knew this would happen."

"I suspected as much."

She stumbled toward him as his image grew increasingly faint, all but his eyes. He stared at her for a moment, his eyes so fierce, green flashing gold. Teague's eyes, with Riordan's passion and so much sadness. Then he dipped his head and he was gone.

"*No.*" She stared, hard, trying to see the outline that used to be there, even passed her hand through it. Not even a crackle of magic, like the first time she'd touched his face. Just emptiness.

She had to do something—"Speak of the devil." She waited, heart pounding. Hoping. Nothing. "*Speak of the devil, damn it!*" Her voice was shrill in the silence of the room. She waited a moment. Nothing. He was really gone.

All thanks to some bossy damn Druids, interfering in her life and her happiness. "Damn it. Damn all of you nature-worshipping, life-ruining hypocrites. How *dare* you dictate my life and my obligations and then rip everything apart when it suits you and your sadistic code of justice? Justice, my big white ass. Who made *you* judge and jury?

"*I* didn't. I'm just a damn schoolteacher and you go and make me guardian to a puca. Without my consent. But I did it and I tried to do right by him. I didn't mean to fall in love with him, but now that I have, we deserve a chance. He's different. He's changed. Whatever he did in the past, he's learned from it. Give him back to me."

*You still want me? But I lied to you.*

She froze, glancing feverishly around the room. "You can still speak to me?"

*Yes. Like this.*

She took a deep breath. And then another. At least she wasn't denied all contact with him. Just the physical kind.

Which really and truly sucked, by the way.

*You don't hate me.* He sounded wondering.

"No, damn it. I don't hate you. I love you. I'm just really, really pissed at you and even more pissed that you don't have a neck I can strangle right now." Still, her throat tightened until the tears slid down her cheeks and she dropped back to the bed. "Oh, Riordan. You knew what would happen and yet you still . . . Was it worth it? One night together like this ending so badly and so permanently?"

*Mina mine. Yes, of course, it was worth it. I love you. Always. I wouldn't have traded this time with you for anything in the world.*

"But this . . . I seduced you and now you . . . I swear I never would have tried if I'd known. But you knew. So why did you tease me early on about jumping in the sack? You didn't know me then. For all you knew, I was the kinky type to jump at a one-night-stand with a shape-shifter. And poof, you'd be back in your stone and I probably would have just tossed the stone and assumed you were a figment of my imagination. What if I were like that? What would you have done?"

*You're not. I knew it then and I know it now. I was inside your thoughts, remember? As for the rest, I was just . . . teasing you. I never knew we'd actually make love.*

"Well, damn it, we shouldn't have. I wouldn't have you tossed back in that damned cornerstone for the world. Don't you know that? All you had to do was tell me this would happen. You could still be at least somewhat free."

*I know. But I have no regrets, other than hurting you. I would have regretted rejecting you, though. I would have regretted not making love to you.*

"Oh." Her heart trembled, just a little. "So. Um." She took a deep breath, trying to choke back the tears that wanted to continue well past the point of productivity. "So tell me, why all of this? Why did you pursue me as Teague? Were you trying to drive me crazy? I thought I was torn between two men for a while there. It wasn't exactly comfortable. Were you intending me to actually marry your mortal half? That's really kind of icky."

*No, I wasn't. It's a lot more complicated than that. First, you have to understand that Teague didn't know the whole story. He really and truly is a human born thirty-four years ago. But he's always felt like his life was incomplete, that he was missing part of himself. In actuality, he was: the magical half of himself. Of his soul. Of my soul.*

"One soul, two consciousnesses. Is that possible? Two minds thinking different things at the same time? Two agendas? Two of everything?"

*Not of everything. Teague's had visions. Always. You were in those visions. And he didn't recognize it at first, but I was part of those visions, too. He knew he had something to accomplish and regain, but he didn't catch on to any details until recently.*

*These experiments . . . we weren't breaking the curse, but I do believe we were breaking through some barriers in Teague's mind—the mind of my other half. He and I were reconnecting in those visions. He was very confused. He still wanted you. How could he not? After all, I'm in love with you and have been almost from the very beginning. As my other half, he couldn't help but have feelings for you, too.*

Mina rubbed her temples, trying to ease the ache building there. She had about as much luck with that as she was having easing the pain in her heart. "Do you know how hard it is to think of the two of you as one?"

*I can only imagine. But Mina . . . I have another confession to make. You may hate me when I tell you, but at this point, I can't lie to you any longer. Because of the lie, I may very well be thoroughly damned anyway. And you have the right to hear all of this from me first.*

Mina tried to brace herself. Could it be any worse than finding out her puca and her studly sometimes-date were one and the same guy?

*Maybe. You see, Teague didn't consciously know about me. But*

*I knew about him. I influenced his visions and pushed you toward him on purpose. I was hoping . . . Well, I was hoping you'd see your puca as an obstacle to anything progressing with Teague. And you'd seek to free me in order to get rid of me.*

"You played me?"

She felt, more than heard his wince. *Honestly, Mina, my intent was not to hurt you. This was supposed to just be a bump in the road for you that could have meant everything for me. But things got complicated.*

Mina remembered all the times Teague woke her from a sound sleep. So coincidental it had seemed, but maybe not. Often, he'd interrupted dreams. Of Riordan.

Other times, he'd made an appearance—even declared his love for her—after an encounter with Riordan or intimate thoughts of Riordan. "Those were all on purpose, weren't they." It wasn't a question. "But what if I'd fallen for Teague? What if your plan had worked so well that I fell for Teague and wanted you out badly enough to break the curse? What then?" But she knew the answer. "Obviously, Teague would disappear from my life as well." Her stomach felt like lead.

*Yes, he would be gone as soon as I was free. But you misunderstand. I didn't intend for you to lose your heart to him. Just be interested enough to want to be free to explore possibilities.*

"But then why did you have Teague say he was in love with me after I confessed my love to you?"

*I didn't want you to fall in love with my magical half either, Mina. That was only heartbreak for you. I tried my damnedest to get you to associate me with animals—remember the ears and tail when I first shifted to human? You weren't supposed to focus on me. And once you did, I was so tempted. It was so damn hard. But I had to muddy the waters, keep you from focusing too long on me.*

"Ah. So that's when you sent the straight man in. Teague. Or would that be the stunt double? And when that didn't work, you turned Jackson loose on me." How humiliating. She fisted the sheet higher.

*Yes. I thought he could distract you from me and from Teague. But more importantly, he could stay behind to be a husband to you after I was gone. I didn't want to leave you alone, Mina.*

"But you promised that you would never abandon me. You, not Jackson. Were you trying to get out of that promise?"

*No. But for your own sake, for the sake of the normal life you wanted to lead, I wanted to give you a human man to love. One who could stay with you, give you children and relate to you completely in your world. I wanted you to have everything you deserved. I'd still give it to you if I could.*

"So what happens now?" A sudden thought had her glancing up in alarm. "*Teague.* Where is he and what's happened to him now that you're like this?"

*I thought you didn't love Teague.*

There, finally, some jealousy. A woman could feel like a regifted fruitcake, passed around from man to man like this. "Well, for pete's sake, I cared about him. I liked him. And now that I know he's part of you . . . Tell me. What's happened to him?"

Gusty sigh. *He's lapsed into an altered state of consciousness. His visions are constant now. He and I are connected.*

"But what does that mean? For him, I mean. He's not dead, is he? He can't be."

*No, he's fine. His condition would be interpreted as a coma. By everyone, that is, except his friend Janelle, assuming she can keep the faith and continue to believe what he's told her for years now.*

"Is she with him? Is she taking care of him?"

*In secret, yes. He was able to tell her what was happening to him before he passed out completely, and she's been prepared. His family believes he's out of the country on vacation for the next two weeks. Meanwhile, she can provide help to him herself and hire more help if need be.*

Mina buried her face in her hands. "So, essentially, he's a vegetable because you and I made love."

*You feel guilty? You shouldn't. Increasingly, he and I have be-come one and the same. I am him and he is me. Unconsciousness is actually a relief to him right now. Ever since you inherited guardianship, the fragmentation has grown increasingly uncom-fortable for him. For me.*

"But his family. My god, his poor parents. What if—"

*I told you. They're not aware of what's happened. Come No-vember first, even should the worst happen, he will come out of it, continue his life, and I will be back in my cornerstone. This is just time out of time for him. He's okay.*

Mina groaned. "This is so freaking involved. With the you-are-him-and-he-is-you thing."

*I know.*

"So what can I do now? Can I still break the curse? It's not completely hopeless, is it? It can't be over yet."

*I'll still have a judgment day, if that's what you're asking.* But his voice was flat, even hollow as it sounded in her head. He'd given up hope.

"Oh, no you don't. Don't you give up now. I'm still mad at you and you damn well owe me an end to this argument in person. I'm going to break the curse just so I can strangle you." And then jump your undeserving bones . . .

*I'd love that. It would be worth strangulation to have you jump my bones again.*

She groaned.

*I'm just trying to be honest.*

"You waited long enough." Angry, heartbroken and con-fused, Mina still found herself believing him. He really would give her everything if he could. But all she wanted was him.

*Even now?*

"Yes, even now. Although, I'm telling you, buster, once I get you out of there you are so living in the doghouse. I'll make that cornerstone look like the Ritz."

*I'd love nothing better than to give you the opportunity to abuse and mock me. Really. Laugh at me, throw vegetation at me, do anything you want to me. Just give me a chance to make it up to you. That's what I want more than anything.*

More than anything?

*More than my powers, more than my freedom, more than my life.*

That's alarming. Don't do anything stupid.

*I already did. Remember?*

She sighed and slumped down on the bed. "Oh, boy, do I. And now that we've done the wild nasty, it's only going to be torture hearing your voice."

*Think so?*

"I know so." Sighing and exhausted, she slipped back under the covers. Tomorrow she'd seek more answers. Other solutions. Obviously, curse-breaking was not the solution anymore. What was? As she wrestled the problem, she felt a soft, soothing voice humming in her mind. Trying to . . . getting sleepy . . . was it . . . Riordan . . . ? And she drifted.

*"Mina mine."*

"Mmm?" *Stretching and feeling her bare skin slide across satin sheets, Mina lazily opened her eyes.*

*To find herself stretched out beneath a softly fluttering weeping willow tree.* "Pretty."

*"So are you."*

*She turned her head toward the voice. And saw Riordan. With Teague's face, and yet more. It was all of him.* "Riordan."

*"And, as you said, Teague. Yes, I'm here."*

*"But how?" She sat up, pulling the sheets with her until he plucked them away from her.*

*"You're asleep. I came to you in your dreams. It's all I can give you now. Speaking in your mind and coming to you in dreams."*

*"But you came to me."*

*"I couldn't stay away. You can send me away still if you want*

*to and I'll go. It's up to you and you have every right to be angry with me."*

*"Oh, Riordan. Like I could stay mad at you. I'm too damn glad to see you. However it happens." She traced his face with her gaze, let it drift over his bare shoulders and lower, over his strong chest and rippled abs, only partially concealed by the sheet. They were both reclining on a pallet of satin, amid grass and the sweeping fronds of the tree. She could smell blooms nearby. Feel the warmth of spring on her skin. Lovely. What if they never saw a real spring together? Judgment day . . . was only a few days from now. She could lose him forever.*

*Squelching that thought, she tried to move closer to him. "So, how does this work? Can I touch you?"*

*"Only if you wish it. This is your dream. You get to dictate what happens."*

*"Oh, really," she whispered, letting her voice lilt just a little. "That's fitting. Did you make up these rules?"*

*"No. You did. Like I said, this is your dream. I'm at your disposal."*

*Carefully, she reached out to touch his shoulder, warm and hard and only barely substantial beneath her fingertips. He was there and he wasn't. Much like the feel of his blurred face before they'd made love. Energy and just a hint of form. Warmth, definitely. She smiled at him. "So this is my dream and you are at my disposal. I kind of like that power balance."*

*He smiled, eyes twinkling wickedly. "Completely at your disposal. What would you like me to do?"*

*"Oh, baby." She growled at him. "I want you to start in the kitchen, scrubbing the floor, since you made such a wreck of it as Teague. Then you can vacuum all the BobGoblin dog hair off the area rugs and couch in the living room and—"*

*Riordan looked completely crestfallen. "Really?"*

*She pondered, eyes narrowed. "It's what I should make you do."*

*He nodded slowly. "Yeah. But there wouldn't be much point to it. Your house would be clean, but only in your dreams."*

*She laughed. "Oh, I get it. Like it always is. Clean only in my dreams."*

*He grinned. "I'm afraid so."*

*"I'll have to figure something else out then. But right now, I'm feeling a little drafty. Why don't you cover me up?"*

*He leaned close, tugging the sheets higher, past her breasts and over her shoulders.*

*"You misunderstood. I meant cover me with you."*

*"Thank God." And he pounced, mouth and hands and tongue touching her everywhere. He was already hard, his erection straining and flinching with every point of contact. His chest heaved into hers with his breath, and her legs moved restlessly against the sheets.*

*"Riordan. Oh, yeah. Just like tha—mmph." She sighed into his mouth, felt him coming into her. Again. And again and—*

Pound-pound-pound—

Huh?

Pound-pound-pound! "Mina! Answer the door! I know you're in there, and you have to stop avoiding me sometime." Pound-pound-pound! "Not returning my calls is one thing, but outright ignoring me when I know you're in there is just rude and hurtful. I won't stand for it." Pound-pound-pound! "Mina!"

Clambering off the bed, Mina stumbled to the front door and swung it open. Her mother. "Sorry. I was asleep."

"But it's almost noon."

Noon? Mina eyed the clock in surprise. She rubbed her eyes. "I didn't realize."

"What's going on in here? I can't believe you didn't hear me knocking and yelling. Are you sick?"

Mina, still dazed and seriously unwilling to leave her dreams behind, backed up so her mother could enter. "I'm fine. Just give me a moment."

"What's wrong? Where's your puca? Does he zap himself back into his cornerstone to sleep?"

Mina closed her eyes again, feeling the aching dread weigh down her heart and soul.

*I'm here. I haven't abandoned you. I'm dying of frustration, thanks to your mother's timing, but I'm here.*

She choked back a sob of laughter then, stronger, opened her eyes again. "Mom, please. Give me some privacy to get dressed and use the bathroom. Then we'll talk. Okay?"

Lizzy, obviously still alarmed, studied her shrewdly. "I don't know if I should leave you alone."

"Wait in the living room. I'm fine and I'll be right out."

Sighing, her mother tossed her hands over her shoulders, fingers fluttering. "All riiight. Blame a mother for worrying."

And she sounded just like a real mom.

*She is a real mom, Mina. You know she is. Open your eyes.*

You're becoming quite the nag in your disembodiment.

*That's not what you were thinking just a moment ago.* His voice, even in her mind, had deepened to a sexy rasp.

Tease. She rifled through nearly empty drawers—when was the last time she'd done laundry?—for a T-shirt and underwear. Jeans. Then she brushed her teeth and finger-combed her ratty mess of curls.

*It's not ratty. It's beautiful. I love it tousled.*

You can see me?

*Only in my mind. Your face is always right in front of me. I like it that way.*

Lord, but you're living up to your gifts now, my sexy poet.

*I'm trying.*

Smiling a moment, she turned to the door and, bracing herself for confrontation, opened it.

Her mother sat on the couch, knees locked primly together and hands gripping each other. The woman looked uneasy. More uneasy than Mina had seen her in a long, long time. In fact, the last time Lizzy had looked this nervous was on her wedding day, when she married the very nice, very loopy man who was so obviously the perfect mate for her.

Lizzy cleared her throat. "You haven't returned my calls."

Mina studied her mom. "No, I haven't. I'm sorry."

"Are you?"

Mina looked away. "I guess I just didn't know what to say to you. I've been trying to get Riordan free and I've been dealing with some . . . surprises on a more personal level."

Her mother's big gray eyes met hers evenly. "You've figured everything out now, haven't you?"

Everything . . . what everything? That Mina had made love to her puca and damned him back to his hellish cornerstone? Surely her mother didn't know that much.

*I think she's referring to our visit with your father.*

Of course she was. That was a whole lot to digest as well. Mina remembered the "everything" that her jerk for a father was kind enough to share with her. Things her own mother had kept from her, when Mina might have taken the truth a whole lot better coming from Lizzy. How dare she let Duncan Forbes be the one to break it, so less than gently, to Mina?

"You mean, do I know that I was some science experiment that you performed once upon a time? Yes, I know. Dear old Dunky was only too happy to tell me once he got an eyeful of Riordan."

"Honey, it wasn't like that."

Mina stared at her.

"Okay, at first it was a lot like that. More an obsession than an experiment, though. I'd heard whispers about the legend for years. A female Avebury descendant from each generation inherited the sacred duty of guarding the puca. It was like our very own princess in the tower fairytale. Except it was a prince in distress and, eventually, a female heroine who would unlock the secret to freeing him. I wanted to be the one to free the puca. I'd heard for years that somebody in the family would have the ability, but a woman can't choose her parentage, I suppose."

"No kidding."

Lizzy had the grace to blush.

"So, what is the secret?"

Lizzy shook her head. "I don't know. I just knew I wanted to be the one to figure it out and free the puca at last. Obviously, it wasn't for me to do."

"So instead you planned to do your hocus-pocus crap through me?"

Lizzy pondered a moment, a faraway look in her eye, then smiled just a little. "Do you remember your ninth birthday?"

"Vividly. Nobody came to my party. Their mothers wouldn't let them. I'm sure you can understand their reasoning."

"Was your birthday that terrible?"

Mina shrugged, remembering more in spite of herself. "You took me to the park."

"That's right. I called you in sick for school so you could stay home and celebrate with us."

"Which was so admirable of you, by the way."

*Mina, give her a break. Just listen.*

"Yes, yes. I failed you as a mother. And see how terribly you turned out?" Lizzy gave her a sharp look before continuing. "Yes, we went to the park. The three of us. You, me and Joe."

They'd brought a picnic lunch with them. Granted, it was some organic mishmash of sprouts and other granola-caliber foodstuffs. Still, her mother had gone to the trouble of putting it all in a basket along with a pretty tablecloth and even—Mina had been so shocked—three genuine bottles of cola to go with the frothy pink-frosted cake Lizzy had made. A lopsided cake, but homemade and with none of the usual, healthier ingredient substitutions that never really worked. "I remember."

"Do you remember that exotic bird some man brought to the park with him? I think it was a parrot. So gorgeous, with that wicked beak, blue and gold feathers. It squawked and chattered and said horrible things while we watched them together. It wasn't in a cage or anything, just perched on the man's arm. And you wanted to know why the bird didn't fly away."

Mina remembered that. The filthy-mouthed parrot making her stepfather chortle and her mother clap hands over Mina's ears. "You told me the man probably had the bird's wings clipped so he couldn't fly away."

Lizzy was nodding. "You were horrified. First, at how much it must have physically hurt the bird—I've been told since then that it doesn't, dear, if this is still concerning you."

Mina just waited for her to continue.

"But then . . . then you felt bad for the bird. Why can't the bird fly free? you wondered. If the man loved the bird, why would he do that to him? Surely he knew the bird would stay with him if he took such good care of him."

"A child's naiveté." Mina shrugged carelessly. "The bird didn't know it was missing anything. It had probably been born and raised in captivity, and was just fine with the man. Probably better off. Even if it had free use of its wings, it wouldn't have survived ten minutes on its own."

Lizzy smiled fondly. "Leave it to you to take that viewpoint. But that's not what you thought back then."

"I was a child. Children take the comforting safety of their boundaries for granted." Mina raised her eyebrows. "I never had that kind of safety net."

"But I never, ever kept you against your will. I never limited you. In spite of yourself. Even as a child, you would have strangled yourself with this passion for boundaries and restrictive tradition. I couldn't let you do that to yourself. So I tried to create a nonjudgmental environment, one full of options that encouraged you to explore the unusual on your own."

"What, by letting me run naked under the stars while you giggled and the neighbors had a cow? That was just great."

"Mina, please don't be deliberately obtuse. You know what I'm trying to say. You just don't want to admit it to yourself or to me. I assumed, given your lineage, that you would have some latent abilities, but you were so shy. I was afraid you'd never explore enough on your own to discover them. What a waste that would have been. So I supplied the props. And a tolerant atmosphere, and watched to see what would click for you."

Mina gazed at her, horrified. "So *I'm* the woo-woo magnet? *I'm* the psychic-witch-doctor-Druid-freak? So what exactly can I do? Make fire? Draw down the moon? Come on, break it to me. I'm all numb by now. I can take it."

Lizzy looked rueful. "Actually, unless I've missed something over the years—and trust me, I've tried it all—I'm afraid the latent ability was all wishful thinking on my part. You really are about as extrasensory as a brick wall."

Riordan snorted a laugh in Mina's mind.

"Oh." Mina blinked. "Well, I could have told you that."

"No, you couldn't. Not until we'd explored all your options. You really are just a normal girl. With unusual heritage. Period."

"And that's all I damn well wanted as a child. A normal life, not some weird collage of paranormal hobbies. I could never bring a friend home for fear you'd be 'sky-clad' or boiling my pet frog."

"Now, that's outright exaggeration."

"You know what I mean."

"Yes, I do know. But I'd like to think I in some way prepared you." Lizzy smiled at her daughter.

"For perpetual dysfunction? Oh, yeah. You got that right. After speaking with dear old Dunky and discovering that not only was I an offense against nature and a reminder of a heritage he hated to acknowledge, but I was also a walking reminder of him screwing around on his wife . . . Yeah, there's dysfunction."

Lizzy shrugged. "I didn't rape the man."

Hearing her own words come out of her mother's mouth, Mina choked in surprise. "That's actually the same thing I told Dunky." And they both had a point. Duncan was the one who'd cheated, and he'd done it willingly. Not that it excused her mother of the other stuff, but—"So, did you know?"

"About the wife or the daughter?"

"Both."

Lizzy sighed. "About the wife? Not at the time. But then, I did trick him about the pill. The daughter? That was a bit of a shock to me, too. But it did make you all mine then."

"Isn't that a little selfish? I had a right to a father."

"You really wanted Duncan Forbes for a *father*?"

"You really took Duncan Forbes for a *lover*?"

"Touché, daughter. I can honestly say I didn't know he was that bad when we had our affair." Lizzy paused thoughtfully. "It's just possible that he *wasn't* that bad when I first met him. Maybe I had a hand in turning him into the ass that he is today. I don't know. He certainly blames me for everything wrong in his life. Do you?"

Mina stared at her mother for a few minutes, weighing everything. It was just too freaking complicated. Nice turn of phrase, that. *Freaking* and *complicated*. She dropped down onto the couch next to her mother. "I *have* blamed you."

Lizzy shrugged, obviously trying not to appear hurt. "I'm not surprised. I know you had an odd childhood. But I always loved you. You may have started out differently than other babies. Your conception was more unorthodox than other children's. But once you were born . . . you were just mine." Her voice dropped to a whisper. "I was going to name you Pandora. Like the curious creature who opened a dangerous box? But then you were mine. Pandemina." She smiled. "My world. I was right in the middle of writing your name for the birth certificate and out it came. Pandemina. Mina. Mine to love."

"Oh." Mina's throat tightened. "Is that true? Really, really true? Not just some story to tell a stupid girl who found out she started life as a guinea pig?"

"You were never a guinea pig. Hope maybe. Excitement, certainly. But once you were born, always, *always* you were my perfect baby girl."

Mina leaned against her mother, felt arms go around and pull her close. "That's . . . God, that's just lovely, Mom. Thank you." She chuckled a little hoarsely. "Not that I can agree with the perfect part. I've made my share of screw-ups."

Lizzy wrinkled her nose. "Jackson? Big screw-up, sweetie. The man couldn't even give you an orgasm."

Mina groaned, remembering the way her mother had tricked that little tidbit out of her. The woman was just sneaky. And impossibly intuitive, though Mina would never imply as much, even in jest. "Just when I think we can have a normal relationship—"

"Your mom goes and brings up sex. You endure so much, darling." Lizzy smiled at her daughter, then regarded her more soberly. "So, what are you going to do with this information your father gave you?"

"Blackmail him with it?"

"Mina!"

Mina sighed. "I'm not sure."

"You have a sister."

"A half-sister."

"She's still your sister." Lizzy regarded her daughter with

understanding. "Sure, Duncan acknowledged her and not you, but somehow, I don't think life as Duncan Forbes's acknowledged daughter would be a piece of cake either. The man has a judgmental streak, if you haven't noticed."

"Tell me about it."

"I would think you'd be curious about this girl."

"Her name is Daphne." Mina murmured it. "He told me."

"You were curious."

"Of course I'm curious. But it just so happens I have bigger things on my mind right now."

"Like November Day?"

Mina stared. "So you know about that, too?"

"I know about the prophecy. I know that you are the one who holds the key to the condemned puca's freedom. But that's all I know. The legends and the rumors have been passed down, but they're all ambiguous and contradictory. You are the key. There is no doubt of that. But the rest . . . is all up to you to figure out. I'm sorry."

"I was afraid you were going to say that."

Lizzy nodded. "Your puca will face the Druid Council very soon. Is he ready?"

Mina blinked back sudden tears. "No."

"Tell me."

"He's disembodied again. He and I . . . we were together . . . and it was against the rules. So now he's disembodied again. He's back inside that damn cornerstone."

As disjointed as her speech was, Mina knew her mother's widened eyes and speculative expression meant she'd understood most of what Mina hadn't said aloud. "I see. And you're scared."

"Desperate. Mom, I love him."

"Oh." Lizzy stared at her, eyes rounding. "Oh, just . . . Damn it to hell and back." Lizzy launched to her feet and strode angrily around the room.

Mina gaped. "What? What'd I do?"

"Where's your head, Mina? First you fall for that idiot Jackson and now you can't even mate within your own species? For heaven's sake."

"What? You're the one who wanted me to jump him."

Lizzy threw her hands up. "Well, there's jump him and then there's go be an idiot and fall in love with him so you can get your heart broken when you can't keep him. Mina. I wanted you to cut loose. Live and learn to laugh and play again. I wanted most of all for you to forget that idiot Jackson. Not get yourself in deeper trouble by losing your heart to yet another lost cause."

"You think I haven't told myself the same thing, over and over again? I fought this. It's not what I wanted and I know how hopeless it is." She shrugged. "So I did fight it."

Lizzy regarded her with frowning pity. "And lost."

Mina shrugged and whispered: "And won. That's the worst part. I wish I could regret the love. I don't. I just regret the consequences of making love to him. I didn't know this would happen."

"I didn't either." Lizzy looked thoughtful. "But apparently he did. Or at least he suspected. And he loves you, too."

Mina nodded.

Lizzy frowned a moment, her eyes bright and obviously concealing a brain operating at warp speed. "All right. Then you fight dirty."

"Huh?"

"Oh, good god, girl. Use what you have. Your father's a Druid. He must have some idea how to undo this curse. And, if I recall correctly, the idiot not only cheats on his wife, but he talks in his sleep."

"What are you saying? You think I should approach his wife?"

Lizzy frowned a moment. "That's an option, but I doubt she would talk. You know what I think?"

"I'm afraid to know."

"I think you should find your sister. You have common ground there. Both innocents and on a level playing field. She'll be able to tell you more than you think."

"You know this?"

"Just a hunch. And if she doesn't willingly cough up the info, offer to ask her unsuspecting mom instead. Play any card you have. You're fighting for your love and your puca's life." She gave Mina a bracing look. "Now is *not* the time to be squeamish."

"You know," Mina murmured. "I think for once you give some utterly ruthless, truly excellent advice. I'll go find Daphne."

"Good girl." Lizzy nodded encouragement, then eyed her daughter with more sympathy. "I am sorry about your puca. I hope things work out for you."

"Thanks, Mom." Mina stood up and hugged her mother. "Really. For the picnic when I was a kid, for Pandemina, for the advice. Maybe you'll even give up on all the crystal crap and we can try to be normal after all this is over."

Lizzy laughed. "Oh, that'll happen. My daughter's in love with a puca. What a weirdo."

"*Mo*-om!" Mina tried to frown at her mother but couldn't quite manage it.

"Besides, I rather enjoy my crystals, even if I can't make them do a damn thing. But good luck with your search and let me know if you need books or resources. I have an entire library of 'woo-woo' at your disposal, dear."

"Thanks, Mom. I may take you up on that."

After she saw her mother out, Mina ran to take her shower. After emerging, she felt the desperate need to check on—

*Mina mine, I told you he's just fine. Janelle's taking care of him.*

"I know, but it can't hurt to call." She dug through her purse for her cell phone and dialed the number.

It rang twice before a woman's voice answered. "Hello?"

"Janelle?"

"May I ask who's calling?"

"Mina Avery."

Gusty sigh. "I thought so. I can guess why you're calling."

"Teague. He's there with you?"

A long silence. "Just how much do you know?"

"As much as you, if not more. Is he out cold?"

"Yes. The occasional mumbling, like an uneasy sleep, but he's been this way for nearly a day now. It's creepy as hell."

"Was he able to explain everything to you?" Yeah, like how Mina having sex with Riordan dropped him into a coma? Mina winced.

*Quit that. You're still thinking in human terms. They don't apply here.*

Well, I am human. I can't help thinking that way.

"Teague left a message for me saying I'd find him out cold, just as he predicted. He saw it in a vision just a few days ago. He knew this could happen and he knew he'd need help."

Thank God for that. "It's my understanding that this is temporary. That everything will be resolved on November first. Whatever happens."

"And that's the question, isn't it?" Janelle spoke evenly. "What exactly *will* happen on November first?"

"A lot, I'm afraid. I'll be working on that. I'm hoping you're okay with taking care of Teague? I can help, you know."

"No. He made money available for a nurse if it comes to that. He'll be fine. But he was very clear on what he wants from you—focus on November Day. Everything's riding on it."

"Then that's what I will do. Thanks, Janelle."

"No problem. Just keep me updated if something's going to happen."

Mina hung up. At least Teague wasn't alone like that, lost in his visions, wandering in his head. Was it a nightmare?

*Not at all. In his mind right now, he and I are one. And I'm with you. Like me, he's content with that, just uneasy about the fragmentation.*

"You're still weirding me out with that stuff."

*I know. So are you going to find your sister?*

"Can't hurt at this point. I figure her office is the easiest place. Assuming I can get around dear old Dunky. Lucky for me he has a doormat for a receptionist."

# CHAPTER FOURTEEN

Glancing in the mirror to apply lipstick and minimal mascara, Mina tucked her blouse inside her jeans and stepped into pretty flats. "Riordan. Are you there?"

*Always. Are you nervous about meeting Daphne?*

"Well." She shifted uncomfortably. "She's my sister. I don't have any other siblings. And she's bound to hate me on sight. What's to be nervous about?"

*She may surprise you.*

"You and Mom keep saying that." She grabbed her purse and walked out the door. "Daphne's probably going to think I'm a freak, just like everyone else did when I was growing up."

*No offense, but you seem pretty normal to me. At least on the outside.*

"Twisted only on the inside, huh?"

*Although, you might want to stop talking to yourself before somebody starts looking at you funny.* There was a smile in his voice.

Should I squint and pretend to be mute, too? She smiled, remembering Riordan the dog. Engaging mutt that he was.

*Now that would draw some stares.*

They continued the casual patter all the way into town. Mina was well aware that Riordan was trying to distract her from her own nerves. It worked to some extent until she parked her car and turned off the ignition. She stared at the sign. FORBES & FORBES. An exclusive little group, there.

*You're not an accountant. What do you care?*

Good point. So, Riordan?

*Yes?*

Look, I'm not sure how to manage this, but I could really use some privacy right now. I'm meeting my sister for the first time, after all . . . and I don't want to hurt your feelings, but . . .

*No problem. Consider me not here.*

"Like really not here? How does that work?"

*Now that I lack a body, you mean? I can just choose to mentally distance myself. I'll treat you as white noise and concentrate on something else. Memories maybe. Grapes, for example. That's a good one.*

Mina smiled.

*So, I'll try to stay out of your way as much as I can until you call me. Call loud, okay?*

Okay. And thanks.

No response.

Focusing now, Mina climbed out of her car, grabbed her satchel with its precious ten pounds' worth of enchanted Sarsen stone, and strode across the street toward the office. She marched in as brazenly as last time, smiled a hello at the receptionist who was busy on the phone, and eyed up the doors behind the woman. Under the receptionist's disapproving but not overtly protesting eye, Mina ignored

Dunky's door and turned to the other. She cautiously opened it to peer inside.

A woman sat behind the desk, her honey blond hair pulled back in a sleek updo. Her face was carefully and discreetly made up, and her suit was obviously expensive and well-fitted. With her svelte figure and careful appearance, this woman made Mina suddenly conscious of her comfortable but inexpensive outfit and occasionally troublesome curves.

"May I help you?" She—Daphne?—smiled slightly.

"I hope so. Are you Daphne Forbes?"

"Yes." She stood up from her chair and held out a hand. "And you are?"

"Mina Avery." Mina shook Daphne's hand. Like Mina, Daphne had creamy, stay-the-hell-out-of-the-sun skin, but the resemblance ended there. Mina didn't discount her own looks—which she considered pleasing, if mostly average—but Daphne was downright gorgeous in a sleek Barbie doll way that set most women's teeth on edge. Until she smiled. A slightly crooked eyetooth drew the eye. It was adorable. A crooked tooth shouldn't be adorable, but there it was. Was Dunky too cheap to get his beloved daughter braces for her teeth? Still, Mina had to admit she thought Daphne wouldn't be nearly as appealing with perfect Chiclet teeth.

"What can I do for you today, Mina?"

Mina pondered her options and her timeline, which was awful damn short. Tomorrow was Halloween—the day before November Day. So, straight up it would have to be. "This is going to sound strange, but I'm your half-sister."

The blonde leaned back in her seat. "I thought your name sounded familiar."

Mina stared. "You know about me? How?"

"My mother told me about you."

"Your mother?" Well, that was a jaw-dropper. So much for reserved ammunition.

"Why, were you going to use her against me? That won't work. She'd eat you alive." Daphne spoke almost conversationally as she studied Mina with wide, curious eyes.

"But I thought—"

"What, that Dad was protecting his wife and daughter from the painful truth? Get real. That man protects himself. As does my mother. That's why she set a private eye on his tail. He dug up everything—and I do mean everything—on my father. Mom claims she hasn't told him a thing, and she and I continue to play dumb about you and your mom. It just works in our best interests to keep Duncan Forbes on his toes."

"That's creepy. All three of you are keeping the same secret from each other."

"Not quite, but close." Daphne smiled at her. "That said—that blackmail just isn't in the cards today—is there anything else I can do for you?"

Mina stared at her sister. *Half*-sister, she corrected herself. "Yeah. You could let me buy you lunch. Are you free?"

Daphne tilted her head, obviously as curious as Mina. Mina detected not one iota of hostility from the woman. Just a disturbingly distant curiosity. A neutral setting might help.

Pressing a button on the phone base, Daphne picked up the receiver. "Wendy? Yes. No, everything's fine. Just letting you know I'll be out for a couple hours. Right. Thanks." She hung up. "Lunch sounds like an interesting idea."

The women stood and filed out of the office. Would Duncan see her there, Mina wondered? By the odd look on the receptionist's face, Mina could only presume that Duncan would find out about it one way or the other. After they left the office for open air and busy streets, Mina turned back to her sister who was, Mina noticed, about two inches shorter than her. Finally, she excelled at something.

"Um, Daphne? In spite of what you might think, I really

did not come here to cause you trouble. Is this—you and me together—going to upset things between you and your father?"

"I think you mean *our* father? And I sure hope so. The man needs an upset on occasion." She pointed toward a building a block over. "How's Italian sound to you?"

"Sounds great." Adjusting the satchel straps over her shoulder, Mina turned and kept pace with Daphne until they found themselves seated at a casual, family-owned restaurant. Daphne, who ordered without looking at the menu, obviously patronized the place frequently.

After the waitress left with their orders, Daphne folded her hands and eyed Mina. "I've been curious about you."

"So why didn't you come find me?"

Daphne shrugged. "Same reason you didn't seek me out when you pissed Dad off at the office a couple weeks ago."

"You knew about that?"

"Sure. Oh, not because he told me. Mom keeps tabs."

"Alarmingly close tabs, apparently."

Daphne smiled. "Sure. I don't know her sources and, frankly, I don't want to know. As long as she keeps her paws off my life. We have an understanding."

Kind of a cold one, Mina decided sadly.

"*Your* mom, however, sounds pretty darn interesting." Daphne widened blue eyes that sparkled with intrigue. "A commune?"

"Only for a few years—"

"And all that occult stuff she's into? Wow."

"You know about that, too?" How unnerving to be so openly investigated.

Daphne gestured vaguely. "I was curious. I've known about you for a few years now and I wondered how you fared without the great Duncan Forbes messing up your life. I think you did pretty well for yourself."

They paused while the waitress served up their food. Lunch, apparently, was on the fast track during the work week to accommodate the business crowd. Mina murmured her thanks then, over two salad and minestrone combos, faced the half-sister who thought Mina had done fairly well without a father messing up her life. Interesting perspective.

Could be Daphne had a point, too. Mina's upbringing might have been unorthodox, but at least her family relations weren't complicated by covert surveillance and subtle blackmail. She supposed that went a long way toward making up for the woo-woo problems and lifelong neglect by Dunky. She stabbed at some greens and chewed thoughtfully. "Yeah, I think we did okay."

"So what is it you want from me, then?" Daphne blew on a spoonful of minestrone and sipped.

"Well . . . I did want to meet you, first. To see who exactly Duncan might consider an acceptable daughter."

Daphne shrugged. "One within wedlock trumps one without every time."

"Ouch?"

"Sorry. Just telling you how he would see it. And, just for the record, I'm not necessarily all that acceptable either. He's pretty rigid."

Mina nodded.

"So what's the other reason you came looking for me?"

"I need your help."

"Look, if it's money—"

"It's not. I need information." Mina paused. "Kind of weird information, actually."

"The Druid stuff?"

"You know about that, too?"

Daphne shrugged. "Just that according to legend, Dad has some big, bad Druid ancestors in his past. I bet that was the draw for your mom. Doing a Druid?"

"Hey, wait a minute." Mina lowered her fork. "That *is* my mom you're talking about."

"What, you dispute it?"

Mina sighed and poked through her salad. "No. But it's a lot more complicated than a fetish. And frankly, I don't think you want to hear or try to believe the specifics. If you could tell me something about the Druid stuff, though, it might help a friend of mine who's in trouble. That's all. Just information that I'd never use against your family. And . . ." She eyed her sister with unexpected wistfulness. "Maybe I'd like a chance to get to know you a little. I've never had a sister. It's probably too late for that now, but I don't think one meeting's going to satisfy my curiosity about you."

Stirring her soup, Daphne regarded her thoughtfully. "That's all? Just harmless information and getting to know each other?"

"I swear it. On my mother's life. And I love my mother, by the way, so that counts."

Daphne nodded. "All right." She set her spoon aside. "The Druid stuff's pretty straightforward, actually. Talk to our receptionist, Wendy Truman."

Mina started. "The receptionist? Why, does she set up all the grove meetings and screen eager wannabes and stuff? I know secretaries and receptionists tend to be the ones who run the office, but this is just weird."

Daphne sighed patiently. "This is more than running an office. She's his protégée. Mentee. Whatever you want to call it."

"His protégée? But I thought—"

Daphne rolled her eyes. "You think your mom's the only one with a fetish for a Druid? Duncan's not into the public Druid scene anymore, but he's agreed to do some private dabbling with Wendy. It was the only way she'd let him bang her."

"Oh, my god." Mina stared. "You're serious."

"Yep. So she'd be a good source of information. I think she's pretty active with the Druid community, too, in spite of Dad. He avoids it like the plague. She may know more about current practices than he does." Daphne shrugged. "And if she's not talking, let me know. I can make her talk. I'll use Mom."

Mina stared at her sister, feeling all kinds of sad. "I'm . . . sorry."

"Why? Because my parents are screwed up? Eh. Everybody has issues. My parents have a power problem. Each wants it. I just want my career and out from under both of them. Give me a couple years and I'm out of here. Just watch me go."

"You'll leave Richmond?"

"If necessary."

"Well, call me selfish—and, frankly, surprised at myself—but I hope it doesn't happen too soon."

"Seriously?" Daphne eyed her, then smiled. "How about that."

Mina smiled back, feeling positive about the future for a change. Her sister was cynical, too pretty to live and completely fascinating. Mina looked forward to learning more.

When the waitress brought the check, Mina paid the bill, then followed Daphne back to the office. After Daphne disappeared inside, Mina waited until the coast was clear, as per Daphne's suggestion, then reentered the building herself. Finding Duncan's door still closed, Mina turned to the receptionist. "Hi." She smiled.

The woman eyed her with less than trust. "If you want a word with Mr. Forbes, you'll have to make an appointment. And I'm afraid he's all booked until—"

"The next millennium. I get that. Good thing it's not him I want to talk to, isn't it?"

"Who do you want, then? Miss Forbes just—"

"I want to talk to *you*."

Big eyes blinked at Mina. Bosom heaved restlessly. "Me?"

"Yes, ma'am. Wendy Truman, right?

The woman nodded wordlessly.

"Can we find an empty office or something? So we can talk." Not lunch again. Mina was stuffed.

"I suppose you could buy me lunch."

It figured. "Sorry. I just got back from lunch. How about just coming out to my car?"

Wendy folded her arms and raised her chin. "You want me to sit out in your car and talk to you? Why would I?"

"That's exactly what I want. Unless you'd rather I call up Mr. Forbes's wife to discuss your odd *apprenticeship*?" Hey, adultery was just wrong. Mina shouldn't feel guilty using it against the woman.

Wendy stared. "I don't know what you're talking about."

"Yes, you do. And frankly, this isn't going to hurt at all. I just need information to help a friend and I need it too fast for me to take the diplomatic route with you or anyone. An hour of your time. That's all I want."

Grumbling, the receptionist picked up the phone, set the calls to voice mail, then announced to her bosses that she was going to lunch. She turned back to Mina. "I'll listen. But that's all I'm promising right now." She reached into a drawer, grabbed her purse and a sack lunch, and stood up. "Let's go." An angry wiggle in her walk, Wendy preceded Mina out the door.

Mina held the door a moment to glance back. She saw Daphne's office door open, just a few inches, and the hint of a smile shone just beyond the opening. Mina smiled back and left.

"Where's your car?" The woman paced impatiently.

"This way." Mina led the way to her tiny heap of a car. She unlocked both doors and slid into the driver's seat. Wendy plopped into the passenger seat and slammed the door.

Still scowling, Wendy opened her bag lunch and peered inside. "So, what do you want from me?"

"Information."

The woman glanced up. "I don't share client information with anyone. It's unethical and illegal."

"Trust me. The information I want has nothing to do with business and everything to do with your personal relationship with your boss."

"I don't know what you're talking about." Reaching into the bag, she pulled out a sandwich wrapped in plastic.

"Oh, come on. Let's not do this. You're sleeping with Duncan Forbes." Mina held up a hand when the woman attempted to speak. "And I know for a fact the man talks in his sleep. I just want to know if he happened to mention any of the following names: Riordan, Teague, Robert Goodfellow or Robin Goodfellow. That's all."

"That's all?"

Mina had seen Wendy's eyes flicker when Mina mentioned the last two names. She knew something. "That's all. I won't even reveal my source for any info that you give me. That would be on your conscience, not mine."

Wendy huffed in annoyance. "My conscience is just fine, thank you."

"So, Mrs. Forbes is okay with the whole infidelity scene? My paying her a visit to discuss you, among other things, wouldn't bother her in the slightest?"

Wendy looked alarmed but tried to brazen through. "You don't have any proof."

Mina sighed. "Come on, Wendy. Do you really think I need proof? All it takes is a whisper and you know she'll be checking up on you. What will she find?"

Wendy flinched. "But Duncan—"

"Doesn't have to know a thing. Wendy, I'm not out to get you. I just need info and I'm willing to do whatever I have to do to get it. Make it easy for me and we're good. Oh, and let me just say that I'll know if you're lying to me or not telling me everything. That would be a problem." And, sure, that was a bluff, but at this point—

"So, if I give you this information, you'll leave me alone and"—she visibly shuddered—"not say anything to Mrs. Forbes?"

"That's right."

Wendy eyed Mina cautiously. "Well, those last two names. They're brothers, I guess?"

"Yes."

"It might be that I know something about that." She bit into the sandwich, chewed a moment, then spoke. "A black sheep and white sheep kind of relationship, right? One's the good brother and the other's the bad one?"

"That's their reputation."

Wendy nodded. "Well . . . lately . . . Duncan's been kind of restless. You see, he's had these guys calling at all hours, trying to pressure him into attending some function. I think that's what has him upset. He's kind of resistant to the whole Druid thing, you know. I'm trying to win him back to the grove, but no luck so far. So, like I said, he's refusing to go to this thing and—"

"Is this function soon? As in, tomorrow?"

Chewing again, Wendy nodded. "Yeah. But he won't go and he won't talk about it. He always hangs up the phone and walks around mad for the rest of the day. Only it's not so much that he's mad as he seems kind of nervous. Are these mob guys or something?" She lowered her sandwich. "I mean, I don't want anything to do with the mob, so you gotta tell me if that's what he's involved in—"

"No, I think it's all part of the Druid thing. Haven't you received an odd invitation for November first yourself?"

Wendy looked startled. "How did you know? So that's what this is about? The Council meeting tomorrow?"

"Like I said, it's not the mob."

"But if it's Druid business, I can't talk about it."

Mina shook her head. "It's not really about Druid business, though. The Druids involved are supposed to be objective. This is more family business for Forbes."

Wendy frowned, obviously torn.

"Seriously, tell me what you know about the Goodfellow brothers and I'm out of here. No strings."

"But if Duncan finds out—"

"If I were you, I think I'd much rather have Duncan mad at me than his wife. And Duncan doesn't need to know any information came from you."

Wendy frowned and slumped in her seat. "But Duncan trusts me to be discreet."

"No problem. I can do anonymous tips." Mina paused. "Do this my way and, like I said, Duncan doesn't have to know anything. And neither does his wife."

Wendy still looked unsure. "All right. As long as we keep my name out of it."

"I won't mention your name. But you'd better be forthcoming."

"Well, he took me to the beach this weekend. And he was muttering and groaning in his sleep, like he's been doing— Really restless, you know? And he kept talking about a mistake. Or a cover-up."

"A cover-up?" Mina's interest heightened.

"Yeah. You know, with the two brothers. And this other guy. Mapes. Meeps. Something like that. Wait a second." Wendy frowned, dug around in her purse and pulled out a card. "This guy." She handed the card to Mina. "He keeps dropping by the office and leaving his cards, so I kept one. Just in case."

Mina read the name, her eyes widening. "What exactly was Duncan saying about this guy?"

"They were arguing in Duncan's office one day. I was the

only one there, so they didn't bother to keep their voices down. And I heard . . ."

Mina leaned toward her. "Go on."

It was like pulling teeth to get the rest out of the woman, but twenty minutes later, Mina had her answers. The only question now was how to use them to Riordan's best advantage. She needed to plan. Strategize. And not get Riordan's hopes up if things didn't work the way she wanted.

Still, she had one more person to visit before this was all done. A Reverend Maepus. It sounded like the man was at least as interested as Mina was in Druids, folklore and ancient vendettas. Now, if the man would just pick up his damn phone. All she needed was confirmation, clarification and some details.

But first things first. Closing her eyes, she visualized a cubicle. With stainless steel walls, combination locked door, no windows, and airtight seals.

Not that discretion was necessary, she discovered shortly thereafter. Clutching the cornerstone to her breast, Mina exited her car and ran through her front door, yelling Riordan's name in panic. He still didn't respond.

Despite repeated entreaties throughout the drive home, she hadn't heard his voice since asking him for privacy to speak to her sister. What had happened to him? Surely they wouldn't condemn him already.

Where was Riordan? Surely he hadn't abandoned her. He couldn't, could he? And even if he could, he wouldn't break his promise to her. He wouldn't.

# CHAPTER FIFTEEN

The first day of November dawned gloomy and overcast. Mina woke moaning from a candy hangover.

The night before she'd considered overindulgence a reasonable remedy for fear and frustration complicated by the usual Halloween mania. So call her a spook scrooge, but given her circumstances, she'd felt completely justified. It was logical that she didn't want to celebrate Halloween, and she didn't want to be nice to cheerful, knock-knock-joke-telling short people who just didn't get it that everything in Mina's world was wrong, wrong, wrong. But she'd handed out candy to the costumed beggars, employing a one-for-you-and-one-for-me brand of fairness until nausea had convinced her to abandon her bowl of candy and go to bed.

Wandering around at a loss now, Mina spent long, useless moments hovering over the cornerstone as if in doing so she could somehow be closer to Riordan. She'd tried repeatedly to phone Reverend Maepus, but his office said he was out of town and he hadn't responded to any of the messages she'd left for him.

Repelled finally by her own whiny helplessness, Mina called Janelle. Apparently, Teague had mysteriously disappeared right around the time Mina lost contact with Riordan. Annoyed—someone could have warned her this would happen, for pete's sake, instead of worrying the crap out of her—Mina begged Janelle to show up at the grove, just in case the Council would accept a character witness on Riordan/Teague's behalf.

"Yes, of course I'll be there. You're sure this is where they're having it?" Janelle sounded upset and distracted.

"I'm positive."

"All right. Look, I'm still on shift. I'll get out of here when I can—oh, shit. I gotta go."

"Be there!" Mina shouted into the phone, eyeing it resentfully when she heard a dial tone.

Mina passed a long day doing, of all things, housework while she rehearsed a variety of speeches in her head. Speeches on Riordan's behalf, possible answers to accusations, and various ways to defend a puca who considered himself already condemned. Still grumbling to herself about possibilities, Mina crammed the dust mop under the couch, shoving and tugging to get the dust bunnies that tended to hide out there.

As she did so, bending low, she focused completely on an unfamiliar brochure set neatly in the middle of her coffee table. A folded sheet of notebook paper had been tucked inside. Notebook paper? No. Not after all their fruitless searching.

Dropping the mop, she grabbed the brochure. It advertised a park—one she fully intended visiting in just a few short hours. Hands trembling, she pulled the sheet of paper free and unfolded it. Then she frowned. "Huh?" She needed help. Interpretation help. The language, copied so carefully in a neat hand, was unfamiliar to her.

Racing for her purse and praying for luck this time, she

rummaged until she found both her phone and a now-worn business card. She dialed the number on it. To her surprise and great relief, the Reverend answered on the first ring.

"Reverend Maepus? Oh, thank God. You're back."

"Yes, and I was just going to call—"

"Look, I'm sorry. I'm frantic. I need your help. My name is Mina Avery and I have what might seem like a strange request—"

"Mina Avery? You mean Pandemina Avery? Pandemina Dorothy Avery?" He sounded as worked up as Mina felt. "Fathered by Duncan Forbes?"

"Er, yes. But how did you—"

"Mutual acquaintances told me to look for you. You left messages, yes? But we should talk in person. I'll come to you. Just give me directions."

Baffled but grateful and by no means questioning her luck, Mina hurriedly gave him directions. Less than half an hour later, Reverend Maepus was sitting at her kitchen table, eyeing Gladys's letter eagerly. "Old English. My guess is your distant cousin, in a bid to be orderly, recopied what was probably a very old, very worn document."

"Great. What does it say?" Mina restrained herself, but it was difficult. Time was running out. Twenty very long minutes later, the Reverend handed over his translation of the document—what he could read of it. The ink had smudged to illegibility at the bottom corner of the document. Dog saliva?

Mina scanned it, her disappointment growing with every word. "That's all? But most of this is useless now." Mina slumped lower into the couch cushions. "I already know all this crap. Don't break the seal on the cornerstone, she tells me. Um, too late? Don't blab about the puca to anyone. Also too late? If he gets free, pull the *speak-of-the* trick, which I've done a few times now, so also duh. Then there are details about the rules for his confinement. More rules for if he gets out of the cornerstone. All stuff we already learned on our own through trial and error. And—" Mina frowned, reading further through Reverend Maepus's translation.

*Human sacrifice . . .*

"No way. That can't be what they intended. To actually—!" She met the clergyman's eyes in horror, but his gaze was steadfast. *No.* She couldn't speak or think it, let alone actually do it. They couldn't ask this of her. She couldn't do this. But how could she not? Mina stared blindly at the paper but the words didn't change. Nor did their implication.

"It's a difficult task they've set before you," Reverend Maepus commented softly. "You love the puca?"

"With my whole heart."

"I thought so. You're so eager to help him."

"But this?" Mina was horrified. "I can't do this. Not even for—" She broke off. "Murder's wrong. Right, Reverend? No ifs, ands or buts."

He sighed heavily. "It's a moral dilemma, all right."

"No, a moral dilemma is deciding whether to send a thank-you note to Aunt Matilda for giving me an insult disguised as a 'thoughtful' early Christmas present." Mina stared at the letter. "But we're talking homicide here. Not much gray about that, is there?"

The Reverend frowned thoughtfully. "Perhaps. Perhaps not. I think, when the time comes, you must follow your heart and your conscience. Think of the greater good."

The greater good. How did one define the greater good? On a personal level or a universal one? Could Mina really kill another human being? Even for Riordan? Trembling, Mina nodded her response, then watched as Reverend Maepus apologetically murmured about another appointment.

Appointment. She had one of those, too. In . . . way too little time to make a decision of this caliber.

An hour later, technically just prior to sunset, Mina was

shoving the letter, along with the cornerstone, into a backpack. Past the shock, she was now just mad. At any target she could conjure in her distress.

Chief at the moment might be Riordan. Mostly because he was the source of her distress.

He just damn well better not give up on his innocence and a chance at life. Determined and increasingly pissed about the stakes of today's stupid meeting, Mina slung the backpack over her shoulder and climbed into her car to drive to the outskirts of town. She paused to nod at a guard as she drove past the gate, then parked in an open space.

"A Druid grove meeting in a state park," she scoffed, throwing the car into park and climbing out. "Now I've seen it all. Maybe Smoky Bear will attend." Mina continued muttering nervously to herself, glancing right and left and ahead. She crossed the lot and stepped off asphalt onto a path that, according to the map that so mysteriously appeared on her coffee table, ran toward the center of the park. Then, as instructed, she veered off and moved farther into the trees, backpack bouncing heavily against her spine. "I swear to God, if this gets me lost or eaten by bears, a certain puca will pay dearly."

*You won't get lost.*

"Riordan." She halted, her knees weakening with relief. "Thank God. Where have you been? I've been terrified that they zapped you completely beyond my reach."

*Well, I was. A gag order to precede the meeting, or so I was told. I'm sorry I didn't warn you. I wasn't given much warning myself.*

"But you're here now. So, are you like here-in-the-park here now? Or just-here-inside-my-head here?"

*I'm in the park. Go a little beyond the big oak tree with the scarred trunk, and you'll see a clearing. Keep going.*

Surer, now, Mina moved more quickly, stepping over roots and around trees. "Any idea what poison ivy looks like? I don't have a clue."

*Little nature girl, aren't you? Your mother would be ashamed.*
"Thank you."

A chuckle echoed hollowly in her head.

"Will I see you again? At the clearing?"

*Yes. I'll be there, in all my manliness.* His tone was self-mocking.

Well, that explained Teague's disappearance. Apparently, right at this moment, Teague and Riordan were one in every sense of the word. "That's great. But . . . why?"

*Why am I whole right now? For practical reasons. The Druids can't judge me unless I'm completely present, in a corporeal sense. Otherwise, the judgment is weakened.*

"What if you didn't show? You could maybe fake your presence, couldn't you? Let them cast their judgment and, whatever it is, try to fight your way free of it later?"

Silence echoed in her mind before Riordan spoke heavily. *Once upon a time, I would have been tempted to try. The man I used to be would have done anything to free himself. I'm not him anymore. I'll be there, body and soul.*

"Oh, Riordan." How could she be annoyed and yet proud of him, all at the same time?

*Sucks to be you, doesn't it?* Riordan's voice was amused, as he echoed a phrase she'd used on him more than once.

"Oh, buddy, you have no idea."

*What does that mean? And why do you have this wall up in your mind? I thought we were done with that.* He sounded hurt.

Mina struggled to harden her heart. It was for his own good that she kept that wall raised. He just didn't know it.

*What don't I know?* Now he sounded grim.

Mina reinforced the sagging wall. "None of your business. A woman has a right to a few private thoughts. I'd hate for your head to swell any more than it already has."

*And now you're bluffing like hell. Do not do anything stupid, Mina. I won't have you hurt by this any more than you already have been. Understand?*

Mina didn't respond.

*Mina, please. I couldn't live with myself if something happened to you.*

She relented. "Nothing will happen to me."

*It better not.*

His words were still sounding in her mind as she stepped beyond a group of trees and came to the clearing. Fully two dozen men and women dressed in white robes and . . . athletic shoes? baseball caps? . . . stood in the clearing. All wore somber expressions and ranged in age from early twenties to elderly. One man, his robe trimmed in gold, stood in the center of the group.

Mina cleared her throat. "Hi. I'm Mina Avery. The, uh, *guardian*." She glanced around the gathering until she saw him.

"Riordan!" She rushed to him.

"Mina mine." He caught her up in his arms.

She wrapped her arms tightly around his neck. "Oh, but I've missed your sorry ass."

"Me, too."

She started chuckling. "'Me, too' as in, you missed me, too, or you missed your sorry ass, too?"

"Both. Behave yourself, woman."

She pulled back and looked up into his dear face, those lovely green eyes. Gold flecks. Both Riordan and Teague, in one man, one man she loved with her whole heart. Moved beyond words, she slid her hands up his neck to cup those lean cheeks and skim his smiling mouth, sharp nose, long eyelashes and noble brow.

"Noble?" He sounded pained.

"Well, damn it, it is. You look like such a freaking aristocrat. It's no wonder that you get all the girls and their daddies all curse you."

"*Precisely*."

Mina jumped and pulled back.

The response had come from the Druid wearing the gold-trimmed robe. He raised his chin. "That's exactly why we're gathered here today. Because this man has wronged a woman in the past. And, as I understand it, a woman in the present."

"What? Who?" She turned an outraged gaze on Riordan. "When did you have time and opportunity to wrong some woman in the present?"

Riordan brushed her hair back from her face. "I think he's talking about you, babe."

"Me?" Baffled, she turned back to the Druid. "How did he wrong *me*? I'm not wronged. And wouldn't *I* be the best judge of that anyway?"

"What he might have snowed you into believing is beside the point. The facts speak for themselves. This man used deception to—yet again—seduce a human."

"What do you mean, he used deception to seduce a human? And how would you know, anyway? Do you go crawling around people's bedrooms, spying on them?"

"Mina—"

The High Druid shrugged. "The puca was sucked back inside the cornerstone, wasn't he? That's a sure sign he violated his *geas*. Akker's probably spinning in his grave right now."

"You think he lied to seduce me?" She eyed him with disbelief. "Well, I have news for you, you backward-thinking naturists. He didn't lie or seduce me. In fact, I'm the one who seduced him. So cram that in your bong and smoke it."

Riordan's shoulders were shaking.

The High Druid looked taken aback, and he glanced at his cohorts, who all looked equally thoughtful. Finally one spoke up. "I assume he resisted you? Said no, perhaps?"

"Could *you*?" That was Riordan, incorrigible as ever, eyeing the male Druid as though sizing him up for a frilly dress. "I mean, look at the woman. Who could resist her?"

"Will you please shut up? You're ruining this," Mina stage-whispered. "And it's important." Torn between tears and laughter herself, Mina turned her back on Riordan and faced the Druid. "There are different kinds of resistance. Riordan resisted gently—not wanting to hurt my feelings, of course—but I can be really, really persuasive when I want to be." She subtly assumed a pose, attempting Mata Hari sluttishness. Given the doubtful look in the Druid's eyes, she had to assume her performance fell short.

"How old are you, Ms. Avery? Twenty-six perhaps?"

She tipped her chin high. "That's very sweet, but I'm thirty-one and proud of every minute of it. Well, most minutes. Certainly the ones I spent with Riordan."

He nodded. "Your defense of the puca is admirable. It's obvious you feel affection for him. But he's very good at playing on a woman's feelings to gain an advantage."

"Oh, come *on*."

A female Druid, who looked to be in her early fifties, spoke up doubtfully. "Listen, honey. At last count, your puca's got twenty-two hundred and change years on you. Do you know how many women he's seduced in that time?"

Mina paused to eye Riordan uncertainly. "No, and don't tell me. I'm feeling a little inadequate now." And maybe . . .

Riordan had eyes only for her. "I've never loved another woman until you. Never."

The female Druid looked unconvinced. "I still say if he landed back in his cornerstone, some deception had to occur, followed by sex."

*I played you, remember? When I used Teague against you.*

Shut up. You didn't use the deception to get me into bed.

*No, but it worked all the same, didn't it?*

Mina eyed the Druids resentfully. "I'm not discussing my sex life with you. Suffice to say that it was consensual. And *spectacular*." So there.

The male Druid studied them both and sighed. "Be that

as it may, there is still the original charge against the puca. The Archdruid Akker condemned you for a crime you certainly did commit, so—"

"No, he didn't." Mina spoke up again.

"What did you say?" The Druid looked disapproving.

"I said, no, Riordan did *not* commit the crime your Druid buddies condemned him for two thousand years ago. Or at least, there were extenuating circumstances. He never did get the fair trial he deserved."

"Mina, honey, I know you want to defend me, but there's no way you could know what really happened."

"And why not?" She glanced discreetly at Wendy before turning her gaze to the rest of the crowd.

"I know of at least a few Druids from this Grove who don't prize your precious Truth as highly as the Druid PR would have us all believe. Otherwise, they'd be calling this trial as much a farce as Riordan's last one was." Mina watched, amazed, as several people besides Wendy nervously averted their gazes. "More than a few? Interesting."

Riordan looked surprised now, then turned back to Mina. "Maybe you'd better just spit it out before somebody has a coronary." He glanced meaningfully at one of the older Druids, who muttered heatedly about today's youth not respecting their elders.

"All right." She turned to the male Druid who seemed to be running the proceedings. "Look." She squinted at what appeared to be a nametag on his lapel and read it: *Hi, My name is Phil, High Druid.* The High Druid was named Phil? Somehow, that just lacked panache.

*Get on with it, Mina.*

"Phil." She met the Druid's eyes. "It's true that Riordan seduced Akker's daughter when she was engaged to another man. But at the time of their encounter," she paused, eyebrows raised for emphasis, "Riordan *didn't know* she was engaged. And, more to the point, *he had no idea that she was engaged to his own brother.*"

"My own brother? She was engaged to Robin?"

"Riordan didn't deliberately impersonate his brother to seduce the girl. He just picked the wrong girl to make moves on. So, I guess you could say he's guilty of the seduction, but innocent of malice, deliberate betrayal and deception." She paused to let that sink in before continuing. "Since your Druid buddies stole Riordan's memory of the encounter and events leading up to it, he had no way of defending himself at his long-ago farce of a trial. So. How's that for a miscarriage of your beloved justice?"

Phil the High Druid stepped forward. He glanced around at his group, focusing momentarily on each of a half-dozen averted faces, then turned back to Mina and Riordan. "How did you come by this information?"

"I'd like to know that myself," Riordan murmured, looking hopeful for the first time.

Mina though of Wendy—poor, weak and misguided Wendy—then turned back to Riordan before facing the High Druid. "I'm afraid I can't tell you."

There came a mild rustling in the bushes behind the Druids. Reverend Maepus stepped forward. "Mina Avery speaks the truth." Phil the Druid frowned at him. "This is a private gathering, by invitation only. What are you doing here?"

"Looking after my kinsman. Besides, it's a state park. Open to the public, remember?" Dismissing the Druid, he turned to Riordan. "Hello. We haven't met. I've met Pandemina, however, who has only the nicest things to say of you. I'm sorry I haven't come to your aid sooner. I've only recently come into certain facts and learned how to use them."

Reverend Maepus turned back to the Druids. "I'd like it noted that Duncan Forbes, Akker's most direct descendant, declined your invitation to attend this meeting. Repeatedly. If I were you, I'd be forced to draw a few conclusions from that, myself. He also wouldn't hand over a set of diaries he kept in his safety deposit box. Word of mouth reports, however, support Mina's suppositions." He turned back to Riordan. "You deserve your freedom and you have any support I can lend you."

"Thank you." Riordan frowned at him. "But why would you do this for me? Who are you?"

"I'm a descendant of your mother's. Your *human* mother. I speak for her family. And for you."

"Thank you." *A champion. One who freely chose me. And a kinsman at that. I have one family member who believes in me.*

Riordan sounded so shaken, Mina grabbed his hand and held it fiercely. There was hope. This could happen. Maybe they really did have a chance.

His actions speaking even more clearly, Reverend Maepus approached Mina and Riordan and squeezed their joined hands. Then he moved away to the edge of the clearing— but obviously on their side of the virtual courtroom. He was in their corner. Against the rest of the gathering.

While they waited, the High Druid turned to his followers and motioned them closer. The Druids gathered around him, talking softly in a weird, white-robed version of a football player huddle. It made Mina want to laugh, in a terrified, surreal sort of way. She shifted her gaze to Riordan, wishing she could move closer to him. Hold him, just for a moment. Riordan's gaze never faltered. He watched only her, hopeful but still resigned to the judgment against him.

The huddle broke apart and Mina returned her attention to Phil the Druid. "Well?" She eyed them all hopefully. "You know, besides all the other stuff, I want to add that Riordan's really changed. He's a grown man who's learned from the mistakes he did make, and he's been great to me. My life was a wreck before he came into it. And now . . ."

She glanced at Riordan, who looked grim now. He finished her statement for her. "And now your life's going to be wrecked again. I am sorry about that. I love you, but I never intended for you to love me back. I'm an impossible risk."

She gave him a crooked grin. "I know. But I couldn't help myself." She watched, with affection and delight, as he shook his head. Then she turned back to the Druids. "Well? Don't keep us hanging here. Don't you have to vote or something?"

The High Druid nodded but seemed resigned. "We can vote, but I'm afraid it's moot at this point. The puca is guilty. We all know it." Nods and murmurs from behind him only confirmed his words.

"But—"

"Guilty *as the facts stand*. Whether he knew it or not at the time, he did seduce his brother's intended wife. Can you deny it?" He glanced from Mina to Riordan.

Silence.

"And then there was the effectiveness of Akker's retaliation against the puca. Unless the puca had violated his *geas* and/or the flow of karma, Akker's efforts would have been fruitless. The puca, however, was vulnerable to them, thus confirming his own guilt."

"But we don't even know—"

"*And*," the Druid interrupted Mina, "Riordan's brother himself confirmed the rest. He confirmed Akker's story and the girl's story. He claimed the girl wouldn't have slept with a man other than her intended. He said Riordan must have impersonated Robin. Otherwise, the girl would have rejected Riordan."

"But—"

"Argue all you want, but it will all come down to puca word against puca word. Any other evidence is all hearsay, since all the parties besides the Goodfellow brothers are dead." The High Druid eyed them meaningfully. "And I know which puca's side I'd be on. It's not the man in front of me, who can't even remember the night anyway. Add to that a reputation of a certain kind and . . . a moot point, as I said."

Fighting her frustration, Mina pondered her options. Really, there weren't any. How could she back up a story when all the principle parties but two were long dead? And of those two, one couldn't remember enough to defend himself, and the other would likely hold a grudge, even if she could find him.

"However . . ." Phil looked reluctant. "Given the possibly mitigating factors you've raised during these proceedings, I feel it incumbent upon me to remind you both of a loophole that exists in Riordan's sentence. Are you aware of this? There is a way to alleviate the puca's circumstances. A verse detailing it was written and passed down from guardian to guardian."

"I know." She didn't look at Riordan. She couldn't.

"So you know exactly what you can do for him?"

"Yes. I found some help and translated the verse." Glancing at Reverend Maepus, who bowed his head, Mina bit her lip. She pulled her backpack off, dropped it to the ground and opened it. She withdrew the cornerstone and turned to Riordan.

Riordan's gaze was drawn, irresistibly, to the cornerstone. "So you know. And the Druid knows. What is this loophole?"

"I found the letter from Gladys," Mina offered reluctantly. "It filled in a few important blanks for me. Remember the part about a human sacrifice?"

"You don't mean—"

"Yes. And no. You see the human that must be sacrificed to free you from the stone . . . is *you*, Riordan. *Your human half*."

Riordan considered her words. "What exactly does this mean?"

"Remember how you believed the letter Gladys sent me contained the means to eliminate you for good? Well, that was a warped view of things. Not exactly the whole story. You see, it's not the puca that would be eliminated but . . ." And here she broke off, unable to continue.

The High Druid took pity on Mina and finished the explanation. "Basically, there are two choices here. You can return to the cornerstone, disembodied and basically continuing the same fragmented existence, going from guardian to guardian after each marries or dies. Or. After a certain amount of, er, ceremony, you could . . . *forfeit* . . . your human life and regain your freedom and other powers. Should you choose freedom, you will be and feel spiritually whole, but you will no longer be able to hold a human form. It's gone from you. The human side your mother bequeathed you would no longer be reborn into another body."

"But that fragmented feeling would be gone?" Riordan asked quietly.

The Druid nodded.

"And what of Teague?" Mina asked hesitantly.

"He and Riordan are one and the same. He would continue his existence spiritually joined with Riordan. It's what his soul has sought since birth. They are one." The Druid paused.

"There's more, though. Isn't there?" Riordan spoke with quiet certainty. "Let's have it."

"I'm afraid so. You would be forever forbidden all contact with past victims. This would include any descendants of Akker and his daughter. Which would include . . ." He turned his gaze to Mina.

Riordan looked horrified. "I couldn't see Mina? Ever?"

"No contact of the minds, the spirits or the bodies. Separate forever. Mina would return to her own life. Alone."

Riordan continued to stare at Mina, who was having a

hell of a time holding it together now. It would break her heart, over and over again, to be separated forever from Riordan. At the same time, she couldn't bear to see him caged any longer. He was so much more than the BobGoblin. He could have everything else back, all that was taken from him, if only he sacrificed their relationship. She was willing to sacrifice it for him.

But Riordan was already shaking his head. He looked, if anything, more resolute than before. "If those are my two choices, I choose the cornerstone. We'll resume my former sentence."

"But—"

"Mina. I swore I'd never abandon you, come what may. And I will not."

"But Riordan, I never meant for you to sacrifice everything to keep that promise."

"Ah, Mina mine. You think I'm being self-sacrificing. But I am not. I can willingly give anything else up. Anything else but you. Freedom is nothing but a cage if I'm forbidden the one and only thing I want. That's you. Unless you don't want me?"

She choked back a sob but couldn't lie. Not about this. "That's not it. God, you know that's not it. But—"

"Would you be better off without me in your life? Would you rather go it alone? Without me? If you decide that you would, either now or later, you could always . . . *marry* . . . and I would just move on to my next guardian. I will not be a burden to you. And I will not break my promise. *I will not leave you.*"

Those words cracked her heart, just as they had the first time he'd spoken them to her.

*I will not abandon you.*

And he would not. She knew he stood by his promise. She closed her eyes, remembering the emptiness of her life just before he'd filled it with himself and his love. It was almost more than she could stand to contemplate going back to that old emptiness.

"You know I don't want to be without you." She licked her lips. "But I could do it. I *would* do it. You can't go back to that rock. Think, Riordan. In fifty or sixty years, I'll be gone anyway. That's all the time we'd have together—just a blink of an eye for someone like you. And you could spend the better part of an eternity afterward, caged inside that rock. I can't condemn you to that. Heck, I could be hit by a truck tomorrow."

"Mina, do you love me?" He gazed patiently into her eyes.

"Oh, Riordan." She broke off on a sob she couldn't quite hold back. "You know I love you. But I can't let you do this."

"Then it's settled." He turned back to the High Druid. "I choose—"

"Wait!" Mina shouted, briefly meeting the High Druid's eyes before turning to Riordan. "Before you go. Before you return to the cornerstone. Could I have something from you?"

Hearing her voice catch again, Riordan caught her hand and pulled her closer. "Anything within my power."

"It's nothing all that difficult." She offered him a wavering smile, trying to memorize his face, the gold-flecked green of his eyes. The feel of his hands on her. Think of nothing but those. Nothing of the future, nothing of intentions and consequences.

*Mina mine, you are still keeping something from me.*

Only my pain, my love. "May I have a good-bye kiss?" She blinked rapidly, trying to clear her eyes of tears and free her mind of anything but anticipation of his lips.

"Can you—!" On a wordless groan, Riordan pulled her into his arms, lowering his face until all she could see was the gold-flecked green of his eyes. They filled her entire world. Threading his fingers through her hair, he lowered his mouth to hers. As his lips softly caressed hers, Mina fought back more tears, tried to concentrate, to memorize.

Then steeled herself.

Tightening her grip on the cornerstone, her mind determinedly clear, she raised it high overhead and slammed it down, with all her might. On her lover's head.

Torn free of her, Riordan stumbled under the blow, a sphere of light settling like a dim halo around his body. He raised his head, managed to focus a disbelieving, almost comically annoyed gaze on Mina—"You *tricked* me?"—just before his eyes rolled back in his head. He crumpled to the ground. The glow began to dim, just as the letter had said it would.

Mina dropped to her knees, feeling the reality of what she'd done and what she'd lost crash in on her. "Oh, god." She let her hands flutter over his beautiful face, slackened now in unconsciousness. She traced his jaw, his cheekbones, her gaze going again and again to the pulse, throbbing so visibly in his throat. It seemed to be slowing already.

"No." He was leaving her. Soon, he'd be free and whole—Teague and Riordan rejoined at last—but lost to her. She'd be alone again. It had to be this way. But *why* did it have to be? Why was she forced to sacrifice a future with the man she loved in order to save him? Never see him, hear him, feel his presence and his love for her. Never again see the flash—

—*shimmer*—in her peripheral vision . . . ?

But she couldn't lift her gaze. She didn't even care who or what—

Riordan's eyelids twitched, then opened. Dazed green eyes finally focused on Mina, then darkened in annoyance. "Damn it, that *hurt*."

Mina fell back onto her rump, feeling a little dazed herself. "It didn't work. But why? The letter said one firm blow with that cornerstone—not even a killing blow—

would be enough to . . ." She broke off. "Damn it. Can't I do anything right?" she wailed, feeling as juvenile as she knew she sounded. "I'm so sorry, Riordan. Your body was supposed to die instantly."

"Um, darn?" He gave her a sarcastic look, already up on one elbow as he rubbed his scalp with the other hand. "I'm so sorry you didn't club me hard enough to kill me?"

"Oh, *there's* gratitude for you." She sobbed openly at him, uncaring of the swollen, mucus-ridden mess she was probably presenting. "There I was, thinking about you and not me, and you can't even cooperate, so now I'm going to have to do it all over again." Angry and feeling mildly unstable, she patted the ground around her, looking for the cornerstone. She tried to gather herself for another round of violence and trauma.

"Looking for this?" The voice came from behind Mina, drawing Riordan's immediate attention.

Riordan looked first surprised, then cautious. "Robin?"

Mina rolled to a knee, her attention drawn upward. The man, who bore an uncanny resemblance to Riordan and held the cornerstone in one hand, offered her the other hand in assistance. Warily, she took it and let him pull her to her feet. Then she snatched her hand free and stepped backward, protectively, toward Riordan.

"Hello, baby brother." Robin studied Riordan as the latter fumbled his way to his feet.

Groaning softly and pinching Mina's backside—*you tricked me!*—until she jumped, Riordan straightened and squinted past his pain at his brother. "You came for the sentencing?"

"I attended the proceedings."

"Why? To ensure that I was punished?"

Robin looked at the brick he still held in his hand. An innocuous brick, really, but such an integral part of Riordan's fate. "I attended to ensure justice."

Riordan sighed, long and hard. "I guess I can understand that." He studied Mina for long moments before returning his attention to his brother. "If I found out Mina and you had been together . . . like they're saying I was with your fiancée . . . I can't say I'd be above tossing your ass inside a cornerstone for eternity either. For what it's worth, I'm sorry."

Robin continued to study the rock, tipping it to the side and eyeing up the measurements of the hollowed interior. "You spent a long time in here."

Riordan winced, his gaze drawn once more to the cornerstone his brother held. "Yeah. And it looks like I'm not done, either."

Robin studied the brick so intently the Druids found enough courage to move closer, the better to listen in on the conversation. Finally he raised his gaze and focused squarely on Riordan. "Yes, brother. You *are* done with this. You won't be condemned to this stone ever again."

Riordan frowned, confused, as his brother turned back to the assemblage. Robin raised his voice. "My brother is innocent of all Pandemina Dorothy Avery says he is. Of all of us—Maegth, Akker, Riordan and myself—Riordan is the most innocent party. Maegth was engaged to me when she slept with my brother . . . fully knowing he was not me, although she claimed otherwise to save herself from her father's wrath. Our engagement was still secret from my family, so my brother was unaware that I was even engaged and I know full well Maegth never told him.

"Akker, I suspect, doubted his daughter's word but feared me and his loss of face enough to condemn my brother in his daughter's name. My brother's betrayal of me was unintentional." He turned to Riordan. "And now forgiven. I only hope he can forgive me, too."

"What are you saying, Robin?"

"I'm saying Maegth accepted my ring, but then later, out

of spite for some imagined slight, refused my bed and slept with you. She betrayed me. You did not. However, your violation of your *geas*, plus the karma infraction of committing the act even in ignorance, left you vulnerable to Akker. And to me. In my pain, rage and jealousy, I allowed your crimes to be exaggerated beyond truth."

Robin stared at the ground a moment. "We also misled you as to the nature of your *geas*. I foresaw the betrayal at your birth and later suggested to Akker that he place a *geas* on the puca christened as Rioghbardon to never have sexual relations outside of wedlock with a descendant of Akker. I thought the geas, plus my foreknowledge, would prevent the betrayal. It did not. I retaliated in rage."

While Riordan just stared at his brother, obviously trying to comprehend two thousand years of sentence based on an exaggeration, Mina stepped forward. Her tears had turned to fury. "Why, you Neanderthal, impulsive, grudge-holding coward. Just because you proposed to a woman who was sleazy enough to sleep with another man while engaged to you . . . you have to go and mete out this kind of torture? To your own brother? What kind of animal are you?"

"Mina." Riordan grabbed her arm and tugged her backward.

"I have no excuse. Other than jealousy and a passion that I realize now was shallow at best." Robin lowered his voice. "I've watched the two of you these past weeks."

"That was *you* out there? All those times I felt eyes on me, that was you?" Mina eyed him incredulously before slanting an annoyed look at Riordan. "You didn't tell me voyeurism was a family trait. Or maybe you did. Perverted pucas."

"Why?" Riordan asked Robin. "You didn't trust the strength of the curse to hold me?"

His brother shrugged. "I was curious, given the prophecy about your lady here, so I watched. I listened. And I witnessed. If anything, little brother..." Robin eyed his brother briefly, then studied Mina. "I'm more jealous now than I ever was over Maegth, God rest her shallow heart. Riordan, you have a treasure in this woman, and you should not be parted from her. You've proven worthy of her and she's proven her commitment and love to you. You have my blessing—if that matters at all to you."

Mina frowned at him. "Are you the one behind the brochure on my coffee table?"

He nodded.

"And the one who stole, at least temporarily, the letter from Riordan's last guardian?"

"Guilty as charged. I wish to rectify everything now."

"But why?" Mina gave him a baffled look. "I mean I'm not complaining, but you did kind of take your time here. Two millennia pass and suddenly now is the time to come clean? Why now?"

Robin gazed past her shoulder, his focus faraway and his expression brooding. Then he shook it off, resuming his former arrogance. "The why is . . . rather complicated. Just know that I'm sincere."

After one long, measuring look at his younger brother, Robin turned back to the hovering Druids. Most fell back a step. Expressionless, Robin offered a shallow bow in their direction. "As you can see, my brother's innocent of most of the accusations against him. I have pardoned him. What say the descendents of Akker and his like?"

A shuffling and then the leader slowly stepped forward. "I say we'd like nothing more than to give his life and powers back to him free and clear—"

Mina whooped.

"*But—*"

Mina froze in mid-celebration, then dropped her arms with an angry smack against her thighs. "Oh, come on.

Why is there always a 'but' on the end of your statements? What is it with you guys? Just give him his get-out-of-jail card and let us live in peace."

A long sigh. "I'd really like to do that, but it's not within my power. Frankly, it's not within anyone's power that I know of. However, I can make his choices more attractive."

Mina folded her arms. "This is completely outrageous."

"*Mi*-na." Riordan grabbed her arm again. "Patience."

"Each of these choices will, effectively, free you from your *geas* for different reasons. Your choices: One remains mostly unchanged. You get your powers back, your freedom back, even your soul returned to you intact. But—"

"Here it comes again." Mina muttered it to Riordan, who pinched her.

"*But*, you can't achieve human form any longer. You can see anyone you want, but the human form will not be substantial and you will be incapable of intimate relations with anyone, let alone a descendant of Akker. I'm sorry. The option of shifting to human form has already been taken from you. Remember the cornerstone? Hitting your head?" The Druid glanced at Mina.

She stared at him in horror. "You've got to be kidding me. *I* did this to him? But you're the one who told me to do it."

"Now, I never told you to do anything. I just reminded you of the existence of another option."

"For the record, your options truly suck." She scowled at him. "So what's his other choice? I'm assuming that's changed at least? The cornerstone is *not* an option."

"No, of course it's not an option. His other choice is a simple one and yet difficult, too." The Druid lowered his voice and glanced between Riordan and Mina. "You can choose to assume the human form only. You can be Teague again, if you wish. You will no longer be puca—and therefore not subject to the *geas* placed upon the puca christened

Rioghbardon. However, your soul and your memories will be intact, and you may keep everything material and abstract that you've built as Jonathon Riordan Teague in this particular human lifetime."

Confused, Mina frowned. "Yeah, but what about the rock hitting his skull? I thought his human half was eliminated."

"No. The permanent separation was made between his magical and human halves. That's why, as your letter instructed, you had to use the enchanted cornerstone to deliver the blow." He paused delicately. "I'm guessing you didn't read the rest of the instructions regarding the loophole? Nothing about separating the head from the—"

"Oh, yech! *No.* No way. We thought the rest was just garbled and . . . I mean, it was stained with saliva and all thanks to a certain mutt I know and—Beheading? Seriously?" She eyed him with disbelief.

Phil shrugged. "So you didn't kill his human self. Just achieved the ceremonial separation by striking him with the cornerstone. The soul can reconnect, but the magic and the mortal cannot."

Meanwhile, Riordan was eyeing Mina with some ire. "That brings up an interesting point, though. Just what exactly did you plan to do to me after I regained consciousness? You know, to kill me dead. Were you going to bludgeon me to death with that cornerstone? And how would that work exactly? You say 'stand still, honey' and so I calmly stand there like an idiot while you clobber me repeatedly?"

"Shut. Up." She turned to Phil. "Please. Continue. You're telling us that if he made this choice, he would be Teague. Human. But also Riordan. Just, with no access to his powers?"

"Right. No access to his powers. *And no longer immortal.* He would live as a human and die after a normal human lifespan expires. A normal, completely whole, human being with no unnatural limitations on his life and relationships as this human." He focused entirely on Riordan. "This way, you could have your Mina and build a life with her if you choose."

"Naturally, that's only if you can forgive my evil plot to bludgeon you to death." Mina couldn't hold back the comment.

"Ssssh." Riordan was frowning. "So I'm choosing between my human half and my magical half, but—"

"But that essential part of you, the part connecting the two, would follow you whichever path you chose. You will have your soul back, intact, whatever choice you make."

"Then the choice is very simple." Riordan's expression cleared, and he smiled as he turned to Mina. "I choose mortality and Mina. Forever, whatever this life or the next brings us. Well, except bludgeoning. We're done with that."

All traces of humor gone now, Mina stared at the cornerstone. It had lit as if from within as soon as Riordan stated his choice. Obviously, the decision was final. She turned back to Riordan, feeling shaky. She'd known he would make this choice, but the reality of it, now that he had . . . "You're giving up your immortality for me? And your magic? Dear god, you're going to *hate* me."

He laughed and picked her up for a wild spin. "Oh, no, woman. You see, I have an evil agenda of my own now. First, I'm going to make you pay for keeping secrets from me. Then you're going to pay for clubbing me. And then you're going to pay for your intention to club me again—"

"Oh, so now you're going to beat me? That's love." But she was laughing through her tears.

He let her body slide low enough that he could whisper in her ear. "Who said anything about beating? Babe, I have only the most exquisite tortures in mind for you. You forget, I've been living in your head and walking through your fantasies for some time now. I know just how to get you."

"Oooooh. Bring it on." She stared at him, dazzled and seriously breathless.

"And then I'm thinking skanky food sex. That's something I've always wanted to try. Ice cream and steak. Let's be creative. . . ."

# EPILOGUE

"I await your pleasure, ladies and gentlemen." Robin surveyed the grove of Druids.

Mina glanced up from Riordan and frowned. "What—?"

"Robin, no." Setting Mina down, Riordan stepped forward.

Glancing in surprise at his brother, Robin chuckled a little, but shook his head. "Imagine. I helped Akker condemn you to a living hell, knowing you didn't deserve it. And now that I've finally confessed to the unforgivable, you still think to save me. Riordan, you have by far surpassed everyone's expectations of you. I commend you for it. Now stay the hell out of this."

The High Druid stepped hesitantly forward. "You seek to right matters."

"I do."

Obviously alarmed, Riordan interrupted again. "But that's completely unnecessary. Robin, I forgive you. There. It's done. My pardon for your pardon."

Robin eyed his brother with a strange smile. "So quickly

you forgive me. After everything. I thank you. But it doesn't work that way, you know. My karma . . ." He shook his head, his lips twisting as his handsome features assumed that odd, faraway look again. "Plus a really inconvenient, newborn conscience. God help me. But it's there. And neither karma nor conscience will be satisfied so easily." Robin turned back to High Druid Phil. "Please. Continue. I do wish to right matters."

The Druid nodded quietly. "And you will abide by whatever retribution we deem appropriate? Without retaliating against us?"

Robin tipped his head forward in acknowledgment.

As the Druids hesitantly rehuddled, sneakers and sandals gathering beneath a cloud of white cotton, Mina heard a rustling in the trees. And a shout.

"Hey!" A thump and then, "Ouch, damn it. Tea-eague! Miiii-na! Are you there? Am I too late? I can be a character witness. I *want* to be a character witness. Just hold your horses till I get there."

Riordan squinted into the trees. "Janelle? Damn it, I told you to stay out of this. This isn't for you to deal with."

"Well, I was the only one who believed in your damned visions before now. While everyone else is reeling from shock and confusion, I'm damn well not going to abandon you to God knows what—Damn it!" Another thump and more scrabbling.

Riordan raised a brow at Mina. "Obviously, she's even less of a nature girl than you are."

"No, I'm just tired. Ouch!" Janelle sounded near violence now. "I just got off a sixteen-hour shift dealing with such idiots you would not believe. I haven't had any freaking sleep in more than twenty-four hours, and I was terrified I'd get here and you'd already be condemned." She stumbled into the clearing, looking ruffled and stained in her wrinkled scrubs. A smudge concealed the freckles on part of her cheekbone. "And now . . ." She froze, staring beyond Riordan.

To glare at Robin. "*You.*"

Robin bowed his head in acknowledgment. There was an odd gleam in his eye as he surveyed Janelle from tousled top to scuffed bottom.

Phil the High Druid cleared his throat. "If you don't mind . . ." He glanced at Robin and Janelle, along with the wildly intrigued Mina and Riordan. "We have a sentencing to finish"—he frowned down at his watch—"before the park closes."

"Oh, that was mystic-like," Mina muttered.

"Mina, hush." But Riordan's voice shook with amusement.

Choosing her own method of silencing, Mina tugged Riordan's face down to hers.

"Yes, of course. Please continue." Robin bowed respectfully to the Druid while Janelle looked on, frowning. She glanced at the embracing Riordan and Mina and obviously decided it was worth holding her tongue for the moment.

"Given your own transgressions and their effect on your brother, we can't let this offense go unpunished. Robin Goodfellow, Akker's legacy must not be blemished by your acts."

"I understand."

"Your brother is no innocent, but neither are you entirely guilty. Your brother has paid dearly for his offenses. You have not." The High Druid frowned, obviously pondering options.

"They're not going to do the football thing again, are they?" Mina stage-whispered. "All right, all right. Stop pinching. Hey, I get it now. Janelle wouldn't go out with you because you looked like some mysterious ex. Do you suppose—"

"Yes, truly, it's your brains and intuition that seduce me every single day." Riordan gave her an ironic look. "Now hush, so we can hear what's going on."

Phil the Druid was quietly consulting with an elderly woman next to him, who eyed Robin and then Janelle with a speculative gleam in her eye. Finally, Phil nodded and turned back to the remaining puca. "I have a punishment that is both compassionate for all concerned and appropriate."

He cleared his throat and gathered his robes and his dignity. "We, the Druid Council, condemn you, Robin Goodfellow, to finish out your years *as a mortal*. You will walk the earth, like your brother does, as a human male adult.

"We will not take your powers from you, as we do not have Oberon's permission to do so, but we can severely limit them. We can require you to be accountable to the human lifestyle, values and laws. No willful and convenient disembodiment, no glamouring. You should use this time to make amends with your brother and others you may have wronged along the way."

"Oh, now wait just a minute." Janelle heatedly stepped forward. "You're going to loose this arrogant, irresponsible, vindictive jerk on the human population with no warning, no way to protect the innocent? How idiotic is that?"

"Excuse me," the Druid interrupted her. "May I ask who you are and what interest you have in these proceedings?"

"My name is Janelle Corrington. I'm a friend of Riordan's. Teague's. Er, Robert Goodfellow." She groaned. "Him." She pointed to the appropriate brother.

"I see. And you know this other man, too?"

Janelle scowled. "You could say that. Briefly and much to my regret. If you want a guy who drops women like flies, though, he's a better pick than my friend is. This guy's a complete loser with women."

"I see."

"And you!" She turned back to Phil and the other Druids. "You want to loose him on the world. How is that fair to us humans? What happened to the 'compassion' part of that sentence—compassion for the innocent? Are you so under this guy's thumb that you're willing to risk the whole freaking planet just to give him a light sentence?" She glanced at the white-robed group behind Phil, who all stood silent. "Surely one of you could be chained to him, like Mina was to Riordan, just to make sure he behaves."

The white-robed group shuffled until finally the High Druid cleared his throat again. "I'm afraid not. You see, we all fear him." He seemed to be choking on his own words, while the elderly female next to him nodded agreement.

"You fear *him*?" Janelle pointed at Robin, her voice arcing high with disbelief.

Phil just shrugged. "His temper is legendary."

"Well, fine, you cowards. Someone else, then."

"Who exactly? Should we tell the police that a condemned puca lives among us?"

Janelle paused at that. "Well, you could just say he's psycho or something."

"Based on what evidence?"

She raised her brows and spoke with mocking simplicity. "His claim to being a shape-shifter, maybe?"

Robin eyed her with amusement. "Do I look stupid enough to tell a human something he refuses to believe? I've been shifting shape for longer than your country has existed. I know how to play the chameleon."

"You know better how to play the heartless *snake*."

He shrugged, his gaze lingering on his brother before returning to Janelle. "Perhaps you're right."

A sudden murmuring in the Druid ranks drew their attention again. The High Druid spoke. "There is, however, another option. Perhaps one of you, present here today, could keep an eye on him." Phil cast an eye upon Robin's brother.

Riordan and Mina stilled.

Eyeing them, Janelle was already shaking her head. "Oh, no you don't. They just got their lives back. They don't need to play keeper for this jerk."

The Druid cleared his throat. "Are you married, young lady?"

"Me? No, but I don't see what that has to do with anything."

"Of course you don't," Robin muttered. "But you will."

"And you are acquainted with the Goodfellow brothers and Ms. Avery here?"

"Well, yeah, but—"

"The solution seems obvious to me, then." High Druid Phil looked satisfied now, as he surveyed his audience. "You, Janelle Corrington, will be Robin Goodfellow's guardian on Earth."

# AUTHOR'S NOTES

Yes, the Avebury Stone Circle really exists. Thought to have been constructed by the Beaker people (*not* the Druids) in Neolithic times, this circle encloses the existing village of Avebury in Wiltshire County, England. It's larger and older than its well-known cousin, Stonehenge, but less well-preserved, with only a fraction of the original number of stones still intact.

During the fourteeth century, and possibly even earlier, Christian authorities toppled and broke many of the stones in their effort to eradicate local paganism. Later, villagers continued to break up the stones to make way for agriculture—even using stone fragments to construct local buildings. Was there ever a family named Avebury or Avery, native to this area? Your guess is as good as mine, but I liked the idea of closely aligning my heroine with the area, so I let her share the name.

The puca really is a creature of Irish and Welsh myth. He's a trickster and a shape-shifter who enjoys surprising and terrorizing unsuspecting travelers. In his form of horse, he has been known to toss the occasional human onto his back for the ride of his life, after which the terrified human returns home "forever changed." What exactly does "forever changed" imply? I never could find any folk tales bold enough to outline the details, so I took a few liberties of my own.

Also according to folklore, November 1 (November Day), also known as the puca's day, is the one day of the year when the mischievous puca can be expected to behave civilly. He may even hand out prophecies and warnings to those who consult him.

In English folklore, the puca is known as Robin Goodfellow, the prankster son of a human female and Oberon, King of the Fairies. He was immortalized more recently by William Shakespeare and Ben Jonson. Some experts have even suggested that the legend of Robin Hood evolved from Robin Goodfellow.

*Robert* Goodfellow—or Rioghbardon/Riordan—whom I named as Robin's half-brother, was a product of my own imagination. And, while the *geas* really existed in Celtic folklore, I know of no legend or myth suggesting a puca was ever burdened by one or otherwise plagued by vengeful Druids.

The Druids themselves are shrouded in mystery, with history recording only a few references to them, many by Julius Caesar. The Druids wrote almost nothing down, each spending twenty years at a "college" learning skills and memorizing everything rather than resorting to script. As the more learned members of their society, the Druids were known as the wise men, the leaders, the judges, the peacemakers and the healers of their times. Naturally, I've taken all kinds of (enjoyable) poetic license in depicting fictional Druids Akker and Maegth, as well as the modern day bunch who judged Riordan and Robin at the end.

# MARJORIE M. LIU

## THE LAST TWILIGHT

A *Dirk & Steele* Romance

### A WOMAN IN JEOPARDY

Doctor Rikki Kinn is one of the world's best virus hunters. It's for that reason she's in the Congo, working for the CDC. But when mercenaries attempt to take her life to prevent her from investigating a new and deadly plague, her boss calls in a favor from an old friend—the only one who can help.

### A PRINCE IN EXILE

Against his better judgment, Amiri has been asked to return to his homeland by his colleagues in Dirk & Steele—men who are friends and brothers, who like himself are more than human. He must protect a woman who is the target of murderers, who has unwittingly involved herself in a conflict that threatens not only the lives of millions, but Amiri's own soul...and his heart.

***AVAILABLE FEBRUARY 2008!***

ISBN 13: 978-0-8439-5767-9

# Sandra Schwab

### Sweet passion...

After a magical mishap that turned her uncle's house blue, Miss Amelia Bourne was stripped of her powers and sent to London in order to be introduced into polite society—and to find a suitable husband. Handsome, rakish Sebastian "Fox" Stapleton was all that and more. He was her true love. Wasn't he?

### or the bitter taste of deceit?

At Rawdon Park, the country estate of the Stapletons, Amy began to wonder. It seemed that one sip of punch had changed her life forever—that this love, this lust, was nothing but an illusion. She and Fox were pawns in some mysterious game, and black magic had followed them out of Town. Without her powers, would she be strong enough to battle those dark forces and win? And would she be able to claim her heart's true desire?

# Bewitched

ISBN 13: 978-0-505-52723-3

## My name is Geri O'Brien, and I'm having a bad hair life.

My last date was with a guy who'd rather make tracks than make love; I work for a publisher who actually thinks a kids' book about the Donner Party is a fun idea; and the closest I'm ever going to get to my dream man is seeing him on the side of a taxi.

When I started writing this, I thought that fabled New York minute was never going to come for me or my friends Maria, Emmy, and Sally. But when one of us got dumped, one of us got shot and one of us threw up on a 4 star restaurant window, I had a run of luck you need to read to believe. I guess it's true what they say: Every time we complain there are no good men out there, a great guy out there is complaining that there are…

# No Good Girls

## Jean Marie Pierson

ISBN 13: 978-0-505-52756-1